For my Daughter Jocelyn

Published by Carnevale Publishing 2009
Carnevale Publishing is a trading name of Carnevale Films Ltd

Papers used by Carnevale Publishing are natural
recyclable products made from wood grown in sustainable
forests. The manufacturing processes conform to the
environmental regulations of the country of origin.

Carnevale Publishing
12 East Passage
Smithfield
London EC1A 7LP

www.carnevalepublishing.com

A CIP catalogue record for this book
is available from the British Library

ISBN   978 0 9563756 0 5

Cover Design & Typeset by Marianne Coupe
Printed and bound in Great Britain by CPI Antony Rowe

THE HARLOT'S PROGRESS

Yorkshire Molly

PETER MOTTLEY

Peter Henry Mottley (1935-2006) was born in Edmonton, London. He graduated from University of Sheffield in with a BA(Hons) Philosophy & English. Peter became a professional actor, theatre director, script-writer and novelist. Several of his plays have been produced professionally, including *After Agincourt*, *The Last Will & Testament of Popsy Petal*, *Before Nell* and *A Matter of Etiquette*.

After Agincourt was also produced on Radio 3, narrated by Bob Hoskins. Other plays on the amateur circuit included *Liz* and *Dead Trouble*. He has had several short stories and one novel, *The Sex Bar*, published.

Peter was a prominent figure in the Oxford theatre world and active member of the Oxford Theatre Guild, where he wrote and directed many plays. His memory is celebrated with a named seat in the stalls at The Oxford Playhouse.

"I was privileged to read and enjoy these novels as they were actually taking shape, the result of several years' meticulous and heartfelt labour. I am so proud to see my father's novel in print, though deeply saddened that he died before he could see it too."

Jocelyn Pulley

Chapter 1

'Keep your heads down!' The wagon-driver's voice was brusque, urgent. 'Two riders coming to meet us. They could be highwaymen.'

Molly's eyes were as sharp as any other seventeen-year-old's, but she could only just make out the tiny specks of blue a mile or more ahead of them on the dirt road stretching through the rough scrub of Finchley Common towards London.

Around her, the half dozen other women passengers whimpered nervously and huddled together under the hooped canvas cover. The four men among them, ranging in age from the callow to the decrepit, with hardly an able body between them, scrambled for their unaccustomed pistols and moved to protect the back of the wagon as they'd been instructed. Molly crept forward, peering past the driver at the road ahead, feeling her heart thudding in her chest.

A high cloud scuttled across the sun, and the sudden shadow mixed all the bright spring colours into a muted palette of greens and browns that spread out to the horizon. The riders blended into the landscape.

Or, perhaps, Molly thought, they've spurred their horses into the trees beside the road ahead, waiting under cover until we've drawn alongside, ready to... Ready to what?

Ready to rob us, of course.

Her dream of adventure slumped into the disappointment of reality. Five days on the road from York, only to be robbed an hour or two from London. She set her jaw defiantly and took a deep breath. If I'm to be robbed, so be it.

Again, her resolve faltered. Robbed, aye. But what else? And how do they go about their business? Are they really gentlemen of the road, or simply cut-throats on horseback? She'd heard tales; she'd read the broadsheets; but she'd never come face to face with a highwayman before, nor even seen one hanged.

After the bright early evening sunshine, the unwarmed breeze seemed unusually chill. She shivered, perhaps with cold, perhaps with fear, perhaps with excitement.

The sun broke free again. The pinpoints of blue resolved themselves into the silhouettes of two horsemen. The Waggoner loosened the pistols in his belt and cocked them, unbuckled the straps that held the blunderbuss tight against the seat and tucked it close to his thigh, lifted a primed carbine onto his lap. He cocked the carbine and rested the long barrel in the crook of his elbow, still clutching the reins of the four heavily plodding horses in front of him.

The parson trailing a dozen yards behind spurred his horse into a gallop and caught up with the driver. 'Let me have one of your pistols,' he demanded. Sweat beaded his forehead.

The driver flicked a dismissive glance at him. 'You could no more fight off a highwayman than I could preach a sermon,' he growled. 'If you're afeared, get in the wagon with the women.'

The parson let his horse drop back to the rear of the wagon, where he might be able to take cover if he had to.

The passengers in the York Wagon crouched down amongst their luggage; but Molly kept her gaze fixed on the approaching horsemen. Fear and a perverse anticipation tingled over her shoulders, down her body, into her stomach. As they came nearer, she could see them clearly. Both unshaven, both in ill-fitting blue topcoats, both with their hats pulled low over their eyes. The evening breeze twitched one of the coats aside to reveal a pistol tucked into the waistband of the rider's breeches.

Eying the wagoner's ready armoury, they separated to pass either side of the wagon. The wagoner followed one with his carbine, and lifted the blunderbuss with his other hand to cover the second. As they passed, he dropped the reins, stood up in his seat and turned to face them over the hooped canvas top, both weapons at the ready. The four trembling but cocked pistols poking out of the back of the wagon supplied the clinching argument, and the two men spurred their scrawny mounts into a trot.

'A safe journey to you,' one of them called.

'And to you, good sirs,' the wagoner replied. Uncocking the two firearms, he sat down again, took up the reins and continued with the journey. 'You can uncross your legs now, girls,' he called back to his passengers. 'Your valuables are safe.' The giggles of relief behind him subsided into excited chatter.

'Were they highwaymen?' Moll asked him.

'Maybe, maybe not. They might just have been honest gentlemen out for a breath of air on the Common - but if they were, they'll be lucky to get as far as Finchley without having their throats cut.'

But there was no doubt at all in the minds of his passengers. The women had survived a brush with not only one but two highwaymen, and had miraculously escaped unrobbed, unharmed and unraped - thanks to the bravery of the men who had held the desperadoes at bay with their pistols. It was a tale enough to make them heroes and heroines in every letter they wrote home for the next year.

And when that topic tired, they could refresh it with a description of the gibbet they'd passed a mile back, the eyeless corpses of four hanged highwaymen dangling in chains, with a court of crows dancing attendance.

How their stay-at-home cousins would envy them!

The wagon lurched and trundled along the rutted track. Molly continued to peer past the swaying driver, drinking in every glimpse of rooftop, every distant spire as London hazed into view.

She smiled to herself, excitement blushing up through her throat and lips and into her cheeks. Stolid, dull York was two hundred miles behind her. Cousin Tom and her brave new life in London were just an hour or two ahead.

London. She closed her eyes and hugged herself, stroking her hands down her upper arms in sensuous anticipation.

London. Fashion. Elegance. Fine manners...

＊

Black husband, black wife, white lover, a squealing baby neither black nor white. And a smell of violence as arousing as musk.

The crowd began to gather. There was sport to be had. Better than bare-knuckle fighting. Better than a cockfight. Almost as good as a hanging at Tyburn.

A husband face to face with the father of his wife's bastard.

'I'm goin' kill you, whoremonger! First you, then her!'

A narrow streetful of spectators roared them on, the sweating anthill of Wood Street, jostling for position, pitiless, laying bets, baying for blood. Thieves, harlots, children, cutpurses, beggars. Dogs of all sizes picked up the bloodlust scent, yelped backwards and forwards, boiled into throat-seeking fights of their own. Two Town-bucks lounged on the fringes, hoping for an amusing tale to tell. A scared lawyer, bewigged in his sedan chair, sniffed a nosegay, pretending not to be interested in the fight while the two chairmen temporarily abandoned him. A swarthily handsome, but impatiently scowling young Jew, balked on his way to the Royal Exchange, clamped one hand on his watch, the other on his purse, and waited. A vinegar-seller's donkey, startled, skittered sideways, its panniered barrels bumping a knot of spectators into a cursing eddy.

And the Watch nowhere to be seen.

The squat negress was screaming incoherent curses at her husband, her cries echoing back from the high peeling walls before being swallowed by the uproar around her.

The two men ignored her, circled each other, looking for a chance to wound, to maim, to kill.

One, Newgate-pale, wiry, wearing the frayed red coat of a discharged soldier, held a broad-bladed knife out in front of him, taunting his adversary, beckoning him with his free hand, half-grinning, half-snarling, his tongue flickering behind yellow teeth.

The other, the shiny-black husband, shaven-headed, older by ten years, stripped to the waist above his grimy breeches, gripped a broken wagon-shaft in his huge fists, setting his feet, holding his balance.

For the crowd, this was more than entertainment. The odds were weighed, the wagers accepted. 'Two to one the Captain! Three to two the blackbird! A shilling says the Watch will get here first!'

The younger man laughed, and put both forefingers up to the sides of his head to make horns. 'Cuckoo!'

The wife thrust her baby into the arms of the red-haired woman next to her and dashed towards the men, screeching in a strange tongue. As the wagon-shaft swung powerfully at the head and the horns, she hurled herself at her husband, cannoned into him, clawed at him. The mocking horn-maker ducked to avoid the blow. But the woman had dragged the shaft downwards. As he raised his arm to defend himself, the thick wood crunched into his forearm, just below the elbow. A sharp crack, a howl of pain, a grunt of victory, a knowing intake of breath from the spectators. In that one second, the fight had been lost and won.

4

The knife wheeled out of his hand, glinting in the evening sunlight, and clattered to the cobbles; hunching himself close, he clutched at the shattered bone, feeling it jagged through his coat; he staggered backwards, desperate to keep his balance.

The fight was over. But the retribution wasn't.

The bludgeon swung again, this time upwards, this time between his spread legs. This time no howl, but a deep, rasping sigh of agony and despair, echoed in sympathy by the watching crowd. He fell to the cobbles and rolled onto his side, moaning.

The negress rushed to him, knelt beside him, cradled his head, her curses diminishing into sobs. The gnarled hand of her husband swatted her out of the way. Flinging the broken shaft aside, he drew back his boot and axed it into the fallen man's groin, then again and again, splintering the protecting fingers, wrenching the already broken arm.

The woman tried again to get between her lover and the crashing boot. 'Leave him! Leave him!' she shrieked.

The back of her husband's hand smashed into her face, splashing blood into the air and sweeping her full length into the foul gutter flowing down the middle of the cobbled street.

'You goin' get no more bastards on my wife!' he growled at the groaning heap. A last kick drove into the already broken fingers, the already crushed testicles. 'Nor on no man else's!' He grabbed his wailing wife by her thick, curly hair and hauled her to her feet. The back of his hand lashed across her mouth again.

Struggling, spitting blood, she stumbled along behind him, away from the main street, down Love Lane towards the wooden staircase leading up to their dark rooms opposite the back entrance to The Bell. 'You be in Newgate for this!' she shouted. 'They goin' hang you!'

'Who goin' believe you, woman?' he shouted back at her. 'The word of a highwayman? The word of a woman taken in adultery?' His fist split her cheek, once, twice, as he dragged her up the steps. He stopped at the plain-boarded door, turned and looked down at the smirking spectators below him. 'She work at The Bell,' he proclaimed from his pulpit. 'She ain't one of their harlots.'

From Cheapside, the elderly Watch gaggled into view. Before they'd hobbled more than a few yards, Wood Street was empty; only the crumpled red rags of the loser bleeding onto the cobbles gave any clue that anything had happened.

'Nobody saw nothing,' said the wronged husband as he kicked open the door. 'You and me and him, that's all. They ain't no one else here to tell!'

'Cuckold!' The bright blood streamed from her nose and mouth and cheekbone, running down her chin and onto the white muslin tucked into the neck of her bodice.

'Better cuckold than eunuch,' he spat. 'Cus that's what he is now.' He looked down at the red-haired woman who had followed them to the back door of The Bell, cradling the now-sleeping brown baby. 'Two hours, Annie,' he called. 'We collect the highwayman's bastard in two hours.' He thrust his wife through the door. 'No need tell Mother Wickham 'bout this.'

The red-haired Annie nodded. No hint of emotion disturbed the pale stillness of her face; nothing stirred behind her withdrawn green eyes.

With a heave of his muscular shoulders, the negro pulled his wife up the rest of the stairs, through the door, slammed it shut behind them.

For several minutes, Annie stood by the door to The Bell, holding the sleeping baby to her, rocking it to and fro as it slept. She could hear its parents' voices, but she couldn't make out the words.

Wood Street and Love Lane were back to normal.

❋

'Whoa!' The wagoner brought his horses to a standstill in front of the spiked tollgate at Hornsey.

Though the thick-wooded, dapple-green hills on either side of the gate were the same, the perils of Finchley Common were behind them, and the safety of Hampstead Heath was all that lay between them and the Great City.

Where the common had been deserted, the heath was bustling with men calling their cattle home for the evening's milking, with rumbling carts labouring under huge casks of water, with shrill-voiced women carrying bundles of firewood. Long shadows stretched away to the east of them. The wind had died, leaving a clear sky and a clean chill that goose-pimpled the skin. Woodsmoke caught at the nostrils, with its promise of warmth and welcome.

'We leave again in a quarter of an hour,' the wagon-driver called, climbing down and walking forward to greet the gatekeeper, counting out his tenpenny toll as he went.

The passengers climbed stiffly out of the wagon, the men to piss against the wheels of the wagon, the gossiping women to traipse out of sight behind the tollbooth and wait their turn at the canvas-covered privy above a slope running down to a sluggish stream. The parson, as bladder-full as the rest, sought the cover of a patch of bramble some yards apart.

Content to be last in line, Molly jumped up onto the second of the turnpike's five bars, the better to see London's skyline. The dipping sun threw the shapes ahead of her into relief, and she tried to guess at them. Was that tall spire St Paul's? Was that great brick building the Tower of London? Whereabouts was her cousin Tom's house?

Cousin Tom...

My Deareft Molly

Your Rooms have been already prepared for your Vifit: which I hope fhall be a long Vifit; and an eager Welcome awaits you at my Houfe in Thames Street.

Think not of returning to York until we both make ye fame Trip together: which I hope and truft will be a moft happy Occafion.

Your loving Coufin

Thos. Heppenftall

Her head was filled with fancies. All the finest folk in England lived in London: King George and his court, members of parliament, famous actors and actresses. Surely they must walk the streets like other folk? Or at least travel the streets in their carriages. Would she see them? Did Cousin Tom know any grand folk? When she was married to him - if she was married to him - would she get to meet them?

My Lord, I don't think you've met my wife. My Lady, would you do my wife and me the honour of dining with us? Your Majesty, may I present my wife?

My wife. She mouthed the word silently, savouring the vowel, caressing the consonants. To change her name from Molly Huckerby to Mistress Heppenstall. Even her initials would remain the same, the same MH that was picked out in brass studs on the lid of her trunk, the trunk that contained everything worth bringing with her from York. Very little of value; but it was hers. Her best gown, her needles and threads and scissors for dressmaking, her Bible and Prayer Book, a palm-sized ink drawing of her dead mother in a chipped gilt frame, a battered rag doll she couldn't bear to leave behind. And twenty carefully saved shillings.

'Don't let the wagon go without you,' said a voice behind her. The gatekeeper unlatched the tollgate, waited for her to jump down from it, then pushed it open.

'Wait a few moments,' she called to the wagoner, and dashed to the privy. Within two minutes she was back and clambering eagerly up into the wagon.

After seventeen years in York, her life was about to change for ever.

❋

The late sun peered over the rooftops, creeping down into Love Lane and sidling past the back door of The Bell. Love Lane was deserted, and Wood Street was already in shadow. But Wood Street was beginning to stir.

'Spare a penny, good sir.'

The polished mahogany cane cracked against the beggar's elbow as the strutting young peacock cleared him out of his way. The twittering lady on his arm twitched up the hem of her silk embroidered gown to avoid a puddle of what might have been rainwater but probably wasn't, and carried on chattering about her piquet-party the night before.

'My Lady This, and My Lady That, and Sir Moneybags, and Lord Own-all... and I won a pitcherful of guineas...'

A single guinea was enough to take a beggar out of begging; but fumbling for a penny would be enough to disturb the flow of the couple's conversation. So the beggar nursed a sore elbow and an empty cup. But without rancour: that was a beggar's life.

The clomp of tired horses and the rattle of iron-rimmed wheels on cobbles, and the street was immediately alive.

The York Wagon. A canvas-covered bone-shaker full of hopefuls who had travelled two hundred miles to The Great City, two hundred miles to escape the cattle and sheep of Yorkshire, two hundred miles to fall prey to the wolves of Wood Street.

Out of the rat-holes crept the cutpurses, the bawds, the pimps, the harlots, all the Cheapside predators who might earn a shilling or steal a florin or gull a fledgling or find a fresh piece of meat to peddle.

And, of course, the beggars. Not with any enthusiasm, of course: since it was the York Wagon, it was hardly worth rattling a cup at. If they had pennies enough to spare for a beggar, they'd have been riding on the stage.

But he shook his cup anyway. It's what beggars do. 'Spare a penny.' He dodged the driver's whip as it flicked idly in his direction. There was no malice; the driver didn't care whether he caught the beggar with the lead tip or not. It was what drivers did. But it was worth taking the effort to dodge. Old Blind Morris who begged on Gracechurch Street was, in truth, only half-blind, with one eye in his head and the other on the end of a wagon-driver's whip.

The first one out of the wagon was old enough to be somebody's grandmother. In less than a second, she was looked over, weighed up and forgotten. As she took her first step down onto the streets of London, the eyes were already hunting beyond her into the wagon for the next dish to be served onto the Cheapside table. They were picking out not only the weakest to feed upon, but the tastiest.

'Is this Lincoln's Inn Fields?' asked the grandmother, her flat vowels sitting oddly on the open-eyed wonder in her words. The outskirts of York were never so magnificent as this, the crumbling brickwork of a London courtyard.

'It's London, missus,' said the wagoner, as he hefted her trunk onto the ground beside her.

'Aye, but is it Lincoln's Inn Fields?'

'As far as you're concerned, missus, it might just as well be.'

'Spare a penny, good lady.' The wagoner's foot kicked out; the beggar dodged; his crutch slipped on the wet cobbles, and he fell sprawling

9

on his face. His cup clattered away from him, the few coins in it scattering; before the pennies had stopped rolling, the barefoot children had snatched them up like mud-spattered magpies, and had skipped away into the waiting alleys. Hot pastries were more important than fallen beggars.

The grandmother protested. 'Eh, y' dint hafta kick un!'

The wagoner dumped her other case beside the first. 'Give your money to beggars, missus, and you'll soon enough be one yourself.' He turned to his other passengers. 'Mind where you tread, girls. The parson's horse has just mistaken these cobbles for a privy.'

The women giggled. Not at the wagoner's joke, but at the sheer thrill of being in London.

Molly stared about her as she climbed from the wagon, excitement bubbling up from her belly and shivering deliciously into her face. At last, she was in London.

The mean houses with roughly washed clothes drying on lines hung high to be out of reach of the thieving children; the untidy piles of straw heaped against the walls; the gutters running with foul water, sloshing into the horse-shit, the dog-turds, the contents of emptied chamber pots.

The stench of an unwashed city, trapped between blackened walls. The echoing cacophony of street-sellers and beggars, dogs and drays, rolling barrels and reeling drunks.

The crowded, narrow streets, overhung with so many painted shop-signs and inn-signs that it was hard to see the sky without looking straight up. A vintner's bush, a tailor's scissors, a shoemaker's last; a surgeon's striped pole, an apothecary's bottle, a furniture-maker's spindle; and a whole menagerie of red lions, white horses, blue boars, and golden creatures that had never walked the earth.

Among them, the silver-gilt sign of an inn. The Bell.

Not ancient and timbered like the inns in York. Not boldly outlined in black and white, not soaking in the spring sun through leaded windows, not jettied out expansively below gabled roofs. Instead, the plaster peeled off The Bell's brickwork like the skin off a leper's face; the chequerboard tiles above the crudely-framed door hid sullenly beneath a layer of soot and grease; the two front steps sagged wearily, worn, rotting.

Like a pearl in a midden, a fine silver-wigged gentleman stood by the door, with fine silver buckles to his boots, fine silver buttons to his coat, a fine silver knob to his cane. And a fawning servant a discreet pace behind him, attentive to his master's meanest wish.

Molly's gloried in the wonder that was London. London was grand. There was so much to see, so much to do, so many dreams to come true in London.

London...!

Annie looked down on the wagon from an upper window of The Bell, holding the black-white bastard in her arms, humming to it without even pretending to a tune.

'All the way from York, Lily,' she crooned to the sleeping baby. Women, mostly. Come to London seeking work. But what work is there in London for a woman? 'Whoring and thieving, Lily, that's all. Whoring and thieving.' She took up her tuneless humming again.

Oh, there's other work to be had. Honest work, with an honest wage. And, in due course, an honest husband, with honest drudgery and, after it all, an honest burial.

But not in Wood Street. 'Whoring and thieving, Lily. That's all the work in Wood Street. And begging.'

'You! Wagoner!' The parson was squinting at the address on a letter, holding it short-sightedly almost to his nose. His half-starved horse, worn out from following the wagon two hundred miles from York, stooped and plucked up a mouthful of hay. The scavenging dogs danced backwards as the horse clattered a pile of buckets to the ground.

'Spare a penny, your worship.' The tin cup rattled.

'Be off, or I'll thrash you with my whip!' More chance of getting alms from another beggar than from a parson. 'Wagoner! Did you hear me?'

'I heard you.' He lifted the tailgate back up into place, and dropped the latch-pegs into their iron rings. 'If you want Cheapside, follow my wagon. If you want elsewhere, follow someone else.' He walked to the front of the wagon, and climbed up into his seat.

The parson coaxed his horse level with the wagoner. 'I wish to call upon the Bishop of London,' he said, loud enough for the remaining travellers in the wagon to hear.

'Well, you won't find him in Cheapside, that's for sure.' He hawked, rolled the phlegm round his tongue and spat into the street. 'Giddup!' The wagon creaked into motion and lumbered downhill towards the Thames, its leather brakes squealing, its horses skidding and neighing, its iron-clad wheels screeching and grumbling over the cobbles, scant inches away from the scarred brickwork of the houses.

'Spare a penny, miss.'

Molly tried to make her reply both apologetic and encouraging. 'I en't got a penny to spare. But I'll give you this ha'penny if you'll tell me where I'll find Thames Street.'

A kindly, middle-aged, motherly voice broke in. 'Thames Street, dear? Did I hear you say you're looking for Thames Street?' Mother Wickham, moving in with a wary anticipation, like a rat sniffing at a new-born chick.

'Aye, that's right, Thames Street. Do you know it?'

In a blink, Mother Wickham had taken inventory. Brown eyes in an outdoor face, full-bosomed and strong-shouldered, pretty in a rustic sort of way, plainly dressed in pale blue and laundered white, the crimson flash of the rose at her breast reflected in the ribbon trimming her wide-brimmed hat. The scissors and pin-cushion dangling from her wrist told her trade: dressmaker. Both the girl and the rose were limp and tired from the journey; but her face was alive with excitement.

An innocent. Fresh, green produce that would fetch a good price at market.

Above them, Annie moved away from the window into the dimness of her room; but she continued to watch the scene being acted out below. God help you, child, if you should fall off the York Wagon into the arms of the most relentless bawd in London.

Mother Wickham oiled closer to Molly. 'You can't be walking all the way to Thames Street, dear - not with that heavy trunk and all the rest of your luggage.' She smiled as she clasped the girl's hand. Long-nosed and bulbous, pock-marked and pallid, her voluminous gown of scarlet sparked garishly against the rose on the dressmaker's bosom. 'Come into The Bell, here. You must be tired. Have some refreshment before you go on with your journey.'

'Oh, I - I couldn't.' The merest pause. Not enough to be a hesitation... 'I couldn't go into an ale-house.' ...but enough for the pin-sharp rat-eyes to spot the weakness.

'Ale-house?' A faint overtone of disappointment, of disapproval. 'Oh, The Bell isn't an ale-house, dear. It's an inn. An inn for travellers - such as yourself. And for gentlemen like Colonel Charnell and his friend, yonder.' Silver wig, silver buckles, silver buttons. 'Real gentlemen. Gentlemen who have the ear of the King.' She gestured to a scowling scar-faced man, who shuffled forward to pick up the coffin-shaped trunk. 'You come in, dear, and rest your bones. There's plenty of time to get to Thames Street before nightfall. Why, I'll take you there myself. And Jed will carry your trunk for you. Later on.' She reached up and touched her ungloved hand to the girl's cheek. The mother's caress of love; the stranger's hand of friendship; the professional's judgement of quality. 'But come inside, now, and I'll see if I can introduce you to Colonel Charnell.' Her hand fluttered down to the young dressmaker's elbow. 'What's your name, my dear?'

'Molly. Molly Huckerby.' She allowed herself to be manoeuvred a few feet nearer The Bell.

'Molly. Such a pretty name.' When the girl stopped, the bawd stopped. Seduction is a patient craft. 'My very own daughter is called Molly. So, Molly Huckerby, I shall call you Moll - so that I shan't get you mixed up with my daughter. Because I can see we're going to get on so well together, I might start thinking you are my daughter.' Her friendly arm slipped through Molly's arm, and they walked a few more yards. 'And you must call me Mother Wickham. Everybody calls me that. Mother Wickham.' Molly halted; Mother Wickham halted. 'You'll be looking for work, I suppose?'

'Aye, ma'am. I'm a dressmaker. And I'm a good dressmaker, too.' Her shyness disappeared as she found something she could talk about without blushing. 'I made every stitch you can see on me now. And I've been sewing for my father and my brothers for as many years as I can remember. Ever since I were a lass.'

Mother Wickham's face lit up with a practised delight. 'What a stroke of luck! Only this very morning, I was saying to my daughter how much we needed a good dressmaker in the neighbourhood. The dress-makers at Lincoln's Inn Fields are so expensive, and the ones in Wood Street are...' She glanced around her and lowered her voice. 'Well, to tell the truth, my dear, they're not very good. Clumsy, every one of them. Haven't had the sort of experience you've had. Now, I've got a petticoat, my favourite petticoat, that needs just a few stitches...'

Up the two sagging steps, out of the early evening sun, into a world where dressmakers didn't stay dressmakers for long.

Mother Wickham's voice echoed out into the once-again deserted Wood Street. 'Colonel Charnell? Colonel, I'd like you to meet somebody...'

Annie turned away from the window and laid the baby down on her bed. God help you, Molly Huckerby.

❈

Candlelight, even though the sun was still edging past the heavy curtain; a dark-panelled room with smoke-dulled picture frames high up near the ceiling; a sturdy oval table set with a dozen square-backed chairs.

The Colonel sat at the table, smoking a long-stemmed pipe. A bottle and glass were in front of him, the remains of a chicken and a loaf at his elbow. Standing behind him, a slightly-built man with thin lips and narrow shoulders rubbed his hands together, ready to serve his master in any way he wished.

'Colonel,' said Mother Wickham, 'this is Moll Huckerby. Such a pretty girl. She's this very moment got off the York Wagon, and I've brought her in for a morsel of food and a glass of ale.'

'Nay,' said Molly. 'My cousin Tom in Thames Street stays dinner for me. Just a glass of water. If you please.'

The Colonel rose, handed his pipe to his servant, touched a hand to his cravat to make sure it was in place. 'Mistress Huckerby,' he said. 'This is London, not York. Any stranger is, to us, a cousin.' His voice was friendly, cultured. He took her hand, the one with the scissors and pin-cushion hanging from it, bent forward in a courteous bow, and raised it delicately to his lips. 'Pray join me.'

The smiling servant pulled back a chair for her; from nowhere, a greasy-aproned, grubby-fingered woman, clearly unused to serving at table, cleared away the chicken and replaced it with a ham, a fresh loaf and an extra glass.

'Thank you kindly, sir, but just a glass of water will do.'

14

The Colonel mirrored his servant's smile. 'As I said, Mistress Huckerby, this is London, not York. If our springs were only as pure as the ones you are used to, we too would drink nothing but God's gift. But this is London. A little brandy, in moderation, is far safer.' He poured a thimbleful into the fresh glass. 'Mother Wickham. A jug of the boiled water you keep. And some honey.'

'Are you sure, Colonel?'

'Of course, Mother. Don't worry about the cost. I could no more let Mistress Huckerby drink undiluted brandy than I could let her drink unboiled water.' He returned his attention to Molly, his manner devoted to her best welfare. 'To the unwary, neither are safe.'

It was slightly warm to the lips, smooth and comforting to the tongue, pleasantly glowing to the throat.

'A little more?'

'Thank you, sir, but I must be getting to my cousin. He'll be waiting.'

'Quince, carve Mistress Huckerby a morsel of ham.' Thick, juicy, studded with cloves, the richness offset by the clean smell of the fresh bread. 'Not as good as your famous York ham, of course, but after a lengthy journey...' He topped up her glass with brandy, honey, water.

She could feel the weariness seeping into her. But, after two hundred miles in the York Wagon, forcing down badly-cooked food and sour ale in the kitchens of coaching inns, the bread and meat were a luxury.

Gratefully, she accepted more ham, more bread, more brandy and honey.

More bread, more brandy and honey.

More brandy and honey...

Chapter 2

She hurt.

It must have hurt when it happened, but her memory was blurred. Now her head hurt, her stomach hurt, and there was an uncomfortable stickiness between her thighs.

She tried to focus on what she could see of the unfamiliar room. The sloping ceiling of an attic; daylight filtering past uneven shutters; slapdash plaster between crudely-hewn beams.

She pushed back the rough blanket, bemused at seeing the bare whiteness of her own breasts and belly; even at home, even in the summer, she never slept naked. The surprise turned to shock as she saw the dried blood on her thighs. Not since she was fifteen years old had there been blood on her thighs; but then her mother had been alive to explain it.

A choking despair smothered onto her, and she dragged the blanket up again. Too ashamed to weep, too ashamed to call for help, far too ashamed to remember what had happened last night. All she wanted now was water to slake her thirst, to wash away the foul taste in her mouth.

The door opened, and Mother Wickham busied in with an earthenware jug. She splashed water into a pottery beaker and thrust it into Molly's hand. 'Drink this, child' she said briskly.

Molly gulped at the water, then gagged as it churned up her stomach. 'Is it safe?' she gasped.

'Safe?' She frowned, then her face cleared with amusement. 'Oh, you mean safe to drink. Safer than brandy and honey, Moll Huckerby.' She threw her head back and laughed coarsely. 'A lot safer than brandy and honey!' She poured water into the bowl on the rickety table beneath the shuttered window, and tossed a rag onto the bed. 'Clean yourself, girl. Be in the kitchen by the time St Alban's strikes the hour.' Almost as an afterthought, she dug into the folds of her skirt; a glint of gold clinked onto the scattered clothes on the floor. 'This is for you, from the Colonel. I always let my girls keep their first purse to themselves.' She chuckled to herself. 'As a memento.' The door closed behind her.

Molly slid cautiously off the bed, wrapping herself in the blanket, even

16

though there was no one to see her. She stood up. The room tilted and blurred, then lurched upright again. For safety, she fell to her knees, clutching the wooden frame of the bed, her head bowed, swimming, buzzing. Slowly, she pulled her surroundings together; and, since she was kneeling, she prayed. 'Our Father, which art...' Swallow and wait for the nausea to subside. 'Which art in Heaven...' Not my fault, God, please God, I were foolish, but it weren't my fault, please God. '...hallowed be Thy name...' I have sinned, God, but it weren't my fault, God, please God, forgive me, please forgive me.

She mumbled her way through the rest of the prayer, the tears running down her face and dripping off her chin onto her clasped hands. 'For ever and ever. Amen.'

Then, since she was on her knees beside the bed, she swept her hand blindly under it, disturbing the dust and dead moths, until she struck something solid. She pulled out the chamber pot, squatted and pissed, still wrapped in the blanket, still sobbing, still hurting. Her bladder eased; her head didn't, and neither did her soul.

As she swabbed herself clean as best she could, she thought of her cousin Tom in Thames Street. He'd have stayed dinner for her. He'd have made a room ready for her. He'd have waited for her - all night, probably.

She'd brought a fine, plump goose from York for him. But, if she allowed her dreams to speak for her, she'd brought herself from York for him. He was thirty, hard-working, respected, widowed. She was seventeen, industrious and an orphan.

And, until just a few painful hours ago, a virgin. What Robert from the neighbouring farm had failed to capture with persuasion, what big Ned Foley had failed to capture with bullying, Colonel Charnell had captured with brandy and honey.

Stooping cautiously, she picked up the coins Mother Wickham had left behind. A frisson of disbelief rippled through her.

Five guineas. Five gleaming pieces of mill-edged gold. More gold than she'd ever held in her hand at any one time. She put one up to her mouth and bit hard onto it. Gold, not gilded lead. Between them, Mother Wickham and Colonel Charnell had shamed her, violated her, debauched her; but they hadn't cheated her.

It took her a head-swimming age to dress. When she was clothed, she drew open the peeling shutters, blinking painfully at the sunlight, then drew back into the concealing gloom. She could see Wood Street below; wagoners, water-sellers, dogs, children, beggars.

But Wood Street, she hoped, couldn't see her. Just one glance, she was sure, and even a stranger could tell.

No more than a dozen yards away, she could see the square tower of a church. St Alban's? St Alban's or not, the hands pointing upright on the face of the heavy iron clock were close together. Two minutes to twelve.

Twelve o'clock! The last time she'd stayed in bed till midday was when she was seven years old, and had the fever. But the fever is something you get over. Losing your virginity is once and for ever.

A tear dribbled down her nose as she put the coins safely in her placket, peered queasily round the room to make sure she'd left nothing, and made her way unsteadily to the door and down the giddy stairs, descending from cramped attic to dim basement.

The low-ceilinged kitchen smelt of fresh bread and hot fat and sweet spices. Her throat and stomach protested, but stopped short of rebellion. The air was warm and humid from the stewpots already simmering in the coal-blackened fireplace, and aromatic from the two herb-stuffed chickens and a rabbit spitted in front of it. The row of bottle-glass, thick-grimed windows tucked up against the ceiling let in hardly any light and even less air. At street-level outside the windows, anonymous feet trudged back and forth along Love Lane.

Half a dozen pallid young women sat at the scrubbed table. A skinny waif of no more than twelve was breaking chunks of yellow cheese onto pieces of bread and eating them with unashamed gusto. Two fair-haired girls who were certainly sisters and probably twins held hands, smiled into each other's eyes, and fed each other scraps of bread laden with porridge. Two more, one pock-marked, one bruised, ate tiredly, mechanically, not speaking, buried inside themselves. A young red-haired woman with a freckle-dusted face poured gin into a beaker, stirred a purple cordial into it, drained it without tasting, reached again for the bottle.

By the huge fireplace, a squat negress with puffy cheeks and a split eyebrow was scraping and washing dishes in a large wooden tub, her movements slow and painful; from time to time, she stretched out a hand to turn the spit. A muscular negro crouched on the floor, mending the leg of a broken chair. Beside the steps that led up to the outside, a slightly-built man with hooded eyes and a scar-puckered face rhythmically chopped wood, muttering under his breath as he smashed the axe down onto the logs.

Molly slipped uncertainly onto a stool at the table. The Waif beamed brightly at her, then tore another chunk from the communal loaf and stuffed it into her mouth. Nobody else bothered to notice her except the redhead, who nudged the gin-bottle towards her with the merest hint of a raised eyebrow of invitation. Molly's stomach baulked at the smell. She shook her head. The motion made the room swirl.

'I have to go soon,' she mumbled. 'Who do I have to pay for my night's lodging?'

The redhead stared at her with, a touch of irony smile playing at her lips. 'Lodging?'

'Mother Wickham said this were an inn for travellers.' Her Yorkshire spirit of independence fluttered briefly. 'I've got money. I can pay.'

'This isn't an inn.' The corner of her mouth twisted ironically. 'Do you see any travellers here?'

Uncomprehending, Molly looked at the self-absorbed girls opposite and on each side of her. What had Mother Wickham meant, 'my girls'? What did she mean, 'I always let my girls keep their first purse'? The Colonel's gold. A purse? A purse?

Slow realisation filtered through the fog inside her head. Instead of saving herself for Cousin Tom, she'd allowed herself to be taken to market by Mother Wickham. And she'd been bought. The Colonel had paid five guineas for her.

Her chest tightened, the blood drained away from behind her eyes, a hoarse cry of despair squeezed out of her suddenly constricted throat as she sagged backwards, crashed heavily to the kitchen floor.

A sharp hand slapped her cheek, then the other, and she could hear Mother Wickham's cold voice telling her to wake up and face the real world, girl, do you think he fucked you because he suddenly fell in love with you, do you think he parted with five guineas out of respect, where do you think you are, girl, what do you think you are?

'Wake up, girl!'

She rolled over onto her face, forced herself up onto her hands and knees, crawled towards the shifting door. The stone flags tilted up to meet her, and she vomited, the hot gush filling her mouth before cascading onto the floor with a flat pattering. Again she vomited, and again, and again, and the pungent liquid bubbled up into the back of her nose, and she coughed and sniffed and the sucked-back sick choked into the top of her windpipe. Again her stomach heaved, and her mouth opened, and her tongue retched, but there was nothing in there to come out except a thin muted howl, and her guts were grinding together, and her cap had fallen from her head, and her hair was draggling in the warm spatter, and her breath was going out but not coming in, and the dogs were milling round her, and she was more wretched than she'd ever known, and...

And in the background was the sound of laughter.

Air rasped into her lungs, and she was able to breathe again. She spat onto the floor, then wiped her tongue round the inside of her mouth and spat again. She crawled backwards away from the lumpy puddle, toppled over into a sitting position and pushed herself against a wall, her legs straight out in front of her, her eyelids squeezed shut, her arms flopping beside her, her shallow breath wheezing, grateful for the stone chill on the back of her neck.

A door creaked. Instantly, the laughter died, replaced by a metallic scraping as an iron-bound bucket was dumped beside her. A mop fell into her lap.

'Clean it up, girl.' Mother Wickham's voice, brisk, unsympathetic. 'Of course, if you'd rather have one of the other girls do it for you, they'd be more than obliging. Wouldn't you, girls?' A muted giggling, more nervous than mirthful. 'But it will cost you five guineas. Now then, what do you say?'

She opened her eyes. Mother Wickham's face swam close to hers; the effort of trying to focus made her retch again, but she had nothing left to bring up. Reeling, she forced herself upright against the wall.

I've mopped floors. I've cleaned up after my brothers when they've had too much ale. I helped look after Great Uncle William when he was dying of dysentery. This is my sick on the floor, and I shall mop it up.

She took the mop that was thrust into her hands.

Mother Wickham stared harshly into her face, the warm stench of brandy on her breath fighting Molly's stomach, then swung away, up the steps and out.

Molly's jaw set stubbornly. This hell-kite will not steal my guineas from me just for mopping a floor. They may have been bought with shame - but they're mine.

She levered herself away from the wall, staggered, splashed her foot into the puddle of vomit, retched, took refuge against the wall again, clinging to the comfort of the cold stone.

The redhead scraped her chair back, stood, took the mop from Molly's slack hands, kicked the dogs out of the way, eased Molly to one side. Molly tried to resist. Five guineas to mop a floor? But she had no strength of body, and little strength of will.

Slop, mop, squeeze; slop, mop, squeeze; slop, mop... In a few moments the floor was clean. The redhead put the mop back into Molly's hands.

'I... I could have...' Her voice was a feeble croak that she didn't recognise as her own. I could have done it myself. But this is London. Where they toss you five guineas for debauching you, and charge you the same to mop a floor. So be it. I shall honour my debt.

She dug into her placket for the Colonel's coins, trusting the word of the bawd.

But the redhead reached out a hand to stay her. 'Don't tell Mother Wickham,' she murmured. She turned to the rest of the girls. 'Don't tell Mother Wickham,' she said again. But this time her voice was charged with menace, violence, hatred. The flicker of animation died again. She sat on Molly's stool, lifted the beaker of gin to her mouth and emptied it in a single animal gulp.

Molly lifted the bucket. 'Where...? Please, what do I...?' Where does London have a midden?

The Waif grabbed another piece of cheese as she stood up and made for the outside door, jerking her head for Molly to follow. Molly lurched after her; the bucket wasn't heavy, but her legs were nearly buckling under her. Up the stone steps, out into the street, among the beggars, the children, the dogs. The air was foul, but it was bathed in sunshine. Nausea washed over her, and she closed her eyes. Instantly, fearing she would fall as her senses whirled, she opened them again. The Waif took the bucket from her, swilled it into the gutter, handed it back to Molly, led her towards the back door of The Bell again.

She summoned up all her resistance. 'No!'

The Waif was sympathetic. 'Do you want to stay out here in the air for a bit before going back in?'

'I don't want to go back in there ever. Except to collect my trunk.'

'Where else are you going to go?' It was a question, not a challenge. This child cared where else she was going to go.

'My cousin Tom in Thames Street.' If she could explain away being a day late, if she could pretend to herself that nothing had happened, if she could convince Tom she was still a virgin, if she could...

'Was it him you sent the goose for?'

'Aye.'

'Mother Wickham had Jed take it to him this morning at seven.'

'Jed?'

The Waif indicated the muttering handyman at the foot of the stone stairs, swinging the short axe into the logs as if he had a grudge against them. 'Come half past, he'd brought it back again. Your cousin said it was tainted.' She frowned. 'Didn't smell tainted to me.'

Sucking in great lungsful of the fetid air through her nose, her teeth clenched, her lips drawn back in a grimace, she stumbled along the crowded streets towards the river, bumping between people and walls, clutching the Waif's dainty hand in hers.

'Tell me when we get to Thames Street,' she panted.

'Which part of Thames Street?'

'I don't know. The part where my Cousin Tom lives.'

The Waif didn't mind being swung from side to side with Molly's erratic course. She skipped alongside her. 'We'll ask someone,' she said. 'What's his other name, apart from Cousin Tom?'

Molly leaned against a shop doorway to catch her breath. 'Heppenstall,' she said. 'Thomas Heppenstall.'

A sharp intake of breath. 'Mother Wickham won't like you going to visit Master Heppenstall.' She tugged at Molly's hand. 'Let's go back to The Bell.'

She shook herself free. What had that hypocritical harpie to do with her? 'I don't care what Mother Wickham likes or doesn't like. I'm going to see my Cousin Tom. Now then, let's get to Thames Street, and ask someone where he lives.'

'No need,' the Waif said. 'I know where he lives. We all know where Thomas Heppenstall lives.'

'But he must see me! We're kin!'

The sour-faced housekeeper stood with the plain oak door half-open, shielding the interior of the two-storey house with her bulky, beef-fed body. 'Master Thomas says that no cousin of his would be content to live at The Bell in Wood Street. He has no cousin named Molly.' She held up a hand to still the protest. 'Nor Mary, nor Mistress Huckerby, nor any of the other names you bade me give him.' She made to close the door. 'Go away, young woman,' she said. 'Master Thomas is an important man. He does not wish to know you.'

Molly's shoulders slumped, and her head drooped. He'd been so friendly when he'd come to York for her father's funeral. He'd made sure the tenancy of the farm was secure in her brother Michael's name. He'd spent his own money on repairing the wall that protected the herb garden from the weather. He'd spent time with Molly herself, teasing her about her plans for a knot-garden, admiring the dress she'd made to impress him, even though he didn't know that. Though he'd probably guessed. Inviting her to come to London on a visit where, possibly, he hinted, he could help make her life comfortable. His secret smile, the private twist to his lips, made her hope that, perhaps...

The Waif planted her doll-like foot in the door. Her eyes were big and round, full of innocence. 'Master Thomas doesn't wish to know Miss Molly,' she piped in her little-girl voice. 'But has he ever known you? Has anyone ever known you? Is that why you look as if someone has turned you upside down and stuffed the lemon in your mouth instead of where it might have been of use? Is that why you - '

The housekeeper's nostrils flared with contempt. 'I see that the children of The Bell, too, are nothing but whores and strumpets.' She dropped her gaze to the Waif's foot where it blocked the door. 'Take your foot away, or I'll have one of the men set the dogs on you.' No anger; it was merely a chore to be dealt with.

The Waif did as she was told. The housekeeper fixed Molly with an implacable stare. 'Master Thomas does not know you. He has never known you. He wishes never to know you in the future.' The door closed with a solid finality.

As Molly trudged back through the bustling river-bound traffic of Thames Street, she became aware of the glowering Jed tailing them twenty yards away.

'Just in case,' the Waif explained. 'Mother Wickham doesn't like her performing fleas to escape.'

✻

My Dear Coufin Tom

I pray you let me vifit but for a few Minutes that I may tell you how I came to be detain'd at Ye Bell againft my Will. I have Greetings from my Brothers and a fine Goofe from ye Farm and I long to fee you again.

Your loving Coufin,

Molly Huckerby

The letter was returned within the hour. An unsigned note in a precise hand was written on the outside.

Mr Thos Heppenftall, Magiftrate, has no Coufin nam'd Molly Huckerby. Further Letters will be conftru'd as a Nuifance and will be dealt with by Procefs of Law.

Molly let her brimming eyes stray from the letter to the unplucked goose where it dangled from its noose in the coolest part of the kitchen.

'Cousin Tom were right,' she said miserably. It didn't matter if the Waif heard her or not. 'It is tainted.'

In York we feed tainted meat to the pigs. Is that what London's got in store for me?

Chapter 3

That first day, Mother Wickham felt Moll's clammy forehead, peered at her tongue, grinned, winked at the rest of the girls, and sent her back to bed. Wretched, lonely, nauseous, she drifted into and out of sleep, weeping when she was awake, running from nightmares whenever her eyes closed.

On the second day, she did whatever she was told, too numb, too weak, too despairing to protest. Without questioning, she tidied the beds, cleared away the brandy bottles, scrubbed the dishes, put poultices on the bruises, oiled the whips, nursed the babies while their mothers took their visitors upstairs. Only with the babies did she sense any of the life she'd known in York.

Even the dogs at The Bell were different. She was used to terriers, foxhounds, beagles, sheepdogs - eager dogs, bright-eyed dogs, dogs with a job to do. The Bell's dogs were slinking, stinking, snapping curs, tail-between-the-legs mongrels, dogs with no line, no purpose, and no names. Matt-haired dogs that came and went as they pleased, ate what was thrown to them, mounted each other and snarled at each other without check. After trying two or three times to make friends with them, Molly gave up and devoted her energies to the babies.

There were four of them. The Twins had one each, though only the Twins themselves knew which baby belonged to which mother. The pale brown one was the child of Abigail and Bull, the negroes. And the smallest of all was, simply, The Bell's baby. No mother, no father (but which of them did?), no right to live except... Except that Mother Wickham had said the baby should be cared for.

Kitchen gossip provided rumours by the dozen. Illegitimate heir to the throne. Mother Wickham's own child, grandchild, godchild. A goblin child that Mother Wickham was powerless to kill.

None of the babies had been baptised, and only the half-black baby had a name: Lily. The others were known as The Twins' Boy, The Twins' Girl, and The Baby. The Twins had secret names for their own babies, but they didn't say them when anyone else was within earshot.

As well as the babies, there was an eight-year-old boy, Okoro, as shiny-black as his parents; a foul-mouthed boy of some ten or eleven years, who ran wild between the kitchen and the gutter; and a deaf-mute girl of about four, who spent all her time with the dogs. Mother Wickham, they said, had plans for her and the dogs.

The babies and the children were cared for by anybody who was free. From time to time, the mute girl crawled onto the lap of whichever Twin was suckling, and suckled when the baby fell asleep. The Twins were content to let her; sometimes she was cuddled afterwards, sometimes she was slapped away. She had no name.

On this afternoon, she'd clambered into Molly's lap as she snatched a few moments rest beside the kitchen fire. 'Poor child.' Molly gazed at the blank-faced, thumb-sucking creature curled in her lap. 'Not even to have a name.'

At the big pine table the redhead, who had mumbled that her name was Annie, looked up from the gin-glass she'd been staring into. 'Why should she need a name? If she had one, she couldn't hear it, and she couldn't say it. A name would be wasted on her.'

Molly stroked the child's hair. 'But what do you call her when you talk about her?'

Annie shrugged. 'Nobody ever talks about her.' She went back to her gin.

The boy was known as The Bastard.

At six in the evening, Molly ate left-overs stew in the kitchen with Okoro, the Bastard, the Deaf Mute, black Abigail, and the Waif.

The Waif kept up a chatter about what if this, and what if that, and who knows what would happen if...

'My name's Helen,' she told Molly. 'Like Helen of Troy.'

But when she'd eaten her fill and skipped out of the room, Abigail grinned affectionately. 'Don't you listen to her, Miz Moll. She got a different name every day. Depends what book she been reading.' Molly was surprised that anyone at The Bell could read at all.

None of the other breakfast girls was there for supper, but she didn't ask why. She didn't ask anything. She carried out the tasks that were given her, and tried to forget the shame of being turned away from Cousin Tom's door.

Returning to York was out of the question. Cousin Tom's letter must already be on its way to her brother and his upright wife, with news of her fall from grace.

Even if her employment were to be as the lowest maidservant in an alehouse, so be it - until she knew London well enough to face it on her own terms.

Every few minutes throughout the day, she fingered the guineas in her placket.

Portugal Street. The Lincoln's Inn Fields Theatre. The Way of the World. An old play. Nevertheless, a full house, buzzing with conversation and laughter, ringing with the cries of orange-sellers, swirling with clouds of tobacco smoke, heavy with the smells of perfume and oranges and sweat.

In the pit, Jenny Diver edged discreetly through the crowd, murmuring her excuses, her gloved false hands clasped over her falsely bulging belly, her thieving real hands striking cleanly and accurately as she brushed intimately past the young gentlemen, as she eased apologetically past the young women, as she blushed modestly past the elderly lechers groping the orange sellers.

A fan, a silk handkerchief, a purse, a brooch, a watch, a pin. One by one they disappeared into the vast pocket of her pregnancy, until she feared that any more booty would cause her to rattle when next she bumped into a gull.

Without fuss, she took her place in the pit, smiling contentedly when one of the women caught her eye, smiling shyly if one of the men noticed her, smiling serenely when no one was looking at her, just in case somebody was. She'd stay at least until the end of the First Act; leaving too early when you'd paid to get in might draw attention.

The musicians struck up the overture; everyone ignored them.

A hunchbacked Jew and his twenty-year-old son sat in the most expensive seats, at the side of the stage itself, waiting for the play to begin. Lace and silk rustled all around them, vying with the velvet and brocade of the men's coats. Crimson and blue, russet and gold, pink and green, gleaming and matt, shifting colour in the flickering light of the tiered chandeliers.

'I've seen it before, Father.' Boredom, not entirely affected.

'So see it again.' He dipped a greeting at a consciously elegant couple as they took their seats on the opposite side of the stage, the man looking around him to see who else was there, the woman looking around her to see who was looking at her.

'I've seen it at least three times.

'I've seen it at least a dozen times. I saw the very first production in this very theatre a quarter of a century ago.'

'So why see it again? Father, I can tell you the plot. I can tell you who marries who. I can tell you - '

'Who?'

'Father?'

The older man beckoned an orange-seller to him. He pressed more than enough money into her hand, sought a response, found none, took two oranges. He handed one to his son. 'Enjoy. So who marries whom?'

'The handsome fellow marries the beautiful lady. At the end.'

'Yes?'

'Well, doesn't he?'

'Indeed he does,' his father agreed. 'As he does in Much Ado About Nothing. In As You Like It. In The Taming of the Shrew. In Twelfth Night. In The Merchant - '

'No.' The son cut the peel with his penknife, stripped off a triangle and dropped it carelessly onto the floor. 'No, I'm sure it was The World's Way. I'm sure I'd remember if it was any of the others you said.' He bit into the orange and sucked the juice noisily.

'Were.'

'Father?'

'If it were any of the others I said.'

'Were.'

His father steered the conversation in a different direction. 'The Merchant of Venice. Now that is a play. That is a wonderful play.' He peeled his orange, stacked the peel in a precise heap on the floor at his feet, separated the flesh into tidy segments and popped one neatly into his mouth. 'The Merchant of Venice.'

'Is that the one where the Jew is the villain?'

'It's the one where the Jew is the hero.'

A puzzled frown. 'Doesn't he ask for a pound of somebody's flesh instead of a thousand ducats?'

'Three thousand ducats.'

'So how can he be the hero?'

28

'Even a bad businessman can be a hero, Isaac. Trust me.' He raised his cane to salute a client on the other side of the stage, an aristocrat with more breeding than cash, with more sense of honour than the means to make it good. His client looked straight through him. The Jew let it pass without losing his composure, without losing his dignity, without reacting to the snub. His turn would come.

His son was not so tolerant. He surged to his feet. 'You, there! Yes, you, sir!' Loud enough to draw the eyes of half the theatre to him.

The Jew rose to his feet, pushed the young man back into his seat, inclined his head in a deferential bow to his client. 'My son mistook you, sir, for someone else. I pray your pardon.' He sat down again, unconcerned, unruffled. 'Don't ever do that again, Isaac,' he said, the smile sitting lightly on his barely-moving lips. 'Our creed is that every man has his price. We are money-lenders, and we live in luxury. But the price we pay for our luxury is to be despised by bankrupts like my Lord Penniless there. Smile, Isaac. Smile and enjoy.'

'But he - '

'But he is a man of rank, Isaac. He has very few guineas, but a great number of powerful friends. We have a great number of guineas, but only a few friends of any sort. Let him despise us, Isaac, let him insult us. As long as he keeps paying the interest on the money we've lent him, why should we worry whether or not he snubs us in the play-house? One day, unless he recovers his fortune, his powerful friends will desert him. And then we'll be the only friends he has. Then you may insult him, Isaac. Then you may challenge him. But by then, there'll be no point in doing either. Because when that day comes we'll own him.'

The young man seethed. 'I can't bear to see you insulted by him!'

His father laid a hand on his arm. 'Isaac, my son, my dear, dear son. Why should I worry about being insulted? Why should you worry about being insulted? In our trade, Isaac, being insulted is good business. But peace, now. Here comes the Prologue.'

The house quietened a little, but not much, as the music ended and the actor stepped out from the wings and onto the stage. Briefly, he struck a pose; then, since the audience showed no sign of giving him any more attention than they were giving each other, he strode to the centre of the stage, positioned himself to get the maximum light from the chandeliers overhead and the floating candles at the front of the stage, flung out his arms and began.

'Of those few fools, who with ill stars are curst,
Sure scribbling fools, call'd poets, fare the worst...'

✻

Backstage, in the only private tiring room, the actress playing Mistress Fainall cocked an ear at the stage, abruptly unclasped her legs from the waist of the actor playing Mirabell and tried to shove him away. 'The prologue's started!' she said.

'Plenty of time,' he insisted, continuing to thrust energetically. 'You're not on till the Second Act.'

'You're on now!' she hissed. 'The prologue's already started!'

'Plenty... of... time...' he grunted. 'Plenty... of... Aaah!... Aaah!... Aaah!'

'Now! Now!' she shouted at him as he bounced up and down on her chest and belly. 'You're on now!'

'Now! Now!' he echoed. 'Aaaah! Aaaah! Aaaah!'

'Get off me! Get on stage! Get off! Get on!'

He collapsed on top of her. 'Aaaah... Aaaaah... Aaaaaah...'

'Now! You're on now!' She heaved at him as hard as she could, and he fell off the couch onto the floor. 'Ow!' she cried as his weight crushed her thigh against the edge of the couch.

'Ow!' he cried as his head banged against a wooden chair. His flailing arm swiped the bottle and two glasses off the table, splashing wine across the room.

'Now! Go now!' She scrambled off the couch and tried to haul him to his feet.

'Ooooh...' Gasping for breath, groaning with pain, sighing with spent lust, he crawled towards the door, his breeches round his knees, his wig lopsided, his head slewing cross-eyed from side to side. He used the door-jamb to drag himself upright, clutching at his breeches, fumbling at his crotch, stumbling out into the narrow corridor that led to the stage.

'Should he by chance a knave or fool expose...' Into the wings.

'...That hurts none here, sure here are none of those...' Onto the stage, hidden behind the movable flats..

'In short, our play shall (with your leave to show it)...' Tuck in the shirt.

'...Give you one instance of a passive poet...' Button the breeches. '...Who to your judgements yields all resignation...' Straighten the wig.

'So save or damn, after your own discretion.' Slide into the chair at the table, just as the Prologue speaks his last line. Enjoy the exasperated relief on the face of the actor opposite him.

On the other side of the curtain, the Prologue took half a pace backwards, and flourished an elaborate bow.

Pick up the hand of cards lying on the table.

Scattered applause, and a slight drop in the level of conversation; since it was an old play, the audience knew when the important part was about to begin.

Take a deep breath.

The blood-red plush curtain was plucked up and away to reveal the elaborate scene-flats of ACT I, Scene I: A Chocolate-Houfe, with Mirabell and Fainall at play.

Throw the cards down on the table with a flourish. 'You are a fortunate man, Master Fainall.'

At the side of the stage, the old Jew settled comfortably into his seat. After twenty-five years, The Way of the World was just as it had always been.

❉

Sunset. Bedtime.

In York. Not in London.

As Molly set foot tiredly on the bottom stair, there was a flurry of movement above her, and she stepped aside for two proud ladies. With a condescending nod, they swept past her. Then, mocking, they swung to face her and dropped exaggerated curtsies.

Painted faces with bright red lips. Lace edging the necks of their flame-embroidered cream gowns, silk bows catching the pleats down the front, tight underbodies pushing their breasts up and out, and pulling their waists in. Ribbon-and-lace caps.

Both dressed identically. The Twins.

More regal gowns, more ribbon and lace. This time she recognised them. Pock-marks, Bruises, Redheaded Annie. None of them acknowledged her as they came down the stairs, along the passage, into the room with the high ceiling.

The Waif was last, clinging to the banisters, jumping down the stairs two at a time, dressed in the fashion, but without the adult frills. Breastless, capless, without stockings, without flounces. A child, her greased hair ringleted down her back.

As she passed Molly, she took her hand and led her after the others. Neither spoke.

Into the brandy-and-honey room. The oval table was now set for company, piled high with meat, bread, cheese, fruit. To one side, a smaller table bore wine, brandy, goblets. At one end of the room, a simple bed with a bare mattress and a single blanket.

Twelve chairs: six empty, six already occupied by the gaudily-dressed girls. Red, pale blue, royal blue, two sets of flame-and-cream, the pink and melted butter of a child.

The Waif sat. Molly made to sit beside her, but the Waif hastily urged her upright again. Not knowing what to do, she stood behind the Waif's chair and, like everyone else in the room, waited in silence. Outside the curtained windows, the clock of St Alban's chimed nine; as the last stroke died away, Mother Wickham entered.

'Good evening, girls.'

'Good evening, Mother Wickham.' Five chorused voices, like the children in the village school outside York; Red Annie stayed silent. Molly hurried to catch up, just in time to say '...Mother Wickham' with the others; she'd done nothing wrong, but she felt guilty.

The bawd prowled the length of the table, behind the girls, hesitated momentarily behind Annie at its head, then stalked back down the other side. 'As you can see, we're to have a feast this evening. Only two gentlemen, but they've bought The Bell for the whole night. Do what they want, whatever it is - they've already paid.' She added a caveat. 'Except beating. They haven't paid enough for that. Of course, you can whip them if they want you to. But to my eye they don't have that aspect about them.' Mother Wickham's eye was one of the best in London. She put her hands tenderly on Bruises' shoulders. 'No beating. We've had enough damaged goods recently.' She continued her journey round the table. 'Remember my rule: at The Bell, we never steal from our visitors.' She smiled to soften the iron in her voice. 'Because, of course, there's no need: they'll be generous enough without that. And anyway, these are men who could cause trouble if they're crossed.' She directed her next remark at Pock-marks. 'If they want to play the chuck-game, don't - none of you is good enough, no matter what you think. Tell them a posture-woman will be here at three, and let them be content with that.' She pointed at the Waif, then hooked her thumb over her shoulder at the door. 'You, go to bed. You won't be needed.'

The Waif eyed the food on the table. 'Can I...?'

'If you're hungry, there's porridge in the kitchen.'

The Waif scraped back her chair, and left without argument. As she passed Red Annie, she let her hand brush against the older girl's shoulder. Almost imperceptibly, the redhead nodded; but her expression didn't change.

'Twins, you'll sit on either side of the one who's paying. He's been here before, but that was before you joined us. He's a bit older than his friend. At least, he looks older. Probably because he's been here before.' She paused for the dutiful laughter before carrying on. 'He's not a lord, nor is he a knight, nor anyone in the Government. But he's got money. And, since he's sworn to spend it, best he spend it wisely with us than squander it foolishly with the South Sea Company.' Another ripple of laughter. 'Nan and Polly,' she continued. Pock-marks and Bruises paid attention; they didn't dare get it wrong. 'You'll sit either side of the other one. Annie, you are to attend on both as they so desire, and soothe them when they become angry.' She turned to Molly. 'Moll Huckerby, you will fetch the wine when they want it, and carve the meat, and clear up any mess, and stay attentive all the while. Annie, I'm leaving Moll in your charge. She can be fondled, but not fucked. She's for the Colonel. I shall join you from time to time. But,' and a lascivious smirk passed across her face, 'for most of this evening, I have other things to do.'

She made her exit, and the girls relaxed. One of them let a thin bee-buzz fart, and the rest giggled, making much of fanning the air and holding their noses.

Molly sagged onto the Waif's vacant chair. Fondled but not f... She'd never spoken the word. And neither would her father and her brothers in front of her. But she knew well enough what it meant.

So, whatever was to happen tonight, she was not to be... tupped. But she could be fondled. Fondled? By whom?

A man's hands on her. A man she didn't know. Of course, she'd been fondled before. Big Ned Foley had made her breasts tingle with his horny-palmed woodman's hands; and Robert Nyes had insinuated his slender clerical fingers into her and almost made her forget her resolve. But this was to be a man who didn't know her, who didn't care to know her, who'd have forgotten her before he woke up the next morning.

The quarter hour chimed outside. A quarter past nine... somebody expected at three... bought for the whole night... How many hours would she have to be here serving? She was eye-burning tired already.

Serving? Serving what? Herself? Offering up her body to the clumsy, groping hands of a stranger? And then what?

No! Better the night streets of a strange city than this.

Shaking her head in stubborn anger, she made to rise to her feet. A hand pressed on her thigh and toppled her back into the chair.

'Nobody will touch you tonight,' Annie promised in her dead voice. 'You have my word. But Jed will come after you if you leave.' She poured more gin into her glass, but no cordial; during the last several minutes the drink had paled from purple to red to pink. 'You can go to bed when the posture-woman comes. After you've cleared the food away. I'll serve the wine after that.'

Molly swallowed, let her anger cool for a few seconds, then accepted Annie's word.

'Don't tell Mother Wickham,' said Annie. She raised the gin to her lips.

There were three of them, not two, and they were already drunk. They were boasting of their brave exploit in routing the Watch on their way here, and they were flaunting their trophies of the encounter.

As they swaggered into the room, all the girls leapt to their feet, and all except Annie rushed to them, squealing with pretended pleasure. Molly rose, not knowing what to do. Annie bunched a cloth into her hands and pushed her into a corner. 'Smile,' she hissed. Molly tried to fix a smile on top of her fright.

Blonde-wigged and silver-coated, the eldest of the three was no more than twenty; he was the leader. Striding through the girls to the table, he scattered all the dishes onto the floor with a single sweep of the Watchman's staff he was carrying. 'Who needs the taste of food when we've got the smell of cunny?' he roared. The girls blushed prettily, and giggled their agreement. 'Let's have wine!'

What to do? Molly's eyes pleaded with Annie. Annie retrieved a boiled ham from among the scattered food and broken earthenware on the floor. 'Take this down into the kitchen,' she told Molly. 'Cut four slices of ham, and two slices of bread, and set it to one side, under a cloth. After you've swept the floor.' She rested the ham on the wine-table, uncorked a brandy bottle and poured generous measures into three glasses.

Molly found a broom, cleared up the mess and took it outside. She salvaged the ham and a roast chicken, and carried them down into the kitchen. She could hear her long-dead father's voice: Waste not, want not, lass. And don't fret if it's been on the floor - we'll all eat a peck of dirt afore we die.

When she returned, the three men were engaged in a contest to see who could first fill up a glass by standing on a chair and pissing into the middle of the table. The girls had chosen their champions and were cheering them on. The tallest of the men lost by dwindling to a trickle that wouldn't reach his glass; the shaven-headed one, whose wig had fallen onto the floor, lost by falling backwards off his chair, spraying all over Pock-marked Nan as she broke his fall; Blonde-wig won by carrying on till he'd not only filled his own glass, but tried to fill both the others as well. He claimed the Watchman's broken lantern as his prize, and stood triumphant on the chair, dripping, shrivelled, dangling white outside his breeches.

As the rest of the girls cheered and applauded, Molly swabbed up the mess, wrung out the cloth and took the bucket down and through the kitchen to empty it in Love Lane.

For an hour she poured wine, emptied the chamber pot when the men could be bothered to use it, wiped the window sill dry after Shaven-head had tried unsuccessfully to piss on a passing beggar, listened without hearing while they boasted of the noses they'd slit, of the Watchmen they'd beaten, of the women they'd raped.

Then Blonde-wig stood, tossed back the wine he was drinking, unbuttoned his thigh-length waistcoat, and banged on the table with his fist. 'Time to do what we came for!' he declared. His two companions whooped their approval. Leaping onto a chair, he surveyed the assembled girls. 'First, I'll have...' He thrust both arms out in front of him, his forefingers pointing at the Twins. '...you two.'

Gleefully, they skipped across to him. One of the Twins unbuttoned his fly, and the other lifted out his erection, almost as if it were a sacred relic. As he stood there, proudly displaying himself, the rest of the girls applauded.

The other two bantams chose which hens to begin with, and scrabbled their flies open.

Molly backed into an unlit corner and watched as the farmyard rutting unfolded into a nightmare, as the nightmare became a vision of hell and, because it seemed as if she were stuck in it for ever, the hell gradually took on a normality of its own.

She watched as one of the Twins straddled Blonde-wig on the bed. She watched Tall-man bend Nan face down over the table and take her from behind, his fingers digging into the flesh on her hips as she pretended to enjoy it. She watched Annie kneeling beside the drunken Shaven-head, teasing at his limpness in a vain attempt to arouse him, while he clumsily poked the Watchman's staff up poor bruised, wincing Polly.

And she cleaned up both the floor and Polly after he vomited without warning and passed out, spreadeagled on his back and ridiculously exposed.

Annie moved to the bed; the Twin who was taking her turn under Blonde-wig arched her back without disturbing her rhythm; Annie pulled the blanket out from under her, covered the comatose Shaven-head with it, and cast a practised eye about the room to make sure everything was in order, that the customers were being satisfied.

'Polly, bed,' she said. 'Moll, clear the glasses, then go to bed. As you pass Kitty's room - ' She read the query written across Molly's face. 'Kitty. Catherine. Helen. Whatever name she's told you. The girl. As you pass her room, take her the ham and the bread that you put aside.'

'But it's three o'clock in the - '

A fondness played at the corners of her mouth, the first sign of softness Molly had seen on her since she'd been at The Bell. 'Time has never been a bar to that child's appetite,' she said.

The door opened, and Jed ushered in the posture-woman, already blank-eyed weary, with her keeper, her outsize candle, her yard-across polished brass plate, her collection of whips. Another bawdy-house, another audience, another performance, another shilling. She sat with her back to the rest of the girls and began to undress.

When Blonde-wig dismounted from the Twin, Annie took him aside for a private conversation. When Tall-man lurched away from Nan, Annie breathed a few words in his ear. As Molly came back from the kitchen for the last time, Annie bent over Shaven-head, opened his purse, took out a single silver crown, held it up for the other two men to see.

She led Moll to the door. 'Be at breakfast. Midday in the kitchen.' Her hand closed over Molly's; a hardness dug into Molly's palm. 'This is for you.' Three crowns. 'Don't tell Mother Wickham,' she said.

Molly plodded, exhausted, up the stairs to her attic.

My father broke his back on a farm, and scraped less than twenty pounds a year. In the last two days, I've lain on my back in a bawdy-house and earned nearly a third of that.

Where's the justice? Where's the honesty?

I should run away. It's not too late. No one need ever know. I still have my skills as a dressmaker.

But...

On the third day, they plucked and cooked the York goose.

Chapter 4

Despite the April sunshine seeping through the kitchen's high windows, Abigail shovelled more coal onto the smoke-churning fire, then returned to the bread-dough she'd been kneading.

The Waif, whose name today was Ophelia, was attacking a plate piled with bread soaking in porridge, and cheese on top of the bread; the Twins were feeding each other with bread and cheese; the rest of the girls, including Molly, had porridge only; red-headed Annie nursed a glass of purple-diluted gin.

The sleepy babble of the seven girls died away as the clock of St Alban's struck for the eleventh time. As it clanged out the twelfth stroke, Mother Wickham entered into the silence. 'Good afternoon, girls.'

'Good afternoon, Mother Wickham.' Molly joined in the chorus because she was afraid not to. She didn't know why, but Mother Wickham frightened her.

Without speaking, the bawd came down the steps, then circled the table until she came to Molly. Her hands rested on Moll's shoulders. 'Such a pretty child,' she said. 'But her clothes...' She clicked her tongue in disapproval. The rest of the girls chirruped their support for her ridicule. Molly could feel the embarrassment reddening her cheeks. What was wrong with her clothes? She'd made them herself. They were well cut, well sewn, well fitted. 'There's nothing wrong with being a girl from the country,' Mother Wickham continued. 'Many of you here were girls from the country once. And you're all cunt...ry girls now.' A familiar joke for the girls; a shocking obscenity for Molly. 'But that doesn't mean you have to dress like a girl from the country.' She gave Moll's shoulders an affectionate squeeze. 'I think that pretty Moll deserves a pretty gown, don't you?'

A burst of chattering and laughter, and a spattering of excited applause.

Molly blushed. 'I - I'm sorry,' she said, though she didn't know what she was sorry for. 'If you can find me some material, I'll make myself another dress.' More laughter. 'I am a dressmaker,' she asserted defiantly to the table at large. What did these common harlots know about an honest trade!

Mother Wickham corrected her. 'Not any more, child.'

'I've learned my craft and - '

'London's full of dressmakers,' Mother Wickham said sharply. 'Every silly child who can thread a needle calls herself a dressmaker. Forget your scissors and thread, girl. The prick of a needle is worth pennies. The prick of a man is measured in guineas.'

Molly's head drooped, and she avoided all the eyes that were on her; under the table, her hand felt for the coins that now lay in her placket. Five guineas and three crowns. As much as a York dressmaker would earn in three months.

She felt Mother Wickham's hands on her shoulders again. 'Let someone else do the sewing, while you do the wearing,' she said. She put her hand under Molly's chin, tilted her face up towards her, surveyed her professionally. 'Brown hair,' she said. She treated the rest of the girls to a conspiratorial leer. 'All over, so the Colonel tells me.' The girls giggled; Molly coloured with remembered shame. 'Dark skin, as befits a country girl. But that won't last in London.' She let her go. 'However, in the meantime, let us use her sunburn to make her special - as special as every one of you. What colour shall we choose for our Moll's new gown?'

'Pink!' called the Waif, her mouth full of cheese. 'With roses and flowers and pink ribbons on it.'

Mother Wickham made a pretence of considering the suggestion. 'Very pastoral, but no, I think not.'

'Red,' said the Twins in unison.

'No, I think not. Too like a blush.' She moved to the head of the table. 'No other ideas? Come, girls, what colour would suit Moll best?'

'Pale blue and white,' said Annie quietly but audibly over the rim of her gin-glass. Molly was already wearing pale blue and white. None of the girls dared smile.

Mother Wickham ignored her. 'Gold' she said. 'Pretty Moll shall have a new gown, and her gown shall be gold, to show off her charming country colour.'

The girls clapped. 'Can we come to the dressmaker's with you?' asked Polly.

'Please, Mother Wickham' said Nan. 'I've got money saved up for new ribbons, and I'd dearly love to see what the fashions are.'

Mother Wickham beamed at her girls. 'Who'd like to come to Covent Garden with me and Moll?'

'Me! Me!' Polly and Nan. Not the Twins. Not Annie. The Waif had her mouth full, but she waved her hand high in the air like an eager schoolgirl who knew the right answer.

'Anybody else?' asked Mother Wickham, the edge worn off her good humour.

The Twins turned down the corners of their mouths. 'The babies,' said one.

'We can't leave them,' said the other.

'Abigail will look after them,' Mother Wickham promised.

'They already see more of Abigail than they see of us,' said one of the Twins. 'We need them.'

'They need us,' said the other.

'We all need each other,' said the first, flashing a sly glance at her sister.

The Waif choked down her food. 'I'll come,' she said.

'You've got a visitor,' Mother Wickham told her. She looked at Annie, challenging her to respond.

Annie gazed back, impassive, dead-eyed. Without speaking, she poured more gin, more cordial, nursed her glass.

With an effort, Mother Wickham became the mother hen again. 'Then the four of us shall go to Covent Garden, and measure Moll for a golden gown.'

Molly's hand strayed to the placket where her harsh-earned coins were hidden. Even in York, she'd heard tell of the fabulous sums London women paid for their clothes. Why waste her money in Covent Garden when she could make a gown every inch as good as the ones the rest of the girls were wearing? She summoned up the courage to speak. 'I... I...'

'Yes, girl?'

'You told me the dressmakers in London were very expensive. And... and...'

'Yes?'

'I only have... I have little money of my own.' Less than six guineas in her placket; twenty shillings more hidden. Twenty shillings brought from York that she didn't want Mother Wickham to know about.

Everybody laughed. Even Annie laughed. Mother Wickham cocked a pitying eye at her naivety and smirked for the benefit of the rest of the girls. Molly looked from face to face, confused, seeking help, seeking a friendly lead.

The Waif came to her rescue. 'Who's going to pay for the gown, Mother Wickham? Is it a present?'

'Indeed it is a present,' said Mother Wickham. 'From an ardent admirer. From Moll's only visitor. From - the Colonel!'

Another dutiful sprinkling of applause from the girls. Except Annie. 'Moll's only visitor?' she said.

Mother Wickham rounded on her, her features tight. 'Yes. Moll's only visitor. Until I say differently, Moll is for the Colonel, and for the Colonel only.'

'Lucky Moll,' Annie said, her voice as expressionless as her face. 'No strangers. It will almost be like being married.' She sipped at her gin, then glanced up at Mother Wickham. 'But never quite.'

Mother Wickham clapped her hands. 'Now, then, girls.' It was business time again. 'Twins, you may stay here. If anyone arrives unexpectedly, Abigail will take care of the babies while you take care of the visitors. Kitty - '

'Ophelia,' said the Waif. 'My name's Ophelia.'

Mother Wickham's face hardened. 'You can be whatever name you like in your own bed,' she told her, 'but in my kitchen you're Kitty.' She softened, and relented; it made no difference to her. 'Ophelia,' she corrected herself, 'you have a visitor at three. You've not met him before, but he's been recommended. He knows you're not a virgin, but he's been told you're ten years old.'

'Ten?' The Waif's voice dripped with insulted scorn.

'Yes, ten. Tell Abigail to let you have one of the rag dolls. And suck your thumb when you first meet him.'

'Wash it first,' said Annie. 'You'll poison yourself else.' They all laughed, including the Waif and Mother Wickham.

Including Molly. The bribe of a bought gown had melted her defiance; but it had done nothing to assuage her suspicions. Her father's voice echoed in her ears: In this life, lass, you don't get owt for nowt.

Mother Wickham clapped her hands again. 'Supper at six, apart from

Polly, who has a special visitor at that time.' She feathered her fingers down the already bruised girl's arm. 'Supper in my room when your visitor has gone,' she said. 'There'll be good ham, and fresh bread, and wine. And,' she added, as if promising sweetmeats, 'Abigail will have some of her best poultices for you.' She patted Polly's shoulder, then issued her orders to the rest of the girls. 'We leave for Covent Garden when St Alban's strikes the hour. Those who are coming, be ready.' Without looking back, she mounted the steps and let the door swing shut behind her.

Taking a chunk of bread and a square of cheese to eat alone, Molly rose, trying not to be noticed, and climbed the three flights of stairs to her attic room.

For the first time in her life, she felt important. And, she confessed to herself, she liked the feeling.

Until today, she'd only ever known two lives. Seventeen years of the innocent, rough-and-tumble, sun-up to sun-down life of York; four days of the brutal, brutalising sun-down to sun-up existence of The Bell.

But now Covent Garden had twitched a corner of its skirts aside and enticed her with a life where politeness was the norm, where the customers were assumed to be superior, even when they plainly weren't, where money was the first matter to mind, but the last to be mentioned.

She'd been measured, flattered, cosseted. She'd been called 'mad-emoiselle' by the deferent dressmaker, and 'dear thing' by the slender, rouged, perfumed, clean-shaven shop-owner. She'd been offered the choice between this gold fabric and that gold fabric and a dozen other gold fabrics, and had ribbons matched against her face, her hair, her hands to determine which was perfectly, most charmingly, absolutely the most exquisite way to transform her into la plus belle, into una contessa, into a blushing advertisement for the dressmaker's art and the couturier's shop.

'Choose the most costly,' Polly had whispered, even though they could only guess at what the cost might be. 'Ask for two gowns. The Colonel's paying.'

If the Colonel paid for a hundred gowns, it would never be enough. Given enough time, I could cut and sew a hundred gowns for myself.

But nobody can ever sew back what he's torn, nor buy back what he's taken from me.

'That one,' she decided, pointing to the gold gown with the most lace, the richest embroidery, the tightest pleats. She set her jaw. 'And that one.'

Mother Wickham inclined her head in the tiniest nod of approval. The girl was learning fast. She opened her purse.

Back at The Bell, Molly scampered up the stairs to her attic room, leaving Polly and Nan behind. Already, her blue-and-white York bodice and skirt seemed dowdy and home-made; but it would do until the golden gowns were delivered tomorrow. In the meantime, she must see what trinkets she had to go with them, what earrings, what ribbons, what -

The room was empty. Her trunk was gone. Her case, her basket, her shawl, all gone.

High excitement plummeted to disbelief, then drained into disillusionment. She leaned her back against the door, and her shoulders drooped. London, where they pressed shoddy on you with one hand while they stole your gold with the other. Her hand strayed to her placket, clutching at the comfort of the few coins still safely lodged there.

Despite the panic probing at her heart, her practical mind sifted through the most likely thieves. Not Polly, not Nan - they were with her in Covent Garden. Not Mother Wickham - though she could have ordered it, and probably did. But who had climbed the stairs and stolen the things she'd brought from York? The Twins? The Waif? Annie? The Bastard or the Deaf Mute? Scarred Jed or black Bull? Abigail? One of the visitors? In a houseful of harlots, who could be trusted?

Onto the landing. 'Abigail? Abigail!' Her voice wailed down the echoing stairwell. 'Abigail!'

A slapping of loose shoes on wooden stairs, and the maidservant called up at her from the floor below. 'Yes, Miz Moll?'

'I've been robbed!' She fought to keep at bay the hysteria probing at the corners of her composure. As the hysteria ebbed, it left dark strands of despair behind it. 'I've been robbed,' she sniffed. She sat down on the top of the stairs, and let the great sobs come. Everything gone now. Robbed of her possessions, her virginity, her hopes of marriage, her hopes of anything. All she had left to escape Mother Wickham's world was the six guineas Mother Wickham's world had damned her with. Even the twenty shillings she'd brought with her had been stolen with her trunk.

Abigail's feet pounded heavily up the remaining stairs. 'No need cry, Miz Moll,' she panted. She knelt beside her and put her muscular, comfortable arms about her. 'No need cry. You ain't been robbed. You just been moved.'

'Moved?' With one huge sigh, the sobs came to an end. 'What do you mean, moved?' Three days away from the York Wagon, and her cramped room had come to be her only security, her only anchor in the threatening sea of Wood Street. 'I don't want to be moved.' Uprooting herself from York to London was nothing compared to this. 'I won't be moved! I won't!' She struggled to free herself from Abigail's grasp.

The big black arms lifted her to her feet. 'You come with me, Miz Moll.' She took her hand and led her down the stairs. 'I wonder Mother Wickham didn't tell you. Maybe she keeping it for a surprise. Maybe I didn't ought to show you.'

Molly steadied herself, sniffed and spoke with a confidence she didn't feel. 'Show me,' she said.

Down a flight of stairs. Past Mother Wickham's own rooms, their doors tightly shut. Along a narrow passageway. Abigail opened a door and stood back to let her pass into...

Into a different world. Sunlight streamed through the polished, small-paned windows onto a canopied and curtained bed with full pillows and an embroidered cloth thrown over linen sheets and a deep mattress. A sturdy wooden chair, padded and upholstered; a mahogany vanity table with a tilting mirror; a pair of framed engravings on the wall; an arabesque rug on the floor. Much grander than she'd ever known in York.

'For me?' There was her trunk, her case, her basket. Her shawl rumpled in a heap on the bed, cheap and white against the expensive red and cream of the over-blanket.

She brushed her fingertips over the furniture, the hangings, the bed-cover. There was a disturbing edge of familiarity about the room, a blurred scene from a half-remembered nightmare. Was this where the Colonel had...? She couldn't remember. She picked up her shawl and held it to her throat, pressing the rough wool against her skin to remind her of reality. 'For me?'

'Mother Wickham said you's to sleep here, and Bull brought all your things down from upstairs.' Her face creased with indignation. 'All on his own,' she added, 'cause that no-good Jed was drunk.'

'For me?' A bedroom bigger than her uncle's parlour at the farm - and only one bed in it. The attic room she'd clung to so desperately only a couple of minutes ago now seemed nothing more than a tawdry memory. The protests tiptoed out of her mind.

'The Colonel's paying.' Abigail shut the door behind her.

Molly took in the room's furnishings, its spaciousness, its comfort. She sat on the edge of the bed, relishing the softness of the mattress, the luxury of the cover. A big bed. Easily big enough for two people.

She caught sight of herself in the mirror, gazed briefly at the familiar reflection, then looked away, too ashamed to meet her own eyes.

Above the muffled cries of Wood Street, a faint but rhythmic creaking came from the room above her, and what sounded like the Waif giving childlike squeaks of delight.

She looked at the room again, this time with her father's voice in her head. A pig may not like its sty, lass. But, come market-time, it'd rather have a filthy old sty than a clean new slaughterhouse.

Chapter 5

The Waif lowered her voice confidentially. 'I'm not really ten. I shall be fifteen on my next birthday. And I've already started having blood-flows.' A hint of grown-up pride. 'But I've got no bubs, and the Twins help me shave my cunny every day.' She stood up from the edge of Molly's bed and hauled up her skirts to show the hairless white flesh at the fork of her thighs. 'See? They love that, some of the visitors.' She dropped the skirts back into place. 'I've already been a virgin a score or more times, and I don't doubt that I'll be a virgin many more times yet!'

Molly sat back in the padded chair. She didn't know what to say. To her, fourteen was a child's age, not an age for someone who'd been known by scores or even hundreds of men. Hundreds of strangers. 'But how can you...?' The shrinking of her body and the look on her face gave away the rest of the question.

The baby-faced girl beamed cheerfully. 'Like Mother Wickham says, if you get a good fucking every night, and a good beating only once a week, then you're better off than all the other women in Wood Street.' She sat back down on the bed. 'And you get money of your own to spend.'

Molly's thoughts flitted to her own purse. She put the shame out of her mind, and thought of a different shame. 'But you might have a...' A bastard. '...a baby.' Fourteen was too young for a harlot, but old enough for a mother. A shudder of cold nausea as her first night in London slipped into her memory. Seventeen was more than old enough to be a mother.

The Waif shook her head confidently. 'Not me.' She leaned forward, the old hand offering advice to the novice. 'I always wash myself out with sour milk afterwards. And I put half a lemon up there first. That makes it safe.' Her face split into a grin. 'Unless I'm being a virgin,' she said. 'Then I put some chicken liver up there. If they've got blood all over them when they've finished, they believe it.' The grin faded to nothing. 'Then they tell me how sorry they are, and some of them tell me they've got daughters of their own, and they give me money to buy some dolls with.' She frowned. 'I don't understand it, Moll. If

46

they come from the other side of London to The Bell, and pay Mother Wickham money to fuck me, and give me money on top of that, why should they be sorry? If they want to fuck their own daughters, why don't they? They probably wouldn't even have to pay.'

Molly opened her mouth to reply, then closed it again. Where to begin? Fornication? Adultery? Incest? Morals? Hopes of marriage? The Word of God?

Their own daughters?

Her father had taught her the value of chastity. If tha's got owt, lass, keep it to tha'sen - and ah'm not talking about thy halfpennies. Once tha's wed, it's between thee and thy husband. Till that day, keep it to tha'sen. A virtuous woman's price is far above rubies.

And what did I do? I traded rubies for gall. Traded virtue for disgrace. Buried my father's advice in a quicksand of brandy and honey.

Even if Cousin Tom hadn't known about The Bell, one look at me would have told him everything - my shame would have been glowing in my face, like a reflection of the fires of hell.

And who am I to give advice to the Waif? A silly country girl who surrendered her maidenhead to the first man who laid siege to it. A simpleton who traded her whole life for five golden guineas and a sick head. Who am I to offer advice to someone who's already sold her maidenhead twenty times, and is set to sell it twenty times more? I'm living in her world now; and her fifteen years have seen far, far more than my seventeen.

'What do you...' What do you say to them? What do you think about while they're doing these things to you? Do they ever realise that they're flirting with eternal damnation? How much money do they pay for you? 'What do you spend your money on?' A thought occurred to her. 'Or do you save it?'

The Waif hesitated, almost embarrassed. 'Books,' she said.

'Books?'

'When I haven't got visitors, I read books. I love books. I've got dozens of books. Homer, Shakespeare, Virgil, Rabelais. Lots of books.' She became oddly shy, almost embarrassed. 'They're all translated into English, though. I don't know how to read Latin and Greek.'

'Shakespeare is English.' She, too, had no classics. But her father had read her passages from Shakespeare when she was a girl.

'Is he?' Delighted surprise. 'Shakespeare's English? I didn't know that.'

'Where did you...' Go to school? That would seem unlikely. 'Who taught you to read?'

'Annie taught me. When I was little.'

Little? 'How long have you been...' A harlot. '...here? At The Bell?'

The Waif shrugged. 'Always, I suppose. Ever since I can remember, anyway. Can't remember being anywhere else.'

'Don't you have a mother?'

'Only Mother Wickham. Not a real mother.'

'Do you remember your mother?' A shake of the head.

Molly's eyes pricked with tears. The young girl's isolation made her feel her own loneliness all the more strongly. She put her hand on the Waif's and squeezed it, offering comfort.

The girl slipped off the bed and sat at Molly's feet, tucked up against her, her head leaning on her thigh, her free hand on Molly's knee. She looked up at Molly and smiled with a little-girl-lost innocence. 'Do you want to kiss me like the Twins do?' she asked.

Molly stared at her, uncomprehending. The Twins? A picture came into her mind: the Twins feeding each other, the Twins gazing at each other, the Twins touching each other the way she'd seen her brother Harry and Beth Fuller touching each other before they were married, the Twins behaving like lovers.

Women, together? Sisters, together?

Pushing the Waif roughly away, she rose giddily from the chair, crossed the room and flung open the window. She stood there, staring down into Wood Street, sucking in great gulps of the stinking air, trying not to be sick.

Oh, God, please God, what sort of world have you led me into?

She felt the Waif's arms circling her waist from behind, and her head snuggling up to her back. She stiffened in revulsion.

'Don't be frightened,' said the small voice behind. 'You don't have to. I was only being nice in case you wanted to. Please don't stop being my friend.'

Friend? The past few days had been such a nightmare, she'd not once thought of her York friends, all the friends she'd promised to write to from the Great City. She'd forgotten all about whispering her secrets to Maddie in the golden-sunbeamed, mouse-rustling hayloft; stirring up clouds of scent as she and ginger Dorothy chased painted butter-flies through the herb-garden; helping Dairy Jill to steal cherries, and looping them over her ears as pretend earrings. All the friends she'd laughed with, shared her dreams with, planned her future with.

All gone now. Brave Molly, seeking her fortune in London. Foolish Molly, plucked clean of everything she had within hours of arriving. Shamed Molly, who could not, dare not, write home to York without lying.

But the Waif had claimed her as a friend. And her claim was just: if Molly was to have any friends at all now, they would have to be the girls at The Bell. Nan and Polly, Annie and... No, not the Twins. There was no room in their hearts for outside friends, and no room in her own provincial morality for the realisation that had been forced upon her.

She eased herself around to face the Waif, whose head was snuggled now against Molly's breast. She smoothed the hair protectively, as if the Waif were one of her own young cousins or nieces. 'I'm still your friend,' she said. 'But this is all so strange to me. So... so...' A tear trick-led down the side of her nose, traced the corner of her lips, dripped down onto her chin. She wiped it away with the back of her hand. 'Helen... Ophelia... What am I going to do?'

The Waif hugged her. 'My real name's Kitty,' she said. 'I'll show you what you have to do.'

In the morning, the golden gowns arrived. In the afternoon, a parcel of caps and ribbons.

Just after sunset, the Colonel.

Molly sat silent, apprehensive at the table with him while he dined; she picked without appetite at the tidbits he cut and passed to her, and refused the wine he offered. Over the Colonel's shoulder, his man Quince leered and bobbed and winked at her, pouring wine when his master emptied his glass, snapping his fingers at Abigail when the bottle became low, removing the napkin from the Colonel's throat when he had finished eating.

The Colonel dipped his fingers into the bowl of water that had been brought for him, wiped them fastidiously with the napkin, stood and offered his hand to Moll. 'Shall we, my dear?'

She stayed sitting, too frightened to take his hand, too frightened to protest. The blood had drained away from her face, her heart was racing, her breathing was shallow, she could feel cold droplets of sweat breaking out on her forehead.

This time it wasn't seduction. This time she was sober. This time she had a choice. This time she could get up and run away, take her chance of escaping Jed, take her chance of eluding Quince, abandon her trunk and everything she'd brought from York. Throw herself on the pitiless mercy of London. Deep inside her, she knew that the choice was no choice.

Seeing her reluctance, the Colonel frowned apologetically. 'Forgive me, Moll,' he murmured to her. 'Quince,' he said reprovingly to his man.

The servant scuttled behind her, scraped the chair away as she started to rise. With no alternative, she stood fully. Left with no alternative as the Colonel continued to hold out his hand, she put her hand in his. And then there was no alternative but to follow him, out of the eating room as Quince held the door open, up the stairs as Quince scurried ahead of them, into her room as Quince held open the door and stood aside.

The Colonel nodded with satisfaction at the room's familiarity. Everything was as it always was. Only the girl had changed. 'Thank you, Quince.' The servant bobbed his head, gave a last leer and wink at Molly, and closed the door behind him.

The Colonel placed his cane with military precision on the vanity table, sat in the padded wooden chair, leaned back comfortably and put his fingertips together. 'Now, then, what shall we do?' he asked Molly. His manner was relaxed, friendly. She didn't answer. 'What shall we do, Moll Huckerby?' he said again. She didn't know what to say. 'Well, my dear, whatever we're going to do, I think you should take your clothes off first, don't you?'

She stood backed up against a carved bedpost, one hand to her breast, the other behind her, nervously playing with the heavy-draped bed-curtain. 'Please...' she said in a tiny voice.

'Excellent.' he said.

Still she made no move. 'I - I can't,' she said.

He reached out a hand towards her, solicitously, courteously, fully understanding. 'Shall I ask Mother Wickham to help you?'

A dead despair settled on her. 'No.'

'Good. You may begin with your cap.'

She untied the strings to her flimsy cap and took it off; her brown hair spilled over her shoulders. She stood facing him, nervously twisting the scrap of linen through her fingers.

'There,' he told her encouragingly, 'that wasn't difficult, was it?' When she didn't answer, he widened his eyes slightly and asked her again. 'Was it?' Almost imperceptibly, she shook her head. 'And taking off your shoes can't be more difficult than taking off your cap, can it? Or your stockings?'

She sat on the edge of the bed and took off her shoes. With trembling fingers, she reached up under her skirts, untied her garters, rolled down her stockings and put them on the floor beside her shoes.

'Or your gown.'

Clenching her teeth to give her resolve, she stood with her back to him, slipped the loose-fitting golden gown over her shoulders, pushed it down over her hips and let it fall to the floor.

'Excellent,' he said. 'Now your bodice.'

She fumbled at the drawstrings with clumsy fingers, managed to loosen them, and pulled the boned bodice over her head. Tucking her elbows tightly to her sides, she let the garment fall onto the bed.

'And the rest,' he said.

'Please...'

'And the rest.'

She untied the strings of her petticoat but clutched the fabric to her, holding it in place.

'And the rest.'

Her face puckered as the tears began, and she let the strings go. But her tightly clamped knees and thighs caught the fabric between them and it simply drooped, falling away from her buttocks but not falling to the floor.

'Move your feet apart, Moll,' the Colonel said. Her muscles didn't want to obey her. 'Now!' he snapped.

Startled, she jerked her foot a couple of inches. The petticoat slid down her legs to the floor, and settled round her ankles.

'Step out of it,' he said, his voice as casual as before. She picked her feet clear of the tumbled velvet and linen, but kept her back to him, hunched into her nakedness. 'Now turn to face me.' She couldn't. This was the moment she'd been preserving for her husband. 'Turn!'

The husband she would probably now never have. Her left arm covering her breasts, her right hand tucked between her legs, she shuffled three quarters of the way round to face him, her head lowered onto her chest.

'Excellent,' he said. 'Now put both hands down by your sides, and stand up straight.' She stayed where she was, statue-frozen. 'Now, Moll,' he instructed her. His voice was conversational, but there was menace in it. 'Now.'

She did as she was told. She knew he was gazing at her, mapping the contours of her exposed body, but she didn't meet his eyes. Even the tears had stopped flowing.

'You're a lovely young woman, Moll,' he said. 'And I can see that you're very sensitive.' He smiled sympathetically. 'And, with the exception of just one aberration, which wasn't your fault, still a virgin. I like that in a woman.' He took a few moments to enjoy his exploration. 'Yes, quite lovely. But tonight is not the night to enjoy all your many virtues at once. A pleasure delayed is a pleasure doubly savoured.'

She ventured a glance at him.

Relaxed, comfortable, the connoisseur's smile of approval. 'Quince!' he called, not much above a conversational tone.

The door of the room opened instantly, and the Colonel's man appeared. 'Yes, Colonel?' Molly twisted away from the intruder, trying to cover herself with her hands.

'Don't be afraid, Moll,' said the Colonel. 'Quince is my friend. You should greet him as such. Allow him to kiss your hand, Moll.' He allowed her a few seconds hesitation. 'Moll?'

She hunched her shoulders forward, making her body as small as she could, her covering hands and arms as big as she could. Quince oiled past her, faced her, held out his hand for hers.

'Your hand, Moll.' Which hand? She squeezed her elbow further across her body, and tried to extend her left hand without exposing more of herself than was already showing. 'Come, now, Moll, that's no way to greet one of my friends. But perhaps you've never learned the rules of etiquette. Perhaps I should ask Mother Wickham to instruct you. After I've left, of course.'

She shrank into herself, offered her left hand to Quince. Still she didn't stand upright, and her right hand stayed spread over her pubic hair.

Quince took her hand and raised it to his lips. He held it there so long she eventually had to look up at him from beneath her tear-heavy eyelashes. Only a few inches away from her, his ferret-thin face was leering and winking at her.

'Quince,' the Colonel said, 'I think Moll has given me what I wanted from tonight. Ask Mother Wickham to send up one of the other girls.' Quince backed out of the room, his smirk never wavering, his eyes never leaving Molly's body. She could hear his footsteps tripping down the stairs.

Molly knelt to pick up her gown. 'Stay as you are, Moll,' the Colonel told her. She halted, slowly stood up again. 'You must think of me as a teacher, my child.' He rose to his feet. 'And we are just about to embark upon the next part of your education.'

She waited. Three minutes which stretched out like three hours. Then she heard the clatter of feet coming up the stairs. Two sets of feet. She stooped for her gown, caught the Colonel's eye, straightened up again. She covered herself as best as she could with her arms, dropped her head, turned her face away.

Quince came into the room, followed by Nan. 'Thank you, Quince,' the Colonel said. Quince left. 'Undress,' the Colonel said to Nan. Unfussily, as if preparing for sleep in her own room, Nan stripped off all her clothes and lay on her back on the bed. 'Watch,' the Colonel said to Molly, 'and learn.'

He unbuttoned his breeches and pulled himself free. He was already erect. Nan opened her legs wide. Without ceremony, without foreplay, he knelt between her thighs, lowered himself onto her and let her guide him into her. 'Come here, Moll,' he said. Reluctantly, she took a pace towards the bed. He snaked out his hand, twined his fingers into her hair and forced her head down level with his hips. On the farm she'd seen bulls serving cows, stallions covering mares, rams tupping ewes. But always from half a field away, never from just a few inches.

Nan wrapped her legs round his waist and pushed against him as he thrust into her. A dozen strokes later, he began to grunt through his teeth. 'Uh! Uh! Uh! Uh!'

Nan matched the Colonel's grunting with encouraging squeaks of her own. His fingers slipped out of Molly's hair and his whole body went rigid. 'Aaaahh...' he breathed. Nan moaned with unconvincing ecstasy.

The Colonel sagged on top of Nan, blowing noisily, then withdrew from her, swung his legs to the floor and stood. 'That's your first lesson, Moll,' he said. He tugged a silk handkerchief from his sleeve, wiped himself, tucked in his shirt and rebuttoned his breeches. 'If you wish to please me, always pretend you've enjoyed it. As she did.' He picked up his cane from the table. 'Quince!' The door opened, and the servant entered. 'One for Moll, one for...' He wafted a hand in Nan's direction. '...the other one. Be downstairs in five minutes.' He paused at the door. 'Get dressed,' he told Molly, 'then see Annie.'

Before the door had closed behind him, Molly had turned her back on Quince and was scrambling into her clothes as fast as she could. Quince stepped past her, put a guinea on the vanity table, and started to unbutton his breeches. She went cold with fear, and clutched her gown to her; but he continued past her to the bed, where the already paid-for entertainment was waiting.

She finished dressing to the sound of his guttural snorting behind her, punctuated by Nan's practised gasping. He was still pounding vigorously at her when Molly grabbed her shoes and stockings and the prize money, and fled barefoot down the stairs to Annie's room.

Chapter 6

The beggar rested his weight on the rough crutch and eyed Annie's bed hopefully. She lifted a finger in a gentle denial. 'Not this time, Jack. It was small news, and I already knew it.' He didn't argue; disappointment was part of a beggar's life. She rose from her chair, poured a glass of gin at the table near the fireplace, brought it back to him. No cordial for the beggar. 'But I'll always listen, you know that.'

No pretence that the gin was anything more than a way of dulling his existence. Tipping his head back, he emptied the glass in one swallow. His breath caught in the back of this throat for a moment; he gasped, then swivelled his crippled neck towards the bottle. Annie gestured an invitation. He hobbled across the room, tucked his crutch under his arm, propped himself against the wall and poured himself another glass of the colourless liquid. This time, he savoured the first sip before tossing the rest back.

She held out her hand for the empty glass. 'I'll always listen, Jack.'

He gave her the glass, levered himself onto his crutch and swung himself to the door. As he reached for the handle, the door crashed open and swept his crutch from under him. He tumbled to the floor, cracking his head against the bare floorboards.

Molly stood a yard inside the door, both hands to her mouth, staring from Annie to the beggar, from the beggar to Annie, not knowing what to say, what to do.

'Get out!' Annie shouted. 'Get out!'

Shocked at the venom in her voice, Molly fled back up the stairs, past the swaggering Quince as he emerged from her room, into her candle-lit haven, where the naked Nan sat spread-legged on the edge of the bed, wiping herself clean with a grubby cloth. After the initial surge of embarrassment, Molly noticed that blood was dripping from Nan's nose, splashing onto her breasts, and running down onto her belly.

At last, something she could cope with. Wringing out a towel in the room's basin of cold water, she sat down on the bed beside her and swabbed the blood away, careful not to press too heavily against the swelling flesh.

Half an hour later, Abigail tapped on Annie's door and waited for it to be opened. 'Here she is, Miz Annie, like you ask for.' She ushered Molly into the room, then shut the door behind her.

'Come in, Moll,' said Annie. No sign of her previous anger. 'Jack's just leaving.' Clinging to the bedpost, the beggar bent awkwardly to retrieve his crutch, then pulled himself upright. 'Go to the kitchen,' she told him. 'Tell Abigail I said you could fill your belly. And take enough bread with you for tomorrow.'

The beggar smiled his gratitude and limped out. The door closed behind him.

'Now, Moll,' said Annie. The heat had subsided, but the firmness remained. 'It's time for you to learn one or two simple lessons. And less painful that you learn them from me than from Mother Wickham.' She indicated the hard-backed chair. Molly sat, subdued. 'After that, you're to come out with me into the Town to continue your education.'

The Town? Education? No! If it's the sort of education Mother Wickham would have me receive, if it's more of the education the Colonel gave me not half an hour ago, then no!

Heart thumping, fingernails digging into her palms, she stood. 'Thank you, Annie,' she said, as coolly as she could, trying to steady the tremor in her voice. 'But I'll not come with you. If you'll ask someone to help me downstairs with my trunk, I shall - '

'Listen to me, Moll.' Annie's voice was tired, uninvolved. She was offering advice, not demanding obedience. 'And sit down.'

Moll stayed standing, her stubborn lips set tight. I'm not going to sit. And I'm not going abroad this evening. My education can wait. God willing, it can wait forever.

Annie sighed but said nothing: it made no difference to her. She moved past Molly to the table, poured herself a glass of gin, laced it with thick, sugary cordial. 'Nobody will help you with your trunk unless Mother Wickham orders them to. You will come into Town with me tonight, because it has already been decided. No harm will come to you, and I will bring you safe back here afterwards.'

'What sort of education?' She could already read and write, her father had insisted she know her numbers, and she was well acquainted with the Bible.

'I'm to take you to the theatre.'

'The theatre? But...' How can I afford to go to the theatre?

Annie read her mind from her words. 'The Colonel's paying.'

'Where are we going?'

'Later.' Back to the subject. 'This, Moll, is a brothel-house.' Molly coloured. She couldn't accept that she was living among harlots. 'You burst in upon me when I was with Stumpy Jack.' Molly opened her mouth to speak, but Annie ignored her and continued. 'I might have been with a real visitor, a paying visitor. I might have been with the Colonel. Would you have liked that to happen?'

Molly dropped her eyes. The Colonel terrified her. 'But it was the Colonel who told me to - '

'I might have been with one of his friends. Someone who might have complained to Mother Wickham. Would you have liked that to happen?'

'No.' Little more than a mouse-squeak. Mother Wickham terrified her even more than the Colonel.

Annie sipped at her gin. 'The rules are few, Moll, and simple. You may go into your own room without knocking. You may go into the kitchen without knocking. You may go into the entertaining room without knocking - but only if you're part of the game. At all other times, at all other doors, you must knock. And if you don't receive an answer, you must go away. Either there's nobody there, or they don't want to see you. Do you need me to explain why?'

She shook her head, staring in embarrassment at the floor. Annie's message was clear. And, of course, obvious.

Annie lifted the gin to her mouth again. 'The Colonel came to see you.' It wasn't a question, but Molly nodded confirmation. 'He made you undress, and then just looked at you.' Molly nodded again. 'And then he had his man bring Nan up to him, and he fucked her.' Another nod, and a hot, swimming flush as she remembered. 'Afterwards, he told you that if you wanted to please him, you had to enjoy whatever he did to you - or at least pretend to.' Another nod. 'Don't.'

Molly jerked her head up. 'What? I don't understand.'

'Don't pretend to enjoy it.' The single candle on the table lit one side of her face with a guttering paleness, leaving the other in deep shadow. 'He's not at all interested in you, Moll, nor your body, nor what you do with it.' She toyed with her glass, tilting it so that the purple liquid inside ran almost, but not quite, to the brim. 'The Colonel plays a different game,' she said. 'Mother Wickham supplies him with virgins, such as you were, and he destroys their innocence. That's what he comes here for, Moll. And as long as you hate everything he does, as long as he can shame you, and make you beg him not to do it, he'll keep coming back to you. But as soon as you try to please him, as soon as you try to become better at it, that's when he'll cast you off.'

Molly glimpsed an end to the nightmare. 'But that's what I - '

Annie stilled her protest. 'No, Moll, you don't want him to cast you off.'

'But - '

'This is a new life for you, Moll. You hate it.' She raised her hand before Molly could speak. 'I hated it, too. But this is the life you've got, now. There's nowhere else you can go.'

'If Bull would help me with my trunk, I could - '

'Believe me, Moll, there's nowhere else you can go.' She came close to Molly and put her hand on her shoulder. 'You hate the Colonel. Quite right. We all hate the Colonel. But life as the Colonel's own private whore is a lot better than life as nobody's private whore. It's a lot better than being everybody's whore, whether you hate them or not. Whether you've ever seen them before or not.' She removed her hand from Molly's shoulder, put her fingers under her chin, tipped her head up and looked into her eyes. 'When you start to enjoy what the Colonel does, or even pretend to enjoy what the Colonel does, that's when he'll cast you off, and ask Mother Wickham to find him someone else. And that's when you'll find out what the life of a harlot is really like.' She clasped Molly to her and hugged her comfortingly. 'The life of a harlot,' she murmured into Molly's ear, 'steals your very self. But there are tricks to make it bearable. Since nobody cares who you are, you can be whoever else you want to be. Like Kitty and her different names. If you hate what the Colonel is doing to you, you can make yourself believe that he's doing it to somebody else, that you are someone else.'

'I could never give myself another name.' Her father's voice welled up in her memory. Be proud of tha name, lass: tha name is who th'art. I've lost my good name - but I shall never lose my real name. She hesitated before speaking again. What questions were allowed? 'The Colonel. Did you ever...?'

Molly felt the hot breath against her face as Annie exhaled sharply. 'Oh, yes. I was the Colonel's whore for several months. Years ago. When I was not much older than Kitty.'

'Why didn't you...?'

'Why didn't I learn my own lesson? Why didn't I carry on pretending?' She pulled away. There was no pretence now. Her eyes were bleak. 'I fell in love. And I ran away.'

Molly said nothing. If Annie wants to tell me, she will. If not, not.

Annie returned to the table and filled her glass. 'Mother Wickham had me brought back,' she said. A hint of pain sharpened her voice. 'The Colonel's men killed my Billy. And I had a baby. And she died.' She swallowed the gin and poured another, not bothering to soften it with cordial. 'That's when I stopped pretending. I didn't care any more who they were, or what they did.' She tipped the gin into her mouth. 'Keep on hating the Colonel, Moll. And keep on hating whatever he does. Because it is hateful. He is hateful.' She poured more gin into her glass. 'But he has money.' A wry smile flickered at the edge of her pale lips. 'Hate him, love his money. Then maybe one day you'll be able to leave him - and take his money with you.' Again she tipped the glass; but this time, the gin barely wetted her lips. 'The pity is, he won't miss either you or the money.'

Knuckles rapped at the door. 'Miz Annie?'

'Come in, Abigail.'

The door opened. Abigail stood there, but didn't enter. 'Visitor, Miz Annie.'

'Who?'

Her shoulders shrugged up round her plump neck. 'Not seen him afore, Miz Annie.'

'Where's Nan?'

'No-good Quince hit her. Her eye all swelled up. She lying down with one of my poultices.'

'Polly?'

'Visitor.'

'Twins?'

'Out with the babies.'

Annie drained the rest of her gin and picked up the bottle. 'While you're the Colonel's whore,' she told Molly, 'you'll be spared this. Go back to your room. Meet me in the kitchen at five by St Alban's.' She turned to the negress. 'Ask him to wait, Abigail. I want to make sure I'm ready.'

As Molly left, Annie was filling her glass again.

She'd never seen anywhere so magnificent.

York was small and medieval. The towns on the York Wagon's journey south - Doncaster, Grantham, Peterborough, Hatfield - were even smaller than York. And all she'd seen of London was Wood Street and Covent Garden.

Until now. Lincoln's Inn Fields luxuriated in its own formality, its stately houses peering down at her with an air of condescension. The Lincoln's Inn Fields Theatre soared above her, three storeys high, its windows as high as a man, its arched doorway promising regality within.

She hung onto Annie's arm, hot excitement coursing through her. 'The folk are all so grand,' she said, her eyes wide with awe. If Annie hadn't been with her, she'd have run away.

Tall men in powdered wigs, rouged ladies in fine-spun gowns, bowing servants. Three days ago, she'd been ashamed of her plain York dress. This night, she was almost ashamed of the golden gown the Colonel's money had bought for her.

'Not so grand,' Annie said. 'If we have money enough to go in, we're as grand as they are.' She counted four shillings into the hand of the doorman, and led Molly into the theatre.

Four shillings? Molly opened her mouth to protest. If she'd married Big Ned Foley, they'd have been glad to get that in a week. But this wasn't her money to protest about.

The noise was deafening: chattering men, shrilly laughing women, rowdy drunks, calling vendors.

A heavily pregnant woman brushed past them and mumbled her apologies. Annie caught her arm, whispered in her ear, let her go; the expectant mother disappeared into the swirling crowd. Annie gave Molly back the ivory brooch Mother Wickham had lent her to go with her gown. Molly hadn't missed it.

Annie shoved and elbowed a path for them into the pit, past the orange-sellers, the fops, the harlots, the bucks, the cutpurses, fending off probing hands, thieving hands, groping hands, inching as far forward as they could, just a few yards from the stage.

Molly gripped Annie's arm tightly. 'I've never been in a theatre before,' she said. Mummers at Christmas, now and then a mystery play (but her Grandam remembered them being performed every year), sometimes a travelling troupe of acrobats. But never a building this big, decorated with such splendour, existing only for the strutting of actors. 'I've never seen a play. Not a real play.'

She stood and gawped. At the stage with its crimson curtain, at the carved cherubs on the proscenium, at the packed seats to either side of them. Above all, at the people. Men and women of class, confident, proud, assured, there to be seen as much as to see. Men of substance, there to meet clients, to discuss business, to worship Mammon. Women of pleasure, there to make what living they could from whoever had money enough to buy them. Men and women from the underbelly of the Town, stalking their victims like cats in a rat-run.

And there, to one side of the stage, the Colonel. He saw her, but showed no sign of recognition.

'Don't acknowledge him.' Annie at her side, drawing her further into the press. 'Pretend you haven't seen him.' Embarrassed, flustered, Molly switched her gaze to the other side of the stage.

And found herself staring at another man, a young man, dark, brooding, chisel-featured, sitting next to an older man who could have been his father. Jews, both of them.

Again, she averted her eyes. But, when she glanced back, the older man had joined him in looking at her. A word was spoken; they both laughed, then turned their attention to other matters. Molly could feel herself colouring.

The hubbub abated as an actor stepped onto the stage. He began to speak.

Molly didn't even hear the words, let alone understood them. Who listens to the words of a spell when magic is being cast?

After the play, the Colonel followed them back to The Bell.

Without saying a word, he took Molly's hand and led her up to her room. His room. Instead of asking her to undress, he simply ripped her new golden gown away from her body. She squealed with fear and backed away from him, trying to hide her nakedness, clutching at the trailing cloth.

Still without speaking, he drove her backward towards the bed. 'Please, no,' she said. 'Please, no.' Her foot caught in the torn velvet, and she fell, landing awkwardly on the floor against the side of the bed, banging her head against the solid wood; the room tilted and went hazy.

Stooping, he grasped her under the arms and heaved her onto the bed. 'Please, no,' she said, sprawling on her back, trying to protect herself.

Again he grabbed her, this time by the elbow, spinning her onto her face. She felt his hands at her ankles, forcing them apart, pushing them up till she was on all fours, her petticoats being snatched roughly up over her waist. A moment's hasty fumbling, and then he was in her, grunting, grating painfully against her dryness, his fingers digging into her hips, his thighs slapping noisily against her buttocks.

Her arms gave way, and she collapsed with her face in her hands, bucking forwards with each thrust, hacking great sobs until he eased, slumped against her, caught his breath, then withdrew. She rolled over onto her side and curled herself into a ball, her eyes tightly shut, the sobs coughing into the silence.

She heard the clink of coins on the dressing table, and the door shutting behind him.

From start to finish, he'd not spoken a single word.

As soon as the Colonel had gone, Abigail busied up the stairs with a bowl of sour milk and a short bamboo pipe with a pig's bladder tied to the end of it.

Numbed, Molly gave in while she was sluiced and dried.

Before leaving, Abigail gave her a small wooden box with a hinged lid. Inside it was a fresh lemon and a penknife. 'Mother Wickham don't want no bastards no more than you does, Miz Moll,' she said. 'I give you a fresh one every day, just for when you needs it.' She collected up her bowl and douche, then offered a cryptic explanation. 'You only use half, and you squeeze the juice out first.'

Midday. Mother Wickham's instructions for the day. Breakfast. Porridge, bread, cheese, ale. Dogs snuffling sullenly under their feet, waiting for scraps.

Molly had no appetite, and spent her time at the table staring up at the door into Love Lane at the back of The Bell, avoiding the other girls. She hurt, and it was uncomfortable to sit. But, nevertheless, she sat, as The Bell's custom demanded.

Annie bent over her as she left. 'Never, never learn to enjoy it,' she told her.

One by one, the other girls left. None of them spoke to her. As the Waif stood to leave, she put her book into Molly's hands. 'The Rape of Lucrece,' she said. 'Shakespeare. It's for you.'

Alone, Molly let her misery overcome her, and the tears rolled down her face, dripping off her chin and into the cold porridge in front of her.

'The Colonel won't need you tonight.' Mother Wickham. Molly hadn't heard her coming in. 'This afternoon, Annie will take you to be measured for a new gown. The Colonel's paying.' By the time Molly had wiped the tears away, she'd gone again.

The next time, three days later, Quince was invited in to watch while the Colonel undressed her, kissed her, laid her gently on the bed and enjoyed her.

The following afternoon, the Colonel sat in his large wooden chair and watched while Quince enjoyed her.

The theatre. Quince went ahead of them, elbowing, shoving, kicking people out of the way, making passage for the Colonel and his bright-eyed companion, clearing a path for them to their seats on the stage itself.

'My niece,' the Colonel said, introducing her to My Lord This, and My Lady That, and Sir Whatever. 'New to Town from the country.'

She bobbed and curtsied the way Annie had taught her, lowering her eyes so as not to seem bold. The discreet silence was tutored; the blush was genuine. Nobody believed any of it.

On the opposite side of the stage, the young Jew nudged his father. 'I've seen her before,' he said.

'Who?'

'The pretty girl with Colonel Charnell.'

The old Jew didn't look up from the orange he was peeling. 'A harlot,' he said.

'How do you know? You don't know who I'm talking about.'

'If she's with Colonel Charnell, she's a harlot.' He bit into the fruit, savoured it, and spat a pip onto the floor. 'Unless she's his wife.' He grinned wryly at his son. 'But, Isaac, no one, not even you, would describe the Colonel's wife as a pretty girl.' Isaac scowled. 'Noble, perhaps,' his father went on. 'A woman to give strength to a man. A woman to trust. But not a pretty girl. Believe me, Isaac, whoever the Colonel has with him, however pretty she may be, she's a harlot. Or,' he added in the interests of accuracy, 'if she isn't yet, she very soon will be.'

The young man studied her. Nothing brazen about her but, yes, possibly a harlot. But, if so, a very pretty harlot.

The Colonel made room for her, guided her elbow with a practised touch, solicitous, attentive until she was comfortably seated; he called an orange-seller to her, helped Molly peel the pungent fruit and divide it into segments. The acid-sweet taste was new to her. She smiled with pleasure. The Colonel noted her reaction with indulgence, encouraging her to eat the rest. But his eyes remained cold and cruel.

A few feet away, the vast crimson curtain lifted to reveal the stage, and the audience hushed.

'I've never been,' said the Waif. 'I've read dozens of playbooks, and lots and lots of Shakespeare's plays, but I've never been to the theatre. Tell me what it's like.'

Molly pulled the blanket up to her chin and leaned back against her pillows. 'Fairies,' she said, remembering. 'And magic. And people being in love. And at the end there was dancing.'

The Waif, sitting at the foot of Molly's bed, hugged her own knees. 'But what was the theatre like? Was it big and grand like Hamlet's castle? Or was it rich and strange like Cleopatra's palace?' An incongruous thought tickled her. 'Or was it like the hovel in King Lear?'

'I don't know.' Molly was awkward in her ignorance; but the Waif's question carried no malice. 'I've never been in a palace, and I don't know what a hovel is.'

'Nor have I ever been in a palace. But I know what they're like.' She looked into the distance, and painted a picture. 'Every room is as big as a cathedral, and they're lined with gold, and paved with marble, and the people are all princes and princesses, and they're all beautiful, and... and...' With all her reading, the Waif didn't have the words to describe her vision.

Molly thought back to her evening. 'The stage was like a palace,' she said. 'And very, very big. And the actors and the actresses were like princes and princesses. At least, they were dressed like princes and princesses.' Her face darkened. 'But the people in the... the people who were watching - '

'The audience.'

'The audience...' Her voice drifted away to nothing.

'Yes?'

She blushed with remembered shame. 'The Colonel told them I were his niece. But they didn't look at me as if I were kin. The women looked at me as if I were a serving girl, and the men looked at me the way my Uncle Barnabas looks at the pigs at York Fair. As if they were judging how much I might weigh.'

The Waif corrected her. 'Judging how much you might cost.'

Change the subject. 'But there were so many people in the... the audience.' She remembered a frisson of excitement. 'And I saw someone steal a handkerchief.' The Waif's eyes brightened; actors, fashion, crime - this was a tale worth listening to. Molly continued. 'When we were going in. There was a man standing there in fine clothes.'

'Was he handsome?'

'Eh? Oh, er, no. Not handsome at all. But very fine. And he was standing with his hands on his hips. Well, behind him, there was a roughly dressed man with a large hat.'

'Pulled down about his face.'

'Aye, I suppose it were. I hadn't thought about that.'

'A disguise,' the Waif said. For her, reality could always be improved by imagination.

'Well, then the rough man tickled the other man behind the ear with the tip of a feather. And when he reached up to scratch his ear, the rough man snatched his handkerchief and wriggled away into the crowd. And the fine man didn't even know.'

'And then what happened?'

'Then the Colonel led me on further, and I couldn't see any more.' Suddenly, she remembered. 'And we had oranges! I've never had oranges before.'

The Waif wasn't to be outdone. 'I've had oranges. I've had lots of oranges.' And then, so as not to spoil Molly's moment, 'But none this year.'

'The next time we go to the theatre, I shall bring you back an orange,' Molly promised. A knot formed in the pit of her stomach. Already, she thought, I'm looking forward to the next time.

A few yards away, St Alban's clanked out midnight. The Waif un-clasped her knees, stood, leaned across the bed and kissed Molly lightly on the lips, the innocent kiss of a child. 'Goodnight, Moll,' she said. She opened the door, but didn't leave immediately. 'When I'm too old to pretend,' she said, 'I shall be an actress in a theatre. A theatre like Cleopatra's palace.' She spoke it as a fact, not as a dream. 'One day, I shall have a theatre of my own.'

The door closed, and she was gone.

❈

It was the Waif's idea. 'Let's go to church,' she said, as St Alban's rang out the three-quarter hour. They were side by side at Molly's open window, leaning on the sill, watching the noisy swirl of Wood Street, letting the warm April sunshine play on their faces.

'When?' Molly asked.

'Tomorrow.'

'Is there a service tomorrow?'

The Waif giggled. 'Of course there is! Tomorrow's Sunday.'

Sunday. And she'd been here since Thursday. No: she'd been here since a sevenight last Thursday. A ten-day tumble from grace into damnation. 'I...' She turned back into the room and began to rearrange the precisely placed trinkets on the vanity table. 'I'm not sure I... How can I go to church when I've... The Colonel...' She left the rest of the sentence unsaid.

'Pray for God's mercy,' said the Waif. Her child's voice was oddly callous.

My cousin Tom couldn't forgive me. I don't think I can ever forgive myself. Why should God forgive me? 'Will God have mercy on me?' she asked; her voice was small, her thoughts far away.

'On you?' said the Waif. Her voice was puzzled. 'No, pray God's mercy on the Colonel. He's so far fallen into wickedness, only God can pull him out again now.' She looked furtively behind her, as if God might be listening, and lowered her voice. 'Best of all, cry God's curse on him, and pray that He'll stamp on his head and push him yet deeper into wickedness, so that he drowns in it.' She stamped her foot on the floor and made a squelching sound with her lips. 'Drown him in a whole midden of wickedness. A whole shit-pit of evil.' She squelched her lips again.

Molly stamped her own foot, and squelched her own lips. 'A shit-pit of evil,' she repeated.

A vision of the Colonel, gasping with fear, trying to claw himself out of a bubbling brown quicksand, his wig plastered close to his head, filth dripping down his face, spitting shit, being dragged under by laughing, howling, mocking demons, crying for mercy, calling for Molly's help, screaming No! No! No!, stretching out his hand towards her, sinking, sinking -

'Moll?'

She swung to face the Waif, her eyes wide. 'Uh?' A whimper of fear, the bleat of a lost lamb.

'Are you unwell?' She came to Molly and took her hands in her own. 'Don't think about the Colonel. Let's think of tomorrow, and church, and God's grace.' She craned her neck, squinting out of the window at the church clock opposite. 'I have to go now. I have a visitor on the hour. I'll arise at six tomorrow morning by St Alban's, and I'll come into your room to wake you.'

Molly demurred. 'But Annie said we must never go into a room unless we've been - '

The Waif squeezed Molly's fingers reassuringly. 'Even if he comes, the Colonel never stays all night. He has his wife to go home to. And I dare not tap on your door - Mother Wickham might hear me. I shall have to creep past her door to get to yours.'

'Where shall we go?' Her voice had dropped, as if it were a conspiracy they were planning.

'St Alban's.' The Waif was quite certain. 'We can hear the prayers and the sermon and be back in bed by nine o'clock, and no one will even know we've left the house.'

Molly was content to let the younger girl make the decision. 'St Alban's,' she agreed.

They looked at each other with a shared mischief. 'Don't tell Mother Wickham,' they chorused.

They crept down the back stairs and out into the black chill of Love Lane, deserted but for a couple of aimless dogs, a sleeping beggar huddled against a wall under a wooden balcony, a lurching last-night reveller pissing into the gutter. The grey glow of pre-dawn spilled into the far end of the lane, but avoided the lingering night outside The Bell's kitchen.

As they turned the corner into the early shadows of Wood Street, a familiar voice above them broke into the near-silence. 'Going out so early?'

Chapter 7

The two girls froze, and their heads jerked upwards. Annie's window was open, and she was leaning on the sill, her long red hair falling loosely about her face.

The Waif checked to see if The Bell's front door was shut, then poked her head round the corner to peer back into Love Lane. 'Please, Annie, don't tell Mother Wickham. Don't let Jed follow us. We're only going to... We thought we'd like to...' She tailed off into silence, awkward, embarrassed.

Molly's glanced up at the tower above them. 'We're going to church,' she said. To her own ears, her voice sounded defiant.

'Don't go to St Alban's,' Annie said. 'It's too near. We remind the congregation too much of the sins they've gone there to be forgiven for. Wait.' She stepped back into her room, then reappeared. A grey woollen cloak floated down, flapping and swooping like a giant bat. 'You should have worn your blue and white dress,' she said as Molly caught it in her arms. 'A golden gown in church is as good as a badge.' She drew back into her room and closed the shutters behind her.

Molly swung the cloak over her shoulders. The Waif took hold of her hand, and they ran lightly along Wood Street towards the river until they were out of sight of The Bell. 'We'll go into the first church we come to,' said the Waif.

'The second,' said Molly.

'The third,' said the Waif.

Molly considered. As long as it was anonymous and safe, she didn't care where it was. 'The third,' she agreed.

The third church they came to was neither large nor small, neither sumptuous nor mean, neither full nor empty. The service had just started; they creaked the iron-studded oak doors open, sidled in and stood at the back, next to one of the cold stone pillars. The smell of the incense swept Molly back to York, to St Margaret's, to the resounding bass voice of Pastor Cartwright preaching love and charity.

As the congregation mumbled their responses, the Waif clutched Molly by the arm and hissed into her ear. 'I know him!'

'Who?'

'The parson. He was one of my visitors.'

Open-mouthed, Molly stared at the black-clad figure in front of the altar. 'He can't be,' she whispered back.

'He is, he is! Whenever Mother Wickham said he was coming, she always said to expect His Holiness, but I never knew why.'

Molly smelt danger. She took the Waif by the arm. 'Let's go.'

As Molly tugged open the heavy oak door, she heard the Waif's piping voice ring out as clear as one of the church's own bells. 'Your parson is a fornicator,' she said. A hundred or more shocked faces swung round. 'Lock up your daughters,' she said. 'He fucks little girls like me.'

Before the horrified gasp had time to boil into anger, she'd grabbed Molly's hand, and the pair of them were out of the church, running furiously, dodging into alleyways, losing themselves in the labyrinth of courtyards and side-streets beyond Cheapside, until they'd run themselves to a standstill, panting for breath, crying with laughter, hopelessly lost.

Molly composed her features into a stern admonishment. 'You shouldn't have said that in church,' she said. 'Not in church. Even if it were true.' Her face cracked again, and she burst into giggles.

Linking arms, they carried on walking, following the downhill cobbles. 'I hated him more than all the others,' the Waif said, making a face. 'He used to preach me sermons while he was taking my clothes off. Suffer the little children to come unto me, he used to say. Then he used to put me on his lap, and put the end of his prick in me.' She curled her young lip in contempt. 'He wasn't even honest about that. He always used to pretend it had been an accident. Then he'd give me a sugarstick, and say Bless you, my child, and sneak out through the kitchen door into Love Lane. And then, I suppose, every Sunday he'd go to his church and preach the evils of fornication. He's a hippo... hippo something.'

'Hypocrite.'

'Hypocrite. That's the word. Annie told me what it means.' She grimaced ruefully, as if she'd made a mistake in class. 'I remembered what it meant,' she said. 'I just forgot what the word was.'

Molly took her hand. 'We'd better go home,' she said. Already, The Bell had become home.

But the Waif had a better idea. 'Let's go down to the river,' she said.

'We can look at the river, and still be home before breakfast.' She challenged Molly's doubtful expression. 'Annie knows where we've gone. She knows we'll be back. And she won't tell Mother Wickham. Or Jed.'

Molly allowed herself to be led by the Waif through the half-deserted Sunday streets that sloped down and away from the church, the City, The Bell.

They turned a corner, and the Thames lay spread out in front of them. Wide, slow, brown; small ships swaying at anchor; bigger ships lying sluggish in the water, their uncanvased masts stark against the clouded sky like a winter copse below the moors; tiny waves slapping at the wharves; muffled voices getting the morning under way.

Molly's eyes widened, and her mouth gaped open. 'It's so big,' she said. Beside this, the Ouse at York was nothing more than a trickle, a paddling stream for children, a gutter to be stepped over.

'It's the biggest river in the world.' No possibility of doubt. The Waif pointed downstream to her left, a dramatic gesture like a magician revealing a conjured apparition. 'There's London Bridge,' she said, with as much pride as if she'd built it herself.

Molly would never have believed a bridge could span banks so far apart. No simple structure to take wagons and horses, this; no up-and-over road across the river to unite two halves of a city. This was a thoroughfare in its own right, a quarter of a mile from one end to the other, stone arch striding confidently after stone arch, supporting huge houses, three, four, five storeys high, water boiling beneath them like all the mill-races in the world.

She picked her way across the flotsam-decked mudflat to the water's edge. She crouched and put her fingertips into the water.

'Don't drink it,' the Waif warned her.

Molly glanced at her. 'I just wanted to feel it against my hand,' she said. The River Thames. As much an act of pilgrimage as if it had been the River Jordan. She stood up again, wiping her wet fingers down the back of Annie's borrowed cloak. 'We ought to be getting back,' she said.

Uphill again, away from the river towards Wood Street. But this time they dawdled.

The Waif stopped to buy two baked potatoes from a street-seller, and they tossed them from hand to hand, blowing on them till the hot, creamy flesh was cool enough to break their fast.

The Bell would remain asleep for several more hours. But the rest of Sunday London had already come alive. They were fifty yards from The Bell when Abigail came rushing towards them, her eyes wide and white in her sweating black face. Seizing their arms, she hustled them off the street and into an alley. 'We got trouble, Miz Kitty. The Watch is looking for you. For you and Miz Moll.' She pulled them down the alley and into a midden courtyard. 'Mother Wickham say you got to come with me.'

She hurried them up a rickety wooden staircase, through a rat-gnawed door into a narrow, fetid passageway and out into the air again. They passed over a creaking veranda, down some stairs, up again, and into a cribbed room reeking of baby-shit and spices. 'Here, Miz Moll,' she said, holding out her familiar but forgotten blue and white dress, 'put this on.' She snatched up a rich pink and cream gown and thrust it into the Waif's arms. 'You wear this, Miz Kitty.' She picked up a loaf of bread, broke it into two and held the two halves out for her. 'And you got to give yourself some tits with these.' She wagged a finger at the child. 'And don't you go eating that bread, Miz Kitty. Your tits get to be big tits. Mother Wickham said.'

It only took a few minutes. But by the time Abigail had finished with her two charges, they were completely different people. The Waif was wigged and powdered, full-bosomed and ten years older. Molly was in her blue and white dress, mob-capped and aproned, her cheeks glowing red after being scrubbed with a coarse towel, her hair scraped away from her face.

Abigail led them down the staircase into Love Lane, then two paces across it into The Bell's kitchen. Down the stone steps, up the wooden steps, along the passage, into the big room with the pictures.

Everybody was there: Mother Wickham, wrapped in a bright red shawl, wisps of hair straying raggedly from under her nightcap; Annie, the Twins, Nan and Polly, all sitting at the table, all in disarray, as if they'd just risen from bed; Jed standing by the fireplace, sullenly glowering; Bull, feet apart, arms folded, beside the door. Even the children were there: the Deaf Mute, the Bastard, Okoro with his brown sister Lily on his lap; Annie nursed the Baby, and the Twins cradled

72

their own.

And the Watch. Two stolid men of the town, armed with staves, and an ascetic, bookish man with a tic that twitched at his lips.

'Come in, Catherine,' said Mother Wickham. 'Come in, Moll.' She indicated two vacant chairs at the table. 'Sit here with us.'

They sat where they'd been told, Molly like a mouse, the Waif like a pampered cat.

'Now, sir,' Mother Wickham said to the leader of the Watch, 'we are all assembled. Do you see here the persons you seek? Do you see here a foul-tongued child? Do you see here a proud harlot in a golden gown?' A professional melange of candour, guile and deceit was plastered thick on her features. She answered her own questions. 'No, sir, you see here the girls I employ at The Bell. Serving girls, kitchen-wenches, scullery-maids.' She painted an indulgent fondness on top of her other lies as she stroked her hand across the Waif's shoulders. 'And my niece Catherine, who has just returned from church. From St Alban's a few yards away, not St... what was the name?'

'St Anselm's,' the sergeant muttered. 'The priest said we were to arrest a child of some twelve years, whose name is Desdemona.'

Mother Wickham pasted a look of incredulity on her face. 'Desdemona? Desdemona? What kind of child do you think is likely to be called Desdemona? Des-de-mona.' The way she pronounced it, it was obvious that even the most careless, the most ignorant, the most depraved mother would never stoop to calling her daughter Desdemona. The girls sniggered amongst themselves, and the two men of the Watch smirked.

But their leader frowned, more troubled than angry. 'I'll be plain, Mother Wickham,' he said.

'I'd expect nothing less.' Her buttered tones shaped her reply into a compliment.

'It's not just the priest, and it's not just keeping a bawdy house.' He held up his hand to cut her off before she spoke. 'Hear me. There were a lot of people in that church besides the priest, and some of them have the power to cause a parcel of trouble.'

'I don't know what the priest - '

'It doesn't matter what the priest did or didn't do, Mother Wickham. It doesn't matter whether or not he came here for the girls. He says he

73

didn't, and his friends in the congregation believe him.'

'If they believe him, why should there be trouble?'

'The priest has been accused in front of his patrons, and he is seeking justice.'

'Justice?' Mother Wickham's voice was a model of disbelief and contrived outrage.

He dipped his head in acknowledgement and admitted the truth. 'He is seeking revenge. He has demanded the full punishment due by law.'

She laughed at the idea with open scorn. 'What, for calling a priest a whoremaster? How many of them aren't?'

He swallowed. 'He's calling on the law against blasphemy.'

There was a nervous, pray-God-it-won't-happen-to-me intake of breath from the girls. 'They hang you for that,' said Nan.Mother Wickham was quick and sharp. 'No they don't!' Her eyes flitted from one shocked face to the next. 'Not since before I was born. King Charlie himself had the law changed.'

The Waif huddled against Molly, her frightened face more babyish than ever. 'It wasn't blasphemy,' she said. She appealed to the rest of the girls. 'It wasn't blasphemy. Please, Mother Wickham,' she pleaded, 'it wasn't. All I said was - '

'Shut up!' Mother Wickham stood and confronted the sergeant, who was plainly out of his depth. 'We need to talk about this,' she said. 'Annie, pour a glass of cordial for Catherine. She seems to be upset about something. Twins, let the gentlemen of the Watch see our rooms. Let them see we've got nothing to hide. The rest of you wait here till I return.' She moved purposefully out of the room. After a moment's hesitation, the leader of the Watch followed her.

The Twins handed over their sleeping babies to Nan and Polly, smiled in a professionally friendly way at the two grinning members of the Watch, and led them out.

Annie left her seat, signalled Molly to swap places with her, and sat down beside the Waif. 'Don't worry, Kitty,' she said. She flung a reproving glare across the table. 'Nan was being stupid.' She put her arm round the young girl's shoulders. 'A vindictive old priest with a taste for kitten-flesh can't do anything to harm you.'

'Then why has he set the Watch to arresting me? Why did he tell them where to find me?' The fear, the panic, was seething under the surface.

'What else could he do? You accused him in front of his congregation. That was silly.' More concerned than chiding.

'What will he do, Annie? What will happen to me?'

'That depends on Mother Wickham.' She hugged the girl to her and softened her voice. 'You'll have to be punished, Kitty, you know that.' The Waif nodded. 'But Mother Wickham will make sure it doesn't hurt you too much. You're too valuable a commodity for her to allow that.' She soothed her hand down the Waif's back, then turned her head towards Molly. 'You, Moll, will have to pay a fine.'

'A fine?' She went cold. A justice of the peace. A magistrate. A court of law. Public exposure. The shame drenched over her like a summer thunderstorm. 'But I did nothing. We only wanted to pray. We only wanted to seek God's grace. We only... We only...' Her lips pressed together, her eyes blazed, her breath shortened.

This is unfair. To be prosecuted in a court of law for seeking out God? That is unjust! But then this is London. What has London to do with justice?

She became aware that her whole body was shaking, that her mouth and lips wouldn't work properly. 'No! I - I will not - will not!'

Annie rested her hand on Molly's. 'You went out without asking Mother Wickham first. She doesn't like that. You're older than Kitty, so you should have kept her out of trouble.'

'But...' But the Waif is years older than I am in her ways. More injustice.

'And you didn't come back here to tell Mother Wickham what had happened as soon as it had happened.' She paused to make sure Molly was taking in what she was being told. 'She was awoken by the Watch, and she didn't know what it was about until they told her. She doesn't like that.'

Molly dropped her gaze, and slumped in her chair. Mother Wickham ruled The Bell. And until there was a chance to escape, her only choice was to bend her knee to the rules. 'I'm sorry,' she said, her voice as small as she could make it.

Annie patted her hand. 'Don't worry about it too much,' she said. 'Mother Wickham will sort it out. But,' she warned, 'there'll be a price to pay, and Mother Wickham won't want to pay that price herself.' Polly and Nan looked at each other knowingly. 'What happens to Kitty depends on what bargain she can strike with the Watch, or with the priest himself. But what happens to you is simple. Mother Wickham will buy the sergeant's silence with a guinea, and she's already bought the rest of the Watch with the Twins.' She took her hand away from Molly's and leaned back in her chair, her arm still draped round the Waif's shoulders. 'You'll have to replace that guinea, Moll. And you'll have to pay Mother Wickham what the Watch would have paid her for the Twins. And there'll be a fine on top of that.'

Her heart sank. 'A justice of the peace?'

Annie reassured her. 'No. The courts have no interest in you. It's Mother Wickham who will fine you.'

Molly's hand strayed to her placket. But she was wearing the blue dress Abigail had given her, and her golden gown was... Her golden gown and her precious coins could be anywhere. 'How much?'

Annie tipped her head to one side and made a face. 'Whatever Mother Wickham decides.' Her sympathetic expression died away, and she became as impassive as she usually was. 'She may decide you didn't know any better. Or she may decide you need to be taught a lesson.' She shrugged. It was nothing to do with her. 'Whatever Mother Wickham decides.'

Mother Wickham decided that Molly needed to be taught a lesson. 'Eleven guineas,' she said. She walked almost soundlessly across the richly patterned rug to the delicate table, lifted the crystal decanter, poured brandy into a gilded Venetian glass.

Molly blanched. 'I haven't got eleven guineas.'

The bawd savoured the brandy, then returned her attention to Molly. Not a glimmer of pity in her gaze. 'You've got nearly twelve guineas,' she told her. 'Think yourself fortunate I'm being lenient.'

Back in her own room, Molly stared down into Wood Street without seeing it. Nearly twelve guineas. Everything the Colonel had given her. Plus her first purse. Plus the twenty shillings she'd brought with her from York.

Nearly twelve guineas. And Mother Wickham was to rob her of eleven guineas of it. She'd be left with even less than she had when she climbed down from the York wagon.

No! Her jaw set stubbornly. I've saved for it, been seduced for it, been ravished for it. I've whored for it, and betrayed everything my father taught me for it. And now it's being stolen away from me. And for what? For going to church to pray forgiveness!

The injustice boiled up inside her. Spinning away from the window, she stormed into the dim passageway outside, and along it to the end. Three doors huddled together: to the stairs, to Mother Wickham's bedroom, to Mother Wickham's parlour. She'd demand that she be allowed to leave The Bell, and take her saved-up guineas with her. She'd defy Mother Wickham to her face.

Screwing up her courage, she rapped on the door to Mother Wickham's parlour.

But it was Annie who opened the door.

Molly was not to be deflected. 'I have to speak with Mother Wickham,' she said.

In her first glance, Annie took in Molly's set jaw, her angry eyes, her clenched fists; stepping into the passageway, she pulled the door almost shut behind her. 'Mother Wickham is busy. But I shall make sure she gets the message.'

'Tell her that - '

Annie hustled her across the narrow corridor, opened the door to the stairs and bundled Molly through it. 'Yes, yes - your monthly courses have started. Abigail will give you some old linen to bind yourself with.'

'But - '

'If the Colonel should arrive, I shall explain that you are at present unclean.'

'I - '

Annie glared at her. 'If it is causing you pain, ask Abigail for some sprigs of feverfew.' She slammed the door.

Her resolve bullied out of her by Annie, Molly sat at the top of the stairs for several minutes before going down to the kitchen and seeking out Abigail. Her blood-flow was two or three days away; but she connived at Annie's fiction. At least it would keep the Colonel away from her for a week.

It was only later that she wondered how Mother Wickham had known exactly how much money she had.

'No,' said the priest, turning away from the glass-doored bookcase that trumpeted his learning in the scriptures, the ancients, the safest of the moderns.

'You could say you were mistaken,' said Mother Wickham.

'No,' he repeated.

'Kitty has already apologised. She knows she was wrong to say what she did.' She couldn't see his face as he stood between her and the mullioned window of the rectory's withdrawing room, the setting sun blurring a red corona around his silhouette. But she knew she held most of the cards. 'Even though we all know she wasn't wrong in what she did say.'

'No.' He stood silent for a few moments. 'My patrons, my sponsors...'

'Money?' she said.

'No, not money.' There was fear in his voice as well as anger. 'She's threatened my office. She's threatened the authority of the Church. She must be punished.'

'What would you have me do to her?'

He took the chair opposite her. His expression told her not to play games with him. 'Punished, Mother Wickham. She must go before a justice, and confess her fault - confess that she lied - and be punished.'

Mother Wickham returned his gaze with one of her own: let's neither of us play games. 'And?'

The priest made his opening bid. 'My patrons are crying blasphemy. They want her dragged through the streets on a hurdle, then exhibited on Ludgate Hill.'

Mother Wickham topped it with a bid of her own. 'But then I'd pay every harlot in Cheapside to swear you'd fucked them and their daughters and their new-born babies.' She stood. 'The justices wouldn't believe them, of course. But your patrons might. And your bishop certainly would.'

He sat back in his chair. 'Let us come to an agreement...'

At the eleventh stroke of the St Albans clock, the girls stopped their chattering. Even the dogs slunk into corners and lay quiet. As midday sounded, the door to the kitchen opened, and Mother Wickham stood at the top of the steps. She pushed the door shut behind her, but didn't come down into the room.

'Kitty is to be charged with blasphemy,' she said. She held up both hands to silence the outburst of urgent whispering. 'She won't be harmed. But this kind of foolishness has to be punished.' She paused to let her warning sink in. 'Stand up, Kitty.'

The Waif stood, her hands clasped meekly in front of her. Mother Wickham had already told her what was to happen.

'Kitty will be charged with blasphemy. Annie will argue that, because of her age, and because she doesn't have a mother, she didn't know any better. Kitty will weep, and beg the priest's forgiveness. The priest will publicly forgive her, and pray Christ's mercy on her. The justice will tell her that the Church is not to be mocked, but the priest will ask him to be merciful. The justice will pronounce sentence.' She paused for effect, her eyes cold, a warning to any of the girls who might transgress in future.

'Kitty's punishment has been arranged,' she said. 'She is to stand an hour in the pillory at St Paul's.'

Chapter 8

The Watch were close to mutiny.

With as much dignity as he could muster, the sergeant led his troop along Cheapside towards St Paul's. Behind him, two lumbering giants shouldered their pikes and fixed their eyes straight ahead. Between them, the Waif broke into a run every few yards to keep up with them; dressed in lilac and white, her pink-ribboned hair tied in bunches on the side of her head and swinging below her cap, one hand clutching a rag doll, the other hand raised to her face so that she could suck her thumb, she skipped happily, gazing wide-eyed at the crowd as it parted to make way for them.

And the people of Cheapside laughed and followed.

They jeered at the Watch, they shouted obscene jokes about the justice, they called bizarre and ludicrous curses down on the head of the priest, they sang ribald verses ridiculing the Church. Apprentices abandoned their work and joined the procession, housewives grabbed their babies and left their laundry to soak, beggars quit their begging, thieves postponed their thieving, harlots scrambled into their clothes and scurried to join the merriment.

The Punishment of Little Kitty had spontaneously blossomed into a holiday.

At St Paul's, the base of the pillory's fat-limbed cross stood three feet from the ground on its stone-block plinth. But when they led the Waif up the steps into position, they found she was at least a foot short of the crossbar, and the Watch had to borrow a stool from a nearby shop for her to stand on. Willingly, trustingly, she put her head and wrists into the semi-circular grooves as she was told. Above her head, the paper pinned to the timber proclaimed Here is Kathrin Bell. So fhall fuffer All who mock the Houfe of God.

The sergeant lowered the top section into place and padlocked it shut. Great Tom, the clock-bell of St Paul's, began to chime the hour. 'Be it known,' he said, reading from the sheet of paper he'd been given, 'that Catherine Bell is found guilty of blaspheming against God, and the house of God, and the servants of God, and shall stand for a full hour in the pillory at St Paul's, to serve as a warning to the subjects of

His Majesty, King George, Defender of the Faith.' He waited for the final stroke of the bell that tolled the hour, and jumped down from the plinth.

The Waif grinned at the crowd.

A beggar put his crutch to one side, stooped, scooped up a handful of mud, hurled it at her. It struck her on the hip, spattering a large brown stain on her white dress.

A big negro shoved through to the front of the crowd. 'Why you stoning her?' he demanded. 'She only a child. What do she know about blaspheming?'

'Blasphemer!' the beggar cried unconvincingly. 'She deserves to be stoned!' He scraped together another handful of mud. Soft mud. The negro dashed it from his hand, and planted his broad hand in the middle of the beggar's chest. The beggar flailed his arms, tripped, fell into the mud. The audience laughed: clowning had been added to the farce.

And then Kitty delivered her masterstroke. 'Mummy!' she cried, her voice thin and high with fear. 'I want my mummy!'

'She's only a child,' called a huddled, bruised young woman. 'Leave her alone.'

'Only a child,' called a gin-sipping woman with red hair.

'Mummy!' cried the Waif.

'Only a child, only a child...' The crowd were on the Waif's side. The big negro took up his position in front of the pillory, folded his arms, and silently defied anyone to hurl anything at all.

He stood there unmoving for the full hour. The only person to approach her was a young woman in a blue and white dress, who held up a jug of water for the child to drink from.

As Great Tom began to chime, the sergeant unlocked the crossbar. In less than a minute, the Waif had been lifted down from the stool, wrapped in a cloak and whisked away. Before she was out of sight, the negro had melted into the dispersing crowd.

The Colonel continued to visit. Molly continued to hate his visits. The Colonel continued to find new ways of humiliating her. In less than two months, she'd replaced the eleven guineas Mother Wickham had fined her. And, despite her Yorkshire carefulness, she'd spent more than six of them.

The first time he made her take him in her mouth, she was sick. The swollen flesh ramming against the back of her throat made her gag, then gag again. But his hands, twined in her hair, pulling her roughly onto him gave her no choice. She clawed at his wrists, tried to wrench her head sideways, tried to twist away, but still he thrust on, faster, more urgent, the full force of his thighs and buttocks crashing him into her, until -

The lumpy brown vomit choked and coughed and spluttered out, over him, down his white breeches, onto the floor where she knelt in front of him.

The first blow caught her above the eye, and split her eyebrow. The second caught her in the mouth, splitting her lip and loosening one of her teeth. The third brushed harmlessly through her hair as she fell.

'Quince,' said the Colonel. Not a trace of emotion. The door opened. 'Fetch Mother Wickham.'

The Colonel stayed to watch because he found it amusing. Mother Wickham stayed to watch because she wanted to make sure no more damage was done to her goods. But they were both agreed: a lesson had to be learned.

First Quince, while Jed held her, wrenching her arms up behind her back. Then Jed, while Quince held her. Then Bull. 'I'm sorry, Miz Moll,' he muttered as he pumped hot and salty into her mouth. Big as he was, he too was scared of Mother Wickham.

Then Stumpy Jack, then another of Wood Street's beggars, then the barely erect, but no less brutal, eleven-year-old Bastard.

Then others, perhaps four, perhaps five others.

Finally, the Colonel.

And Mother Wickham stayed to make sure the lesson had been thoroughly learned.

'I hate him, Annie! God forgive me, but I wish he would die!' Her voice sank to a ferocious growl. 'I shan't stay, Annie. Within this week, I shall be gone.'

Annie gripped Molly's elbow so tightly that it hurt. 'Hate him,' she hissed. 'That is right and proper.' Her voice deadened as she stared into the past. 'But if you run away, Jed will find you and bring you back.' She dropped her hand to her side. 'You wouldn't want that.'

May, June. The King died, and the Colonel's official duties kept him away from The Bell for more than a week. A week of freedom in which to hone her hatred.

July, August. And a pattern was in place.

The Colonel visited at least three times a week, sometimes in the afternoon, sometimes in the evening, sometimes as late as four in the morning, when he'd been playing cards at Button's Coffee House in Covent Garden.

The evenings were easy. Usually he was in a hurry, and took her perfunctorily before tossing a couple of coins onto the vanity table as he left. Sometimes, he took her at his leisure, seeming to enjoy it; these were the evenings he escorted her to the theatre.

When he woke her - and most of the household - at four in the morning, he could rarely do more than fumble his way into her for a few moments, then stagger off again into the night, supported by the ever-present Quince.

It was the afternoons she dreaded, the afternoons when he probed her, dug into her life, uncovered the things that frightened her most, invented new ways to make her question herself. The afternoons when, with a smile that invited her to trust him, he did things that made her wince with pain or shame or despair.

And yet, no matter how painful, how shameful, she remained too frightened of him and Mother Wickham to run away. Annie's words rang in her head. 'Mother Wickham had me brought back. And the Colonel had my Billy killed.'

Dominated, bullied, used, shamed, scared; but, despite the fear, the secret places in her head stubbornly refused to give in.

Gradually, as she became familiar with life at The Bell, her role as the Colonel's whore became simply her side of the bargain, the price to be paid for security, the cost of a comfortable day-to-day living. Unlike her virgin days in York, she now had more gowns than she could wear, she had guineas hidden and guineas to spend, she was recognised and greeted at all the playhouses in the Town.

But inside she felt cheated; and she burned for revenge, however slight that revenge may be.

'Piss in his wine,' the Waif suggested. Then, with a grin, she changed her mind. 'No. Even with the wine Mother Wickham serves, he'd know the difference.'

But she did, anyway. A single drop from her chamber pot, just enough to drip from the end of her finger. Enough to know that she'd done it, not enough for him to notice. But there was no satisfaction. It was a small victory, but it wasn't revenge. He hadn't suffered.

She wanted him to suffer. At night, she dreamed of the Colonel being dragged down to Hell. By day, in her room, she made up stories for the Waif, stories in which Quince went mad and killed his master, in which the Colonel was trampled under the York Wagon, in which he was torn to pieces by ravening wolves.

The Waif was more practical. 'Maybe he'll seduce one virgin too many, and she'll cut his throat,' she said one afternoon as they sat alone in Molly's room. 'Or her father will come with a troop of soldiers and shoot him down. Or she'll be betrothed to a bishop, and a whole army of parsons will surround him and cut his balls off, like they did to Peter Abelard.' She made a face. 'Most likely he'll die of the pox - and serve him right!'

Molly sucked in a deep breath. She'd not thought of that. With sex went disease. With disease went death. With death went... hellfire? For a harlot, yes: hellfire.

'Leave me now, Kitty,' she said. 'I need to rest. I need to think.'

The Waif, stood, then left without speaking. She understood.

The Colonel never visited on Sundays. Whenever she could, Molly went to her bed early on Sunday evenings, rose at dawn on Monday and went out alone, exploring the crowded streets of London, seeing for herself all the famous landmarks she'd heard about in her York schooldays. Mightily-domed St Paul's; the thrusting monument to the Great Fire; the Tower that had been built by William the Conqueror, imprisoned Queen Elizabeth, and murdered the two young princes. Nearby Aldersgate and Cripplegate, standing guard over the remains of the old Roman wall. She ventured across London Bridge and back again. She strolled round the squares: stately Leicester Square, grand Soho Square, fashionable Hanover Square. She dawdled past the prisons: a few yards from The Bell, the debtors idling in the Wood Street Compter; a few streets to Bridewell, the Fleet, notorious Newgate with its mock-castle front; an hour's walk to gaze in awe at Tyburn's triple-beamed gallows, three times the height of a man.

It was a rainy Monday in September, before noon, and she'd been to marvel at the soaring stonework and stained glass of Westminster Abbey. On her way home again, she heard the clatter of horses' hooves behind her and stepped back against the high brick wall to avoid being splashed by a chaise as it rattled over the wet Whitehall cobbles.

As she resumed her journey towards the chequered stone and flint towers of Holbein Gate, the driver reined the chaise to a halt, and waited until she caught up with it. Jumping down, he opened the monogrammed door. 'Get in,' he said.

Harlots in golden gowns are invited into chaises for only one reason. However, no matter how much she hated it, she was the Colonel's private whore, bought and paid for. She ignored the driver, and walked on.

'Get in,' he said again, striding along beside her. Again she ignored him. He ran back to the chaise, shut its door and climbed back up into his seat. 'Giddup!' The chaise drew alongside her.

Again the door swung open. 'Get in,' said a woman's voice.

Surprised, Molly turned her head to look into the plush-padded interior of the chaise. A woman, nearly old enough to be her mother, immaculately wigged, elegantly gowned, clear-skinned, thin-lipped.

'Get in,' the woman said again. A command, not an invitation. 'Don't worry. You'll come to no harm.'

Still Molly demurred. 'Who are you?' she asked.

The woman shifted herself to the opposite side of the chaise and patted the seat beside her. 'You have my word that you'll come to no harm,' she repeated. 'I am Lady Charnell. I'm the Colonel's wife. You'll take tea, of course.' It wasn't a question.

They sat at a small round table, its central pedestal splaying into three carved feet which sank their cushioned claws into the Persian rug. Caught in a moted beam of early September sunshine, the ornately-carved fireplace beside them was glowing with coal and logs. Below a sugary oil-painting of Cupid and Psyche, the mantelpiece was crowded with statuettes and ornaments. On one side of the table, Lady Charnell poured from a silver teapot into two delicate china cups; on the other, Molly sat upright in the upholstered wheel-backed chair, noting the position of the doors, planning her escape should the Colonel himself arrive.

The Colonel was dangerous. Despite her assurances, the Colonel's wife might be equally dangerous. And she clearly knew about the Colonel's visits.

Beyond Lady Charnell, Molly could see through the columned arch, with its mock-Ionic gold-leaf capitals, into the high-ceilinged, picture-hung gallery beyond. She had never imagined that a private house could be as big as this. In York, only the Archbishop's palace was this opulent. Everything around her reeked of money and power. She took the tea that was offered her, but didn't drink it.

'I shall be blunt,' said Lady Charnell. 'I am mistress of all this...' She made a vague gesture that took in their entire surroundings. '...as well as a house in Soho Square and a large estate in Hertfordshire. You, on the other hand, are a Cheapside whore. However, we have some-thing in common.' Relaxed, encouraging, almost conspiratorial. 'My husband,' she said.

Molly's could feel herself colouring.

Lady Charnell continued. 'His taste lies in seducing silly little girls like you, and he pays that old bawd Wickham a mountain of money to search them out for him.' Irony crept into her voice. 'Or did you think you were the first?'

Molly said nothing. The question didn't require an answer.

'You may not be aware, child, but the money my husband showers on you and Mother Wickham and that creeping toad Quince is my money.' Seeing the startled questions racing through Molly's head, she raised her eyebrows and pursed her lips in cynical confirmation. 'I married the Colonel for love. In those days, of course, he was merely a captain. But I was much more than just another silly little girl for him to seduce.' Her lips smiled, but there was no laughter in her eyes. 'Oh, no. I was a silly little girl who had inherited a fortune.' She lifted her teacup and sipped delicately from it. 'You are wondering why someone of my rank and wealth should be discussing my marriage with a Cheapside whore.'

'No, my lady.' Aye, of course I am. Why have you brought me here?

What do you want from me?

The older woman ignored her. 'We have something else in common, you and I,' she said. Her face sagged briefly into the tiredness of disillusionment before regaining its mask. 'We both want to make him pay. Am I right?'

'I... er... I... well, I...' Keep your secret curses to yourself, Molly Huckerby.

Lady Charnell recognised the hesitation. 'Yes. You're too frightened to say as much, but yes. Yes, you'd like to make him pay for what he's done to you.' Delicately, she placed her teacup and saucer back on the table. 'During the years of my marriage there have been dozens of whores,' she said, 'but that is what one expects in London. Many of them, like you, were virgins when they were first brought to him.'

'How...?'

'Give me leave to know my own husband.' She leaned back in her chair. 'None of them have ever been a threat to me.'

'But I'm only... ' A Cheapside whore.

'Yes, you're only the most recent entry in his catalogue of betrayals. But that isn't why I've brought you here. You are, after all, only a harlot, and I don't invite harlots to my house. You're no threat to my marriage. You're no threat to my position. But...' Her lips tightened. 'You've become a threat to my dignity.'

'I don't understand - '

Suddenly passionate. 'He's been parading you in public!'

'The theatre,' Molly murmured.

'Yes, the theatre.' She glared at Molly. 'I don't care for the theatre, so I never go. But that doesn't mean that my friends never go. It doesn't mean that my neighbours, my acquaintances, my family never go to the theatre. It doesn't mean that your masquerade with him is believed, just because I'm not there.' She refilled her own teacup, ignoring Molly's, which was untouched. 'Do as I say,' she said, 'and we'll both have our satisfaction.'

Danger. 'Please, my lady, I don't... I mean, I...'

'Look at me girl.' Molly raised her eyes, but not her head. 'You'll come to no harm. In fact, I'm offering you an escape. If you want an escape, that is. I've never known any harlots well enough to know what it is they want. Apart from money, of course.' She took Molly's silence for acquiescence.' Very well. I shall now tell you a secret.' She held up her hand to stifle Molly's protest before it could be voiced. 'I'm not entrusting you with the secret. I'm merely telling you. In fact, I want you to reveal that secret to everybody you know. Tell your fellow harlots. Tell them to tell their customers. Tell the beggars, and let them peddle the news in Covent Garden. Tell the coachmen, tell the link-boys, tell the actors in Lincoln's Inn Fields. But...' She lifted a warning forefinger. 'Nobody must so much as hint at it in front of my husband. The Colonel must not find out about it until I tell him. The whole Town must know - except the Colonel.'

She had no reason to trust the Colonel's wife. But neither had she any reason to be loyal to the Colonel. Not knowing whether she was accepting salvation or damnation, Molly nodded.

'Good. Then know this - and tell this.' She rose to her feet. 'While my husband has been taking his pleasure in your bed, I've been taking my pleasure elsewhere. For the past month, I have been cuckolding the Colonel.'

Molly's eyes and mouth opened wide. Her stomach knotted at the thought of what the Colonel might do to her if he found out that she had started such a rumour.

'But,' said Lady Charnell, 'there's more. Oh yes, there's a great deal more.'

Chapter 9

'I don't know what to do, Annie,' Molly said.

Annie stood with her back to her. For the best part of a minute she thought before speaking. 'While you're the Colonel's whore, you have money in your purse. But after you've betrayed him...' She continued to stare out of the window, down into Wood Street. 'Is his wife going to pay you?'

'She said I should never need for money if I did what she said.'

'Did she say how these riches would be earned?' No reply from Molly. 'Will she give you a fat purse? Will she settle an annuity on you? Will she take you into her service?' Still no reply. 'And what do imagine Mother Wickham will say about all this?'

'She said she'd take me away from The Bell.'

'Ah. Can you trust her?'

Whatever the outcome, the Colonel's wife is using me just as much as the Colonel uses me. 'I don't know.'

'If she takes you away from The Bell, Moll, where will you go? Where will she put you? Will you go to work for her? In the Colonel's own house?'

I hadn't thought of that. 'I don't know.'

Annie turned from the window, leaned back against the sill. 'What is this secret she told you? Tell me now, and I'll help you decide whether or not you should do as she asks.'

Molly swallowed. 'She's cuckolding the Colonel.'

Annie tilted her head and laughed. 'Is that all? If she weren't cuckolding her husband, then that would be a tale to be told. But...' She shrugged.

Molly's shoulders drooped. This was a world away from what she's known in York. 'What should I do, Annie?'

'Who's the Colonel's rival? Some penniless young buck with strong thighs and a big prick? If the Colonel finds out, the boy will either be found in an alley with his throat cut, or be made a groom to the household, depending on whether the Colonel's wife has tired of him or not. If he doesn't find out, the people who do find out will think nothing of it. This is London, Moll. That is what wives do in London.'

London or no, it didn't make sense. 'He's not young, Annie.'

'Who?'

She blurted it out. 'He's not young, Annie. He's old, he's ugly, he's crippled, he's a hunchback, he's a Jew, and the Colonel owes him money. His name is Abraham Asher.'

It was Annie's turn not to know what to say. 'Then why...?'

'She said that were the point. She wants the Colonel to appear ridiculous. She wants everyone to laugh at him. But she doesn't want him to know that they're laughing. Not until she tells him.'

'Dangerous, Moll,' Annie said. 'Very dangerous.' Her anxiety became leavened with a hint of mischief. 'But I think we should do exactly as Lady Charnell has asked you. Let's tell everyone in the world. Except, of course, the Colonel.' She pushed herself away from the window sill. 'Leave it to me. I'll tell the rest of the girls. But I won't say where I heard it.'

As she reached the door, she delivered a warning. 'And we won't tell Mother Wickham,' she said.

✳

Molly noticed the difference - but then, she was expecting it.

When they greeted him, the Colonel's friends smiled more broadly, knowingly, enjoying the secret. Strangers smiled as he passed, and occasionally broke into laughter behind him. Whenever an actor poured scorn on a cuckold, his lines seemed more pointed, and the audience laughed more loudly.

And still the Colonel saw nothing unusual.

Once she'd told Annie about the Colonel's wife, Molly never mentioned it again. There was no need to: having started the hare, there were hundreds of other dogs to chase it.

For two months, she acted her part, submitting to the Colonel, being polite to his friends, blotting the open secret from her mind, constantly fearing discovery. And, during that time, she never once saw the Colonel's wife.

✻

Another week of freedom while the Colonel attended the new King.

Molly had been summoned to eat supper with Mother Wickham, to help her celebrate the Coronation. The table was covered with damask; the cutlery was silver; the fare was rich. Tench, boiled beef, goose, a pie, a pudding of apples and cinnamon. Ale, French wine, gin, brandy, Jamaican rum. The table of a woman who could easily afford luxury. In a room that betrayed the self-satisfied excess of a cheap mind.

'To King George the Second,' Mother Wickham said, raising her glass. Coronations put people in a mood for enjoyment. Coronations were good for business.

Molly picked at the food without enjoyment. But she smiled and made grateful comments, as befitted a servant to her mistress, a harlot to her bawd, a prisoner to her warder.

Mother Wickham forked a sauce-dripping nugget of fowl into her mouth, savoured it, gestured to Molly, encouraging her to try it. 'What do you dream of, Moll?' She prided herself on getting to know her girls. Understand which strings to pull, and the puppet will dance to whatever tune you care to play.

'Dream, Mother Wickham?'

'Kitty dreams of being a princess. Polly dreams of ribbons and lace. The Twins dream of each other, two wives with no husbands. Nan dreams of running away - but she never will.' She tilted her head to one side, gauging Molly's reaction; but Molly already knew not to give anything away. Mother Wickham reached across the table and caressed her fingertips delicately down Molly's cheek. The same gossamer touch that had drawn her through The Bell's front door and into the Colonel's web. 'What do you dream of, Moll?'

'I don't dream, Mother Wickham.'

Her eyes narrowed, then widened into a professional openness. She tried again. 'Do you enjoy being fucked by the Colonel?'

Molly concentrated on the plate in front of her. No, I hate it. I detest him. I wish I had the courage to kill him. And Quince. Above all, I wish I had the courage to kill you, Mother Wickham.

Annie's advice was burnt into her being. Never learn to enjoy it. He wants you to hate it. When you stop hating it, he'll stop protecting you.

And then you'll be Mother Wickham's.

'No, Mother Wickham.'

On the bawd's face, a frown of sympathy. Inside her mind, a glow of approval. With the Colonel's tastes, an unhappy harlot meant a happy customer. She continued her gentle inquisition. 'Then what do you dream of while he's fucking you? The golden guinea he'll leave on your table? The ribbons and lace you can buy with it? The dowry that will tempt a handsome young man to take you away and marry you?' So sympathetic, so caring, so cynical.

All the time the Colonel's in my bed, I dream of an old, ugly, crippled Jew tupping the Colonel's own wife. I dream of the sneers on the faces of his friends, and the contempt on the lips of his enemies. I dream of the look on his face when his wife tells him what she does at night. I dream of his anger being as great as mine. I dream of the day when I can drag him down into the midden. I dream of revenge. 'I dream of the moors up above York, Mother Wickham.'

Mother Wickham returned to her goose. This girl was even more simple than she'd thought when she plucked her off the York Wagon. 'There's no profit in sheep and mountains, Yorkshire Molly,' she said, pouring more of the rich red wine into her glass. 'All the sheep and all the mountains in the world haven't got a penny between them. It's men that have the money.'

'Aye, Mother Wickham.' Courteous, contrite, humble. But, inside, enjoying the victory to come.

It was cold when they left the theatre, with a November fog reducing the link-boys' torches to a scattering of eerie glows across Lincoln's Inn Fields. The Colonel's carriage was waiting for them. Quince climbed up beside the driver. Smiling, the Colonel handed Molly up into the luxurious interior, then climbed up beside her.

As the driver cracked his whip, and the carriage moved off, the Colonel rounded on Molly and seized her throat with one hand, ramming her against the cushions. His fingers dug deep into her flesh, choking her, squeezing her tongue out, making her eyes stand out wide. 'Who?' he snarled. 'Who is he?'

She croaked incomprehensibly, trying to claw his hand away.

'Who is he? Why did Quince overhear the word Cuckold tonight?'

His hand squeezed tighter. 'Who is he?'

His face, thrust close to hers, began to swim. The carriage around her turned red, then black. Her hand lost its strength and fell away from his.

And then the fingers loosened. Great gasps of air howled into her starved lungs. Racking coughs tore at her and rasped her throat.

'Who is he?'

Terrified, her mind whirled. How much did he know? How much could she conceal? How much would he make her tell? What would he do to her when he knew that she'd known from the start? Choking, spluttering, she tried to speak, but fear and pain had locked her throat shut. 'I... I... I don't...' Tears ran down her face.

His fist crashed into her mouth and nose. 'Who else have you been rutting with? You ungrateful slut!'

As she feebly wiped the blood from her chin, she could feel the hysteria welling up inside her, and laughter bubbling its way past her lips. Her shoulders heaving, she managed to disguise the laughter as sobbing, and bought herself a few moments in which to think.

His hand gripped her throat again, but this time he left her enough air to speak with. 'His name!'

'No - nobody. I haven't... I wouldn't... Please...' She tried to break free, but his powerful fingers were locked beneath her jaw. 'Ask Mother Wickham,' she pleaded.

He threw her away from him, and she huddled, weeping, in a corner of the carriage until they arrived at The Bell.

Mother Wickham was quite adamant. 'She wouldn't dare.' She gazed without pity at Molly, slumped in a chair with Abigail bathing her bruised face and neck. 'And she hasn't had any chance. Believe me, Colonel, the nearest Moll has ever come to disobeying me was when she went to church without my permission.' She opened the door of her room and called down the stairs for Jed to come up.

'Yes?'

'Has Miss Annie got a visitor?'

'No.'

'Fetch her.'

Annie was just as certain as the bawd. 'Moll does what she's told. You must have discovered that for yourself, Colonel. And she's too simple to lie. No, Colonel, if Moll says she's not lain with another man, then she's telling the truth.' She sidled close to the Colonel, out of Molly's earshot. 'Apart from that, as you must also know, she hates what you do to her. Why should she want anybody else to do it to her as well?'

Mother Wickham joined them. 'Quince must have been mistaken, Colonel. Whoever spoke must have been speaking of somebody else.' Time to insinuate a solution to the problem. A bawd always had the answer to a client's problem. 'Now, before you go home, why don't you go down to Annie's room, and she'll help you back to your good humour again.'

Annie's eyes, lively in her excuses for Molly, deadened again.

But the Colonel preferred the cowering Molly.

Once in her room, he undressed her with less lingering savour than usual. He kissed her bruised lips more eagerly, more painfully, than usual. Afterwards, he lay beside her longer than usual, recovering his breath.

And he left twice as many coins on her table as usual.

❋

'Get in.'

Startled, Molly eased her aching neck to one side so that she could see the liveried driver with her right eye; the left was closed, puffed, rainbowed from yellow to blue to purple to black above her swollen nose and cheekbone. She hadn't expected anyone to recognise her or speak to her in Spitalfields, over a mile from The Bell. Mother Wickham's visitors neither lived in the crowded tenements outside the city walls to the north and east of Bishopsgate, nor needed ever to go there.

The driver was holding the carriage door open for her. 'Get in,' he repeated. She let him help her up beside Lady Charnell. The carriage set off, the horses ambling as if they had nowhere in particular to go.

Lady Charnell touched her gloved hand to Molly's bruised face. The bawd's gesture. 'Does he know about me and Abraham Asher?' Molly shook her head. 'Did he do this to you?' Molly nodded. 'Why?'

'He thought I'd been with another man,' she mumbled, her voice thick and slurred through her split lips.

'Had you?'

94

'No. Quince heard someone mention a cuckold. Your husband thought I must have betrayed him.'

Lady Charnell dismissed the idea with a short, unforgiving laugh. 'Who is he to talk of betrayal?' She composed her thoughts. 'It's time,' she said. 'Not quite yet, of course. We must give your bruises time to heal. I want you to be there when I bring this matter to its conclusion.'

'No!' Molly implored her, fear puckering her lips. 'Please, no.'

'You'll come to no harm. My husband won't even notice you're there. And he'll have forgotten all about you afterwards, just as soon as Mother Wickham finds some new virgin for him to satisfy himself on.' She rapped three times with her fan on the lined roof of the carriage. Despite the clopping hooves, despite the wheels rattling over the cobbles, despite the other carriages, the driver heard her and reined his horses to a halt. Moments later, he'd opened the door and was offering Molly his hand to help her alight.

As she stepped down to the street and swivelled her head slowly and painfully to see where she was, Lady Charnell called to her. 'Girl.' She waited for Molly to face her again. 'You'll be leaving The Bell,' she told her, 'and Mother Wickham will be unhappy at losing one of her whores. But don't worry for your own safety. I shall take care of Mother Wickham.' She'd made her decision; the matter was closed. The driver shut the door, climbed up into his seat and urged the horses onward.

Molly was alone in Spitalfields again.

❋

In the cramped dressing room at the Lincoln's Inn Fields Theatre, the rakehell Sir John Brute moaned with content as the virginal Bellinda straddled him and the straight-backed chair he was sitting on, her skirts riding her waist, her fingers gripping his shoulders. An out-of-place sound caught his ear, and his attention wandered; he put his hands on her thighs to halt her practised manoeuvrings, and cocked his head at the door.

'Don't worry,' she said, plucking his hands away and carrying on, 'there's ten minutes yet before the Prologue.'

Again he stayed her. 'Listen.'

She kept still for a few reluctant seconds. 'They're laughing,' she said. She was just about to get down to business again when a puzzled frown creased her forehead. 'Laughing?'

'They're applauding,' he said indignantly. He stood up, lifted her off him and set her down on the floor. 'What's going on?' Buttoning his breeches as he went, he strode out of the dressing room and along the narrow, peeling corridor that led to the rear of the stage. Wriggling her feet into her shoes and smoothing her petticoats, the actress followed him. She didn't bother with her stockings; there was, after all, nearly ten minutes before the Prologue.

✳

The Colonel had insisted that Molly wear a green and gold bird-beaked vizard mask. Such masks had long since passed out of fashion, and were now the badge of married women looking for an adventure or seeking to conceal their involvement in one. But at least it helped to disguise the remaining discoloration around her eye. She peeped anxiously at the Colonel from behind her mask.

But he, like everyone else, was gazing open-mouthed at the couple making their way towards the stage-seats, the seats where one sat to be seen.

Abraham Asher, sharp-faced, hook-nosed, bow-legged, hunchbacked, leaning heavily on his gold-topped cane; on his arm the tall, proud, stately figure of Lady Charnell.

No vizard mask for her: she wanted to be recognised. Greeting acquaintances, curtsying to Abraham's friends and clients, she allowed herself to be guided nearer and nearer the stage. Nearer and nearer to Molly and the Colonel.

From a suppressed giggle to a muttering snigger, from a delighted snort to a drunken guffaw, the laughter grew as everyone joined in the joke. First the pit, then the gallery, then the orange-sellers. Only Jenny Diver and her fellow pickpockets and cutpurses ignored them: they were far too busy at work, making the most of the distraction.

Lady Charnell and her unlikely lover paused in front of the Colonel. The house whispered into an expectant silence. 'Good evening, my dear,' she said, her words ringing round the auditorium as clearly as any actress.

The Colonel said nothing.

'I'm sure you already know Master Asher,' she went on. She turned to Molly. 'And this must be your Cheapside whore.' She inclined her head in a polite greeting. 'I'm pleased to meet you, my dear. Come, Abraham.' She moved on, and the house erupted into laughter again.

And when, in order to reach their seats, the Colonel's wife and the elderly Jew had to cross the stage, the audience broke out into a spontaneous storm of applause. With a benign smile, Lady Charnell acknowledged them, took Abraham's arm again, and allowed him to conduct her to her seat.

The play that evening was The Provok'd Wife. She'd chosen the occasion with the utmost care.

✻

Four days. No visits from the Colonel. No punishments from Mother Wickham. Annie said nothing, the Waif stayed in her room, the rest of the girls avoided her eyes.

Overnight, she'd changed from a Cheapside whore to The Cheapside Whore.

Eventually, the suspense was too much for her to bear on her own. 'What's going to happen to me, Annie?'

Breakfast was finished; apart from Molly and Annie, the kitchen was empty. In the scullery, Abigail was scrubbing the dishes, singing a dimly-remembered African song; outside the door at the back, they could hear Jed mechanically chopping wood, unconsciously keeping time with the maidservant's rhythm. When Abigail climbed the steps and opened the door to throw out the dirty water, they could see his breath clouding in the freezing November air.

Annie dropped her voice. 'You've become notorious, Moll. Half the men in Town want to say they've also had you. They want to describe in detail what they did to you. They want to boast about what they made you do for them.' She decided to speak plainly. 'The truth is, Moll, half the men in Town are already saying they've had you. They're already describing what they did, what you did. And most of them will be boasting that you were so smitten by the size of their prick that you begged them for it, and didn't charge them a penny.'

A tiny frisson. Mostly shame; but with a seductive edge of pride.

All her life she'd been Molly the little sister, Molly the little dressmaker, Molly the little country girl who said no. In the past few months she'd become Moll of London, Moll the girl with guineas in her purse, Moll the Colonel's whore. And now she was The Cheapside Whore, the woman at the centre of a scandal, the harlot who'd helped bring the Colonel low.

The frisson shuddered into a sudden fear. Did the Colonel blame her for what had happened? What would he do to her? 'What's going to happen to me, Annie?'

There was no way of breaking it gently. 'Mother Wickham will auction you off to the highest bidder.' She played with her ever-present glass of gin before continuing. 'You'll have to learn fast, Moll. Whoever buys you will be expecting a great deal from you. Unlike the Colonel, they won't be looking for innocence.'

Highest bidder? 'But I know nothing of such matters! The Colonel is the only man who's ever - '

Annie cut her off. 'After six months or more of the Colonel, there's nothing anyone can demand that you've not done already. All you have to do is offer it before they ask for it.'

Her jaw clenched stubbornly. 'I am not a harlot!'

Annie was unimpressed. 'The Colonel fucks you. You take his money. That's what harlots do, Moll.'

'I did not choose to lie with the Colonel! He ravished me!'

'But you did choose to keep his guineas afterwards!' She relented, took Molly's hand. 'If a harlot could take the money and keep her body to herself, she would. We all would. Believe me, Moll, I know.' She tipped gin into her glass, but didn't drink from it. 'If men paid a guinea a time for turnips, I'd become a gardener. But you and I, Moll, have something worth a lot more than turnips. And that's why we're harlots, and not gardeners.' She looked Molly fully in the eyes. 'Or dressmakers.'

Molly countered her logic with defiance. 'I will not be sold at market like one of my uncle's pigs.'

Annie spelled out the alternatives. 'You could run away, and wait for Jed to bring you back to Mother Wickham for punishment. You could stay here and let Mother Wickham sell you piecemeal to however many visitors want you. Or you can take your chances with whoever offers her the most.' She stood, her chair scraping on the stone floor. 'It's your choice, Moll. The devil you know, or the devil - '

She was cut off by a shriek of despair and a sudden clatter from outside the kitchen door. Where Abigail had been, a metal plate was spinning noisily on the stone flags, a sodden cloth beside it. The back door was open; Jed's axe lay on the icy cobbles where it had fallen. The dogs scrambled to their feet and bounded up into the alley outside to see what was happening.

Molly and Annie followed them up and out into Love Lane.

The huge black figure of Bull. His left arm draped over Jed's neck, his right shoulder scraping along the side wall of The Bell, his right arm bent up behind him into the small of his back, his right foot dragging, his shaven head drooping onto his chest, his thick lips contorted with pain, his breath labouring, groaning. And a trail of bright blood all the way back to Wood Street.

'No, Bull, no!' Abigail howled. 'No, Bull, please, no, Bull!' She broke into a guttural chant, keening, hugging herself, rocking backwards and forwards. Molly rushed to comfort her, drew her into her arms.

'Captain Jack,' Jed muttered as Annie stood back to let him hump Bull's collapsing bulk down into the kitchen. 'Took him from behind.'

'Shut up, Abigail!' Annie yelled over the negress's moaning. 'Get some hot water!' She grabbed Molly, pushed her towards Wood Street. 'Get the surgeon! Now!'

She stood her ground. 'Where? I don't know where he lives?'

'Cheapside. At the back of the baker's yard. If he's not there, find out where he is, and get him here. Get him here!' She swung away and hurried down into the kitchen after Jed and Bull, kicking the excited dogs out of the way.

Heaving up her skirts, Molly ran as fast as she could down Love Lane, into Wood Street, barging between street-sellers, skidding on frozen cobbles, splashing through ice-skinned gutters, skipping between slow-moving carts, ducking under the necks of horses.

The chaise stopped ahead of her as she careered into Cheapside.

'Get in,' the driver said, jumping down and holding the door for her.

'No!' she panted. 'Surgeon... Bull... dying...!'

'Get in, girl.' The voice of Lady Charnell. A command, not a request.

'No!' She strained to see inside the chaise's dim interior. 'Please, my lady. Bull is like to die. He must have the surgeon!'

'At The Bell?'

'Aye, my lady.'

An irritating hiatus in her plans. 'Tell the Watch to get a surgeon,' she told the driver. 'Make sure he goes to The Bell.'

'Please - it must be now!'

An impatient sigh. 'Now.' The driver beckoned to the Watch, who were already hovering near the chaise in case there was service to be done, and delivered his instructions. 'Now, girl, you can get in. And don't keep me waiting,' she added as Molly hesitated. 'It's cold. And I have no wish to be seen loitering in Cheapside.'

Molly climbed up beside her. 'I did as you asked,' she said. 'You saw me there at the theatre. I did as you asked.' She shivered, and rubbed her hands briskly up and down her arms. Lady Charnell eased a woollen rug towards her; gratefully, she swung its warmth round her shoulders.

'I am a woman of my word. The Colonel will make no effort to see you again. Mother Wickham has been paid off. My driver will now take me to my Lady Tunbridge's house in Berkeley Square, and will then convey you to your new master in Chiswick.' She smiled with cynical humour. 'Your new whoremaster.'

Molly looked back over her shoulder at The Bell with a flash of dismay. What right had this woman to uproot her from her life, to tear her away from her home and her friends -

She caught herself. Her home? Her friends? A Cheapside brothel where she was bullied by Mother Wickham, debauched by the Colonel, and mocked by the other harlots when she tried to hang on to the values her father had taught her. Even if she no longer had her chastity, she still had her modesty, her honesty, her awareness of right and wrong.

And an unwillingness to let go of what was rightfully hers. 'Please, ma'am, what of my...?'

'Your possessions? Your cheap gowns? The trappings of your trade? Don't worry about them: you'll have new ones.' The anxiety stayed in Molly's eyes. 'What else do you have that could grieve you in the losing of it?' Her sneer was unconcealed.

Without thinking, Molly's hand strayed to her empty placket.

Lady Charnell tilted her head back and barked a scornful laugh.

'How much did you have saved?'

'Eight - ' Eight; but a lightning thought changed her mind. 'Eighteen guineas,' she said. This wasn't dishonesty: this was justice.

The older woman was surprised that a common harlot could even talk in terms of such a sum. 'Eighteen guineas of my money,' she said. 'He was either a lot more generous or a lot more active than I thought.' But the money, to her, was irrelevant. She didn't question Molly any further. 'When I arrive home, I shall write a note. You shall have your guineas, girl. I'm sure you must have earned them.'

'Thank you, my lady.' Was it always this easy? 'And...'

A raised eyebrow. 'There's more?'

'My trunk. From York.'

A dismissive, humourless grunt. 'Very well. It will be delivered. Though what it could possibly contain that...' A bemused shake of the head; what possible value could there be in the possessions of a Cheapside whore?

Delivered. To Chiswick, she'd said. In the country, outside London. Who lives in Chiswick? Play the frightened rabbit. 'Please, my lady.'

'Yes?'

'Why am I being taken to Chiswick?'

'I thought I'd made that obvious.' A thoughtful frown skittered across her aristocratic features. 'Perhaps I didn't. You, girl, are a farewell gift to someone who has been of service to me.' A hint of amusement twisted the corner of her lips. 'I've bought you for Abraham Asher. You now belong to the old Jew.'

Chapter 10

'It's business, my dear,' Abraham Asher said.

Molly sat where she'd been invited to sit, beside the imposing stone fireplace, her hands in her lap, feeling the warmth on her right side, feeling the chill of the large, oak-beamed room on her left. She said nothing.

He poured glowing red wine into a plain Venetian glass, lifted it by the elaborate stem, passed it under his hooked nose to savour the bouquet, then handed it to her. 'I am old,' he said. 'I am crippled. I am no longer handsome.' A self-deprecating smile flickered at his lips. 'If I ever was. And I'm a Jew. Not quite an outcast from society, but...' He shrugged, spread his hands wide, dipped his head to one side. 'On the other hand, I am wealthy.'

Molly held the wine glass steady, not drinking from it.

He poured wine for himself, and sat down in a hoop-backed walnut chair facing her. 'You are young and pretty. But you have no money - at least, not enough money to lead the sort of life I can offer you. However...' He leaned forward; she could smell the mixture of garlic and perfume that hung about him. 'I want your youth and your prettiness, and I am willing to pay for it. You want my money, and you are willing to earn it.' He sat back in his chair. 'Business.'

Still she said nothing.

He understood. 'You're frightened.' He stood up and limped away from her, his footsteps cushioned by thick rugs, then clacking unevenly across polished floorboards, then onto rugs again. Stopping by one of the large windows, he wiped a patch of condensation away with his sleeve and peered through the frosted patterns on the outside of the glass; he stood quietly, considering, choosing his words, barely seeing the cropped meadow sweeping away from the house down to the ice-fringed river, the empty branches of the oaks and elms, the leafless orchard. 'I'm not Colonel Charnell,' he said. 'I don't want to hurt you.' He turned away from the bleak scene outside and attempted a joke. 'I should buy a work of art, and try to ruin it? That would not be good business.'

And still Molly remained silent.

Abraham Asher read the situation. Best not to attempt too much too soon. He tugged at a silken rope. 'Hannah will show you to your room.' His good humour surfaced again. 'Unlike the rest of the house, she's not Jewish. But she's got a good Hebrew name. If there's anything you need, she'll get it for you.'

A discreet knock, and the maid came in. No more than sixteen, a few inches shorter than Molly, dressed in pale blue and white, her straw-coloured hair gathered tidily under her cap, her alert blue eyes quickly summing up the scene. She reminded Molly of herself just... what? A few months ago.

'Hannah,' said Abraham. 'This is Mistress Molly. You are to serve her. She will sleep in the Racehorse Room.' He offered Molly an apologetic explanation. 'A foolish name for a room. But there's a portrait of a race-horse in there, and it's easier than drawing a map to say which room on which floor.'

Molly rose to her feet. 'My...'

He waited. When she didn't continue, he said 'Your nightclothes? Your trunk?' A wry smile. 'Your woman's aids to beauty?' He beckoned to the waiting maid. 'Hannah is here to serve you,' he said to Molly. 'She will find you nightclothes. Tomorrow your trunk will be here.' He took her hand in his and brushed it with his lips. 'And I cannot believe that you ever have any need for a woman's aids to beauty.'

Molly tried to echo his smile. But it was a thin echo, and soon faded. She followed the waiting Hannah.

'Tonight is yours, my dear,' Abraham said as she reached the door. 'I shall expect you at breakfast.' He gave her a curt but courteous bow.

As the panelled oak door closed behind her and she set foot on the bottom of the broad, picture-flanked staircase, she wondered how the world would regard her now. The Chiswick Whore?

The address may change, the paymaster may change, the demands may change. But, constant in the midst of flux, the whore is still a whore.

In the half-second between sleeping and waking, the silence fooled her into imagining she was back in York. It was already light, but there were no street cries, no near-at-hand church bells, no clanging clock-chimes, no rumbling of cartwheels over cobbles. Just the faint spitting of the fire in the grate.

The smells were different, too. Dried lavender, wood smoke, the appetising warmth of fresh-baked bread.

She peeped out from beneath the soft woollen blankets and blinked at the morning, enjoying the contrast between the warmth cocooning her body and the cold air against her face.

Without disturbing her, Hannah had drawn back the heavy blue curtains of the bed, and was now sitting by the fire, crouched on a footstool, waiting for her new mistress to wake.

Not wanting to drag the maid away from the warmth, Molly lay still. Instead, she eased her head left and right to take in her surroundings. The room was large, twice as big as her room at The Bell, and filled with colour. Opposite her, beyond the two curtain-hung posts at the foot of her bed, the blue and gold figured wall was broken by two leaded windows. Between them the arched stone fireplace with, above it, the sleek outlines of the racehorse that had given its name to the room. Against the wall to her left, oaken chests for her clothes. To her right, a low, bow-legged table, its polished walnut glinting in the grey daylight; two cream and blue tapestry-padded chairs, bright against the muted reds and browns of a woven rug; a blue and gold draped vanity table reflected the wallpaper, and its mirror echoed the walnut of the furniture. Gilt-framed paintings filled the room: themes from the Old Testament, stories from Greek mythology, portraits of famous men. Tilting her head further, she could see the plain panelled door, and a narrow opening leading to -

A startled gasp. 'Mistress!' Hannah leapt to her feet and rushed to the bed. 'I didn't realise you were awake! Please forgive me!' She stood there, her head hanging in contrition.

Molly stared at her in surprise. 'Forgive you?' She reached out from the warmth of the bed and took the girl's hand in hers. The cold air brought goose-pimples springing to the bare flesh of her arm, and she shivered. At the Colonel's insistence, she had long since given up wearing nightclothes; after lying awake for an hour the previous night, she had peeled off the constricting nightshift Hannah had provided, and settled comfortably to sleep. 'What for?'

'I - I didn't realise you were awake.'

Molly squeezed the young girl's fingers. 'Until a few moments ago,

I weren't.' She let go, and drew her arm back into the warmth of the bed. 'Now then, Hannah, if you could pour me a glass of something wholesome to drink, I should be most grateful.'

The maid eyed her apprehensively. 'Wholesome?'

Molly put her at ease. 'Boiled water. Tea. Small beer.' She wrinkled her nose. 'No, not small beer. Something hot. And some boiled water. Cold boiled water.'

Hannah bobbed. 'Yes, Miss Molly.' She scurried to the door, squeezed through it and shut it quickly behind her to keep in such warmth as there was, and clattered down the stairs.

Molly lay in bed, listening to the crackling fire, breathing in the scents, admiring the luxury of the room's individual features. The paintings, the ornately carved furniture, the tapestry hangings, the dark wood against the cream plaster.

She wriggled onto her side, pulled the blankets up to her ears again, let her eyelids drift shut. So quiet, it might almost be York again.

Too quiet! Her eyes sprang open, and her ears strained. No dogs barking. No sheep, no cattle. Not even any birds. Silence.

She sat up, swung her legs clear of the bed, wrapped herself in the blankets, and padded in her bare feet across the polished wooden floor to one of the windows.

Snow. From the house to the river, the bowed black skeletons of oaks and elms spread their branches over an unbroken white carpet that frayed untidily at the edges as it gave way to the slate-grey Thames.

Pure white. Clean. Virginal. Sunday linen. Confirmation dress. Christmas in York. Goose feathers. Sugar icing. Her head swam as the images of childhood flooded over her. Sagging forward, she clutched at the stone window-sill; the blankets slid from her shoulders and fell to the floor. She leaned her forehead against the ice-cold glass, and let it shock her awake again. As her naked body started to shiver, then tremble, then shake, she reeled back into the room.

The door opened. 'What are you doing, girl?!'

Oblivious, she looked through him and the maid, beyond them to York. She made no effort to cover herself.

Abraham hurried to her, snatched up the blankets, draped them round her and led her to the fireside. 'Hannah - fetch hot water from the kitchen, and a bowl for Miss Molly to put her feet in.' As the maid scurried out, he lowered Molly onto the footstool, returned to the bed and retrieved a pillow to keep her feet from the floor. Gripping the fire-iron in both hands, he wrestled the logs over and poked them into a blaze. Stooping, he tucked the blankets tight under her chin, then smoothed her hair with his hand. 'Should I capture a bird of paradise and let it freeze to death?' he mock-chided her. He knelt, took her foot between his hands and chafed it to bring the blood back into it.

A minute passed. The fire, the gentle massage, the warmth of the blankets lulled her almost into sleep again. 'I had a bird of paradise once,' he murmured, more to himself than to Molly. 'No bigger than a fluffy chick. But oh, so beautiful.'

Her father had seen a bird of paradise once, in a travelling fair. She allowed the image to form from his description. Glowing gold and red, with a tail that swept the sky, and a voice that sang like angels, and proud wings that sailed the sky like an archangel's galleon and -

The fire spat. She jolted awake. 'What happened to it?'

'She was stolen away from me.'

She watched him. His hands continued to massage her foot, but his thoughts were fixed on a long distant scene. He's not talking about a bird. 'I'm sorry.'

He came back to the present. 'Don't be sorry, my dear. Just be careful.' He took her other foot in his hands. 'You have a lovely body,' he said.

Keepers don't pay compliments out of politeness. She gazed past him at the fire. 'Do you want me now,' she asked. Not inviting, not rejecting, simply asking. After all, that's why she was there. She'd been bought and paid for.

He hesitated, oddly shy, then nodded. 'Yes,' he said.

She stood. Clutching the blankets round her, she shuffled towards the bed.

'No,' he said. 'Here. Where it's warm.'

She came back, let the blankets fall open, felt the fire's warmth play over her skin.

On his knees, no more than a yard away from her, he nodded approvingly. 'A moment, my dear,' he said. 'Keep warm.' Rising to his feet, he hobbled away from her to the bed, sat, removed his shoes and placed them together on the floor; next his garters and hose, neatly rolled up and placed on the bed; finally, with his back to her, he took off his breeches, folded them and put them next to his stockings.

Molly watched him. How ridiculous he looked, his wasted buttocks and scrawny legs looping white and bandy beneath his hump-backed silver-grey coat and embroidered waistcoat.

He looked back over his shoulder, waiting until she averted her eyes. With her back to him, she let the blankets slip to the floor, lay down on her side, and let the fire's warmth caress her body. She heard his footsteps pad across the floorboards; a diffident awkwardness as he lay down behind her, and she felt the chill of his body against her. Flesh stirred against her buttock; she rolled onto her back and parted her knees, avoided looking at him, stared instead into the leaping flames. When he was ready, he could take her however he pleased; but she made no move to help him.

With a gentleness that surprised her, he took her chin in his fore-finger and thumb and turned her face towards him. 'I've heard tales about Colonel Charnell,' he said. 'Unpleasant tales. But I'm not Colonel Charnell, Molly. I don't want to hurt you. I want to savour you. I want to nurture you, to please you, to...' He frowned, as if remembering some past pain. 'I want you to respect me, Molly.' He touched his finger to her lips, partly deflecting anything she might say, partly caressing the outline of her mouth. 'I'm old, Molly. And I'm ugly. You're young and pretty. So very pretty.' He paused. 'I was wrong yesterday. It's more than business. It's...' He sucked in a breath of courage and lifted himself on top of her, between her knees. 'Please, Molly,' he mumbled as she felt for him and guided him into her, 'please pretend. Just pretend.'

But she had no time to pretend. Almost instantly, his thighs were ramming at her, his bony chest crushing her breasts, his garlicky breath gasping, his lips drawn back in an agonised rictus, his whole body shuddering, his fingers clawing into her back.

Beyond the bed, the door bumped open; Hannah backed in with a steaming bowl of water. 'Here you are, Mi- ' Her voice caught in her throat as she saw Molly and Abraham in front of the fire. Not knowing what to do, she stood there, gaping, her mouth frozen mid-syllable.

Flat on her back, Molly caught the maid's eye over Abraham's hunched shoulder; she flapped her hand at the door, telling her to get out. Hannah, mindful of her duties, crept into the room, put the bowl down within two feet of her master's humping buttocks, then tip-toed out, closing the door mouse-quiet behind her.

Abraham collapsed across Molly, remained there for a minute before rolling away from her and lying face down on the rug in front of the fire. 'Forgive me, my dear,' he said at last. 'It's been a long, long time.'

She was puzzled. 'But I thought Lady Charnell...'

'No. That was nothing more than an invented story, a lie to help her accomplish her revenge.' He lapsed into his own thoughts. 'I was in her debt. Not financially, but nevertheless, a debt that needed to be repaid. It was a transaction, my dear, that's all.'

And I was part of the price. 'But you're rich. You could afford...'

'As many harlots as I want. Yes, I could. More transactions. I spend my life making transactions, little Molly.' He drew his finger down from her temple to her chin, tracing the curve of her face. 'I've rescued you from Colonel Charnell. I've given you sanctuary. And you have nowhere else to go.' As if shy, he avoided her eyes. 'In the circumstances, I could have told you to make yourself available to me. And, in the circumstances, I doubt not that you would have done. But that would have been just another transaction. I'm tired of transactions, my little Molly.' He stood. Keeping his back to her, he retrieved his breeches from the bed and pulled them on. When he spoke, she had to strain to hear him. 'I'll try not to make many demands on you, my dear. In return, all I ask is that try to feel kindly towards me.'

She snuggled into the blankets. 'You're not so old,' she said. It didn't make sense. 'You could marry.'

He looked back over his hunched shoulder at her. 'I have been married.' The way he said it put an end to the topic. Neither spoke as he rolled his stockings up his legs, tied his garters and pushed his feet into his shoes. He crossed to Molly, knelt, put his hand inside the blankets and took her hand. Lifting it, he touched it to his lips, then tucked it back into the warmth. 'Breakfast will be ready as soon as you've dressed,' he said. A touch of embarrassment twitched at his lips as he noticed the steaming bowl of water on the floor. 'And Hannah seems to have anticipated your need to wash yourself.' He levered his twisted body upright and left.

After he'd gone, she remained cocooned on the rug, enjoying the warmth. Despite what he says, she thought, her eyelids growing heavy, it is just another transaction. And he doesn't even require it to be an honest one.

But one thing is true. He isn't the Colonel.

At The Bell, it had been last night's bread, stale cheese and porridge; at Abraham's house, the bread was fresh-baked, there were hard-boiled eggs, salt herrings, cider, ale. At The Bell, in the rough stone kitchen; at the Asher house, in the panelled eating room. At both, breakfast was a ritual to be observed at the start of the day. In Cheapside, the day began at noon; in Chiswick, as in York, at dawn.

Hannah had dressed her, tied up her hair, brushed rouge on her cheeks, towelled her hands dry after she'd washed them. Molly followed the maid down to the eating room, and sat where she was told by the cold-eyed butler, halfway along the plain, tree-length, square-sided, polished table, big enough for a score of guests or more. Within a minute, Abraham entered and sat opposite her. His eyes were bright, glistening; the corners of his mouth curved upwards; his head was high, his shoulders were as far back as his hunched back could hold them, his white wig was newly combed into ringlets.

'Good morning, my dear,' he said, as if he hadn't seen her for twenty four hours. 'Hannah, serve your mistress some breakfast. I'm sure she must have an appetite.' He smiled warmly, knowingly at Molly. 'I most certainly do.'

No porridge, no cheese. Molly chose herring, bread and ale, and watched as Abraham piled some of everything onto his plate, swilled it down with cider, then refilled his plate twice more.

At last, he leaned back in his chair, wiped his lips with a cloth, dropped it onto his plate. 'It's months - years since I ate like that,' he said. 'Isaac would have been proud of me.' A shadow of disappointment flitted across his face. 'If, of course, he'd managed to rise from his bed in time.' The butler bent beside him and whispered. 'Ah,' said Abraham. He put both hands to his chest in a gesture of contrition. 'Silver tells me I do my son an injustice,' he told Molly. 'He hasn't failed to rise for breakfast, after all. He's simply failed to come home in time for it.' He shrugged indulgently. 'That's what happens when boys become men.'

Molly smiled politely, said nothing.

'Today I have business,' Abraham told her with a different kind of shrug. 'But that means the day is yours, my dear. You can do whatever you'd like to do. Let Hannah show you the house, let her go into Town with you, let her help you choose some new gowns. You'd like some new gowns, wouldn't you?' His smile, as generous as it had been for his absent son, faded and took on an apologetic aspect. 'I don't mean that the gown you're wearing isn't becoming. But I thought...' He shrugged again; he had an entire language of shrugs. 'Hannah is a sensible girl. She'll help you decide.'

The day was hers, she could go anywhere, she was totally free. As long as Hannah was there with her. She chose to play snowballs on the meadow at the back of the sprawling, three-gabled house. And she chose not to be the mistress.

Dressed in Hannah's workaday cloak, in some elderly and anonymous boots, in the cook's almost-discarded hood, in a pair of oversized gloves borrowed from Silver the butler, she scooped the snow, rolled it into fat, loose balls and hurled it at the maid.

It took Hannah several minutes to grasp the difference between an obedient target and a snowball warrior; but when she did, she proved an accurate and energetic opponent. As she drove Molly giggling backwards with a white flurry, a male voice roared into the dead stillness.

'Stop!'

They each dropped their snowballs. Picking his way down the icy steps at the back of the house was a tall young man in a silver-grey cloak, his short powdered wig topped by a pale blue three-cornered hat. Confident, handsome, lean, swarthy. Molly was sure she'd seen him before, but couldn't think where. Not at The Bell.

'Stay where you are,' he said. The tone of his voice allowed no argument. As he waded through the ankle-deep snow, he lifted his hands to quell any worries. He halted some ten or twelve feet away from them, glancing to either side of him as if gauging his exact position. 'Come to me,' he said. With his hands still raised, he beckoned to them. They walked forward. As they came near him, he grinned reassuringly and stretched out both hands to them. Obediently, they each put a hand in his.

The powerful jerk as he tugged them towards him took the two girls by surprise. Completely off-balance, they both stumbled and fell. Hannah sprawled face down in the snow; Molly cannoned into the young man and brought him heavily down on his back, falling on top

110

of him.

As she did so, she felt the ground beneath her crack and shift. Looking over her shoulder, she saw several square yards of the white lawn peel away from her feet and swirl into the fast-flowing water. Instinctively, she flung her arms round her saviour and clung on to him. She could feel the water pushing against the toes of her boots as her feet dangled over the flood.

'Well, my dear,' he said after a few seconds, his warm breath close to her ear, 'this is very pleasant and very encouraging but, alas, very cold.' His hand caressed her back. 'Perhaps we should continue this intimacy elsewhere.'

Molly clawed herself up his body to solid ground, scrambled to her feet, scampered away from the water and brushed the snow away from her skirts. Her heart was pounding; not all of it was fear.

The young man stood, stooped and helped Hannah to her feet, collected her fallen cap for her, waited while she tucked her straggling fair hair back under it. This done, he put an arm about the shoulders of each of the girls and guided them towards the house. 'You must take care,' he said, charming each of them in turn. 'Skating on thin ice is a pastime only for those who know the risks beforehand.' The two girls looked back over their shoulders at the two lines of footprints that led to the jagged edge where the snow met the river. And, with a sickening lurch of what-might-have-been, beyond. 'Come into the kitchen and get these wet cloaks off,' he said.

He let Hannah go. 'And who's this pretty creature?' he asked Molly. 'Another maid to swell the household's complement of beauty?' He took her hand in his and, with an exaggerated gesture, bent low to kiss it. 'My name's Isaac, my lady,' he said. 'Son to the master of this house, the ancient and venerable Abraham. And are you a maid of the kitchen? Or the scullery? Or...,' and he allowed his eyes to meet hers directly, '...a maid of the bedchamber?'

'She en't a maid, Master Isaac,' Hannah blurted out; then blushed and put a hand to her mouth as she realised what she'd said.

Molly decided that boldness was the least complicated policy, and returned his gaze. 'No, sir,' she said. He'd find out at the next mealtime, anyway. 'I'm not a maid. I'm your father's new whore.' She bobbed an ironic curtsy; he was, after all, only the son of the house. 'Come,

Hannah.' Despite her plain cloak, her shabby boots, her greasy hood, she swept grandly up the steps to the back of the house, praying she wouldn't slip on the ice and spoil her exit.

Her trunk was waiting for her in her room. When she opened it, she found a silk purse lying on top of her clothes, together with a letter addressed to Ye Cheapside Whore. Her jaw tightened at the insult, then relaxed as she picked up the purse. It felt full.

She broke the letter's wax seal and opened out the expensive cream-coloured paper with its crested heading. There was no salutation.

That you can read, I have asfum'd. That you can count beyond ye Number of your Fingers, I am asfur'd - elfe would you be alone among all ye Harlots in Chriftendom. Ye Purfe bears 15 guineas. This is fomething lefs than ye 18 Guineas you tried to rob me of; twice ye 8 Guineas you left at ye Bell, for you muft have earn'd them dearly; and a Moiety lefs than twice for your Impudence.

The letter was unsigned.

Molly untied the purse and shook the gold coins onto her bed. Setting then aside one by one, she counted them. Fifteen, as promised in the note. She plucked up three and held them out to Hannah. 'For you,' she said.

The younger girl shied away. 'But - but why?'

Like a reflection in a mirror, Molly could see the child she herself had been in York. 'One day you'll lie with a man,' she said. 'If you haven't already.' Hannah blushed; whether from embarrassment or guilt, Molly was unable to tell. 'You'll lie with him for love. Or for lust. Or because he forces you. Or because he swears he'll marry you.' For the first time in her life, she'd become the cynical voice of experience. She took Hannah's hand in her own, turned it palm upward, dropped the coins into it. Three gold coins. 'You'll lie with him. And he'll lie to you.' She began shovelling the rest of the coins into the purse. 'Men lie and cheat, Hannah. Guineas forsake you only when you let them go. If you look for constancy, look to gold.'

Hannah clenched her fist to her breast and searched for something to say. She'd never had so much money in her life. 'How - how can I thank you?' she stammered.

'One day,' Molly said, 'I'm sure you'll find a way to thank me.'

She could hear her father voicing one of his guiding principles: In this life, lass, you don't get owt for nowt.

Later that day, another letter arrived for her, addressed to Mrs M Huckerby, at ye Houfe of Abm Afher, Efquire, Chifwick. A neat, simple hand, written on cheap paper, unsealed but tied with a pale blue ribbon.

'Meet me at St Paul's,' it said, *'any Day at 2 of ye Clock after Noon.'*

It was signed

Anny.

And, at the bottom, there was a roughly scrawled addendum, smudged by a teardrop.

'Bull died.'

Chapter 11

Two days since Annie's note.

As the carriage approached St Paul's, the colonnaded dome sank out sight behind the twin towers that flanked the huge portico. She could see the tall figure standing halfway up the cathedral steps, the only point of stillness in the scurrying crowds, strands of red hair straying from under her hood and whipping in the raw wind, the eyes screwed up against the squalling snow, peering, searching, hoping.

Molly rapped on the roof with her knuckles, copying the imperious gesture of Lady Charnell. 'Drive on,' she called. She pulled the shade down over the window to avoid being seen.

The carriage swung alongside the cathedral, past its eastern end, into Cheapside, back again the way they'd come, to the foot of Ludgate Hill. The horses began to labour up the slope, their hooves slipping on the melting snow covering the cobbles.

Another smart tap on the roof.

'Whoa!' The horses stomped to a halt, blowing great steaming breaths into the air.

'Wait here,' Molly said to Hannah.

'But Master Abraham said - '

Molly touched her forefinger to Hannah's lips to silence her. 'I'll be a quarter of an hour, no more.' She waited for the driver to open the door and help her as she climbed down from the carriage. 'I shall not be long,' she told him.

She wrapped her heavy new cloak round her, ducked her head and butted against the cutting east wind towards St Paul's, avoiding the worst of the filthy, half-thawed slush, but still getting splashed up to the knees.

Annie saw her when she was thirty yards away, waved anxiously to attract her attention, stayed where she was until Molly had climbed up beside her.

'Moll. I wasn't sure you'd come.' She reached out, almost as if to touch her face; then she drew back, plucked at Molly's sleeve, and led her the rest of the way up to the cathedral's towering doors. 'Let's talk inside, out of the wind.' They threaded past the shivering beggars, past the heavy-cloaked citizens discussing business matters, past the suspicious scrutiny of the lurking curates, into the dim interior.

Annie knelt on the stone floor, bowed her head and mumbled a few words. Molly couldn't hear what she said; it might have been a prayer, it might have been a ploy to satisfy any of the clergy who might be watching her.

Molly knelt beside her and tried to pray. Please, God, forgive me for... There was so much. Too much. Please God, forgive me.

The numbing cold was seeping through her cloak, her gown, her petticoats, her stockings. She stood up. Together, they huddled to the side of the nave. 'I had your letter,' she said.

'Bull died,' Annie murmured; her voice was tense. 'We did everything we could, but the wound turned bad. It turned bad inside and...' She straightened. 'Bull was special to me, Moll.' Her lips quivered, and her eyes glistened with unfallen tears.

Molly had no doubt what she meant. 'Does Abigail know?'

'No.' Her face became dead, emotionless. 'She knows he used to come to my bed sometimes. But that's what harlots are for. She's never paid any mind to that. But she doesn't know that we...' She shrugged. 'It doesn't matter now.'

Molly laid a hand on her arm. 'It does matter, Annie. Otherwise you wouldn't have asked me to come here.'

A querulous voice interrupted them. 'Move on, girls.' A deacon, thin-lipped, red-nosed, weepy-eyed. 'This is no place for you now.' Two unaccompanied young women led to an obvious assumption. 'Doctor Trencham is preaching soon.'

As Annie started towards the great doors, Molly kept hold of her sleeve and stopped her. She let her cloak fall open to reveal the embroidered gown beneath, the silk bows at her breast, the stones sparkling at her throat. The caparison of a mistress, not the trappings of a whore.

Her heart was racing, but what did she have to lose? She stared haughtily at him. 'Why else should we be here?' she said, squeezing her flat York vowels into what she hoped might pass for an aristocratic accent. 'My husband is one of Doctor Trencham's patrons.'

'My - my apologies, my lady,' he stammered. A foreigner, no doubt of it: her distorted pronunciation proved that. A countess, even a minor princess. 'If I can be of service, my lady.'

She arched her eyebrows into a dismissive expression she hoped was reminiscent of Lady Charnell. 'My husband will arrange what needs to be arranged.'

'Yes, my lady.' His feet echoed as he scuttled away, fleeing in case she asked his name.

She gripped Annie's arm with a fierce resolve. 'Don't say a word!' she hissed. With a dramatic flourish, she gathered up her cloak about her. 'Follow me.'

Head high, with Annie trailing behind, she sailed majestically to the main door, paused while one of the deacons heaved it open for her, paused again while she took a handful of coins from her purse and scattered them for the beggars to fight over, then marched into the icy outdoors, aware that an entire coven of priests and deacons was pointing at her and whispering as she left.

'Why?' Annie was indignant. 'We've as much right to be in God's house as they have.'

'Aye,' said Molly. 'But I lived at The Bell until just a few days ago, and you still do. Priests don't like harlots - at least, not in their churches. And especially not in their cathedrals when Doctor Whatever-his-name-is is coming to preach.'

'I'm not ashamed!' A flash of red-haired temper.

'Neither am I.' Aye, I am - but I don't want Annie to know that. 'But a harlot in a cathedral is tempting trouble. Young Kitty were pilloried for it. And how long do you think Abraham Asher would keep me if I made an enemy of half his clients? They tolerate him being a Jew. Would they tolerate him if his mistress mocked the Church?'

Annie's temper subsided. 'You've changed, Moll.'

'No.' She thought for a moment. 'No, I've not changed, Annie. Inside me, I'm the same Molly Huckerby that left York. But I'm not frightened any more.' That's not true. I am frightened - but at least I now know what I'm frightened of.

She sought out a chestnut-seller, grateful for the warmth of the brazier, grateful that her proffered coins prevented her being chased away, grateful that the hot chestnuts stung her fingers through her gloves. 'It's only been a few days, but I've had time to see what my life could be, what it should be.'

They stood downwind of the brazier, enjoying its warmth as they broke open the split shells, popping the hot meat into their mouths, juggling it on their tongues, blowing to cool it, dropping the charred remains to the cobbles before savouring the sweet, earthy taste. 'Nothing's changed, Annie. I'm as much a harlot as I were last week.' The redhead glanced down at the quality of her clothes and shoes. No emotion; but Molly could sense the scepticism. 'Nothing's changed,' she insisted. 'I still sell my body for money. The way you do, the way Kitty does, the way I did when the Colonel did vile things to me and left guineas on my table.'

This time, Annie was openly scornful. 'Then why not come back to The Bell?"

Molly raised her hand to acknowledge the hit. 'Aye, there is a difference. But it's not the gowns, it's not the...' Annie doesn't know about the carriage. '...it's not living in a big house. The difference is Abraham. He's older than the Colonel. He's crippled. But he treats me like a...' No, not like a wife. Less than a wife. But more than a mistress. 'Abraham treats me as if he cares about me.'

Silence while they peeled and ate the chestnuts. 'And...' she looked sideways at Annie. 'And he's got a very handsome son.'

Annie swung to face her, saw the glint of mock-mischief, and grinned with delight. Scandal, intrigue, secrets. 'Has he taken a fancy to you? Have you got a handsome lover as well as a rich protector? What's his name?'

Molly arched her eyebrows mysteriously, teasing her friend. 'His name's Isaac.' Then she relented and confessed the truth. 'But I've only met him once - and then he saved my life.'

'Your life?' She obviously didn't think it likely.

'He saved me from falling into the river, and - ' And Hannah, my maid. I mustn't tell you about my maid. My own maid. Not a maid for everybody, like Abigail, but a maid for me and me alone. 'But he doesn't care for me.'

Annie held her thumb and forefinger five inches apart. 'Not even this much?'

Molly sniggered, enjoying the lewd joke. 'Not even that much.' Her mood died. 'But even that much would be more than the Colonel ever cared.'

'The Colonel?'

'The Colonel never cared for me at all. Not even that much.' She mimicked Annie's gesture, but reduced it by half. 'He cared only for the tricks I could perform at his bidding. I were his dog, his horse, his trained monkey.' More chestnuts. Her thoughts slithered into the dark corners of her memory. 'Mother Wickham doesn't care for anybody. She cares only for what can bring her money. She owns people. She owned me. She could make me do whatever she wanted, no matter how...'

A ripple of disgust tremored across her face. No matter how degrading. Her afternoon in hell that had gone on for ever, hour after hour, man after man, the stiff flesh sliding, ramming, crashing against the back of her throat, the coarse hair chafing her lips, the rigid fingers dragging her head forward, the muscles cramping in her jaw, the sick-sweet seed dribbling down her chin, the nausea welling up inside, the choking, the spitting, finally the vomiting, the uncontrollable sobbing, the unanswered prayer that she might die.

And Mother Wickham and the Colonel watching, smiling, cooing with satisfaction.

She flicked her head sharply to one side, to fling away the memory, then breathed the cold air deep into her lungs before continuing. 'Abraham doesn't want to own me. He's different. It's a different kind of...' Abraham's own word summed it up. 'A different kind of transaction.'

They stood in silence while they finished the chestnuts; there was no need for words. At the foot of Ludgate Hill a carriage stood, the horses blowing clouds of steam and stamping their hooves.

A nearby church clock began to chime. Molly caught sight of the carriage, put her hand to her face in chagrin. She'd forgotten. 'Oh!' she said.

'What's the matter?'

'Nothing. Annie, I've got to go. I'm late.' She leaned forward and pressed her face against the older girl's cheek. 'I'll send word to you. Go now.' She didn't want Annie to see her climbing into a carriage like a grand lady. She didn't want to flaunt her Chiswick good fortune within sight of Wood Street. She didn't want to remind her friend of the difference between a mistress and a harlot.

But Annie put her hand on Molly's shoulder and held her back. 'You

118

didn't ask me why I needed to see you.'

Molly could feel herself colouring. All this time, and she'd spoken only of herself. 'Forgive me, Annie. I thought... Bull...'

'Yes, Bull. Bull's dead. And without Bull, Mother Wickham doesn't want...' Annie twitched her head to one side in anger.

Molly prompted her. 'She doesn't want Abigail?'

Annie swung back fiercely. 'She needs Abigail. But Abigail won't give up the baby. She'd rather be cast out into the streets than part with Lily.'

'So - '

Annie interrupted her. 'Mother Wickham doesn't mind that.' She breathed a near-silent laugh. 'Lily's a girl-child. Mother Wickham's looking to the future. A touch of the exotic for her more discerning customers.' The way she said it made it sound almost like a direct quote. The cynical smile died. 'But she says without Bull she can't afford to keep both Okoro and Lily. Or, as she puts it, Abigail has to choose between her husband's boy and the highwayman's bastard.'

And she won't give up the baby. 'But what will happen to Okoro if he has to leave The Bell?'

'An eight-year-old boy on London's streets?' Annie pretended to consider the options. 'He can steal. He can beg. He can die. Or...'

'Or...?'

There was a challenge in her eyes. 'Or he can be a Chiswick lapdog. Isn't it fashionable for Chiswick ladies to have little blackamoor attendants to wait on them?'

Molly was stunned. It had never occurred to her that the girls at The Bell could see her so differently, so soon. 'I don't know. I'll have to think about it. I'll have to speak to Abraham.'

'Please, Moll,' said Annie. 'I owe it to Bull. He's Bull's son.' She swallowed. 'If things had been different, he might have been my son.'

'I'll speak to Abraham.' She took Annie's hand and squeezed it. 'Meet me in two days time, here at St Paul's.'

She waited till Annie was out of sight before sloshing towards the carriage.

Abraham listened attentively, then clapped his hands in delight. 'Charming, my dear,' he said. 'Charming. What could be more charming than a little black slave? You'll be the envy of Chiswick. I'll arrange for him to be collected at once.'

Molly nestled into the blankets to keep warm while she waited for him to undress. 'No,' she said. 'I haven't spoken to his mother yet.'

'What need to speak?' He was genuinely puzzled. 'His mother must know the ways of a slave.' His face cleared. 'Ah. You want me to speak to her master.'

'No.' Why won't he understand? 'His mother isn't a slave. She's a servant, but not a slave.' Her jaw was set, and she was ready to defy him if she had to. 'And Okoro will be my servant. Not my slave.'

He acceded, happy to give her the victory. 'As you wish, my dear. Your servant, not your slave. I'll arrange for him to be collected after the sabbath.'

'After - '

'Yes, of course.' He accepted the rest of the agreement. 'After you've spoken with his mother.' He turned his back on her and began to unbutton his breeches. 'But first, my dear, a rather more pressing matter.'

The deal was settled. Now it was time for her half of the transaction. She leaned over and blew out the candle.

❋

Friday afternoon. Molly sat in the leaded oriel at the back of the house and watched the sun's pale blur sink down through the mist to meet the sweeping bend of the river at Chiswick. Enough light to reflect off the snow; not enough to make it glisten.

She pulled the woollen shawl tight against her throat, up around her ears, huddled inside its warmth.

The metallic click of the door-latch behind her drew her gaze from the bright whiteness outside to the dimness of the room. Abraham bent his head in greeting.

In the week she'd known him, she'd never seen him so finely dressed. Intricately-figured golden waistcoat; fitting breeches; cardinal red coat with cuffs that reached from the lace at his wrists to the crook of his elbow, stiff cuffs embroidered to match the waistcoat; white stockings, yellow garters, high-heeled shoes with square toes and silver buckles. Old-fashioned, but so very fine.

120

And no wig. On his close-cropped head, a simple black skull-cap, edged with gold braid. Draped over his arm, a black-striped white shawl.

She leapt to her feet. 'I'm sorry - are we...? Should I...?' Had she forgotten? Were they to go abroad? Was she late already?

He held up his hand to reassure her. 'Be still,' he said. 'Sometimes there are things we take for granted, things we forget to mention.' He crossed the room and took her hand. 'Do you ever go to church on Sundays, Molly?'

'Church?' What's church got to do with it? It's only Friday. 'Aye. Sometimes.' In York, always. In London, just once.

'Good. So you understand about the sabbath.' He raised her hand to his lips and kissed it; holding on to her fingers, he spoke candidly. 'We are Jews, Molly. I am a Jew, my son Isaac is a Jew. Everybody in the house is a Jew. Except you and Hannah and Curtis my footman and one or two of the farmgirls. And our Jewish sabbath isn't on Sundays like yours. Our sabbath lasts from Friday night to Saturday night.' He let go of her hand. 'When you're preparing to speak to God, we've already spoken with him. But that is how it should be. It's his way of talking to both of us without getting confused.'

What did he want of her? 'Is there something I should do?'

He held up his hands in apology. 'I should have told you before.' He looked past her at the darkening snowscape outside, the horizon clouds obscuring what was left of the sun, the first glimmers of link-torches on the road to the City. 'From now until the sun goes down again tomorrow night, we celebrate our sabbath. We have prayers, Molly, which - please forgive me - I would not wish to share with you. You are a Christian, a gentile. We have the same God, but our prayers are different.' He softened the apparent rejection. 'Though, God knows, we're all praying for the same things.'

'What do you want me to do?

'Do? Why, nothing, my dear. Enjoy our sabbath in your own way. After all, that's what we do on your sabbath.' He led her to the door. 'Hannah!' he called.

The slam of a door below, the patter of flying footsteps, a pounding up the stairs. 'Yes...' Pant. '...yes, Master...' Pant. '...Abraham?' Pant.

He wagged a mock-severe finger at the out-of-breath girl. 'Sometimes,

Hannah, my bidding requires dispatch. Sometimes it merely requires dignity. You must learn to distinguish between the two.'

'I'm - I'm sorry, Master Abraham.'

He lifted his hand to dismiss her apologies. 'Don't be sorry, child. How can I blame you for getting here as soon as you could? Now,' he said, changing his tone to make sure she understood his instructions, 'tell Mistress Silver that you are to serve Mistress Molly with whatever she has prepared for Isaac and me.' A possible objection occurred to him. 'Unless Mistress Molly doesn't like it. In which case, Hannah, prepare for her whatever she does like.' A fleeting smile at Molly. 'Except pigmeat. I dare not have it in the house. I might lose all my servants except Hannah and Curtis.' He felt the need to explain. 'The reason Hannah and Curtis work here in the house is because they're not Jews. Somebody has to light the fires on Saturdays.' He saw the blank expression on her face. 'We Jews are not allowed to do any work on the sabbath, not even...' He glanced at the fireplace, then gave up. 'Have your meal served wherever you want to eat it, my dear. In your room, in the picture gallery, in the kitchen.' He lifted a hand towards the window and the wintry dusk beyond it. 'In the garden. Anywhere, in fact, except the eating room. That is where we shall be celebrating our... our barbaric rites.' The self-mockery in its turn mocked her and all peoples who had ever mocked his people.

He looked again at the darkening sky outside. For a second time, he kissed Molly's fingers. 'I must go now and light the candles. Until to-morrow evening, my dear.' He stopped at the door with a mock frown, pretending to allay any fears. 'And don't be alarmed at the wailing noises you will hear. The household is in no danger of being murdered. We will simply be singing our prayers.'

The door closed behind him. Molly considered this new develop-ment. If she'd understood him aright, every Friday night was to be her own, right up until Saturday dusk.

Suddenly, she felt hungry. 'Come, Hannah,' she said. 'Let's eat.'

Abigail stood outside the kitchen door and wept.

Tears of joy at seeing Molly; grief for the death of her husband; sorrow at losing her son; relief at seeing him taken into a rich house rather than cast into the streets; anger at the ingratitude of Mother Wickham;

frustration at having no remedy.

Molly hugged her, and slipped two secret guineas into the pocket of her apron, two guineas she'd previously tied into a handkerchief so that they wouldn't clink together.

Minutes earlier, she'd plucked up her skirts and picked her way through the foulness of Love Lane to the door at the back of The Bell. But this time her carriage waited openly at the end of the lane, outside the front entrance in Wood Street, where everyone could see it. Where Mother Wickham could see it. Where Abigail could see her first-born being taken out of beggary and into the safety of slavery.

Some of the girls came out to see her, but not as friends. Polly and Nan hung back inside the kitchen door, eying her enviously, not daring to greet her, feigning not to notice when she waved to them. The Twins fingered the fabric of her cloak, then went back inside, giggling their sneers to each other. Annie wasn't there; but Molly knew she was watching. Nor was the Waif there.

'Kitty?' she asked Abigail.

'Miz Kitty got a visitor.'

Molly hid her disappointment. 'Tell her to write me a letter. Annie knows where I live now.' She stretched out her hand to the eight-year-old Okoro, waiting just inside the kitchen door, more subdued than she'd ever seen him. 'Time to go, my brave little lion,' she told him. Reluctantly, he came to her.

His mother knelt beside him and hugged him to her. 'Okoro, child,' she said, the tears running down her nose and dripping onto his back, 'Miz Moll goin' take care of you now. You goin' live in a big house with a fine gentleman. You goin' be safe now, child. You goin' be safe.' She choked back the sobs, stood, put Okoro's hand in Molly's. 'You take care of him, Miz Moll.'

'I'll keep him safe, Abigail, I promise. And we'll come to visit.' At the end of the lane, the horses stamped their hooves impatiently. 'Come, Okoro, let's go home.'

As she walked away from The Bell, she never once looked back. As Okoro walked away from his mother, peering over his shoulder, he never once looked forward.

Inside the carriage, Molly could feel Okoro rigid against her, his slight frame trembling. 'Are you cold?' she asked him.

He shook his head, said nothing, stared at his feet.

She put her arm round him and smoothed his tight black curls with her free hand. 'What's the matter, my little jungle tiger?'

Still he wouldn't look at her. After a while, he said 'The fine gentleman you taking me to...' His voice tailed away.

'Aye? What is it, Okoro?'

'Is he going to...' The half-whispered mumble became inaudible.

'Is he going to what, little man?'

Okoro's shaking became more pronounced. 'Is he going to hurt me? Is he going to...?'

She hugged him to her. 'He's a good man, Okoro. He won't hurt you.'

Tears were flowing down his cheeks. 'Do you promise, Miss Moll? Promise he won't hurt me. Please promise.'

She tilted his face up to hers, wiped away the tears with her sleeve. 'What's happened, Okoro? Why are you so frightened? What do you want me to promise?'

His tears turned into huge sobs as he buried his face in her bosom. 'Please, Miss Moll, don't let him stick his thing into me like the Colonel did.'

Molly wrapped him close, hushing, soothing, comforting, feeling her breath shorten, her teeth clenching, her lips tightening.

She remembered the searing pain when the Colonel had done it to her. She remembered the disbelief - surely he'd mistaken, surely he didn't mean to... She remembered him kneeling behind her, his hands forcing her buttocks apart so that he could drive in deeper. She could hear her own voice crying out, pleading, whimpering.

And now Okoro. Not a harlot, not paid for, just a child. For the first time since she arrived in London, she could feel raw, burning rage welling upwards from her belly, into her throat, into her brain, flooding red behind her eyes.

How dare he do that to a child!

How dare he!

Tight-lipped, she made her decision. Hatred and loathing were no longer enough. Now she wanted vengeance. And Abraham moved amongst the Colonel's equals.

There were yet more transactions to be agreed.

Chapter 12

Going to the theatre with Abraham was different.

Unlike the Colonel, Abraham went there to enjoy the plays, not to heckle the actors. To conduct witty conversation with his educated friends, not to swap obscene oaths with the orange-girls. To enjoy the author's jokes, not to disrupt the performance with ribald comments of his own.

From the moment she'd pushed through the high entrance, with Isaac ahead of her clearing a way with his cane, and Abraham limping behind her, protecting her from the gropers and pickpockets, it was different. For the first time in her dozen trips to the theatre, she'd felt neither ashamed nor embarrassed.

She'd laughed at the comedy, she'd sighed at the lovers longings, she'd clutched Abraham's arm when the duel was fought, she'd applauded the actors when they took their bow, she'd tossed a shilling onto the stage for them; then, thinking she was being mean-spirited, added another.

She'd come home elated, her whole body tingling with the drama, the players, the people.

But that was a week ago. Tonight she'd found it difficult to concentrate on the stage.

And Abraham had noticed. 'Did you enjoy yourself this evening, my dear?' he asked her when he came to her room later. He sat on the edge of the bed, slid his hand under the bedclothes and took her hand in his.

She lifted his hand up to her lips and lightly kissed his fingers. 'Oh, Abraham, I enjoyed myself wonderfully. Before I met you, I never knew the theatre could be so much...' She searched for the word. 'So much fun. Thank you.' She wriggled herself a few inches away to make room for him.

Instead, he released her hand, stood and crossed to the fireplace, gazed at the glowing embers over the fire-screen protecting the room from any lingering sparks. With his back to her, he said 'I'm not a young man, my pretty Molly. I don't have...' He thrust his hands out in front of him to warm them. 'I'm not wise in some of the world's ways.'

He rubbed his hands together, held them towards the fire again. When he spoke again, his voice was older, more tired, tinged with pain. 'Do you miss him so very much?'

Miss who? She frowned at his back, puzzled. Alarmed. Was he jealous? Jealous of who? 'Who?'

'You spent almost as much time looking at him as you spent looking at the stage.'

'Who?'

When, at last, he faced her, his features were composed, his emotions under control. 'Why, Colonel Charnell. You hardly took your eyes off him all evening.'

Had it been so obvious? She took time to think what to say. Then, having rehearsed the words in her own mind, she reached out her hand to him. He left the fire and came to her. But he didn't take her hand.

She understood. 'I do not miss him at all.' Her voice was calm, but she could feel her body tensing. 'Yet I confess he is constantly in my thoughts. Tomorrow morning, I shall tell you why.'

'I am here. You are here. Why not tell me now?'

But she'd made up her mind. 'Tomorrow morning. There is someone else who must be here.'

'This... this someone else?' A resigned apprehension.

She took his hand, traced her thumb along the line of his knuckles. 'Don't fear for my loyalty, Abraham. Even after tomorrow morning, I shall still be yours.'

Bought and paid for.

Throughout breakfast, Abraham had been polite, attentive, talkative. Never once had he mentioned last night's conversation. Now, their meal completed, they stood together by the fire.

Hannah was helping the two kitchen girls clear away the dishes, but Molly stopped her. 'Fetch Okoro,' she told her. 'When the child is here, Abraham, I shall tell you.'

'Yes,' he said. But first the stage had to be set. 'Miriam. Rebecca. Tell Master Silver that no one is to disturb us until we call.'

The girls bobbed obediently, loaded the dishes onto their trays, and left. Molly and Abraham waited. Neither spoke. Molly remained still.

Abraham was nervous, adjusting his cravat, fiddling with his coat buttons, tugging at his cuffs.

Hannah came in, Okoro trailing behind her, holding her hand. His clothes and hair were clean, his polished shoes as shiny as his face, his eyes big and white and frightened.

'Thank you, Hannah,' Molly said. 'You can go now.' Hannah released Okoro's hand; he scurried to huddle beside Molly. She gathered him to her and waited until Hannah had left before speaking. 'This is the person who had to be here,' she said.

'The child is why Colonel Charnell occupies your thoughts so much?' He didn't understand. She could see his mind racing, trying to imagine the connection between her and the Colonel and Okoro. White woman, white man, black child. Any sensible link was far from obvious.

'You were right, Abraham,' she said. 'I were looking at the Colonel all night. I were trying to fathom the man. He's not like you, Abraham. He's not like any man I've ever met. He's not like any man I've ever heard of. He is evil.' A tiny shiver. 'Let me explain. The Colonel seduced me. He debauched me. He did shameful things to me, Abraham.' She could feel her jaw tightening as she thought of some of the afternoons she had spent with him. With difficulty, she squeezed the memories into the back of her mind. 'With Mother Wickham's help, he turned me from a simple Yorkshire lass into a Cheapside whore. For that, I hate him.' Her mouth twisted, a bitter tic that vanished instantly; her misfortunes were not what this conversation was about. 'I were foolish and trusting and frightened, so perhaps it were partly my own fault.' She straightened her shoulders, and strengthened her resolve. Okoro clutched at her skirts. 'I know now that London expects all its women to be whores, including the respectable married ones. But there are some things that even London should not allow.'

Abraham understood. 'I, too, have commandments I must keep. What has Colonel Charnell done to you?'

'Not me, Abraham.' The anger inside her welled up, and the accusation burst from her lips in an explosion of loathing. 'He buggered Okoro. He committed sodomy on an eight-year-old boy.' She gave Okoro an encouraging squeeze. 'Isn't that right, lad? The Colonel stuck his thing into you.'

Okoro shrank into himself. He nodded his confirmation, but he didn't speak.

She lifted her head again. 'I want him to pay, Abraham.' Her voice was low, almost a growl. 'I want him punished.'

He weighed her words, balancing justice against the consequences. 'The punishment for sodomy is hanging,' he reminded her.

'Aye.' She had as much pity for the Colonel as he had had for her and for the child at her side.

He weighed the situation. 'He's a powerful man, Molly. With powerful friends. And I'm only a Jewish money-lender. But you are right: he is evil. What he has done is unnatural. It's against the law of God.' The corner of his mouth cocked in a sardonic smile. 'It's even against the law of King George.' He took her hand in his, rested his other hand on Okoro's head. 'It will be difficult. But I shall find a way.'

Despite her resolve, she started to shake. 'Please, Abraham,' she said. 'Find a way.'

She clung on to the bedpost while Hannah tightened the laces in her stays. 'Did you come into my room last night?' she asked casually.

She'd already checked her cache of guineas, and they were all there. Yet something had disturbed her, deep in the night. The click of her latch, the creak of a footfall outside her room, a hint of candlelight beneath the door. Enough to disturb her, not enough to wake her.

'I helped you undress for bed, mistress. Don't you remember?'

'No, much later than that. During the night.'

'No, mistress.' A hint of fear in the maid's voice. Was she being accused?

The laces tied, she waited to step into the petticoats Hannah was collecting from the linen chest. 'I'm sure somebody did.'

'Perhaps it was Master Abraham.'

Molly laughed. 'No - I'm sure I would have remembered that.'

Hannah blushed and lowered her eyes. 'I meant... Forgive me, mistress.'

Molly reached out and touched the younger girl on the arm. 'Don't be embarrassed, Hannah. Everybody in the house knows why I'm here. And you,' she reminded her, 'have even seen why I'm here.' She turned her back so that the maid could tie the petticoat strings.

Hannah still needed to explain. 'Sometimes Master Abraham gets up

128

during the night to check that the house is safe. So some of the other girls have told me. Some of the men have seen him. So they say.'

'It might have been nobody at all.' Molly moved to the oaken chest against the wall. 'The blue velvet, I think, Hannah.' Put the poor girl at her ease. 'I might have been dreaming. And I'm not used to this house yet.' A strange house settling at night can conjure up its own ghosts.

And the dreaming ghosts at Chiswick were far less frightening than the waking ghosts at The Bell.

Four weeks since she left The Bell, and it should have been easy to forget. Her new life was entirely different from her previous life - and from the life before that.   Whatever she wanted now she could have.

She was mistress of a large rambling house. She could wander wherever she wanted: through the original, oak-beamed, uninhibited halls of King Henry's time; into the elegant, high-ceilinged rooms added just twenty years ago when Queen Anne was on the throne; down into the vaulted undercroft that housed Abraham's wine, built - so the servants assured her - by William the Conqueror himself; even into Mistress Silver's noisy, non-stop kitchen, though she'd never yet had enough courage to venture into that holy of holies. Only the servants' quarters at the top of the old house were out of bounds, even to Abraham himself. And, of course, the eating room from Friday dusk to Saturday nightfall.

She had servants to command: not only her own maid, Hannah, but all the other servants, too. (Though she would never have dreamt of trying to command Silver or Mistress Silver. The house and everybody in it was theirs. Abraham merely owned it.)

She had money to spend, clothes to wear, playthings, a pet monkey. The monkey, Abraham explained with exaggerated gravity when he gave it to her, was named Babu, because it wasn't quite a baboon.

From York virgin to Cheapside whore, from Cheapside whore to Chiswick mistress, from Chiswick mistress to lady of fashion. All in less than a year.

And still her provincial imagination wasn't big enough to trouble the purse of a London usurer. Stockings in fine silk, the latest and lightest shoes, gowns so fashionable they revealed not only her arms but her breasts as well. A carriage to take her to Bond Street, to Covent Garden, to Lincoln's Inn Fields. A wish, a half-wish, was enough for Abraham to make it appear.

Okoro accompanied her everywhere, dressed in silk and lace, embroidered coat and feathered turban, his foppish English clothes hanging oddly on the taut directness of his African body. He was her badge of taste, her talisman.

And he was her constant reminder of the Colonel.

She had become so used to having her own way that she became impatient. One afternoon, after she'd had an extra glass of wine with her dinner to help keep out the chill, she became bold. She and Abraham had left the servants to clear the table and, with Isaac, had retired to the smaller, cosier comfort of her bedroom, where the glowing fire was hot enough to fight the December weather outside.

'Abraham,' she demanded, as she poured tea, 'what have you done about the Colonel? You promised me he'd be hanged.'

Isaac swung round in surprise from the window where he'd been staring sullenly out into the late afternoon mist coming off the river. Hannah hastily busied herself with the coal-scuttle, replenishing the fire.

Mild as ever, Abraham corrected her. 'I promised you he'd be punished.'

'The punishment is hanging!'

'The judges don't like to hang a man for doing what half the nobility are doing. To tell the truth, my dear, what half the judges themselves are doing.' He picked up his cup and saucer. 'They insist on proof. And even when they get it, they prefer to soften the charge into something less.'

'Such as what?' Anger, contempt, scorn. 'Showing too much affection for a dear little child? Forgetting which way round a woman should be when he tups her?' An overwhelming blaze of temper. She lashed out her foot in front of her, kicking the veneered tea-table inches into the air; the china leapt from it and tumbled to the floor. 'Damn the judges!' she shouted. 'And the sheriffs! And the magistrates!' She snapped her fingers. 'I don't care that much for them!' All hypocrites like my Cousin Tom!

Okoro cowered away from the outburst of violence. The monkey scampered squealing for cover behind the vanity table. Isaac took a step towards her, concerned. Abraham put his cup and saucer back

130

on the table, then stood. He waved Hannah away as she moved uncertainly to clear the broken cups. 'Leave it until later,' he told her. 'Isaac, I would like to be alone with Molly, if you please. Okoro, go down to the kitchen with Hannah.'

He waited until they had closed the door behind them, then came to her and placed both his hands on her shoulders. 'I've not forgotten, Molly. But everything takes time.'

She pulled away from him. 'How much time? Months? Years?'

He caught hold of her again, and his voice sharpened. 'As long as it takes.' He waited till she looked at him. 'You are young. You want everything to happen now.' Reaching up to cup her chin between his thumb and forefinger, he attempted to soothe her. 'Whispers have been whispered. In their own good time, those whispers will become a murmur. The murmurs will become a rumour.' He ducked his head in one of his expressive shrugs. 'And rumours have their own way of becoming a well-known truth.'

'And then?' Challenging.

'And then we tell whoever wants to know whatever it is they want to know. Reluctantly, of course. After all, he wields a great deal of influence.' His eyes set resolutely. 'On the other hand, Molly, I must obey the laws of Moses. I must not bear false witness against my neighbour.'

'False witness?' Is this your resolve, your promise? Her lips drew back in a snarl. 'Do you call Okoro a liar? Do you call me a liar? Do you say that the Colonel didn't - '

He interrupted her. 'In this instance, Molly, Okoro is my neighbour.' The irony amused him. 'A black gentile, and only a child. But, nevertheless, in the sight of Jahweh, my neighbour.'

Breath by breath, the anger began to subside. 'You're an honourable man, Abraham. A good man.' She broke away from him, walked to the window, focused on the pinpoints of light from the link-torches further down the river towards London. She heard the faltering scuff of his feet as he crossed the room.

'There's more.' His voice was prompting, concerned. 'What else is troubling you, Molly?'

'Where's to be my house, Abraham?'

She could see his reflection in the glass; he was clearly puzzled. 'Your house?' He spread his hands in an expansive gesture. 'It's here, Molly.

Do you not like it?'

She turned to face him. He was a couple of paces away from her. Whether through respect or wariness, she couldn't tell. 'When we last had guests, I overheard you talking with one of your friends from the Royal Exchange. And I heard you mention Molly's house, as if it weren't here. Are you planning to get rid of me?'

He stared at her, bewildered, concerned; then his frown melted and he threw back his head and laughed, as much in relief as amusement. 'My innocent little girl!' He drew her to him and hugged her. 'A Mollies house is a house where Mollies go. Men who would rather lie with other men than lie with women.' He shrugged. 'A dreadful slur on a lovely name, my Molly. But that's the name the Town has chosen. And that's the name I chose to speak of.' He held her at arms' length and lowered his voice conspiratorially. 'Whispers, Molly. Whispers, and murmurs, and rumours.'

❋

The judge sat at one end of the high-ceilinged open court of the Old Bailey, gazing complacently down at the benches on the general floor, a posy of flowers held up to his face to keep the gaol fever at bay. In front of him, the Clerk to the Court sat at his desk, shuffling papers to find out which accused was next after the present one had been convicted.

Facing them a dozen feet away, his hands resting on the wooden bar that separated him from the rest of the court, the prisoner. Plainly dressed in wool, linen and leather, he was a man of substance, a tradesman, a householder, a husband and father.

A man accused of sodomy. A pale, sweating man with an invisible noose tightening around his neck as he awaited the verdict.

The judge rested his elbows on the arms of the chair and put his fingertips together. 'John Eccles,' he said. 'On Thursday night last, you took the young man Robert Campbell to several ale-houses in the City of London and plied him with drink. You've not denied that. You had never met Robert Campbell before that night. You've not denied that. One of the ale-houses you took him to was the Bull Inn beside Bishopsgate, where you bought him not only ale, but noxious spirits, too. You've not denied that.' He leaned forward to emphasise the gravity of the next piece of evidence. 'The boy tells us that you then took him out into the yard behind the Bull Inn, where you forcibly took down his breeches and buggered him. The pot-boy tells us that he came out to see what all the commotion was, and that you tried to bugger him as well. The landlord of the Bull Inn has told us that he heard such a squealing and a shouting that he ran out into the yard, thinking to find a murder, and caught you in the very act of sodomy. Whereupon you fell down upon your knees and begged him not to report you for, you said, if he swore against you, he swore away your life.' He leaned back in his chair again. 'And I cannot deny that. The penalty for sodomy is hanging.'

The prisoner slumped against the bar, his knuckles white in anticipation, his limbs trembling, his teeth chattering.

'However...'

The prisoner's head lifted. However? Was there hope, no matter how small?

The judge continued. 'Robert Campbell was drunk. He could not deny that. The pot-boy was very young, perhaps too young to know what was happening. The yard behind the Bull Inn was very dark, and the landlord may have been mistaken. That you had your privities in your hand may have been, as you have claimed, because you needed to piss.' He smiled at the rows of spectators to either side. 'Though I wonder which of us here is able to piss through a member as stiff as yours has been sworn to have been?'

Laughter flittered round the court. Molly turned to Abraham with a question in her eyes. Jokes about buggering young boys? Jokes when a man was on trial for his life? Was this justice?

Abraham put a finger to his lips; he would explain later.

The judge tapped his gavel to bring the court to order. 'John Eccles,' he said. 'In order to find you guilty of the crime - and the sin - of sodomy, the jury must be satisfied that you penetrated Robert Campbell inter anum.'

Abraham put his head close to Molly's. 'In the arse,' he told her, keeping his voice low so that only she could hear.

Once again, the judge put his fingertips together and leaned back in his chair. 'There is doubt about what you were able to do,' he said. 'But there is no doubt about what you intended.' His performance over, he gave his instructions to the twelve good men and true who were to pass their verdict. 'Gentlemen of the jury, you will find John Eccles guilty of attempted sodomy.'

The judge was a powerful man. The members of the jury were not. But even before they could do what they were told, the judge had passed onto the next stage of the proceedings.

'You will be fined twenty pounds,' he told the prisoner. 'You will stand for an hour in the Temple Bar pillory. You will then be detained for six months in Newgate.'

A low rumble of approval from the court.

John Eccles stared at him, blank-faced. He had stopped trembling. But the blood had drained from his face, and his skin was the colour of parchment.

Abraham put his hand on Molly's. His face was pinched with compassion. 'Better to have hanged him,' he said. 'He's not evil. He's just a man with a vice that is fashionable but not legal.' He took her hand in his. 'Pray for the soul of John Eccles.'

She didn't understand. 'Why? The judge said he's not to hang.'

He took her hand. His grip was hard, as if he wanted to give strength not only to her but to the man in the dock. 'Pray for your Christian fellow, Molly,' he said. 'He's a gentile, a goy - but I shall pray for him.'

The disgust and shame of his wife as she paid over the twenty pounds. The riven sobs of his children as he was led away to the pillory. The hatred on the faces of the crowd pelting him with stones and dung. The four brutal, bleeding days in Newgate, four days of being held down and buggered by pickpockets and highwaymen, by catamites and their pimps, cheered on by the gaolers, watched by the Governor himself.

A world of unforgiving faces filled the air in front of John Eccles as he knelt, took a farewell look at the stone walls crushing in on him, took a last shuddering breath, took the knife resolutely in both hands and gouged it into the side of his throat, slicing as deeply as his strength could carve it.

A hundred inmates watched the life spurting out of him as he fell gurgling backwards. Nobody moved to help him.

Some, perhaps, envied his escape.

134

'Whispers, and murmurs, and rumours, Molly,' said Abraham.

She stroked the side of his face. He was, little by little, fulfilling his promise. So, feigning willingness, she lay back and pulled him onto her.

Another transaction. Though he didn't realise it, he too was being bought and paid for.

Chapter 13

To my dearest Sister in Iniquity.

Mistress Anny said you were desirous that I send you a Letter tho' upon what Matter she did not say.

I am in Health, & have not ye Pox, which is not so with Polly, who is like to die says Mother Wickham, but I think she says it only to frighten ye poor Girl, for Polly said she would not be beaten by her Visitors any more after a drunken Fop burn'd her on ye Arse with a hot Lantern & made Blisters so big she could not lie on her Back for nigh seven Nights, & Mother Wickham had to feed her even tho' she was not earning her Keep. Mother Wickham found another Virgin for ye Colonel whose name was Julia but after he fuck'd her ye first time she jump'd into ye River & was drown'd.

My Bubs are beginning to grow & soon my accustom'd Visitors will not want me. Mother Wickham does not know yet because I have bound them tight with some old Stockings & I weep piteously when my Visitors ask me to take off my Dress but ye Twins know and they are often spiteful & it can not be long before Mother Wickham puts me to Work in some different Way that I will not like because my new Visitors will not give me Presents. I may run away: but do not tell Mother Wickham this for she always pursues & catches & punishes any of her Girls who runs away as a Warning to ye Others. I have more Wit than Polly & Nan & ye Twins, & I hope she may not catch me.

I pray you, write to me about your Life in a Mansion, & tell me about ye Plays you see at ye Theatre. When I run away I shall become a famous Actress.

God be with you at this Christmastide.

Your loving Friend,

Miranda

In York, Christmas was a day for rag-tag friends in their Sunday best, for once-a-year uncles bearing gifts, for tipsy aunts who talked only of the past, for marriageable cousins, for a Noah's ark of children squealing and laughing and crying.

In Chiswick, a simple Wednesday breakfast.

'Happy Christmas, my dear,' said Abraham. Silver slipped her chair under her as she sat.

'Happy Christmas, Miss Molly,' said Okoro, his scrubbed face beaming up at her. She put her hand on his shoulder, leaned down and kissed the tight black curls on the top of his head. He squirmed with pleasure and took his place proudly behind her chair, as Silver had trained him.

'Happy Christmas,' Isaac muttered sullenly. He, too, had been instructed.

Molly smiled, embarrassed. Was it good manners to wish a Jew happy Christmas in return? Would she be repaying their kindness with an insult? By the time she'd thought of something to say, it was too late to say anything.

Abraham tucked a napkin under his chin. 'At Christmas, you are required to worship your Jesus. Am I right?'

'Er, yes.' And Easter. And...

'Then today you shall fulfill your religious obligations.' He hesitated, a piece of herring halfway to his lips. 'But only if you wish to.' He put his fork down on his plate. 'You see, Molly, we are aware of your special Christian day. It means nothing to us, but we want you to enjoy it.' He picked up the fork, put it down again. 'I have ordered the carriage to take you to the church here in Chiswick. I believe it is named after your Saint Nicolas. I thought that... Since this is your first Christmas... your first winter...' He lifted the fork to his mouth and ate the herring, covering his mild embarrassment. 'Hannah is a Christian. She may go with you. If you wish. If, of course, she wishes.' He shrugged. 'It is difficult for you Christians to understand we Jews. But it is just as difficult for we Jews to understand you Christians.' He recovered his normal self-confidence. 'Perhaps that is why so many of us have become money-lenders. In our profession, Jews speak the same language as the Christians who borrow from us.' He indicated her empty plate, a touch of concern in his voice. 'But you've taken nothing to eat, my dear. Are you not well?'

How to explain? 'Christmas and Easter are... I always take Holy Communion at Christmas and Easter. The bread and the wine. But I don't eat beforehand. So if I might have a glass of boiled water...'

Instantly, Abraham put down his fork, swallowed what was in his mouth, and pushed his plate away from him. 'Silver! Some boiled water, if you please.' He looked sharply at Isaac, who was about to spear another helping of fish. 'Enough for three.'

Isaac withdrew his hand, then dropped his fork noisily onto his plate. Dabbing ostentatiously at his lips, he rose to his feet and stepped away from the table.

'Isaac!'

He glared at his father with ill-concealed anger. 'I am not hungry, father,' he said. 'This... Christianity spoils my appetite.'

'Enough!' Abraham's chair went crashing backwards as he rose angrily to his feet. 'Be mindful of your vows of hospitality!'

Isaac faced him, equally furious. 'Hospitality? She's not a Jew - she's a goya! She's not even a guest - she's a harlot!'

'She is not a harlot! She is your father's companion!'

'Harlot, companion, mistress - call her what you will, she is - '

'Whatever she is, she's your father's companion, your father's mistress! Remember the fifth law of Moses, Isaac!'

'And remember the seventh law, father!'

They stood there glaring at each other across the table, tension crackling between them. Molly rose to her feet. 'I know nothing of Jewish law,' she said, 'but I was taught that Jesus said Love thy neighbour as thyself. And He was a Jew.'

Father and son dragged their eyes away from each other towards Molly, weighing her words. Isaac was the first to break the silence. He turned back to his father, bowed his head and sat. 'Forgive me,' he muttered.

'Forgive us both,' Abraham said to Molly.

She spread her hands in a gesture she'd captured from Abraham himself. 'There's nothing to forgive,' she said. 'Please, Abraham, let the coachmen have the day to themselves. Hannah and I will walk to St Nicolas - if you will tell us how to get there.'

Isaac stood again. 'I shall escort you,' he said. Then, to explain his change of heart, 'On a festival day, there are apprentices and other ruffians at large. I shall escort you. Not into the synag-' He corrected himself. 'Not into the church itself, of course. Only to the door.' His own explanation demanded the rest of the commitment. 'And back again. I shall wait for you.'

'We shall escort you,' Abraham decided. 'And during your Holy Communion...' He savoured the exotic phrase. '...my son and I will debate the finer points of Mosaic Law.'

Molly and Hannah and Okoro came out of the medieval ragstone church alone and made for the lych-gate, where Abraham and Isaac were waiting for them. The other communicants lingered in the doorway and greeted each other, gossiped together, wished each other Happy Christmas.

Molly made a rueful face. 'I could forgive them for not speaking to us, Hannah. We are strangers. But did you notice that nobody even looked at us?' She grinned wickedly at the uncomprehending maid. 'I'll wager they're all looking at us now.'

Hannah glanced back over her shoulder, then bubbled into laughter. 'Mistress, you're right! But the moment they saw me turn, they were all busy talking again.'

A spark flared inside Molly. Outrage, defiance, indignation. 'They wouldn't talk to us, Hannah. So let us talk to them.'

She took Okoro by the hand and turned back. But before she could take a second stride, a hand caught her elbow.

'Let them be,' Isaac growled. 'They are righteous. You are the companion of a Jewish money-lender. Speak to them if you must, but they won't speak to you. Your very words might poison them.'

She paused before answering him. Her father had told her always to count up to ten before speaking when she was angry. 'You're right, of course. Come, Hannah. Okoro.' She allowed Isaac to lead her away from the church. But first, she dipped her head towards the congregation in polite greeting.

And still they didn't notice her until her back was turned.

A biting wind cut into them as they climbed from the carriage. But, within seconds, they had crossed the Lincoln's Inn Fields pavement and were warm inside the noisy theatre, breathing the rich smells of people and perfumes, tobacco and gin.

'We are promised something quite different this evening, my dear,' said Abraham, following Isaac as he cleared a way for them.

Molly felt the flutter of a hand at her waist, a butterfly tug at the lace decoration on her gown. Not Okoro: he was in front of her. Without allowing her attentive smile to waver, she struck downwards at the slim fingers, crushed them until she heard the whimper and felt the knuckles crack, then released them. In another life, Annie had taught her how to deal with pickpockets. 'Different?' she said.

'Yes, we are promised a beggar's opera. A satiric device, no doubt.'

An opera. She liked opera. The Colonel had taken her to see opera. The music, she remembered, was difficult. But if it were difficult, it must be worth the studying. If only she'd accepted Aunt Grissom's offer of lessons at the spinet.

She craned her neck and squinted past the shifting rainbow of colour-ful coats, embroidered gowns, powdered wigs. Through the haze of tobacco and candle-smoke, she could see the vaulted arch of the stage, the gilded pillars, the gold-tasselled plush-red curtain.

Opera. Spectacle, romance, passion, tragedy. The noble sentiments of noble characters...

❊

In the whitewashed dressing room, Polly Peachum knelt between MacHeath's knees and fumbled at the front of his breeches. 'Why so worried?' she asked him. 'There's half an hour before the Prologue - and you're not on till nearly the end of the first Act.'

He made no effort to help her. Nor to dissuade her. 'I like it not,' he said.

'You liked it well enough last night,' she said, worrying him free and bending her mouth over him. 'Last night you would have killed your mother for it.' Her head plunged down. And again. And again.

'I like not this play,' he said, two minutes later.

'It's one of the best parts you've had for months,' she said, trying not to swallow. She tipped some wine into her mouth, swilled it round her tongue and teeth, spat it back into the goblet. 'The hero.'

'A highwayman.'

'But a hero nevertheless.'

'A low-life hero in a low-life play.' He grimaced with distaste. 'With street ballads.'

'Satire.'

'Satire is safe enough for the listeners. It is not safe for the singers.' He stood and buttoned his breeches, ignoring her disappointment. 'This play mocks some important men. I like it not.'

She snorted huffily, stepped into her petticoat, pulled it up under her gown. 'If it runs, you'll make money. If it doesn't, these important men you speak of won't take any notice of it. What can you lose?' She struggled to tie the strings of her petticoat under the back of her gown.

'What can I lose?' he repeated indignantly. 'Why, my reputation as an actor.'

So young, so pompous. She didn't stop him as he gravely raised the goblet and sipped from it.

❉

Macheath had betrayed both Lucy and Polly. Peachum had betrayed Macheath. Lockit had cheated most of his prisoners and hanged the rest. When they hadn't been whoring, the whores had been stealing.

The Beggar, whose opera this was, faced out front. 'Macheath is to be hanged,' he said. 'And for the other personages of the drama, the audience must have supposed that they were all either hanged or transported.'

But...

'An opera must end happily,' declaimed the Player.

The Beggar agreed. 'Your objection, sir, is very just.' And Macheath was reprieved.

'All this we must do,' the Player added, 'to comply with the taste of the town.' Laughter and applause.

The Beggar felt the playgoers were owed an explanation. 'Through the whole piece you may observe such a similitude of manners in high and low life, that it is difficult to determine whether, in the fashionable vices, the fine gentlemen imitate the gentlemen of the road, or the gentlemen of the road the fine gentlemen. Had the play remained as I at first intended, it would have carried a most excellent moral. 'Twould have shown that the lower sort of people have their vices in a degree as well as the rich.'

The lower sort of people in the pit erupted. Cheers, shouts of approval, whistles.

The Beggar stood his ground, and waited until they quietened. 'Twould have shown that the lower sort of people have their vices in a degree as well as the rich,' he repeated. 'And that they are punished for them.'

The happy ending, the dance, the final song, all were drowned by the audience. Their mood teetered on the knife-edge between rowdiness and riot before a loud reprise of the overture tipped the balance in favour of good humour.

Molly, seated at the side of the stage, was near enough to hear the words of the closing chorus.

'But think of this maxim, and put off your sorrow:
The wretch of today may be happy tomorrow.'

❋

They argued all the way home.

'It was us they were mocking, father!'

'Are you dishonest, Isaac? Do you betray your friends? Do you get women with child, and then cast them off? Are you a thief? Are you a murderer?' In the near blackness of the coach, he peered at his son. 'Am I any of these things?'

Isaac snorted in disgust and turned away. 'Of course you're not! Of course we're not.' He stared out of the window of the coach into the bumping darkness beyond.

'Then how can they possibly be mocking us?'

With his back to the rest of the carriage, Isaac muttered a venomous retort.

'I didn't hear you, my son.'

Still he wouldn't look at his father. 'I said, ask Molly who they're mocking. It's her world, not ours!'

Abraham banged on the roof of the carriage with his cane. Within a few paces, the horses came to a halt. Okoro stirred, but didn't waken. 'Do you say that Molly is a thief?'

No reply.

'Do you say that Molly is a cheat? A liar? A betrayer of trust?'

No reply.

'Answer me, Isaac!'

No reply. But, in a blast of anger, he shoved open the carriage door and jumped out, his boots splashing noisily into the mud. He swung back towards them. 'I say nothing except that a harlot is a harlot!' The door crashed shut, shaking the rest of the carriage. They heard his voice from the darkness outside, loud but muffled. 'I shall walk home.'

After waiting a full two minutes for Isaac to change his mind, Abraham tapped on the roof with his cane. 'The author was satirising Walpole, not us,' he explained to Molly. 'His target was political, not financial.' The horses lumbered into motion again.

The political implications had passed over Molly's head. But, on the other hand, she couldn't help but notice what a handsome fellow MacHeath had been. If only he'd had Isaac's fire, he would have had no need of the Player's intervention.

'Why does Isaac hate me so much, Hannah? I can think of nothing I've done to displease him.'

The servant-girl hesitated, then continued brushing Molly's hair. 'I don't think Master Isaac hates you, mistress.'

A short, scornful laugh of contradiction. 'Meal after meal, he sits opposite me and scowls. If we play at cards, he can barely summon up a grunt for me. When we go to the theatre, he trails behind Abraham and me like a whipped dog. At home he calls me harlot and goya - and I long since learned what Jews mean by goyim.'

'It only - '

'Aye, I know it only means 'strangers'. It only means 'not-Jews'. But when they use the word, it means a lot more than that. Listen to the way they say it, Hannah. They say it with contempt.'

Hannah reached past her to put the brush on the vanity table, and picked up a crimson ribbon. She looped it under Molly's hair and tied it in a bow. 'Master Isaac doesn't hate you, Miss Molly,' she said again.

Molly regarded her reflection in the mirror. 'Then why does he insult me whenever he can?'

'He...' She was in deeper than she'd intended. 'It's not for me to say

143

anything, mistress.'

Molly reached forward and tilted the mirror, angling it so that she could see Hannah behind her. 'Speak, Hannah. Please.'

'He's angry, Miss Molly.'

'Aye, Hannah, I can see he's angry.' Her voice had an edge of impatience to it. 'But what have I done to make him angry?'

'He's not...' She held back, not sure how to continue, or even whether to continue at all.

Molly prompted her. 'Aye?'

'He's not angry with you. He's angry with himself.'

Molly stood. 'Well, then, the remedy lies with him.' She padded across the chill floor and climbed into her bed. 'If he behaved in a more gentlemanly manner, he wouldn't need to be so angry with himself.'

Hannah smoothed the blankets, and flicked Molly's hair so that it lay prettily on the pillow. 'Will Master Abraham be coming to your room tonight, mistress?' There was the slightest hint of tease in her voice.

'What day is it? Wednesday?' Hannah nodded. 'Aye, I'm sure he will. Master Abraham is orderly in his life.'

Hannah's face remained impassive. But her eyes had friendly mischief in them. 'Goodnight, Miss Molly.'

'Goodnight, Hannah.' As the younger girl opened the door to leave, Molly called her back. 'Hannah, why did you ask me whether Master Abraham was coming to visit me tonight?' That hateful word, 'visit'.

Hannah smiled knowingly. 'Master Isaac will be even angrier tomorrow morning.' A creak of the hinges, a rattle of the latch, and the door had closed behind her.

Chapter 14

The summons was peremptory. And it was brought by Silver himself, not one of the girls. 'Master Abraham wishes you to join him in his withdrawing room immediately.' He held her door open for her.

She tipped her monkey onto the floor, and slapped it away when it tried to climb back onto her lap. 'No, Babu.' It sulked away from her then, forgetting its rejection, clambered lithely up to the top of one of the bedposts, grinning and chattering. She picked up a comb from her vanity table. 'Thank you, Silver. Tell Master Abraham - '

'Now, Miss Molly.' She was surprised at the commanding note in his voice. In the three months she'd been in the house, his attitude towards her had never been more than cold, never less than polite.

She touched a hand to her dressing gown, then up to her loose hair. 'If you will call Hannah for me, I'll - '

'Now. Master Abraham is waiting.'

How dare he? How dare a servant give her orders? Nevertheless, she stood and followed him, flouncing with indignation. An indignation that changed to apprehension as she entered the high-ceilinged room.

Abraham had a guest. A woman. A furious woman. 'I said I wanted him punished. I said I wanted him to look ridiculous,' she was saying. 'I did not say I wanted him hanged!' She swung on Molly as she heard her footsteps behind her. 'You, girl! What lies have you been telling about my husband?'

Molly stopped half a dozen paces away from her. 'Lady Charnell.' She bobbed a curtsey. 'Lies?'

'Molly,' Abraham said. 'Have you been telling lies about Colonel Charnell?' The corner of his eye twitched, a wink so slight that only someone watching for it could have detected it. Molly caught it; the Colonel's wife, whose avenging gaze was fixed on Molly, didn't.

'No, sir.' Now she knew she had Abraham's support, she could play the innocent. 'The Colonel seduced me when I first came to London. But you know that, my lady. Everybody knows that. The Colonel has told them himself.'

She brushed Molly's words aside. 'That was nothing.'

Nothing? As the anger flashed through her, Molly opened her mouth to speak.

With a commanding movement of the hand, Abraham silenced her. 'You have her word, Lady Charnell. At no time has she lied about the Colonel.'

'The word of a harlot?' The scorn was open.

'The word of my companion, Lady Charnell.' His voice, though respectful, was reproving. Instantly, he was his emollient self again. 'But consider what you accuse her of. How could she tell the Town that Colonel Charnell commits unnatural acts with men and boys?' He shrugged. 'You speak no more than the truth: your husband used my companion as his harlot. She's a woman, Lady Charnell. How could she know what your husband does with men and boys?'

'Then where did the stories come from? Tell me that!'

'Jealous rivals, perhaps?' He drew Molly into the conversation again. 'Do you know where these tales could have started, my dear?'

'No, sir.'

'Did Mother Wickham ever provide catamites for her visitors?'

She professed her ignorance with an open-handed gesture. 'I don't know. I only know about the girls. And the girl children.' A helpful thought occurred to her. 'Perhaps...'

'Perhaps?' Abraham prompted her.

'Perhaps what?' Lady Charnell snapped.

'Perhaps if you asked Quince,' she suggested. 'He goes everywhere with the Colonel.' Two birds with one stone.

The Colonel's wife ignored her. 'First you ask me to trust the word of a harlot,' she said to Abraham, 'and now you expect me to gather intelligence from a pimp.'

'Where better to hear the rumours of the Town than from a pimp?' he suggested. 'The Town is all rumours, Lady Charnell. Whispers, and murmurs, and rumours.'

In the darkness of her bed she put her mouth close to his ear. 'Anything, Abraham. Anything. Tell me what you want me to do.' After all, a transaction was a transaction.

'Ssshhh.' He placed a finger on her lips, then eased himself onto her. As she did every Wednesday, every Saturday, she pushed her legs apart and reached for him.

Less than ten minutes later, he had dressed and left her to sleep

146

alone.

'Half a lemon,' Molly said.

Hannah blushed and avoided Molly's eyes.

The monkey swung itself down from Molly's shoulder and scampered up into the branches of a bare elm. 'Babu!' she called. 'Here, Babu!' It ignored her, swinging higher and higher, almost out of sight. She let it go. It would come down in its own time. It didn't love her; but it did love warmth and food.

'Put half a squeezed lemon in your jewel beforehand,' she continued, 'and douse it greatly with sour milk afterwards. Immediately afterwards.' She glanced at the open door of the dairy as they passed, and waved at the black-haired girl inside, who was beaded with sweat despite the late autumn chill as she wrestled the paddles round in the butter churn. 'I'm sure Hephsibah would always be pleased to curdle a jug of milk for you.'

'It seems so... planned.'

'If you can be sure he'll marry you, Hannah, then perhaps it doesn't matter. But what man can you be sure of before you're married?' They skirted the silent beehives on their racks outside the stillroom, breathing in the warm smells of cordials and spices, dried herbs and steeping fruit. Without speaking, they carried on past the cooing dovecote, alongside the leaf-scattering orchard, down to the river and looked out over the Thames. A boatman toiled upstream with a well-bundled passenger. 'What man can you be sure of after you're married?' She was fast learning the manners of a mentor. 'In the meantime, better a lemon in your jewel than a bastard in your cradle.'

Hannah defended her lover. 'He's a good man, Miss Molly. And he's promised to marry me, just as soon as he's finished his apprenticeship.'

Molly took the younger girl's hand and continued walking along the bank. 'Then until he has his freedom, he won't mind sharing you with half a lemon.'

They reached the high, brick-built wall protecting the vegetable garden and began to retrace their steps towards the house. As they passed the elm, Babu dropped out of its branches and lolloped after them.

Molly leapt from her chair by the fireside with a burst of laughter, clapped her hands in delight, kissed Abraham on the cheek.

Isaac bared his teeth in disgust. 'It's a ridiculous notion, father! It will make us the laughing stock of the Town. You're bringing disrepute on our name.'

Abraham allowed Molly to help him to his feet. 'We're Jews, Isaac. To goyim, the word Jew means disreputable. Anyone who's a Jew is already a laughing stock. What can we possibly lose?' He touched his son lightly on the arm. 'We won't lose money, that is certain. Our debtors may laugh at us, but they still have to pay their debts.'

'I shall have nothing to do with it. And I shan't join you.'

'At your choice, my son. But Molly and I will enjoy ourselves. Especially when we see the ill-humour on the faces of those who count themselves superior to us.' He turned to Molly. 'Now, my dear, it is your task to draw up the guest-list.'

✽

Voice by voice, the audience grew from a burble to a buzz, from a buzz to an excitement, from an excitement to a rowdy anticipation.

And then to an incredulous swell of laughter.

A sullen Isaac and two self-conscious coachmen cleared a path for Abraham's theatre-guests.

Abraham himself led the procession with Molly. Then Annie and the Waif. Polly, Nan, the Twins. Abigail. Scar-faced Jed, shifty and scowling. Stumpy Jack. More beggars. More rogues. More harlots.

Enough of the Cheapside gentry to fill half the stage seats.

But not all on one side of the stage. On Abraham's instructions, they sat some on one side, some on the other, mingling with the wealthy, greeting them with extravagant bows and curtsies, mocking them in elevated tones, scattering smiling curses upon them, choking them with foul breath and contrived farts, driving them up and out and away until the harlots and beggars had the stage to themselves.

'You, sir!' cried a fop from a safe distance, holding a nosegay up to his face. 'What do you mean by this?'

Abraham rose and bowed courteously. 'The play is put out as a beggar's opera, sir. It treats of matters wherein my guests may boast of

148

being more than usually schooled. Pray be not put out of countenance, sir.' Flinging his arms out wide, he encompassed everybody left on the stage. 'Consider them not as beggars and harlots and thieves, but as critics.'

He sat down to roars of approval from the stage, to angry curses from the gallery, to howls of mirth from the pit.

The play had finished, but the entertainment had only just begun. Abraham had bought The Bell for the night.

From his position at the head of the huge oval table, he banged his stick on the floor to gain attention. 'My honoured guests!' He waited until the whoops and cheers subsided. 'My honoured guests. The food is free. The wine is free. The girls are free - to do whatever they wish. It is their night also. If they wish to lie with you, that is their choice. If they don't wish to lie with you, that is also their choice. But, if they do agree to lie with you, that is between you and them. It is not covered by the fee I have paid Mother Wickham.' He banged his cane again to quieten the burst of good-humoured obscenities that had broken out. 'But, for this night, you have food, you have wine, you have gin, you have shelter from the cold.' His welcome tightened a fraction. 'You see how generous I can be when everybody behaves well. Pray do not oblige me to show how ungenerous I can be when people abuse my hospitality.' He spread his arms to indicate the laden table. 'Mother Wickham has provided for us. Enjoy.'

The table was immediately besieged by grasping hands, by gulping mouths, by the desperate greed of men and women who expected it all to be snatched away from them, or to turn to dust and run through their fingers.

Molly backed away, uneasy. She didn't belong here. Her embroidered gown stood out like a butterfly among flesh-flies.

Like a cornered rabbit, she searched for a bolt-hole. Everything here was familiar, but none of it offered comfort. Less than a year ago, she'd stood in this same room and watched powdered gentlemen behave like farmyard animals. This was the room in which the Colonel had tempted her with fresh bread and moist ham, with honeyed words and strong brandy.

This room was the watershed between her York innocence and her London experience. I don't belong here.

149

'Not here,' she said, panic rising in her throat. 'I don't belong here!' She scrambled towards Abraham, clawing harlots and beggars out of the way, clutching at shoulders, cannoning into backs, pulling at arms, sleeves, gowns...

...and was hustled sideways, away from Abraham, into a corner.

Annie and the Waif led her to a bench, one each side, drawing her into a private world. Abigail stood in front of her, blocking her off from the rest of the room. All three stood guard while Molly's breathing slowed.

Abigail was the first to nudge her thoughts into a new direction. 'Okoro, Miz Moll,' she said. 'How my boy?'

Gradually, Molly's agitation dissolved; she took the black woman's hand in her own. 'He's a fine boy, Abigail. A good boy. He works hard, and all the serving girls want to be his mother. Only he says,' and she imitated his thin Cheapside voice overlaid with his mother's African accent, 'I gotta mother already.' Annie and the Waif enjoyed the impersonation and tried it out for themselves, to the mock consternation of Abigail. 'He's ten feet taller,' Molly continued, 'and half a house fatter. And he will come to see you soon. I promise.'

Abigail lifted Molly's hand and pressed it to her broad bosom. 'Bless you, Miz Moll.' Her face radiant, she bustled away to the table. 'No need squabble like that,' she called. 'You want more, I get you more. Master Abraham already paid for it. You ain't goin' be left out.'

Annie to the left of her, the Waif to the right. Molly held their hands, but said nothing. There was no need.

The Waif was wriggling with delight. 'The actors were so handsome,' she breathed. 'And the songs so pretty. And the tale so sad until the beggarman let Macheath not be hanged.' She stared into the distance, beyond The Bell, into the future. 'I shall be an actress,' she announced. 'I must be an actress. To come forward at the end of the play and be applauded like Mistress Lockit and Mistress Peachum, that must be... that must be the most...' The world didn't have enough colours to paint her dream. 'Ohhh...' She squeezed Molly's hand tight and snuggled close against her.

'Your Master Abraham is an unusual man,' Annie said. Standing at the table, he was host as well as paymaster, cutting beef for a one-armed beggar, filling the glass of a disfigured harlot, giving his lace-edged handkerchief to a wasted man with transparent skin, who coughed blood into it before palming it into his own pocket.

Molly nodded, proud of him. 'He is. He's kind. He's giving. He harms no one except...' No. Not even Annie must know about the plot against the Colonel. 'Except villains who deserve to be harmed. He's one of the most Christian men I've ever met.'

There was the tiniest moment before they realised what she'd said, then the three girls exploded into wide-eyed laughter, hugging each other, rocking helplessly backwards and forwards. She'd never known Annie laugh before. Abraham looked up from his serving and smiled at them; their laughter renewed itself in a fresh chorus of spluttering and whooping.

Abraham cut generous slices from a boiled ham and piled it onto a plate. 'This place,' he said as he passed the meat to a raddled beggar, withered down the whole of one side. 'Is this the place where Colonel Charnell...?'

'The Colonel?' The beggar sniggered to himself at Abraham's innocence. 'Is this where Mother Wickham feeds him with a fresh diet of virgins? Oh, yes, this is the place.'

Abraham dismissed the information with a shake of his head. 'No, no, not young girls. Everybody knows about that.' He poured some gin into a cup. 'Young men.' He handed the cup to the beggar. 'I've heard certain whispers, certain rumours about Colonel Charnell, and I thought...' His head moved briefly to indicate the high-ceilinged room, his raised eyebrows hinted at the bedrooms above, his manner threw suspicion on the whole of The Bell itself. 'I thought this might be the place where he met his... his... what do you call them?'

'Mollies?'

'Mollies. Yes, that was the name.' He poured some wine into a goblet, but didn't drink from it. 'Mollies.' He pretended to consider the matter. 'But, surely, Colonel Charnell wouldn't...? I mean, with all this at his choice...' His gesture encompassed The Bell, The Bell's whores, the Cheapside whores, the Ludgate Hill whores who had come with the beggars, the beggars themselves, the cripples. 'Aren't there women enough in the world without...? Why should Colonel Charnell want to...?' He tailed off, convincingly puzzled. Without warning, his manner changed. He grabbed the beggar by the arm. 'Never mention this to anyone. Anyone, do you hear?' His voice was sharp, commanding. 'Colonel Charnell is not a... a molly, or whatever you call them. Do you understand me?'

The beggar plucked Abraham's hand away. 'Of course. This is Mother Wickham's house. If he wants mollies, he won't get 'em here.'

'Not a word, do you hear?'

'I've forgotten it already.' He held out his glass. 'Is it all right if I have some more gin?'

'Here, let me pour it for you.'

Within an hour, most of the women and all the men were drunk. The room stank of bodies and gin, and the raucous songs had given way to grating snores. Against the wall, partly hidden behind the open door, a pale woman that Molly had never seen before balanced on tiptoe, holding her skirts up round her waist while a bent-backed man with an eye-patch rammed into her with more hatred than pleasure glinting in his remaining eye. A mask of anger clouding his face, Isaac left the room with one of the Twins; he returned less than a quarter of an hour later, his anger unabated.

Annie was struggling to stay awake, and the Waif had fallen asleep.

'Help me,' said Annie. Between them, they coaxed the slumbering Kitty up to her room, put her fully-clothed into bed. Annie stroked her fingers over the Waif's forehead, oddly maternal, then beckoned Molly out of the room. 'Write to me,' she said.

'I will.' Then she changed her mind. 'No. I shall meet you.'

No good-byes. As Molly made the familiar journey down the stairs, she could hear nothing but the creaking of the house as it settled. It was a world away from her life in Chiswick. Yet her memories of The Bell still had the power to frighten her.

As did Mother Wickham. The bawd glanced briefly at her as she came into the big room, then returned to the gold coins Abraham was counting into her hand. No sign of recognition.

'Leave the food where it is,' Abraham told her. 'Let them fill their pockets with it when they go.' He turned away from her and held his hand out to Molly. 'Come, my dear. Isaac should have the carriage ready for us by now. I'm sure you would welcome some sleep.'

Taking his hand, she followed him out into the passageway, then out into the icy night. She didn't look behind her.

'It cost you money, father, and it made us ridiculous!'

Abraham relaxed into a corner of the carriage as it echoed through the deserted streets of pre-dawn Chiswick. 'It bought us friends in low places, it showed our independence, and it demonstrated our power.'

'Power? Anyone could have done that!'

'But only we would have dared to do it.'

Isaac slouched sullenly in his corner of the carriage, pretending to be trying to sleep.

Abraham lowered his voice almost to a whisper. 'Molly, my dear, are you awake?'

'Aye, that I am.' Tired to exhaustion, drained from being at The Bell again, but unable to sleep.

'What do you think, Molly? Did I make a mistake tonight?'

She thought carefully before replying. 'How can I know? Despite the Colonel, The Bell is no more my world than it is yours.' But Abraham wanted her opinion, and she felt she owed it to him. 'Isaac is wrong,' she said. 'You weren't ridiculous. Neither of you.' She paused. 'And you, Abraham, you are also wrong. You made no friends tonight. If they catch you unprotected, they'll still slit your throat for whatever few pennies you may have about you.' Harsh memories turmoiled behind her eyes. 'In their world, mercy has no value.'

Abraham considered her words. 'Nor does it in ours, Molly,' he said. 'Nor does it in ours.' But he was no longer thinking of the beggars and thieves at The Bell.

✿

The snow cleared, the river dropped, the trees unfolded. Lady Day came and went.

Abraham came home from the City more than two hours earlier than usual, and called for Silver. 'The best wine in the cellar,' he instructed. 'And please ask Miss Molly if she will join me. I have some news that I am sure will brighten up her day.'

When Molly found him in the gallery, he was admiring one of the paintings. 'Leda and the swan,' he said. 'Do you know the myth?'

She picked into the past, into her half-remembered school lessons. 'Zeus?' she guessed.

He beamed with delight. 'Yes, my dear, Zeus.' He lifted his hand to point out a detail. 'Not a masterpiece. But a competent rendering of the subject.' He let her study it for a moment. 'Leda and the swan. Europa and the bull. Isn't it odd, my dear? Zeus had power and position, and he could be as handsome and as cultured as he wished to be. And yet, when he saw a woman he lusted after, he chose to become an animal.' He took her arm and led her to a prepared table at the end of the gallery. 'Possibly because he, too, had a jealous wife.' He poured two glasses of wine, handed one to her and raised his own. 'A toast, my dear,' he said. 'To justice.'

She raised her own glass. 'To justice? To justice in what?'

He rolled the wine round his tongue to savour it, swallowed it, put down his glass. 'Colonel Charnell is to hang,' he said.

Chapter 15

She'd never seen Abraham angry before. She'd never seen him drunk before.

His face was flushed, his gestures ungainly, his voice taking on a shrill edge as he leaned his clenched fists on the oak dining table.

'Damn him!' he gritted. 'Damn him to the deepest depths of Gehenna! Damn him to the worst torments that hell can devise!' He levered himself upright, snatched up his glass and sloshed wine into his mouth.

She moved towards him, but stopped a couple of paces away, as she would from a docile dog that had unexpectedly bared its fangs. 'Who, Abraham, who?'

He flung back his arm, splashing wine high into the air, then swept it forward as he hurled his glass into the fireplace. The crystal shattered against the logs and tinkled onto the hearth; the remains of the wine hissed into the flames.

He whirled to face her, his hunched shoulders bunching closer together than ever, his mouth twisted, his eyes blazing with anger. 'Colonel Charnell!' The words spat into the air with hatred dripping from them.

She took a step backwards. The very mention of his name sent a chill of fear icing through her. 'What has he done?'

'He has done nothing. But his friends have bought him a pardon.' The anger subsided into disappointment, and his shoulders drooped in defeat. 'Please forgive me, my dear. I have failed you. Colonel Charnell, after all, is not to hang.'

As the summer faded into autumn, Lady Charnell fell into a decline and died. The physician declared the cause of death to be the wasting disease. The funeral was extravagant, and attended by hundreds. The Colonel grieved mightily, and publicly.

The whisper was poison.

Molly dashed through Covent Garden, pushing citizens and harlots alike out of the way in her frantic rush to get to the gaudily dressed boy huddled weeping against the wall of Tom King's Coffee House.

Reaching him, she scooped him into her arms and hugged him to her. 'I'm here, Okoro, I'm here. Hush, now, hush.'

Gradually, his tears dwindled to sniffs. 'I want to go home, Miss Molly.'

Standing, she took his hand and led him away. 'Where did you go, Okoro? I was worried. I thought I'd lost you.'

'They said they was goin' kill me, Miss Molly!' The frightened black face was tilted up towards her, seeking an assurance of safety.

'Who did?' Other children, finding someone they could bully? 'Who said such a wicked thing to you?'

'The men.'

She frowned. 'Which men, Okoro?' Stallholders, chasing him away in case he stole an apple?

He wiped his sleeve across his nose. 'I not seen two of them before. But the other one was Master Quince, who used to sit in the kitchen with my mammy when the Colonel come to call.'

She went cold, looked anxiously about her, hurried him along with her. She tried to comfort him. 'It's all right, Okoro. There's no need to be afraid.' There was everything to be afraid of, but she mustn't let him see her own fear. 'What else did they say?'

'They said...' Sniff. 'They said the Colonel hated little boys who told lies about him, and he was going to punish them.'

'And why did they let you go, Okoro? What did you tell them?' Her pace quickened, and she swung her head from side to side, searching the piazza for anyone who might be following them, observing them, looking to harm them.

'I said I never told lies about nobody, 'cause I'm a Christian, and Christians don't tell no lies, and they said did I know the Colonel, and I said What Colonel? and they said did I ever live at The Bell, and I said Where's that? and they said I was a lucky little boy, and then one of them got hold of me, hard, down there.' His hand dropped to his groin. 'But it didn't hurt me,' he added defiantly.

'And then?'

'And then the one who was holding my thing gave me a penny, and they went away again. And then you come and found me.'

Her jaw tightened; but she smothered her anger. She knelt and took both his hands in her own. 'Don't let anyone know you've ever met the

Colonel,' she told him. 'He's a wicked man. But he can't hurt you now. You're safe now.'

The haven of her dressmaker's was just a few yards away. She slammed open the door, dragged Okoro inside, found a chair and sat, waving away the solicitous attentions of the rouged proprietor. Her whole body was trembling. As Okoro dissolved into tears again, she gathered him to her and let him sob on her shoulder.

Safe? With a man like the Colonel, what was safe? Who was safe? Where was safe?

'I thought he was with me, Abraham,' she said. Her agitated pacing brought her almost to the arch leading out of the picture-hung gallery before she turned. 'I thought he'd come into the dressmaker's with me. I thought he was by my side, when all the time he was... when those men...'

He took her by the shoulders. 'Calm yourself, Molly. They did him no harm.'

Despite herself, she started to shake. 'Only because he had more wit about him than a nine-year-old boy should have! Only because he told them he'd never met the Colonel, that he'd never lived at The Bell! What if he'd told them the truth, Abraham? What then?'

He drew her to him, cushioned her head against his chest, smoothed the back of her neck with his hand. 'They knew who he was, Molly. If they'd wanted him to be dead, we'd already be grieving over his body.' He continued to caress his hand over her neck, her back, her shoulders. 'Nothing they said was for him to understand. Everything they said was a message for me.' He hugged her closer. 'And for you, Molly. For both of us.'

'But they could have...'

'Yes, they could have beaten him. They could have killed him. But they preferred to let him tell us what happened.'

'I don't understand, Abraham. I don't understand.'

Pressed against him, she couldn't see his face. But she could feel the shrug. 'It's a game, Molly. And Colonel Charnell has just raised the stakes.'

She straightened and pulled herself clear of him. He opened his arms wide to show he wasn't trying to imprison her.

'A game?' Disbelief, indignation, the beginnings of anger. 'A game? He sets his... his dogs on a child and threatens to kill him, and you say it's a game? Is that the world you and the Colonel live in, Abraham?'

'No, my dear. It's a world that Colonel Charnell lives in, and it's a world I understand from the outside.' He tried to defuse the conversation with self-mockery. 'Where else should I understand it from? I'm a Jew. I can only understand anything from the outside.' He became serious again. 'You've played piquet with me, my dear, and with my friends. You've seen how we begin by wagering a few pennies, and end by wagering a few guineas. Where's the harm in that? It's not the money that's important, but the excitement of the wager, the thrill of winning or losing.'

She stared at him. 'I don't understand.' Her voice was tight, squeezing out through her tense lips.

'Without even knowing you'd joined the game, you gambled your virginity. And you lost.' He held up his finger to hush her before she could interrupt. 'After that, you could have run away from the game at any time. But you didn't.' Again he stopped her before she could speak. 'True, you could never win back that particular stake; but there are other stakes to be won. Not as valuable. But not without value.'

'A woman's most precious asset - '

'- is her honour, Molly, not her maidenhead. Did Lucrece lose her honour when Tarquin ravished her? No, it was he that lost his honour, not her.'

She coloured in confusion. 'I don't know them. Are they... were they friends of yours?'

He was quick to apologise. 'Forgive me. It was a classical allusion.' He waved his hand vaguely at the paintings on the walls. 'Like Zeus and the animals he turned into.' His forehead creased in thought. 'Colonel Charnell is playing a game. The game is to see how deeply he can deprave another human being. And the more their innocence at the beginning, the further they have to fall. The further they fall, the greater his triumph. A virgin, a nine-year-old boy, a nun in holy orders - oh, yes, Molly, Colonel Charnell is more than a mere dabbler. But his debaucheries are only the cards he plays with. The spice is in the wager.'

She tightened her jaw. 'I lost everything to the Colonel. What did he stand to lose?'

'Against you, nothing. Seduction isn't a crime. But against all his rapes, his buggery, his blasphemy - and, I have no doubt, his murders - he wagers his reputation, his fortune, his life. Every time he commits some further barbarity, he pits his very existence against the law, against the Church, against the society he lives in. He's teasing them, Molly, defying them.'

He took her arm, led her to a couch, stood in front of her, his hands on her shoulders. 'He wasn't threatening Okoro,' he said. 'He was merely shuffling the cards.'

❋

'Ten guineas... fifteen... twenty...' The evening's gambling at Button's Coffee House had already begun, but the stakes were, as yet, low.

Candlelight hazed through the smoke drifting upwards from two, three dozen clay pipes. Bewigged and aproned serving men flamboyantly poured boiling coffee from chin-high spouts into waist-high bowls. Others plucked two-foot long pipes from a chest, filled them under the miss-nothing eyes of the owner's wife, and presented them to the coffee-drinkers, seated on plain wooden benches at plain wooden tables. A cauldron of coffee bubbled over the spitting coal fire, with triveted coffee-pots warming in front of it, ready for the next call.

At one of the smaller, less fashionable tables, Abraham lifted his bowl with both hands and sipped gingerly at the blistering brown liquid. 'I thank you for your warning, Sir Christopher,' he said. 'But why should Colonel Charnell choose to revenge himself on me?'

The pinch-faced man opposite him gave a snort of disbelief. 'Come now, Abraham. You cuckolded him. In public.'

'This is not about being cuckolded. He was to hang because of his liking for young boys. Am I not right?' He lowered his bowl of coffee to the table. 'All I know is what I hear.'

'However...'

He acknowledged his companion's point. 'True, I was seen abroad with his wife.'

Sir Christopher wagged a finger at him. 'At the same time, and at the same place as he was seen abroad with his whore. The same whore who is now your whore, Abraham. He must suspect a plot. Anybody would suspect a plot.'

'Yes, but why now? Why not then?'

His companion blew gently onto the steaming bowl in front of him before replying. 'I shall be blunt, old friend. Then, he was a cuckold; now, he's been branded a catamite. Then he faced the laughter of the Town; now, he's just escaped hanging.' He put his coffee on the table, sat back and met Abraham's gaze direct. 'Then, he danced to his wife's tune, because it was her money. Now, she's dead. And the money is his. All of it is his. She had no children to claim a share of it.' He checked left, right; everyone else in the room was engaged in his own business. 'Take care, Abraham. When that happened, he had powerful friends. Now, he's powerful in his own right.'

Abraham lowered his bowl to the table. 'Am I his sole enemy?'

'Great heavens, no.'

'Who else?'

A slight tilt of the head, a moue of the lips, an open-hand gesture. 'Anyone who might have cause to want him hanged. Anyone who might wish to blacken his name. Anyone who owes him money. Anyone he owes money to. Anyone who is privy to his debaucheries. Anyone he doesn't care for. Even those people he does care for.' He leaned forward. 'Anyone at all, Abraham. The man is not only wicked, but mad. And now, too, he is wealthy.'

Abraham stood. 'I'm grateful to you, Sir Christopher,' he said.

His companion also stood. 'I'd not wish to see you come to harm. We've known each other many years.'

'We have.'

'Look to your safety, Abraham. Look to your son's safety, to the safety of your household. If you care for her, look to the safety of the harlot you shared with him.'

'I will.'

'Look behind you as often as you look to the fore, and trust no one. The Colonel's notion of honour is not yours, nor mine, nor any frame of honour we would recognise. But such honour as he has demands revenge. And he is a patient man, with a long memory. Never sleep, Abraham, until he's been hanged in good earnest.'

'I thank you, Sir Christopher.' Abraham walked with him to the door. 'You're right. We've been friends for many years. During which time you've come to owe me... how much? Three hundred and eighty guineas?'

Sir Christopher cleared his throat. It was a large sum of money. 'I have some investments in which I have high expectations,' he began.

Abraham stopped him. 'When you have enough to cover the principal,' he said, 'then that will be time enough to repay me. And for a friend there will, of course, be no question of interest.' He offered his hand. 'I'm grateful to you, Sir Christopher,' he repeated. 'I truly am grateful.'

Another transaction had been concluded.

❉

Annie didn't understand. 'Why me? Why should I beware of the Colonel?'

Molly sat on St Paul's steps, and let the early September sunshine warm her. 'You told me once that he and you...'

The corner of Annie's mouth lifted sardonically. 'Yes, me - and you, and a hundred others. If he's bent on punishing all the women he's seduced and debauched and depraved in his time, there'll be scarce a harlot left in London, and not many more of their betters.' She poured ready-mixed gin and cordial from a bottle into a glass, replaced the cork, swallowed a mouthful of the purple liquid. 'No, Molly, he won't harm me. He's got no call to suspect that I harbour a grudge against him.'

Molly was curious. 'Do you?'

Annie took some more gin. 'If it hadn't been him, it would have been someone else.' She uncorked the bottle and refilled her glass. 'And when you're eight years old, it hurts every bit as much, whoever he is.'

'Eight?' Losing her own virginity at seventeen had seemed aforetimes. But to lose it as a child.

'Eight,' she repeated. 'Mother Wickham must have got an excellent price for me.' She pushed the cork back in with the heel of her hand, set the bottle down on the step beside her, nursed the glass of gin while she looked into the past. 'Yes,' she said, almost to herself, 'I harbour a grudge. I would like to see him hanged.'

Molly hesitated before asking her next question. It was none of hr business. But her curiosity got the better of her manners. 'What did he do to you?'

A shrug. 'Nothing he didn't do to you. Just sooner, that's all.'

The silence stretched between them. 'And Kitty?'

Annie shook her head. 'No, not Kitty.'

Molly was surprised. 'But if you at that age, why not Kitty?'

'Somebody else put in their bid first.' As the clock of St Paul's began to strike the hour, she swallowed the gin that remained in her glass, put both bottle and glass into a battered leather satchel and stood. 'I have a visitor,' she said. 'Mother Wickham doesn't like me to keep them waiting.'

Molly stood and embraced her. 'Be careful, Annie. You say the Colonel has no cause to suspect you, but please be careful anyway.'

Annie gripped her tight, reluctant to let her go. 'Tell your Jew to watch over you. You are more in danger than I am. You have more recent cause to wish him dead.' At last she released her. 'He's more evil than any of you can understand,' she warned. 'Tell your Abraham to watch over you, Moll. And tell him to watch his own back.'

As the bell chimed out its sixth and last stroke, she skipped down the steps and was gone.

This time, Molly didn't wait until her friend was out of sight. This time, darting quick glances about her, she ran to the carriage waiting for her at the foot of Ludgate Hill.

❋

The eighth day of September. A clean-aired autumn day, crisp and bright, glowing with the promise of warmth. Her nineteenth birthday.

Molly was the first to rise.

She was the first to take a stroll in the garden.

She was the one to find Babu, the monkey, dangling from the branch of an elm, its arms pinioned behind it, its blackened tongue and blood-filled eyes protruding, its neck cut through to the bone by a tiny but perfectly-crafted hangman's noose.

When they cut the animal down, it was still warm.

162

Chapter 16

For weeks, Hannah barely left Molly's side, eating with her, walking by the river with her, sleeping next to her, waiting outside during Abraham's brief visits on Wednesdays and Saturdays.

'I'm frightened, Hannah,' Molly told her. 'Even now.' They were sitting in the kitchen, drinking milk and nibbling at plum-cake while Mistress Silver was at market. Two great mastiffs prowled around their feet, sniffing for crumbs. 'How could the Colonel or Quince or one of his men have got into the house? Why didn't the dogs bark? Why didn't Babu make a noise? He never stopped chattering when he was with me, yet he didn't make a sound when they took him and hanged him. How did the Colonel do it, Hannah? Is he really in league with the devil?'

'I don't know, Miss Molly. All I know about the Colonel is what you've told me.' She dropped her voice almost to a whisper, in case she conjured him up. 'Perhaps he is the devil.'

'Perhaps he is.' Aye, perhaps he is.

Christmas came and went, all jollity and no gaiety.

And still the dreams persisted. The Colonel being sucked into a roiling midden, the mire itself alive, hugging him to it, closing over his head - then spewing him forth again, shit moulded into an obscene ape-human, his arms clawing in triumph above his head, his fingers hooked into talons, his bulging red eyes seeking hers, his black tongue poking out at her, his slime-dripping mouth screaming hatred, screaming 'Moll Huckerby! Moll Huckerby!'

Sweating, quivering, howling with fear, she awoke. Night after night, she awoke, clutching Hannah to her.

The only mark of disapproval on Silver's oak-carved face was an almost imperceptible flaring of the nostrils. Otherwise, he was as impassive as always. 'There is a beggar at the door,' he said.

'Give him some money,' Abraham told him. He had second thoughts. 'No.' Silver waited. 'It's January. Take him into the warm, and tell Mistress Silver to give him food and drink. And then give him some money.'

'He wishes to speak with you. He claims you have already met.' The idea was clearly ridiculous.

Abraham looked quizzically at Isaac, then at Molly; after a moment's thought, he nodded to Silver. 'Send him in.'

The assurance faded from Silver's lips. 'In here?'

'In here.'

'But you've not...' A subtle movement of hand and eye drew their attention to the table. They hadn't yet finished breakfast.

'Then he may join us.'

A clattering of cutlery. 'Father!'

Abraham held up his hand to cut the protest short. 'He is a stranger.' He lowered his hand, palm-upwards, changing the gesture from one of authority to one of compromise. 'Perhaps nearly a stranger. And we do not turn strangers from our door, do we?' Isaac clenched his jaw stubbornly. Abraham sought an answer from the waiting manservant. 'Do we?'

A stiff reply. 'No, Master Abraham.'

Abraham spread his arms, palms upwards, cocked his head and smiled. 'Forgive me, Silver. I was teasing you. He will earn his breakfast, I promise you.'

An unconvinced bow. An over-dignified exit. A brief absence. A stiff entrance. A reluctant introduction. 'Your... guest, sir.'

Molly recognised the beggar. The eye-patched hunchback who'd been with them at The Beggar's Opera, and afterwards at The Bell. She remembered the hatred that had burned in his every feature. Now, the hatred was fragmented by greed, by servility, by fear. But she didn't trust him. However cowed, a whipped dog is still a dog. And it's the nature of a dog to feed where it can.

Abraham beckoned him to the table. 'Eat.' A hunchback with money offering food to a hunchback with none.

The beggar shuffled forward, hesitantly broke off a large chunk of the fresh-baked loaf, stuffed it hastily into his mouth. The crumbs sprinkled down his chest and onto the floor.

Abraham indicated a chair. 'Sit.' The beggar lowered himself uneasily onto it. Abraham pushed the dish of herring towards him. 'Take what you want.'

Within minutes, the beggar had eaten his fill; yet still the dish seemed untouched. A belly used to starving is soon satisfied.

'What is your name?' Abraham asked him.

'You can call me... Giles,' he said, conjuring a name out of the air. 'Yes, my name is Giles.' He lapsed into a tense silence.

Abraham prompted him. 'You have news for me?'

The beggar swigged from the tankard of ale Abraham had poured for him, wiped his sleeve across his mouth. 'There's a new play in Lincoln's Inn Fields tomorrow. A play about a merchant.'

'The Merchant of Venice. That, my friend, is not news. It is not even a new play.'

Giles slid a sly glance sideways at Abraham. 'Neither is it news that you never miss the first night of a play.'

Abraham conceded the point. 'Go on.'

He wiped his sleeve across his mouth. 'The Colonel's got an entertainment of his own planned. He's buying entrance for all the brothers and sisters of St Giles his man can muster. And we're each to have two shillings afterwards.'

Abraham was relishing the moment, and he drew Molly and Isaac into it with him. 'Such a lack of imagination. I fill the stage with beggars and harlots, and now Colonel Charnell fills the stage with beggars and harlots. I give them food and drink, and Colonel Charnell gives them money.' He wagged his head with a feigned sadness. 'It is rare for a jest to be amusing at the second time of telling.'

The beggar strove uneasily to find something of significance. 'We won't be on the stage. We'll be in the pit.'

Isaac dismissed his story with an abrupt laugh. 'Wherein lies the jest? At least my father - '

Abraham cut in, renewed his command of the conversation. 'My son is right. Wherein lies the jest?' He put his fingertips together, regarded the beggar over the top of them. 'You've walked nearly ten miles through bitter weather to tell me that Colonel Charnell will take you into the theatre, you and your... what d'ye call 'em... your brothers and sisters of St Giles.' He shook his head in disbelief, his eyes never leaving the beggar's. 'Your story must have more substance to it than that.'

He grudged out a further morsel. 'We are to shout.' Beggars can't afford to give away anything for nothing.

'You are to shout what?'

The beggar waved his hands, shrugged his shoulders, made a face, played all the games of pretended confusion. 'I don't know yet.'

Abraham was insistent. 'You are to shout what? Hurrah for Shakespeare? Bravo to the actors? Free tobacco at Button's Coffee House? Long live the King? What are you to shout?'

'I don't know.'

'Then why have you walked so far to tell me this? Has Colonel Charnell paid you an extra two shillings to bring me this message?'

The beggar scowled. 'I like the Colonel no more than you do.' He sat up as straight as his crooked back would allow. 'We're to take our cue from his man.'

'Quince,' Molly said.

His head swung round, startled, and he squinted past his eyepatch. How much did she know? 'Yes, Quince. When he shouts, we shout. We shout whatever he shouts. It's to do with... I don't know. I heard him mention your name. I know not what is planned.' He grimaced. 'But what is planned is mischief. Mischief towards you. And yours.'

Isaac broke in. 'Father, if this man speaks true, and the Colonel plans mischief against you, then your answer is simple: don't go to the theatre.'

'Molly?'

No need even to think. The answer was obvious. 'Isaac is right. Don't go to the theatre. If the Colonel is planning mischief, then someone will suffer. I don't want you to suffer, Abraham.'

He reached out and rested his own fingers lightly on hers. 'But you see, my dear, I always go to the first night of a new offering. If I don't go to the theatre tomorrow night, he will have won. He will have bullied me out of my pleasure.'

'But if you do go to the theatre, and he does whatever it is he means to do, then you will also lose. And you may lose more than you'd lose if you stayed at home. Much more.' She softened her voice. 'I don't want you to be hurt, Abraham. And the Colonel is more able to hurt you than you are able to hurt him.'

Abraham acknowledged the hit. He had already tried to inflict harm on the Colonel, and failed.

Silence as they all considered her words. Isaac spoke first. 'She's right, father.'

Abraham looked across the table at the beggar, his eyebrows raised in question.

Giles confirmed Molly's fears. 'The Colonel wishes you ill.'

'And what is your part in his purpose?'

'I don't know.' The beggar stood. 'All I know, I have told you. Tomorrow night, we are to shout whatever the Colonel's man shouts. And it bodes you no good.'

'Why do you tell me all this?'

The beggar turned his face away. 'I owe you nothing.'

Isaac had recognised him. 'He was at The Bell,' he warned his father. 'He was at the playhouse, then at The Bell. Don't trust him.'

The beggar's head snapped round to face him. 'Is that your thanks?' he challenged him. 'Yes, I'm a beggar. But nobody has bought me. If you toss me a glass of gin and a crust of bread, I'm grateful. But it doesn't buy me!'

Isaac's face darkened at this ingratitude. 'We also tossed you a night at the theatre.'

His challenged broadened into a sneer. 'Do you think any of us cared what those prancing actors were doing and saying? What have they got to do with us? When were they ever without food? Without bread? Without a glass of gin to dull the pain of their lives?'

'Without a harlot to give herself up against the wall,' Molly added. She remembered, and she understood.

He misunderstood her understanding. 'I owe you nothing!' he spat. 'You could pay for it all, and never miss a penny. What do you know about being poor, about being a beggar, about whoring for enough to eat or for a roof to keep the snow off you? What do you know about life in St Giles?' He stood, looked down at her. 'I thought to help you. I thought maybe to save you from the Colonel. But you're no different! You're the same as he is!'

A red haze of outrage boiled up behind her eyes. 'I am not the same as he is!' The chair went tumbling as she leapt to her feet and advanced angrily on him. 'I am not the same as him!' she said, pushing him in the chest with both hands and forcing him backwards.

'Molly!' Abraham was also on his feet, and trying to get between them.

'Molly!' Isaac.

'I am not the same as he is!' Another push. The beggar staggered, but

kept his feet. 'I am not the same as he is! Don't you ever dare say I'm
the same as he is! Don't you dare!' A flurry of slaps and punches to his
head and face, kicks to his shins, her voice rising to a shriek. 'Don't you
dare!'

'Molly!' Isaac was in front of her, trying to block the flailing fists,
grabbing her by the arms, hustling her away from the beggar. 'Molly!'

'Molly!' Abraham. 'Enough!'

She stiffened, allowed Isaac to hold her while she fought down her
anger; still trembling, she allowed him to lead her back to the table;
gulping mouthfuls of air, she let herself be eased into her seat again.

'Calm yourself, my dear.' Abraham stood over her, gently massaging
her shoulders, quietening her. He waited until her breathing steadied
before speaking. 'I shall go to the theatre tomorrow,' he said. 'You and
Isaac shall remain at home.'

But Isaac chose to disobey his father. 'If you go, I go.'

Molly stood; her legs felt like jelly, and she had to hold on to the back
of the chair. 'And I.'

Abraham acceded to their decision. 'You are not my slaves that I
should tell you what you must and must not do. We go all three to the
play.' He inclined his head towards the beggar. 'I thank you, sir. What
you have told me is of value, and Master Silver will see that you are
rewarded.' It was a dismissal; but he beckoned him back. 'My son and
I will be going into Town within the hour. If you wish, you may ride at
the back of the carriage with my footman.'

The beggar glowered. 'As far as Tyburn,' he accepted grudgingly. 'I
cannot be seen with you.' Even a beggar must be careful of the company
he keeps.

Molly moved to him. Still breathing shakily, she kissed him on the
cheek. His warm fetid breath washed over her, and his stubbled flesh
grated greasily against her lips. She didn't shrink. 'Giles,' she said.
'Forgive me.'

*

Shylock lifted Portia's hand away from the front of his breeches. 'Not
now,' he said.

'There's time enough,' she wheedled. 'The acrobats always take at

168

least a quarter hour.'

'Something's wrong.' He sipped from his glass of wine. His brow furrowed in concentration. 'You were on before me. Did you sense it?'

She made a face. 'Some drunkenness in the gallery. Some lewdness from the pit, but no more than usual. The seats on the stage full with people who know the play well enough to speak the best lines in a ragged chorus behind you. But nothing untoward.' She touched him on the arm. 'What's troubling you?'

'There's a muttering, a restlessness.' He screwed up his face, trying to pin down a vague feeling. 'They seem to hate Shylock already, yet they shouldn't really hate him till the Fourth Act.'

'As you said, they know the play.'

'No.' He put his glass down on the table. 'The seats on the stage perhaps, but not the low-life in the pit. I've already heard cries of Usurer and Christ-killer, and every time one of them shouts out something, the rest shout along with him.' His frown deepened. 'There's something wrong.'

After the acrobats had tumbled and whirled their act, the audience cheered them off, and waited for the play to recommence.

Throughout the second act, they sympathised with Portia, laughed at Launcelot, urged on Lorenzo. But Shylock's scene with his daughter Jessica was greeted with catcalls.

In the third act, Shylock stepped forward to make his impassioned plea. 'I am a Jew,' he declaimed. 'Hath not a Jew eyes? Hath not a Jew hands, organs, dimensions, senses, affections, passions?'

A voice rang out from the pit. 'Hath not a Jew the smell of carrion about him?'

Molly went cold with fear as she recognised the shrill baying of Quince. She scanned the faces below her, but she couldn't pick him out in the sea of faces. Beyond the swirls of tobacco smoke, she could see the familiar shape of the Colonel standing at the back of the pit.

'If you prick us, do we not bleed?' They clamoured their approval. 'If you tickle us, do we not laugh? If you poison us, do we not die?'

'Die, Jew!' Quince again.

'Ah.' Abraham nodded. There was no surprise in his voice. 'Now the tale begins to be told.'

'That's the Colonel's man!' Molly's voice was tense. 'He's trying to turn the audience against you, not Shylock.'

He continued to watch the stage, enjoying the performance. Then he leaned towards Molly and whispered to her, as if pointing out some amusing reference in the play. 'When I take your hand and tell you to come with me, don't question me. Just do as I tell you.' He leaned away from her and whispered to Isaac.

The fourth act, and Shylock stood up in court to demand his forfeit. The pit grumbled sullenly to itself, the low growling of a pack of curs whipping up their own courage, a rumbling undercurrent punctuated by the occasional animal snarl.

'Take thou thy pound of flesh,' said Portia. 'But, in the cutting it, if thou dost shed one drop of Christian blood, thy lands and goods are by the law of Venice confiscate - '

The muttered undertones coalesced, began to take form, killed the rest of the line.

The actors raised their voices, fought against the noise as more and more voices joined in.

The tenants in the pit, the debtors in the gallery, the gamblers in the boxes, all rising to their feet, cursing and pointing, bawling insults, drowning the lines, hurling threats.

Portia grabbed Shylock by the hand, stormed to the front of the stage and confronted the audience. 'Soft!' she bawled. 'The Jew shall have all justice!' She waited till the noise abated a little. 'Soft, no haste. He shall have nothing but the penalty.'

A roar of encouragement.

'If thou tak'st more or less than a just pound...' A seething of anticipation and obscenities. '...nay, if the scale do turn but in the estimation of a hair, thou diest, and all - '

'Aye, thou diest!' Quince. 'Kill the Jew!'

'Kill the Jew!' The claqueurs bought with the Colonel's money.

'Kill the Jew!' The Colonel's acquaintances in the gallery and the boxes.

'Kill the Jew!' Everybody else who realised that the hatred wasn't aimed at Shylock.

The rest of the audience, sensing the beginnings of a more exciting entertainment than The Merchant of Venice, joined in the chant. 'Kill the Jew! Kill the Jew!'

Molly could feel the fear washing over her like a tide of ice, and she plucked at her protector's sleeve. 'Let us go, Abraham,' she pleaded.

Unhurried, he patted her hand. 'Not yet,' he said. 'Not until everybody else is leaving.'

At a signal, the first piece of fruit was thrown. An orange sailed onto the stage, well wide of its mark. More followed. Tomatoes and apples, which couldn't be bought inside the theatre, betrayed the planning behind the attack.

'Why doth the Jew pause?' said Portia, but nobody heard her, not even Shylock.

Time for a decision. 'End of Act Four!' Shylock yelled. A tomato spattered a sunburst onto his cloak.

Portia plucked up her skirts and dashed upstage. An orange thumped her in the back.

As they scrambled out of sight into the wings, the barrage sought a new target, and veered to one side, the side where Abraham sat with Molly and Isaac. Rotten fruit showered onto the playgoers in the stage-seats; they leapt to their feet, backing away, tripping over the benches behind them, squealing with indignation.

Abraham stood, but still he did not flee.

A few inches above their heads, one of the missiles crashed into the proscenium and showered splinters from it.

'That was no orange,' said Abraham, clutching Molly's hand tightly in his. 'Come. Now.' Pulling her along behind him, he hobbled in the opposite direction from everybody else, elbowing aside anyone who got in his way. Edging past the board that separated the seats from the actors, he hurried her onto the stage, past the proscenium arch.

Putting one hand on top of the dividing board, Isaac vaulted it and followed them.

Quince's voice sailed over the top of the pandemonium. 'Don't let them escape!'

As they dodged past the heavy curtain into the wings, the smell changed from perfume, tobacco and sweat to dust, grease and candles. The brightness of the stage plunged into a murky dimness. The illusion of Venice crumbled into the reality of a playhouse in Lincoln's Inn Fields.

Abraham was at home backstage. 'Here!' He weaved past the painted flats, barged between the panicking actors waiting in the wings, ducked past the tied-off ropes holding the scene-cloths aloft, through a peeling door, down an unlit wooden staircase, under the stage itself. Above them, the stage-lighting cut down in thin, straight beams between the gaps in the stage floorboards, just enough to let them pick their way through the carelessly-stored clutter. 'Isaac!' No attempt at conceal-ment: everybody knew by now where they'd gone.

'Here, father.'

'Run ahead. Kick open the door to the courtyard.'

Isaac burst between them, skipped past gilded eagles the size of a carriage, clambered over wicker baskets, trampled through urns and cherubs and plaster statues. Abraham and Molly followed him, scram-bling and stumbling in the half-light.

Above them, the stage thundered and bounced as a hundred feet pounded across it.

'Kill the Jew!' The words drifted downwards with the dust-motes in the knife-edges of light.

Crash! Crash! Crash! At the third time of kicking, the door splintered at its jamb and flew open. 'Here, Molly! Father!' He held the door open for them.

Abraham beckoned him onwards into the bowels of the theatre. 'Not that way! Follow me!' As he passed the door, he snatched off the figured blue silk shawl that Molly was wearing, and flung it into the icy courtyard beyond.

She didn't argue. She could hear the feet clattering down the wooden stairs.

Abraham pushed open a door, dragged Molly into the confined space beyond it, waited for Isaac, then eased the door shut behind them.

In the total darkness, she could hear the double click of a lock engag-ing. Why does a cupboard have a key on the inside?

'Now we have silence,' Abraham urged them. Low, direct, compelling.

Outside, the voices babbled, then faded. 'Here!' Muffled. 'Don't let them escape!' The baying of paid hounds with a trail in their nostrils. 'Kill the Jew!' The pack moved away, faded into the distance.

'Yes, father, you fooled them!' Isaac, triumphant.

'Hush!' Abraham hissed.

'But -

'Hush!' His whisper was life-and-death urgent. 'Not all of them have followed the false scent!'

In the blackness, Molly fumbled for Abraham's hand and hung on to it tight with both hers.

For two, three minutes they stood there in silence. Then, no more than the scratching of a mouse, the tinkling rattle of a door being tried. A tip-toe footfall, another tentative rattle. The faintest scuff of a shoe. Outside their own rabbit-hole the breath of the stalking fox. A finger-width of lanternlight shone through the keyhole. Instinctively, they cowered away from it.

Molly stopped breathing. The handle turned, the door shook once, twice, bumping gently against the locked frame.

The softest of footsteps tip-toeing away from them. Mouth wide open to avoid any noise, Molly released her breath and carefully drew more air into her lungs.

The door beyond them rattled. When it resisted, a voice cursed, not loudly, but with venom. 'Damn!'

With every muscle tensed, Molly buried her head against Abraham's chest.

'Damn!' The Colonel's voice, low and dangerous. 'The Jew is not as cunning as I thought.'

'Nor is he as fleet as he would wish.' Quince. 'The brothers and sisters will soon catch him. And the girl.'

'And if they don't?' More the scavenging growl of a jackal than a question.

'Where can they go without being seen? There are more beggars and harlots in the Town than money-lenders and their mistresses. A shilling will buy any one of them. Two shillings will buy the Jew, his son and his whore.'

'The Jew's son means nothing to me. The money-lender and his whore, that's who I want punished, Quince. And I want them punished so that the rest of the world will say The Colonel is a loyal friend - but an unforgiving enemy. The guineas aren't important, Quince. I have had a surfeit of this Jew.' The footsteps passed the door again. In the silence of the now empty theatre, they stamped up the stairs and faded into the distance.

Abraham made them stay in the cramped, airless space for nearly two hours before cautiously, silently turning the key and letting them out. Pausing every two or three paces to listen for the slightest sound, he led them back the way they'd fled. His penknife severed the cord that now secured the splintered door, and they crept into the frozen courtyard at the rear of the theatre. The narrow space plunged from ice-blue moonlight into smothering darkness as the clouds scudded overhead, then reappeared, etched in sharp outlines.

'Here,' Abraham said, dropping an armful of rags onto the frost-sparkling flagstones. 'Now we can see what we're doing, sort these out and put them on.' He kicked off his shoes and wriggled out of his hose and breeches. 'Put your clothes with mine,' he said. 'Then Isaac will lock them in our own recent prison. They'll not be discovered in there for a month or more.' He took off his coat and waistcoat, tore away his lace cravat, pulled his shirt over his head, stood naked in front of his son and mistress. 'This is no time for modesty,' he said, the bite of accustomed command in his voice. 'Molly. Isaac. Change into these rags!' Stooping, he tore open the bundle he'd brought out of the theatre, and quickly dressed himself in a rough coat and a ragged pair of trousers, together with a pair of broken-heeled shoes.

Molly stepped into a patch of deep shadow, turned her back on Isaac, and stripped off her clothes, shivering as the January air pricked her skin into gooseflesh and hardened her nipples.

'Isaac!' Abraham hissed. 'Make haste!'

Isaac was a jangle of uncertainty, torn between desire and decency. A young woman in the nude. His father's mistress unclothed. As Molly bent to unroll her stocking down her leg, Abraham scuttled across the courtyard and draped a torn, stained gown over her shoulders.

Isaac scooped up the discarded clothes. 'I'll take our clothes into the... I'll...' He scurried into the back of the theatre. When he returned he, like Molly and his father, was dressed in the rags of a beggar.

In the past-midnight gloom, they crept from the back of the theatre into the deserted darkness of Little Lincoln's Inn Fields, felt their way along the rough brick walls behind Portugal Row, scuffed through the stinking fish and flesh remains of Clare Market, ventured into the openness of Vere Street. At the southern end, towards the river, there was light and noise.

The light of more than torches, the noise of more than revellers.

'Keep your heads down. Hunch your shoulders. Shuffle your feet,' Abraham instructed them. 'Don't look anyone in the eye. Don't speak. Just follow me. If we are separated, there is a carriage waiting in Drury Lane. It is not our carriage, but a carriage I have hired. They are expecting a Jew, his son, and his wife. If I am not with you, you will have to convince them that you are who they are waiting for.'

'Why should you not be with us, father?'

'The jungles of Africa are like a pleasure garden compared with the streets between here and Drury Lane. Pray God our journey be swift and safe.' Quickly, he hugged first Isaac, then Molly. 'We are fortunate,' he said to Molly. 'Despite our differences, we both pray to the same God.'

From the deserted street behind the theatre to the link-lights of Drury Lane, they were alone. But the quarter mile was punctuated by shifting shadows, by corner-of-the-eye movements, by hints of the lawless underbelly of London eying them, weighing them, choosing to disregard them before going about its secret business. Molly could feel the fear creeping up her back and prickling into her neck and shoulders.

Just one voice challenged them, beyond Stanhop Street in the night-silence of Black Mare Street, a hoarse croak, pitched to carry no further than it needed to. 'How much for the harlot?'

Abraham put a restraining hand on Isaac's arm. 'She's not working tonight,' he called, roughening his voice to a croak. 'She has the pox.' A riffle of fading footsteps, and they were alone again.

When they reached Drury Lane, the carriage had deserted them.

In the stumbling darkness, it took them over six hours to walk the eight miles of frozen ruts to Chiswick, with Isaac and Molly taking it in turns to support the lame Abraham.

They arrived home as dawn was glinting off the deep white frost. With a single gesture, Abraham dismissed Silver, who had waited up. Without a word, they each went to their separate beds, their eyes swimming, their muscles aching, their feet blistered and bleeding.

When, at last, he rose, Abraham spent the rest of the day in his room, scribbling in his books. His left foot was stretched out on a stool, swathed in wet bandages to alleviate the burning gout the previous night's journey had brought on.

Isaac didn't emerge from his room at all. Only he knew what he did there.

Molly soaked in a tub of hot water, let Hannah scrub her with a sponge, then soaked all over again in a fresh tub. When at last the water began to cool, there was time only for a slice of salt beef and bread with an unusually subdued Abraham before she felt her eyes and her mind start to drift into oblivion. Before the pale sun had gone down, she was in bed again.

The blankets twitched aside. A body slid into the bed beside her. Night-chilled flesh huddled against her back.

'Hannah?' she murmured, still more than half asleep.

No reply. Just a stirring against the back of her thigh.

'Abraham?' It wasn't Wednesday. It wasn't Saturday.

'Ssshhh,' said Isaac.

Chapter 17

'No!' Shock, confusion, fear. Suddenly awake, she swung herself over to face him, forced her arms between them, her clenched fists against her cheekbones, her elbows covering her breasts, her thighs clamped tightly together. 'No!'

'No!' he hissed. 'No.' Holding, soothing, giving his word. In the darkness, his hand strayed over her shoulder, smoothed across her face until he found her mouth. He laid his finger against her lips. 'No.' Despite his words, she could feel his stiffness butting against her belly. His hand retraced her cheek and shoulder, and his arms closed round her, his fingers pressing into her back. 'No,' he whispered. 'Not until you want me. Only if you want me.'

Gradually, the tension ebbed out of her. Her arms relaxed, and she rested against him. For a long, waiting, silent time she lay against him. Breast to breast, belly to belly, male to female, hammering pulse against hammering pulse.

Why hadn't she seen it before? Hannah had hinted at it often enough. Isaac's sulks, his curtness, the way he'd avoided her - she'd seen the same sullen unsureness in her own brothers when they were growing up, when they'd become infatuated with a local girl who wasn't available, or who didn't notice them.

But this is a grown man, not a growing child. Can I trust him? Does he want me - or just my commodity? Is it love or lust? Am I a person or a purchase?

Her mind flickered back to the bullying, honeyed words of the young bloods in York... to the Colonel's casual guineas... to the nightmare on her knees at The Bell... to Abraham's genteel pretences... Was this simply the same transaction in a different guise?

The images melted away as Isaac stroked her back, his fingers fluttering across her skin, tenderness in every touch.

Can I trust you? Can I trust any man? If I give myself to you, will you, too, toss me a guinea when you leave? If I told you to leave now, would you go?

Aye, you'd go. You'd show me that much respect.

But you'd never come to me again. You're too proud for that.

This, then, is the difference. It may be that you're the same as all the other men who have betrayed me, debauched me, bought me. But this time I'm different.

This time I don't want you to go.

Her eyes filled, and the tears trickled over her nose, into her hair, onto the pillow.

She caressed her fingers down the side of his face, feeling the scratch of his yesterday-shaven cheek against her fingertips. A tremor shuddered down the length of her body. She could feel a warmth in her belly, a warmth she'd fought against in York, and had never felt since. Her breathing shallowed. The warmth became a heat, the heat turned to fire, the fire focused, burned her thighs apart, blazed into an inferno that had to be quenched.

She thrust her hand down between their naked bodies, seized him, guided him. 'Now!'

He eased himself onto her and into her. 'Yes,' he sighed, his breath warm against her ear. 'Now.'

❖

She was scared. She was fighting to remain calm, but her breathing was irregular, her pulse racing, the blood flushing into her face.

Abraham limped back and forth, back and forth, leaning heavily on his cane, the pain from his bandaged foot pursing his lips, his brows knitted, his jaw set. The table was set for breakfast, the food was ready in its dishes, but neither of them had taken so much as a piece of bread nor a glass of water.

After three, perhaps four, minutes the tension was too much for her. 'Abraham,' she blurted. 'What is it?'

He continued his pacing. Tap, tap, tap. 'We'll wait until Isaac joins us.'

She could feel her body beginning to tremble, now with more guilt than fear. How had he found out? Hannah? But Hannah wouldn't...

She composed herself, put her hands in her lap and waited for her fate to be announced.

Where next? Cousin Tom had already rejected her. She'd be among friends at The Bell - but at the mercy of the Colonel. There was nothing

178

for her in York; with her father and mother dead, and her brothers married, the crude attentions of Big Ned Foley and his friends were all that awaited her. And if Cousin Tom had written home to his family about her months at The Bell, the homecoming would be unbearable. Better the cunny-warrens of London than the back streets of York.

But where next? Without Abraham's protection, where could she go that was safe from the Colonel?

Isaac? Would Isaac protect her? In the dull grey daylight, last night's passion seemed as flimsy as a dream. He'd sworn to die rather than forsake her. But she remembered one of the Waif's favourite jests: when a man's balls are full, his promises are empty.

Where next? Once a mistress had betrayed her master, who'd ever trust her again? Or is that what whores were expected to do? What did she know about harlotry? Treated like a beast by the Colonel, pampered like a pet by Abraham, a single night of gasping abandon with Isaac - that was all she knew of men.

Oh, God, please - where next?

Isaac hurried into the room, buttoning his coat. 'Father?' He glanced at Molly long enough to register her presence, not long enough to pass any message between them. 'Silver said it couldn't wait.'

'Sit down, my son.'

Isaac drew himself upright behind Molly and put his hands on her shoulders. 'I'll stand, father. What have you to say?'

Abraham hobbled to the table. Painfully, he lowered himself into the chair at the head of the table. He gestured at the food. 'Eat,' he said. 'This can be said on a full belly as well as on an empty one.' Neither Molly nor and Isaac had any appetite. Abraham forked a piece of fish onto his plate, but made no attempt to eat it. 'The night before last,' he continued, 'I said you were not my slaves that I should tell you what you must and what you must not do.' He looked from Isaac to Molly, then back to Isaac. 'Since then, the world has changed.'

Isaac's fingers dug into Molly's shoulder. She resisted the urge to reach her hand up to his.

Aye, the world had changed. Overnight, she'd become a woman instead of a whore. Or, perhaps, a woman as well as a whore. But what had Isaac become? Where were his loyalties now? If Abraham cast her out, would Isaac stand by her, or stay with his father?

Abraham appeared to be studying the fish on his plate, but she knew his mind was seeing something else. 'After we left the theatre, we heard noises. We heard people shouting.' He looked up at them. 'A Jew was caught in Covent Garden. He was stripped and beaten. And then his throat was cut.'

The shock hung between them. 'Who?' said Isaac. His fingers slipped away from Molly.

'I've never met him. A tailor. With a wife and children. Silver tells me he was an honest man.' He was clearly troubled as he spelled out the implications. 'An honest Jew. A Jew with a family. A Jew who was hunted down and killed because they couldn't find the Jew they were looking for.'

He doesn't know! Isaac and I - we're safe!

The brief flare of elation died. God forgive me. I'm rejoicing in the death of an innocent man.

'What now, father?'

Abraham's features were steady and determined. 'Now you do as I say. Neither of you is to leave the house until I say you may. Neither of you is to spend any time alone, not even inside the house.' He levered himself to his feet. 'Colonel Charnell didn't simply copy me,' he said. 'I filled the playhouse with beggars. He filled it with assassins.' He limped painfully towards the door. 'I have matters to attend to. The tailor's family must be provided for. But I shall take men with me to protect me.' He paused at the threshold. 'Since you are both to remain here, why not protect each other?'

Molly felt her blood rising upwards from her belly into her face, warming her cheeks, pricking behind her eyes. Despite the threat of danger, of death, she felt happier than she'd felt since she'd left York. As Abraham left the room, she clutched Isaac's hand and pressed it to her face. His thumb caressed the side of her hand.

Before Molly had decided whether or not to tell her, Hannah already knew.

They stood by the swollen river, their clouded breath hanging in the bright January sunshine, looking upstream to the distant prospect of Richmond. Down by the water Okoro and two of the household's children played ducks and drakes, skimming the flat stones out over the river to squeals of delight, disappointment and laughter. The two mastiffs, Crab and Berry, milled about them, barking and snuffling, joining in the children's enjoyment.

Light-sailed gigs and hoys drifted downstream, a wherry toiled upstream, a skiff hauled itself across the current. On the frozen mud-flats opposite three men, stripped to the waist in the biting cold, worked on the upturned hull of a small boat, repairing, caulking, tarring, sweating to make it good so that they could sweat in it to earn a living. The unbroken blue sky reflected blue-grey off the muddied water.

Molly gripped her shawl tight up under her chin. 'Do you love your apprentice, Hannah? Do you love Richard?'

A melting smile. 'Yes, Miss Molly.'

'Do you really love him, or are you just dreaming of a husband?'

Confusion. A question she'd never considered before. 'I hope he will be my husband. And I believe he will be my husband. But if anything should happen that he can't be my husband, I shall still love him.'

Molly pressed her point. 'And does he love you?'

'Yes.' A moment of hesitation; but no doubt. 'Yes, he does.'

They stood in silence, huddled against the cold, watching the glinting river race past them, hearing nothing but the raucous cries of seagulls driven inland by storms, the excited shrieks of the children, the distant calling of the boatmen.

Molly was the first to speak. 'I'm in love, Hannah.'

'Yes, Miss Molly.' Neither looked at the other. 'And he's in love with you.'

Again they said nothing, watched the river, the seagulls, the boatmen. At last, Molly said 'Really?'

Hannah nodded. 'Really. Very, very much. I've seen it for months.'

Molly stretched her arms wide, closed her eyes, and lifted her face to the sun, allowing the bright redness through her eyelids to fool her with its mock-warmth. A deep, ecstatic sigh breathed from her lips, bubbling into a light flutter of pure happiness as it died.

'Mistress?' When she opened her eyes again, it was to see Hannah in front of her, a mischievous twinkle at her lips. 'Shall I ask Mistress Silver to get you a sack of lemons?' she said.

They hugged each other and laughed so much that the children and the dogs left their games and came to see what the matter was, envious of anything that was more fun than ducks and drakes.

Wednesday and Saturday, Abraham. Gentle, courteous, paid for. Monday, Tuesday and Thursday, Isaac. Snatched hours, animal passion, but never a sound lest Abraham hear them.Friday, the Jewish sabbath. Isaac and his father with another common purpose. Sunday, her own sabbath. No visit from Abraham. No visit from Isaac. But, since it meant leaving the house, no visit to the church, either.

And, while Abraham made his daily trips into the City, Molly and Isaac obeyed his instructions and stayed at home.

✳

Isaac's voice was soft in her ear; but she could hear the intensity in it. 'We can't deceive him for ever, Molly. It's been half a year already. Everyone in the household knows, except him. And he must suspect. He's not a fool.'

Her arms tensed, and her fingers dug into his back. 'No,' she whispered, more a prayer than a denial.

'It must be resolved,' he said, disengaging himself and sitting up. The linen sheet fell away from him, and his lean body gleamed pale in the summer-dawn light.

Molly clutched the sheet to her. The feel of the cloth was comforting, the way it had been when she was a child. 'Don't go,' she begged. Don't go now. Don't go ever. What would she now do without him?

'I must. My father will be rising soon.' He swung his legs to the floor, stooped, plucked his shirt from the floor where he'd dropped it last night, pulled it over his head.

She laid her hand on his arm. 'Wait till he goes down to breakfast,' she coaxed him. 'He'll expect you to be late. You always are.'

Still sitting on the edge of the bed, he twisted towards her, teased a strand of hair away from her face, then feathered his fingers down the side of her face, across her shoulder, onto the top of her breast. With a flick of his fingers, he twitched the blanket aside and gazed down at her body. Her firm body. Her strong body. For him, her willing body.

From where she lay on her back, she could see over the horizon of his thigh to where his circumcised member was springing up to fullness. Reaching out, she touched its swollen tip, and smiled to herself as it jumped. Easing her legs apart, she opened her arms to him. 'Come to

182

me, Isaac,' she said.

They were both late for breakfast. Only Abraham was surprised.

✻

Molly wiped her forehead with a lace-edged handkerchief, then passed it to Annie. They stood on the wharf steps at Billingsgate, perspiring in the moist August heat as they looked out over the Thames to Southwark, the arches of London Bridge to their right, the massive walls of the Tower to their left, six burly Chiswick men grouped protectively behind them.

'The Twins' Boy is dead of the smallpox,' said Annie, 'and the Twins' Girl is sick and like to die. Mother Wickham is nursing The Bell's baby herself, but it's already showing the signs.' Her own eyes were bloodshot, and her pale skin was stretched thin over her cheekbones, her freckles standing out like a spray of dried blood against silk. She twined a cotton handkerchief endlessly through her fingers: wind, draw tight, retrieve; wind, draw tight, retrieve...

Molly put her hand on Annie's shoulder. 'And you? Have you been sick?'

'No, I'm safe. I've had the smallpox.' Wind, draw tight, retrieve. 'When I was a child.' Wind, draw tight, retrieve.

'Me too.' If not the smallpox, then what? 'What's troubling you, Annie?'

'Nothing's troubling me,' she mumbled. 'The gin...' Molly had to strain to hear her.

'Gin? You want some gin?' Molly swung towards the men Abraham had assigned to her for her safety. 'I'll get you - '

'No!' She grabbed at Molly's arm. 'No gin!'

'Something's troubling you,' Molly insisted. 'What is it, Annie?'

Almost imperceptibly, her shoulders straightened. 'I don't drink gin any more,' she said. There was a painful resolve in her voice. She stood up. 'Now, every day, I know what's happening to me. I see the faces of my visitors. Sometimes, I can remember them afterwards.' She moved down the steps to within a foot of the greasily lapping water. 'Since I was younger than you, Moll, the gin has helped me to live inside a dream. A dream which helped me pretend my life at The Bell wasn't really happening. But even inside that dream, I had another dream. I dreamt that my dream was itself a dream, that I wasn't yet born, that one day I would wake to find myself a baby, that I was... that I was a princess, that people... that men...' Tears were flooding down the side of her nose, onto her top lip, dripping onto her chin. 'I dreamed I was a princess, Moll, and not a harlot. I dreamed that somebody loved me, that they married me in a church, that they...' Her voice tailed away.

Molly said nothing. What was there to say?

Annie climbed back up the steps, sat down on the top one. Molly followed, sat beside her. A bead of sweat formed on her forehead, dribbled onto the corner of her eye. She brushed it away.

A droplet ran down Annie's face. A tear, not sweat. 'The gin made me think I was escaping. But all it did was stop me remembering.' She played with the handkerchief: wind, draw tight, retrieve. 'I've been loved twice, Moll.' She was looking out at the boats plying the river, but that's not what she saw. 'Twice. First by my Billy. But the Colonel had him killed.' Her voice faded away almost to nothing. 'Mother Wickham had him killed.' She sniffed, and dabbed at her eyes with the handkerchief. 'And then by Bull. But he was stabbed in the back by a coward in revenge for the beating Bull had given him.' She snorted a humourless laugh. 'And why were they fighting? They were fighting, Moll, because that murdering thief had been bedding Abigail while Bull was bedding me.' She rose again, controlled herself. 'Mother Wickham is right,' she said. 'There's good money to be made from men. But never let them know who you are.'

Molly stood and climbed up to stand beside her. 'Kitty gives herself a different name for every visitor,' she said. 'Could you not do the same?'

She kept her head averted. 'Kitty doesn't drink gin. Kitty enjoys being had by men.' Her shoulders sagged. 'No, that's not true. Kitty enjoys the play-acting, she enjoys becoming whatever her visitors want her to be. But no matter what she has to do to please them, Kitty stays Kitty inside her own head.'

'Despite being Ophelia and Desdemona and Miranda?'

'And Eve and Delilah and... and, for the past few weeks, Polly Peachum.'

Molly stared at her, incredulous. 'Polly Peachum? From The Beggar's

Opera? The virgin who gets tricked by a highwayman?'

When she saw Molly struggling to keep a straight face, Annie let herself be caught up in the farce of the very idea. Her face wrinkled, her lips pursed, her shoulders lifted up round her neck, her breath exploded through her nose in a pent-up sneeze. She hugged Molly to her and let herself laugh. The laughter was still laced with tears; but when they sat down on the steps again, the handkerchief dangled loosely from her fingers.

'And what of Kitty?' Molly asked. 'Or should I say Polly Peachum?'

They both giggled; then Annie's face darkened. 'She's restless,' she said. Molly frowned an unspoken question. Annie screwed up her face: she didn't know the answer. 'She's not a child any more. She can't even play the child.'

'We all of us grow up at some time. But Kitty's play-acting keeps her younger than she is.'

'Not any more,' Annie contradicted her. 'Mother Wickham's customers may be depraved, debauched, evil. But they're not fools. All the stockings in The Bell aren't enough to make her flat-breasted now. Even if the Twins carried on shaving her cunny, her tits would mark her out as a woman, not a child. Just another harlot. But,' she added wryly, 'a harlot with a bald cunny is something to be avoided.'

Molly dipped her head to show she understood. The pox made all your hair fall out.

Annie continued. 'Kitty used to be there for the men who wanted something special, something only a child could offer.' Her lip curled. 'They used to treat her differently from the way my visitors treat me, differently from the way the Colonel treated you. Now, they treat her the same way they treat Nan and Polly and the Twins.'

'But she used to be a different person for every visitor. Why must she change now?' Part question, part despair for Kitty. What was the Waif without play-acting?

Annie smiled; but the smile was humourless, tired, cynical. 'When she was a child, her visitors treated her like a child - because that's what they were paying for. But now she's a woman, and her new visitors are a different breed. Now, she's just another piece of meat. They come, they fuck her, they leave. They don't see her when they're there, they don't remember her when they've gone. Usually, they're drunk.

185

And once they've paid their money, as long as they've got something warm and wet to stick their pricks into, they're content.' She was no longer talking about the Waif. 'A cunny is a cunny. It doesn't matter whose face is above it. If it belonged to a goat, most of them wouldn't notice.' She was twisting the handkerchief again: wind, draw tight, retrieve. 'If they ever come to The Bell again, the only person they'll recognise is Mother Wickham.'

'But Kitty has friends.'

'Kitty? Friends?' Contempt washed over Annie's face. 'The bishops and magistrates who used to visit her have already forgotten her. To Mother Wickham, she's an item for sale. To Nan and Polly, she's the harlot who doesn't have to work late into the night. To the Twins, now they don't get the pleasure of shaving her every morning, she's of no interest. Oh, once upon a time she was useful to them. She used to sit with the babies when the girls were working. But one baby's dead, and the other's dying. The Twins have got no use for Kitty any more.'

Molly thought carefully before speaking. 'And you?'

Annie flashed a glance at her, then turned back to the river. 'I taught Kitty to read and write,' she said. 'I told her stories to quiet her when she didn't know why these men who said they loved her did things that hurt her. I remembered all the dreams I'd had when I was young and frightened, the dreams that helped me get through the bad days, and I told them to Kitty. We pretended that... I told her she was a princess who'd been stolen by gypsies, that one day a handsome prince on a white horse would carry her away to an enchanted kingdom, and she'd be... she'd be...' Her voice broke, and she started to sob.

Molly gathered her friend in her arms and hugged her to her. 'Kitty needs you to be her friend,' she told her.

Annie wiped the back of her hand across her eyes, sighed deeply, lost herself in her own world. 'When I was not yet eighteen, my handsome prince carried me away,' she said. 'We lived as man and wife for so very few months. And we had a baby. A little girl. My Caroline.' A minute or more while her memories tumbled from joy to despair. 'The happiness I had in those few months can never make up for the misery I've had since. I lost my Billy, and I lost my baby. And all because I ran away from Mother Wickham.' She disengaged herself from Molly's embrace and rose to her feet. 'Kitty needs you to be her friend, Moll, not me.'

Molly stood. She didn't understand. 'But I live in Chiswick now, You live with her, at The Bell.'

'Yes, I live at The Bell.' There was no life in her voice. 'And Mother Wickham can read my thoughts as easily as she can read a ledger. If Kitty ever told me a secret, Mother Wickham would be sure to find out.'

'What secret?'

Annie paused before replying. 'Soon, Kitty will run away. And Mother Wickham will send Jed after her. When that happens, the only chance she'll have of escaping is if none of us at The Bell knows where she's running to.' She climbed away from the river, up towards Thames Street, where Abraham's footmen stood guard. At the top, she looked down at Molly. 'I dare not be Kitty's friend. You're the only friend she's got, Moll.'

Chapter 18

The eighth day of September. A Wednesday. Her birthday.

Without noticing, she'd sped from seventeen-year-old virgin to the twenty-year-old mistress of father and son.

She lay awake in the pre-dawn darkness, and tried to remember the birthdays between. What had she been doing two years ago today? Lying on her back for the Colonel? Kneeling on the bed while he took her from behind? Standing against the wall, feeling the plaster scraping rough against her buttocks as he thrust brutally into her, jolting her off her feet with every stroke? Being caressed or beaten, rewarded or punished, tempted with peaches or gagging on his seed? Had she been paraded at the theatre, or ravished in her room?

She couldn't remember. Whatever the Colonel had been doing, he'd stolen her eighteenth birthday from her. And her nineteenth, too. That was the day he'd chosen to hang her monkey.

Her jaw tightened and her lips clenched with the obstinacy her father used to tease her about. The Colonel frightened her to whimpering, but never once in all her time at The Bell had she tried to please him.

Despite everything he'd done to her, she'd won. So far.

The weather was fairy-tale perfect, as birthdays are in dreams. Dawn was misty but bright, and soon cleared into a crisp, clear morning with a promise of warmth to come. The birds, muted at first, soon busied themselves outside her bedroom window and under the eaves, chirruping and singing, never once squabbling the way they did in spring.

Hannah hinted at a surprise to come. 'I think something cotton, Miss Molly.' She plucked the silk out of Molly's hand and laid it on the bed, smoothing it free of creases.

'It's my birthday, Hannah,' said Molly. She picked up the shimmering olive green gown again, feeling it slide sensuously against her skin. 'Today, I wish to feel like a princess.' Unlike Annie, unlike the Waif, she had someone to clothe her dream for her.

'But cotton will be more comfortable in the sunshine.' Practical Hannah, reminding her of reality. Again, the silk was taken from her.

Molly accepted the maid's judgement, and worked her hands and arms into the simple pink dress she held out for her. 'Are we to be in the sunshine today, Hannah? What do you know that I don't know?'

A broad grin, and an easy chuckle. 'A secret, Miss Molly.'

'A secret secret? Or a telling secret?'

'A secret that everybody knows but you, Miss Molly. And you'll know it within the hour.' She turned her mistress away from her and began to pull the laces tight on the back of the dress.

Breakfast was, as usual, simple. For once, Isaac was there to eat it with them. Abraham had no work in the City that day, and was more jovial than Molly had seen him in several weeks.

At the end of the meal, Abraham rose to his feet and made an announcement. 'It is Molly's birthday. And, since the morning is fair - as it should be for Molly's birthday - we shall all spend the day together.'

Her face shone with excitement. 'In London?'

No, not in London. The Colonel remained a threat. She was to spend her birthday in Chiswick. She managed to keep the enthusiasm on her face, but she could feel the disappointment dragging her back to earth. Despite its dangers, London was London; Chiswick was smaller even than York.

Abraham had hired a waterman for the day to row them the short distance upstream to Chiswick Eyot. As the oars splashed rhythmically in and out of the water, Abraham pointed out all the landmarks of interest as they passed them. 'Mark that spire... That large house is the home of... Behind that copse there was a notorious murder... Beyond that hill lies... See where the fish make ripples as they feed...'

While Abraham conducted Molly round the willow-dripping island, not much larger than his own modest estate, the waterman rowed back and forth between the island and the waiting cart on the north bank, ferrying first Isaac, Hannah and Okoro; then Silver and a dozen large wicker baskets; and finally the two mastiffs, Berry and Crab, and a large, muscular man Molly had never seen before, a man who said nothing, whose eyes were never still, and whose waist bulged with uneven lumps beneath his unfastened coat.

The sun climbed high up into the sky. They strolled or sat or idled under the trees, masters and servants alike, chatting, laughing, enjoying the warmth and the tranquillity. Only the stranger stood apart, occasionally sharing a pipe of tobacco with the waterman.

Near the water's edge, Molly sat with her back against a willow, her legs stretched out in front of her, Abraham, Isaac and Hannah ranged about her like a court.

She looked beyond them to the drifting Thames. So different from York, so different from The Bell. She admired the elegant houses on the opposite bank of the wide river, watched the water swirl the early yellow leaves of autumn past her, sipped at river-chilled French wine, nibbled at fresh bread and spiced beef and pungent horseradish and earth-smelling tomatoes.

The iridescent turquoise of a kingfisher flashed from nowhere, skimmed the surface of the river, then revealed a glimpse of vermilion breast as it swooped up into the overhanging branches on the bank and became invisible again. Butterflies danced, dragonflies hovered, bees hummed from clover-head to wild thyme, from the mauve bells of mallow to the pinhead white stars of chickweed.

Lazy in the sun, sleepy with wine, Molly dozed content. Abraham gazed on her with affection, and smiled. Isaac gazed on her with love, and scowled.

Mistress Silver had been busy while they'd been in the sun, and the table in the eating room was a cornucopia of food. Beef, mutton, capon; eels, perch, pike; pies and puddings, sallets and vegetables, sweetmeats and fruit. And, rearing up in the centre of the table, a poached salmon, poised as if leaping a weir.

Molly gaped in at the magnificence of the feast. 'All this for us?' Her eyes were wide in disbelief. 'We can never eat as much as that!' Abraham steered her past the open door to the staircase. 'Perhaps if we had some help?' he suggested.

Hannah was on hand to lead her, protesting, to her room. Then to take an age over dressing her hair. Then to take even more time arranging her in her finest deep-red gown, a gown not as luxurious against her body as the silk, but sumptuous with embroidery, square-necked, pleat-fronted, lace-cuffed, caught up at the side to reveal the pink and gold striped taffeta petticoat. A gown to impress. Last of all, a linen cap trimmed with lace, interwoven with a red ribbon to match the gown. The picture of fashion, dressed, coiffed, perfumed.

As Hannah stepped back to admire her, Molly yawned and pretended to take her revenge for not being told the secret. 'The sun... the fresh air... the river... the wine...' she said. 'I'm so tired, Hannah. I think I shall go to bed now.'

She enjoyed the maid's look of dismay for a moment, then relented and hugged her to her. 'Who's coming? How many? Is it to be a ball?'

Hannah put her finger to her lips, forgiving her, but maintaining the charade. 'It's a secret, Miss Molly,' she whispered.

Molly made a grand entrance down the main staircase, her gown flowing out behind her, Okoro in golden tunic and feathered turban, holding her skirts clear of the stairs, the musicians playing a dignified pavan. Hannah, having transformed her duckling into a swan, stayed up in the gallery to watch until Molly had safely mingled with the knot of admirers waiting for her. The house was full of friends, all there to celebrate Molly's birthday. All there to applaud when Abraham fastened a magnificent necklace of graded pearls round her neck.

All Abraham's friends.

But then, what friends of her own did Molly have in London? Only, by an accident of debauchery, Annie and the Waif. Two other Cheapside whores. Not the sort of friends the 'companion' of a City-rich landowner should have. Certainly not the sort of guests who would be invited to a birthday celebration.

So only Abraham's friends were there to share her joy when she opened Isaac's present, a modestly-wrapped package containing a simple ring of gold and rust-coloured striped agate.

She stood on tiptoe and kissed him on the cheek, to a pattering of applause. A chaste kiss, as was appropriate between a harlot and the son of her keeper.

'A witch told me it would make you invisible, and turn your enemies' swords against themselves,' he muttered.

The ring cost much less than the pearls.

It meant much more.

Her twentieth birthday had been very nearly perfect.

Weather more suited to summer than autumn, Chiswick and Barnes from the river, a day of idleness on the Eyot, expensive gifts, a banquet, a ball. Very nearly perfect, but not quite.

In the early hours of the morning, when the last guests had left, when Hannah had taken the princess's gown and stowed it away in the oak chest, when Molly was naked in her bed, her left hand caressing the ring on her right hand, the bedroom door opened.

The shape silhouetted against the candlelight was unmistakably male.

But it was Wednesday.

It was Abraham who came to her bed, not Isaac.

Chapter 19

The day after her birthday ball, Molly rested.

She slept late. Then, dozing, she indulged herself with dreams of what might have been, what might yet be, fairy tale dreams of happy ever after. When, at last, she decided to wake, she gave Hannah the day to herself. She splashed water on her face, but she didn't dress. For the rest of the day she read, dozed, read. But The Fortunes and Misfortunes of the Famous Moll Flanders prompted too many uncomfortable thoughts, and she put it aside.

As the sun went down, she sat at the window and gazed out across the meadows, watching the shadows creep towards her, watching the light change from gold to pink to warm grey, and then to cool silver as the swollen moon took over from the sun.

She could feel her mind emptying, her eyelids closing. Enjoying the sensuous slide out of lazy day into indolent night, she faltered her way to her bed and fell asleep.

It was Thursday, but Isaac didn't come to her.

Monday at dawn. As she'd asked, Hannah woke her for what the girls called Squish-day.

Silver protested. It wasn't right, harvesting fruit was a job for servants, Master Abraham's companion should set an example, she'd distract the other girls from their work, the day promised to be hot.

But Molly insisted. 'I don't know much, Silver,' she said, 'but I know about dressmaking, I know about pigs, and I know about fruit and vegetables. I've been gathering everything from strawberries to apples since I were able to pick up my first windfall.'

And, before the sun was fully up, she'd joined Hannah and the rest of the women working in the orchard.

The tasks were mechanical, her muscles soon began to ache, Silver's prediction about the hot sun came true, and the perspiration was soon trickling down her face, under her armpits, between her breasts.
But, for the first time in weeks, she wasn't bored.

It had been more than six months since the riot at the playhouse, and Abraham still wouldn't let her leave the house without his permission, and without at least six or seven guards. It wasn't the scale of harvest she'd been used to, but her choice this day was simple: join them, sit and watch them, or hide away somewhere in the house and sulk.

In York, harvest was a gradual affair, each fruit being gathered at its peak of ripeness. In Chiswick, harvest meant a mass assault on the orchard to strip it of everything not yet gathered, before the birds, the wasps and the cloudless nights claimed it.

Plump pink and yellow peaches; purple damsons; acid greengages; late-ripening plums and apricots; the last of the gooseberries. Even a few early apples; but most of them stayed on the trees for the next harvest, six weeks later at the end of October.

Okoro and the other children gathered up the fallen fruit and piled it into huge wicker baskets for Mistress Silver to pick over and load into the bubbling vats that later solidified like magic into sweet jams and sharp pickles, steaming pies and sticky puddings. The younger servant girls squealed as they gathered in basket after basket of blackberries, staining their fingers purple and painting each other's faces with the juice whenever they had the chance.

Nobody touched the crabapples, more like large, blush-golden rose hips than apples. They stayed on the branches, waiting for the expert hand of Silver himself to determine when they were ready to be transmuted into his highly-spiced and jealously-guarded jelly.

Molly was happy to be working, hitching up her skirts and clambering up into the trees to stretch for the red-black starbursts of elderberries near the top, balancing on forked branches several feet above the ground, remembering the childhood harvests in York.

When Isaac joined them, they'd already breakfasted on cheese and bread, and were slaking their thirsts, swigging from flagons of small beer, sitting in the sun by the river before attacking the next swathe of trees.

He sat down on the grass beside her. As the other girls began to rise to their feet, Molly waved them to sit down again. 'Master Silver will tell us when it's time to start work again,' she said. 'Master Isaac has joined us so that he can look up our skirts when we're climbing in the trees.'

There was a shocked silence. Then Rebecca put her hand over her mouth; a strangled snort squeezed through her nose, gasping into a helpless wheeze as her mouth opened. Though her lips were pressed shut, Hannah's eyes bulged and her shoulders crept up almost to her ears before she was at last unable to contain the laughter, and it burst out of her in a barnyard squawk. Prompted so audibly, the rest of the girls collapsed, hooting and heaving and cackling and guffawing, holding each other and rolling on the grass. The dogs barked and wagged their tails, enjoying the enjoyment.

Isaac leapt to his feet, his face clouding. Then he, too, relaxed, sank back onto the grass, and joined in the joke at his own expense. His hand strayed out, and he brushed his fingers against the back of Molly's hand.

When Silver called the giggling girls back to the orchard, Molly stayed with Isaac.

'You didn't come to me last night,' she said.

'I did,' he protested. 'You were asleep. I didn't want to disturb you.'

But that wasn't what was on her mind. When, at last, she spoke, it was in a low voice, and she didn't look at him. 'You mustn't tell him,' she said.

'I have money of my own,' he replied. 'He can't hurt me.'

She lifted her head sharply. 'If he finds out, it will hurt him.' She waited for her point to strike home, then continued. 'He's a good man, Isaac. He's been good to me, and I don't want to repay him with unkindness. We must not hurt him. You must promise me you'll never let him know.'

He said nothing, weighing her demands against his own. At last he gave in to her. 'I shall never tell him. You have my word.' He watched the fruit-picking girls for a while. 'Everybody else in the household knows. How can we be sure they won't tell him?'

'They won't,' she told him. 'Silver might - but only if you drive him to it. He hates us for it. But he loves your father more than he hates us.'

'Silver? He's just a servant. He can't - '

'No! He's not just a servant. He's part of your father's family. Far more so than I can ever be.'

'But you're - '

'I'm just your father's mistress, Isaac. I'm just a whore who was lucky.' She could hear Silver's voice saying it. 'But Silver is your father's friend. And he's a Jew, while I'm just a - '

Isaac dismissed the point with an irritable flounce of his hand. 'So you're a Christian. So what difference should that make?'

She held up a finger to correct him. 'Not a Christian, Isaac. A goya. I'm just a goya.'

'My father doesn't think of you as a goya. And neither do I.'

'No. But Silver does. And that's why you must never provoke him into telling your father about us. If he did, he could badly hurt him. But he'd have righteousness and truth and justice on his side.' She stared resolutely at him. 'Everybody has a line they won't cross, Isaac. Even faithful old servants like Silver. Don't draw that line for him.'

Isaac picked up a pebble, flicked it into the shallows at the edge of the river. For several moments he watched the ripples as they were caught by the current and swirled into nothingness; then he nodded his agreement. 'I won't,' he said.

She rose to her feet. 'Good.' She mouthed a secret kiss at him. 'Now there are plums to be gathered.' She turned away to join the servant girls in the orchard.

They sat in the eating room, the tea-table set near one of the windows, facing south towards the river across the tangle of pink roses fringeing the late-September gardens.

'I've become used to it, Isaac,' she said, 'but I still wonder at it. This is the wealthiest house I've ever been in.' Apart from the Colonel's. But she could remember nothing of that except the delicate teacups.

She looked round her at the room they stood in, and spread her arms. The gesture took in the high, decorated ceiling, the bas-relief frieze below it, the classical architrave above the door and the Doric columns supporting it, the red and gold figured wallpaper, the carved chairs and footstools, the exotic rugs on the polished wood floor. 'Where did all your wealth come from?' She was genuinely curious. In York, the people with money either owned land, or sported a title, or wore a bishop's mitre. None of them were Jews.

He sipped at his tea, buying himself time in which to think, then placed his cup and saucer down on the slender-legged table at his knee. 'We lend money,' he said, almost embarrassed to admit it.

'Aye, I know that.' And she understood the principle of loans and interest. Her father had been in debt. In less than two years, he'd paid more than twice what he'd borrowed - but the problem the borrowed money had been intended to solve hadn't gone away. 'But where did you get the money to lend in the first place? Have you always been rich?'

'No. Not always.' The tension in Isaac's face smoothed into something akin to pride. 'Father invested in the South Sea Company.'

Molly wrinkled her nose ruefully. 'So did mine. That's how he nearly lost the farm.'

Isaac rose and walked about the room, seeing it for the first time in years, noticing the treasures he had come to take for granted. 'That's how father made so much money. He didn't trust them. When they raised the share value to a thousand pounds, father said it was far too much. So he sold instead of buying. He bought at a hundred and twenty eight, and sold at over eight hundred. And then the bubble burst.' He stopped on the opposite side of the room. 'I invested, too. But father made me sell at less than seven hundred.' His shoulders bunched and his eyes darkened. 'I have money of my own, Molly. But I could have had even more if father had left me alone.'

She was reluctant to contradict him; he didn't like to be wrong. But she had a point to make. 'No, Isaac. Your father was right. He gambled, and won - but only just in time. My father gambled, and left it just too late. Your father was protecting you, Isaac.' She softened her voice. 'He's a good man. And he loves you.'

Silence. When, at last, Isaac spoke, his voice was tight. 'He loves you, too.'

She shook her head. 'No. He doesn't love me. He treasures me.' A sweep of her hand took in the entire room. 'His paintings, his porcelain, his fine wines - they're all there for display, to let people see what his money can buy. And so with his mistress. I'm a possession, Isaac. I'm here to be displayed when necessary, and to be kept safe at all other times.'

'You're wrong. He loves you. I've known him with...' He hesitated. '... others. He never loved any of them.' He swung away from her, his fists clenched. 'My father loves you, Molly.'

She crossed to him, laid her hand on his sleeve. 'Why are you so angry?'

He shrugged his arm away. 'I shall never love you.'

'Isaac?'

'Kubed et awichah,' he muttered, resentment staining his voice.

197

'Honour thy father. Commit no adultery. Covet not thy neighbour's wife. Nor his ox, nor his ass, nor his whore!' He rounded on her, a savage snarl on his lips. 'I can never love you, Molly! The laws of my people forbid me to love you!'

Without looking back, he strode past her, out of the room, out of the house. A few minutes later, she heard his horse leaving at breakneck speed.

Chapter 20

Abraham's skinny frame was silhouetted against the dying fire as he dressed himself. She waited until he'd put on his stockings, breeches and shirt before calling softly to him. 'Abraham?'

Safely covered, he turned to her. 'What is it, my dear?'

'Isaac says you conduct your business at the Royal Exchange.'

He bent to pull on his shoes. 'The Royal Exchange. Garraway's. Change Alley. The Custom House. A man does business wherever there is business to be done.' He reached for his waistcoat, folded neatly at the foot of the bed. 'Why do you ask Isaac about my business?'

From the darkness of the curtained bed, she said 'I don't ask him about your business. I asked him about the Royal Exchange.'

'You wish to become an investor?' She couldn't see his face, but she could hear the gentle mockery in his voice, almost see the smile on his lips. Mockery without malice. She imagined herself a child, knowing that it changed the pitch of her voice, knowing that it made Abraham willing to give her anything she wanted. 'I've been in London for two and a half years, Abraham,' she pleaded, 'yet I've never seen the Royal Exchange.'

In her heart she begged forgiveness for the lie: the Royal Exchange was less than half a mile from The Bell, and she and the Waif had often gone there to wonder at the fashions, to mock the fops, to observe the women of the town so that they could ape their manners. But, after so many months of being cooped up in the Chiswick house, she had to escape. Luxury was no substitute for freedom.

Abraham's response surprised her. His head shook vehemently against the firelight. 'No! Forgive me, Molly, but no. It's a place for thieves and idlers. A place for wastrels and harlots. Please believe me, Molly, the Exchange is no place for a respectable woman.'

Her abrupt laugh had an edge of irony. 'Respectable, Abraham? Me?' The Colonel's cast-off? The harlot who's shared by father and son? The Chiswick Whore?

He hurried to the bedside, blotting out the light from the fire. 'Never doubt it, Molly.' In the deep shadow, she couldn't see the concern in his face.

199

Neither could he see the torment in hers. 'Others do.'

'Others see nothing but their own failings reflected in the people around them. What do these others know of you?'

What indeed? Hannah knew about her and Isaac. Despite her promise of secrecy, Hannah had undoubtedly whispered it to Rebecca and Miriam. Silver and Mistress Silver must have guessed. Who else knew? The rest of the household, the rest of Chiswick, the rest of London probably. Everybody except Abraham.

She took his hand to reassure him. 'You're right, Abraham,' she said. 'They know nothing of me.'

'Always remember that, Molly. They know nothing of you. Only you and I know the truth.'

She pressed herself against him, and kissed him on the lips. 'Please, Abraham, please may I go to the Exchange? Just once, so I can write to my brothers and tell them I've been to the famous Royal Exchange. Please?'

'Colonel Charnell has already tried to harm you, and - '

'No - the Colonel tried to harm you, Abraham. And when he couldn't find you, he killed another... He killed somebody else.' He killed another Jew.

In York, the Jews were different. They didn't join in the routs, or the May Fair, or in any of the other festivals. Perhaps, because most of the festivals were Christian, they weren't invited. For whatever reason, until she came to London, she'd never spoken to a Jew, and rarely had occasion even to think of them. But what was a Jew? Apart from their Friday prayers and their Saturday sabbath, Abraham and Isaac were people like any other people. And, especially Abraham, kinder than most.

'The Jew and his whore, that's who I want punished,' said Abraham. It took her a moment to realise he was quoting the Colonel.

'But that were seven or eight months ago, Abraham.' Little girl, whee-dling. 'Surely it must be safe now?'

'While Colonel Charnell lives, it will never be safe.'

'Please, Abraham.'

He remained statue-still, his head cocked to one side, his business-man's mind weighing the risk against the reward. His fear against her need; the possibility of her being attacked against the certainty of her becoming bored. 'Yes,' he said at last. 'Isaac shall take you to the Royal Exchange. That should be safe enough.'

✻

Dogs barking, horses whinnying, carriage-wheels, street-cries, curses. Perfume, horse-shit, sweat, tobacco. Silk cravats, embroidered petticoats, velvet cloaks, brocaded waistcoats. And, of course, rags and begging bowls, cutpurse knives and the greedy promises of harlots.

The sounds, the smells, the colours of Cornhill were unmistakable, a witches' brew of salon and gutter, coffee-house and Tyburn. Sweeter than Wood Street, coarser than Covent Garden, richer than Chiswick, predators and prey bonded publicly together by the itch for money.

'There,' Molly said to Hannah, pointing. 'The Royal Exchange.' She crouched beside Okoro and pointed again. 'All the money in the world passes through the Royal Exchange,' she told him. She couldn't remember where she'd heard it said, but it was easy to believe it was true.

Ahead of them, the soaring stone arch at the entrance drew their eyes up and up to the three-tiered tower above it, framed by wispy white clouds and a September-blue sky. Below, the colonnaded walk was packed with traders exchanging services for silver, goods for gold: fruit-sellers and brokers, prostitutes and pewterers, ship-owners and musicians.

Molly and Hannah followed Isaac through the archway and into the main courtyard, each tightly clutching one of Okoro's hands.

Just a few feet, and they were inside the Royal Exchange itself: a hundred yards long, fifty yards wide, and not a square inch unoccupied.

The pervasive smell of money. Money earned, money gambled, money won, money lost. Money hoped for, despaired for, whored for. Etched into every face, the bright-eyed risk of bankruptcy, the feverish risk of disgrace, the reckless risk of hanging.

They jostled a path over the flagstones towards the pagoda-like pavilions at the far end; but the effort soon proved more than their progress warranted. Molly forced herself in front of Isaac. 'Where does Abraham conduct his business?' She had to shout above the transactions going on around her.

'Not here,' Isaac growled, defensive, almost embarrassed, his voice too low to be heard.

But she read his lips. 'Where then?'

Isaac's mouth and eyebrows were tense, sullen, frowning. 'Have you seen enough?'

Abraham had money, he dealt in money, and the Royal Exchange was where people dealt in money. Yet not where Abraham dealt in money. Was there some secret to be hidden? 'If not here, Isaac, then where?'

Without speaking, he turned and pushed back through the crowds, ill-temperedly elbowing his way towards the archway. Molly and Hannah followed him, dragging Okoro with them.

Out of the Royal Exchange, across crowded Cornhill, dodging the prancing carriages, tugging free of the child-beggars' plucking fingers, plunging into the sunless ant-swarm of Change Alley.

The air was just as pungent as the Exchange, but there was more sweat, less perfume, more desperation. The cacophony of voices had an overtone of pleading, and an undertone of calculation.

Change Alley, like Smithfield, like Billingsgate, was a market. But instead of meat or fish, its commodity was money. Stalls built ramshackle against the walls, housing jewellers, money-lenders, pawnbrokers. Tables in the street, with creditors poising their quills above agreements, and debtors slumped miserably opposite them. Blustering losers trying to bully impassive-eyed winners. Married women begging on behalf of their ruined husbands, their breasts blossoming out of their bodices in vain hope of diverting the issue, in equally vain hope of paying off the debt in kind. Children weeping their entreaties while their anxious parents peeped from behind the stalls and prayed for the first time in their lives. Loudest of all, the huckster temptations of harsh-voiced brokers in gaudy fashions, flourishing leather-bound, gold-blocked prospectuses.

'Here?' said Molly.

'Not here!' Isaac cleared a path for them through the petitioners, the buyers, the sellers. And, inevitably, the harlots, the pickpockets, the cutpurses. Wherever there's money, there's somebody looking to steal it. Ahead of them a slab-stone wall of round-arched, twelve-paned windows, separated by Palladian pillars. Above the door, a carved name. Garraway's.

'Where is this?' bawled Hannah above the noise.

'Garraway's!' She'd heard the name before. 'Coffee-house!'

Hannah was puzzled. 'Coffee?'

'Isaac will explain!'

Instead, Isaac thrust open the door and pulled Molly inside past the protesting steward, and strode to the middle of the high-ceilinged room. One hand gripped in Molly's, the other in Hannah's, Okoro was drawn in with them. Like a danse macabre, the four snaked into the hot and heady, smoke-laden atmosphere of London's unofficial financial centre.

'Father? Father!'

'Isaac?' Abraham made his way between the tables to them. 'What is the meaning of this?' His voice was friendly; his body was relaxed. Only the set of his jaw betrayed his anger. 'Why have you brought Molly in here?' His lips smiled; his eyes didn't. 'This is not a peepshow, Isaac. Garraway's is not Bedlam, nor Newgate, nor anywhere else for bored ladies to pass an idle afternoon. Now, Isaac, if you have money to invest, stay. If Molly has money to invest, I will ask Master Garraway if she may stay. Whether they have money or not, Hannah and the child must leave.' He shrugged an apology. 'Please forgive me, Molly. The rules are those of the proprietor, not mine.'

Molly accepted the ruling without disappointment. 'Of course, Abraham. Please don't blame Isaac. I insisted he brought me here.' She took Hannah's arm and ushered her and Okoro ahead of her. At the door, she turned back to Abraham. 'We are here only because Isaac has business here. We'll wait outside for him.'

Isaac, caught between Molly and his father, delayed a fraction of a second too long. By the time he'd made up his mind, it was too late. Molly, Okoro and Hannah were outside, and Abraham was cursing him for making them both look fools in front of important clients.

By the time their argument had resolved itself, Isaac's charges were several minutes gone.

It was eerie.

Middle of the day, middle of the week. And Wood Street almost deserted. No drays, no street-sellers, no beggars. Just echoing walls, gently creaking shop-signs and the occasional cry of despair from a debtor in the Compter.

'There, Hannah,' Molly said, pointing. 'There's The Bell. That's where my life of infamy began.' Half-teasing, half-bitter. Hannah already knew the story. She could never know the truth.

Hannah shrank into herself, sidled to her left, putting Molly between her and The Bell. Her voice tremored into a croak, catching in fright. 'Is that Mother Wickham?' In her mind, Mother Wickham could debauch a nun simply by looking at her.

Molly whirled, defensive. 'Mother Wickham?' She eased and straightened. The fear on her face melted away. 'No, Hannah, not Mother Wickham.'

Annie stood beside the front door with Jed, the house keys in her hand. The Bell's girls came tumbling out into the street, chattering excitedly. The Twins, Polly, Nan. Last of all, Abigail.

Molly called out. 'Annie!' All the girls looked behind them to see who was calling, waved perfunctorily, carried on down Wood Street in the direction of the river.

But Abigail had caught sight of her son. 'Okoro!' Her shriek of joy bounced back off the walls.

The turbaned boy let go of Hannah's hand and rushed to greet his mother. They collided in the middle of the street, and she swept Okoro up into her arms, hugging him to her, tears flooding down her wild-eyed but beaming face. A jabber of Nigerian dialect washed over the boy.

Annie called out. 'Moll! Go ahead with Kitty - I'll follow you once we've locked up. Let Okoro stay with Abigail till we get back.' She turned to give Jed the keys.

The Waif came flying out of the house. 'Moll?' She caught sight of her, sprinted across the street and hurled herself into Molly's arms, driving her backward.

'Ow!' Hannah hopped away, bending to nurse the foot Molly had trodden on.

The Waif wrapped her legs round Molly's waist and covered her with kisses - her face, her neck, her throat, her ears, her lips.

'Kitty!' Molly held her away from her, astonished at the younger girl's exuberance. 'Are you that pleased to see me?'

'Yes, Moll! Yes, I am, I am!' More kisses. 'And,' her voice dropped to a

204

murmur, 'I want to make the Twins jealous.'

'You're starting to get heavy,' Molly told her, swinging her to the ground again.

The Waif caught her hand and hustled her after the rest of the girls; Hannah trailed behind, hobbling painfully. 'It's my bubs,' Kitty explained, using her free hand to push her breasts upwards as she skipped down the sloping cobbles towards Cheapside; laced, whale-boned, squeezed together, they still did little to disturb the straight line of her bodice. 'I haven't grown, but my bubs have. They're bursting out like a pig's bladder, only filled with lead. If I don't beware when I get out of bed, I pitch over onto my face with the weight of them.' She giggled, then called to the limping Hannah behind them. 'Giddy-up, cart-horse - we don't want to miss it all!'

'Slow down, Kitty!' Molly implored her, struggling to keep up with the excited girl. 'Why are we in such a hurry? Where are we going?'

The Waif let go of her hand, raced ahead a few paces, leapt round to face her again, flung her arms dramatically aloft. 'To Southwark Fair!' she proclaimed.

Molly waited for Hannah to catch them up. 'Southwark Fair?' One of the biggest carnivals of the year. 'Won't you be expecting visitors?'

The Waif grinned. 'Not till this evening,' she said. 'The sixpenny harlots in the alleyways take all the daytime trade during the Fair. So Mother Wickham's given us the whole afternoon off.' She took Molly's hand again and led her onwards. 'We've got until six o'clock to enjoy the sideshows!'

To Cheapside and along, in the same direction as everybody else. Through the maze of midden alleys to Thames Street. Past Coal Wharf, with the rotting-fish stench of Billingsgate drifting downwind, upstream. Onto London Bridge and across, out of the City of London, into the stews of Southwark.

The noise, the press was as great here as it was at the Royal Exchange; but here, it was all laughter and drunkenness, music and abandonment.

As they passed under a painted wooden arch that spanned the road, the Waif stopped and pointed to it. 'This,' she read out, derision taint-ing her voice, 'is the inn where Sir Jeffry Chaucer and the nine and twenty pilgrims lay, in the journey to Canterbury, anno 1383.'

Molly let her gaze go up to the inscription. 'Is it?' She remembered from her schooling that there had been some travellers who were famous for having gone to Canterbury.

The Waif pointed at the signboard hanging outside the inn. 'This is called the Talbot Inn,' she said. 'Chaucer's inn was called the Tabard Inn. Everybody knows that!' She tilted her nose and chin upwards like her vision of a grand lady. 'We shall not patronise such wanton false-hood, my dear Countess Moll,' she said. 'Let us walk on!'

But, in a moment, her resolve was shattered. As she skipped aside to avoid a brawl which spilled noisily out of the inn and into the road, four men with more ale than malice in them, four drunks content to deliver more threats than blows, there came the sound of a drum.

At the entrance to the inn's courtyard, a crippled black boy, some two or three years older than Okoro, stood on an empty barrel and banged on a drum nearly as tall as himself. Beyond him, on a rickety, curtain-backed trestle-stage, stood a pasty-faced young woman with loose greasy hair, several deep pock-marks on her forehead, two crudely-cut fabric stars on her left cheek, and a weeping sore at the corner of her mouth. She was dressed in a crumpled robe that had once been white, and was crowned with a flaking gilt circlet, a cobra's head rearing above it. A live brown and cream snake draped itself lethargically over her shoulders.

The Waif seized Molly's arm and dragged her forward. 'Cleopatra!' she said, the excitement lighting up her face.

The woman's voice shrilled above the hubbub of the crowd. 'Good people, draw near, and you shall see a famous tragical history.'

The Waif bobbed up and down, pulling Molly along with her, ducking beneath elbows, squeezing between couples, bumping the unwary, worming herself and her friend as near the front as she could. 'Did I not tell you!' she said. 'Tis a play! We must see it!'

The boy beat the drum again, and the actress continued. 'Cleopatra, gracious Queen of the Nile, was great Caesar's paramour for a while.' She waved a hand, and a middle-aged, balding actor with gin-soaked eyes stepped from behind a roughly-hung curtain. The noble pose he struck was marred by the food-stains down the front of his toga. 'And after Caesar, you must know, was loved by - '

'Mark Antonio!' The Waif spoke the name in unison with the actress, who flashed a searching look at her, deciding whether she was audience or rival. Kitty's glowing excitement convinced her, and she again stretched out her arm. This time, a pale youth in a knee-length tunic and battered breastplate made an uncertain entrance. His face screwed up into a spasm as his haughty expression dissolved into a dry cough.

The actress waited for the smattering of applause to die away. 'And then, denied her wanton passion, did kill herself in fatal fashion, and her own life did cruelly take by biting her breast with deadly - snake!' With a rehearsed lurch, she thrust her hand out towards the audience, and the snake yawned its mouth wide, hissing, its tongue flicking in and out. The crowd reared back, some squealing in delicious fright, some cheering it on in gin-bolstered bravado. As the pattern of bodies eddied about them, Kitty wriggled Molly nearer the stage.

Cleopatra held the tame snake out at arm's length, and flung out her challenge. 'Does any among you dare approach this vile serpent?'

The Waif squirmed to the front and stretched out a hand to touch the listless reptile. But the actress knew her trade. She snatched the creature away, and called 'Protect the poor child! She knows not what she does! Only the Queen of the Nile can tame this savage beast. And even she succumbs to its treacherous poison in the end. Now, good people, who will come to see our play? For only sixpence, you can witness for yourself the glorious loves and the lamentable tragedy of Cleopatra, Queen of the Nile. Good people, give your money to -' She flung out her hand in a dramatic gesture. '- the Grand Eunuch of Egypt!' The Grand Eunuch swept the curtain aside and stepped onto the stage.

This was no pale and puffy, squeaky-voiced gelding. At first glance he appeared short and squat, his shaven black head seeming to spring direct from his naked, oiled shoulders with no neck to support it, his shoulders the same width as his loin-clothed hips, his colossal thighs turning his measured gait into a waddle. But, as he moved forward to join Cleopatra, he became bigger and bigger until, when he stood beside her, her head came up no higher than the bulging veins outlining the massive biceps crossed against his chest.

This was no eunuch. This was a titan. And, to complete the effect, a glinting scimitar dangled at his waist. If the good people listening to Cleopatra had any thoughts of watching the play without paying, those thoughts vanished the instant her fellow actor appeared.

He drew his sword and brandished it, jumping down from the stage to threaten the crowd back to the very entrance of the courtyard.

The Waif scrabbled in her purse. 'Here!' she cried. 'Here! Sixpence!' She urged the coins into the negro's hand, then counted again. 'And sixpence for Moll!' More delving, more coins. 'And another for Moll's friend!'

Hannah held back. 'Is it safe?'

'The snake is a tame snake,' Molly promised her, 'and its teeth have been drawn. It can't harm you.'

'And neither can the eunuch,' the Waif added. 'He's lost a lot more than his teeth!'

Laughing with bawdy-coloured excitement, the three girls ducked under the Grand Eunuch's arm, and worked their way to the edge of the stage, where they could see the play from the closest position possible.

They had already forgotten Annie. And the rest of the girls were gone, swallowed by the crowds, sucked into the fair's centre near St George's church.

Over the past two years and more, Molly had seen the finest actors of the age playing the greatest roles in the language on London's most celebrated stages. Compared with The Provok'd Wife and The Recruiting Officer, she told the Waif, The Lamentable Tragedy of Cleopatra, Queen of the Nile was fustian stuff, scarcely meriting any applause at all. And, compared with Mistress Bracegirdle and Mistress Barry, the insignificant drab in Cleopatra's robes might just as well have been selling oranges.

But the Waif had never seen a play before. To her, the poor players strutting their hour on the makeshift stage were Cleopatra and her lovers, the daubed cloth was Egypt, the tame python was a poisonous asp.

To the Waif, a magical dream; to Molly, a tedious interlude; to Hannah, an incomprehensible ragbag of history and poetry. But, as they followed the rest of the audience out into the street after the performance, all three girls agreed giggling on one thing. They would have loved dearly to know exactly what lay beneath the Grand Eunuch of Egypt's loincloth.

Daredevil tightrope-walkers skipping from the tower of St George's to the roof of an inn; Punch and Judy swapping blows alongside a quarter-staff competition; dwarves and giants, freaks and grotesques, wax effigies and peep-shows; fire-eaters, jugglers, acrobats, wrestlers - all the entertainers in England were gathered here in Southwark.

Together with all the harlots and pickpockets in London.

And there were more plays. In the courtyard of an inn, The Fall of Bajazet; in the room above a lodging house, The Siege of Troy; under a canvas awning in a churchyard, The Temptation of Adam. The Waif insisted on seeing every one of them, and adored every one of them, no matter how inept the writing, how poor the acting, how shoddy the backcloth.

The Waif's purse was soon empty. And, since Molly and Hannah hadn't expected to be separated from Isaac, they had no money with them.

'We must go,' Molly said. 'I shall repay you, Kitty. As soon as I get back to Chiswick, I shall send you money.'

'But we haven't yet seen The Labours of Hercules,' she protested, pointing to the painted sign hanging over the heads of the cheering crowd surrounding two bloody-faced, raw-knuckled boxers. 'The hydra, the Nemean lion, Cerberus - we can't go without seeing them!'

'Kitty, we have no money left.'

'I want to see how they show Hercules stealing the girdle of Hippolyta.'

Doggedly trying to reason with her. 'But they won't let us in to see it unless we pay for our entrance.'

The Waif's shoulders drooped as she sulked. 'I want to see how they pile up a mountain of shit from the Augean stables,' she grumbled. 'I'll wager they don't use real shit.'

'I'll wager the actors smell as if they do,' said Hannah.

The mood broke. They fell on each other and laughed so much that some of the spectators urging on the fighters turned to see if they were missing an even better sideshow.

The Waif broke away from Molly and Hannah. 'We shall see it,' she said. Molly recognised the reckless tilt of the girl's chin. 'Wait for me here. Don't go anywhere else, or I shall never find you again.' Before Molly could question her, she'd disappeared into the crowds, dodging hurdy-gurdy players, skipping past dice-throwing gamblers, squeezing between tankard-swilling revellers.

For more than a quarter-hour, Molly and Hannah stayed where they were, admiring the dancing bear, watching the potted scenes acted out to advertise the comedies and tragedies on offer, listening to the cacophony of barrel-organs and bagpipes and drums as each entertainer vied with every other for the fairgoers' pennies. And ignoring the ribald comments of the drunks, declining the protection of predatory bucks, refusing offers of sexual adventures that varied from the exotic to the gross, from the crudely unimaginative to the patently impossible.

With each new lewd suggestion, Hannah's colour heightened. Molly was on the point of abandoning the afternoon and taking Hannah away from the Fair when the Waif appeared beside them, an impish grin on her face and a fist brandished in triumph above her head. 'The Labours of Hercules,' she said. She held her hand out in front of her and opened it to show the other two girls; a fistful of pennies. 'Eighteen pence,' she announced.

Molly didn't understand. 'But where did you get it?'

The Waif's eyes opened wide with simultaneous innocence and mischief. 'Three apprentices,' she said. 'One after the other. Up against the wall at the back of the church. Sixpence each - enough for all of us to see the play. Come along.' She grabbed Molly and Hannah by their hands and set off for the board advertising The Labours of Hercules, breasting the crowds like the figurehead on a ship.

She jerked to a halt as a pair of grimy hands reached from behind her and moulded themselves over her bosom. An unshaven face swayed into view, and a gap-toothed mouth tried to kiss her. Letting go of Molly and Hannah, the Waif put both hands in her assailant's chest and shoved as hard as she could. Hooting with delight, he staggered back into the arms of his friends. 'Now, that's worth more than sixpence!' he roared. 'How much, girl? How much for me to dabble in your stream for an hour? Eh? A shilling?'

The Waif beckoned him to her. She lowered her eyes with feigned modesty, and murmured something in his ear. He nodded eagerly, and the rest of the men crowded in to hear what she had to say. A look of bewilderment came over the petitioner, and the rest of the men erupted into lewd guffaws. Kitty rejoined Molly and Hannah, and resumed her progress towards the actors.

'What on earth did you say to him?' asked Hannah.

The Waif re-enacted the encounter. 'I said to him If you have half a crown to spend, I said, and he said I have, I have!, so I said Then buy yourself a broken down, diseased pig, and fuck that - if you can find one that isn't disgusted by you. And then I said - '

'Bitch!' A woman's voice split the air like the cry of a raven.

The three girls swung to face the accusation; the crowds parted; for a moment, the Fair itself seemed to fall silent. Five yards away an accusing, bony finger stabbed in their direction. The face beyond the finger was flushed with gin, raddled with the pox, ugly with rage. Beyond the face stood two more, both braying alliance with the first.

Molly and Hannah took a step backward; the Waif took a step forward. 'I beg your pardon, madam,' she said, shrinking, melting, becoming the child her visitors had enjoyed for so many years. 'If we have offended you in any - '

'Yes, bitch, you have offended us!' The rags-clad harpy advanced on her. 'Ply your cunt on your own side of the river, not ours.' The other two growled their support.

'Why, madam, whatever can you mean?' Innocence.

Molly clutched Hannah's hand. She felt sick. She knew what was to happen. She couldn't leave her friend to fight three alone. But she'd never fought in anger in her life.

The woman thrust out her open palm. 'Give me the eighteen pence you had from those 'prentices,' she demanded. ''Tis rightfully mine. I saw 'em first!'

'True, madam,' the Waif agreed. 'But I fucked 'em first.'

'What's that to me? Give me the money!'

From innocence to mischief. 'May I suggest, madam, that you find yourself a broken-down, diseased pig, and - '

She'd misjudged her audience; no one is disconcerted by their own everyday language. The Southwark harlot's ears filtered out the form and heard only the meaning. Without warning, she responded with a stooping, hook-nailed attack, already upon the Waif before she could defend herself, tearing off her cap and grabbing her hair with both hands, forcing her head down, viciously driving her own knee upward, looking to smash Kitty's nose, but Kitty shoved out her hand to deflect the blow and found her fingers caught under the woman's skirts, and as the foot came to earth again the Waif's fingers scraped up the harlot's calf and between her knees, and the Waif dug in her fingernails and ripped upwards, furrowing into the soft upper-thigh flesh and tearing at the fur-fringed crotch.

Molly dashed forward and tried to wrest the woman away from the Waif, and was attacked in her turn by the other two women. One hand twined itself in her hair while another clawed at her face; two fists rained punches on her arms as she tried to cover her breasts; kicks landed at will on her shins and calves.

Hannah tried to help; but a flailing fist sent her tumbling onto the cobbles.

The two harlots worked as a practised team. One scooped Molly's arms together and pinioned them behind her with one hand, dragged her head back by the hair with the other, exposing her throat.

Helpless, Molly seemed to have time to take in all the details of the scene, from the blood-triumphant snarl of the harlot facing her to the upraised arm above her, from the shard of broken glass clenched in her assailant's fist to -

To the batten of wood that smashed into the woman's face, to the blood that sprayed into the air, to the sound of teeth splintering.

To the sound of men cheering. A brawl between women had an erotic savour to it that even the best boxing match could never equal.

As her arms were released, Molly fell onto her knees. From the corner of her eye she could see Kitty locked together with the third of the harlots, slewing backwards and forwards as they tried to trip each other, aiming kicks, screaming and cursing. As Molly scrambled to get up, she saw Annie swing the wood again, catching her previous captor on the thin flesh at the back of the knee. The harlot fell, clutching her leg, howling obscenities.

The third woman let go of Kitty's hair and shoved her aside, aiming a kick at her as she scuttled clear.

Instantly, the battle-lines were redrawn. Two, three more drabs joined the Southwark harlot. A phalanx of furies hell-bent on vengeance.

Behind Annie, the Twins had appeared, hovering together like two birds of prey, scenting the danger, relishing the chance to hurt someone, eager for the opportunity to act out their own retribution on everything they hated about their own lives.

'Run, Moll,' Annie shouted. 'For the love of Jesus, run! This is no fight for you! Run!' She snatched off her cap and let her red hair flow freely like the mane of some wild beast. Crouching, she hefted the club menacingly. 'Kitty! Get here!'

The Waif dodged another kick, and fled to join the Twins. Her fist was still closed tight round the eighteen pence.

Red panic blinding her to everything except escape, Molly hauled Hannah to her feet and shoved her into and through the crowd of whooping onlookers.

As she fought her way out of the arena, a jostling spectator cannoned into her, spinning her halfway round. Over her shoulder, she took in a frantic slice of the fight that was now in progress.

She saw the Waif butt an opponent in the face, then Annie's club crashed into the same woman's ankles, sweeping her feet from under her. Polly had joined the affray, and her foot crashed viciously into the side of the fallen harlot's head, splitting her cheek. Behind her, the Twins had wrenched the dress of one of the Southwark whores down over her shoulders, exposing her breasts and pinning her arms to her side, leaving her helpless as one Twin held her, and the other raked her talons down her face with calculated relish, gouging four channels of blood from temple to chin, down over the neck and shoulders, down almost to the waist, narrowly missing tearing the nipple as the woman writhed in her attempts to get clear, her answering screech more of rage than pain.

As Molly's view was blocked by the jostling, fast-gathering crowd, she caught a glimpse of Nan hurling herself into the fight with harpie-like venom, her normally withdrawn face distorted with hatred, her flailing arms sweeping aside the nails that slashed at her.

Oh, God, please save me! Hanging on to the hand of the shocked Hannah, she battled desperately against the tide of fairgoers rushing to see the new attraction, fought clear of them, bolted for any escape route, fled from the fight, away from St George's, away from the crowds, into the labyrinth of alleys, skirting the courtyards, scrambling blindly round any corner, into a cramped market of trinket-sellers, scattering trays and baskets, escaping from the outraged protests, ducking into a foul-smelling passageway between two crumbling houses, out into a deserted lane, staggering to a stop, gasping for breath.

They clung to each other, not speaking, trying to control the fear that was shaking their bodies like an ague.

At the end of the lane, where it met a street broad enough for a carriage to pass, the door of a tavern slammed open, and a knot of men bundled out, laughing and swaggering as they turned towards the two girls.

A knot of men led by Quince.

Chapter 21

This was more than fear. This was blind terror.

Through a door and crashing past a family at table; spinning a mother and her child to the cobbles; into a harlot's room and out by the window, oblivious to the humping buttocks as she passed; barging anyone, everyone aside, her legs buckling, her lungs heaving, the world ahead of her tunneling down to a red blur.

An acrobat danced out of her way and lost his rhythm; a street-play fell into confusion as she blundered into the scene; a fighter's attack faltered as she fell at his feet, dragged herself upright by his breeches and lurched away.

Behind her, Quince. Ahead of her...

Ahead of her was Annie, Kitty, the Twins, Polly, Nan. They were crouching, mopping the blood away from their fallen adversaries, binding their wounds, holding cups of wine to their lips, comforting them as if they were children who had fallen and grazed their knees. Around them, jugglers were juggling, hurdy-gurdies were grinding out their tinkling tunes, dancers were skipping and laughing. The cheering, jeering drunks had dispersed, and the biggest crowd was now gathered to watch a troupe of tumblers.

She didn't understand. The nightmare had become a madman's dream. She stumbled towards them, tripped, fell, sank into red, then black...

'Qui...' she squeezed out. 'Qui...' She took a mouthful of wine from the goblet Annie was holding to her lips, then coughed, spluttered, spat. 'Quince.'

Annie's head snapped up. Her eyes widened, and se swung right, left, far enough to see behind her. 'Where?'

Molly waved an uncertain arm, pointing everywhere and nowhere. Quince was somewhere but, thank God, not here. The Colonel was everywhere. Everywhere. The Jew and his whore, that's who I want punished.

'Hannah!' She pushed Annie's hand away, spilling the wine. 'Where's Hannah? Where's Hannah?'

When they found her, it was too late. Quince and his men had found her first.

It took them more than an hour to trace their way back to where Molly had last seen her, searching for the scant clues she could give them. A shop that sold pies... an inn with a lantern outside it... trinket-sellers... a butcher's shop with strings of sausages looped above the door... the same narrow street, the same tavern...

'Here!' She took her bearings, searched her memory, made sure she was right. 'Aye, here. This is where we saw Quince.'

Annie was pragmatic. She understood people like Quince. 'They won't have taken her far. Or, if they have, we'll never see her again.'

Nan found her. She was slumped against a gravestone in an over-grown churchyard, the tall grass and weeds trampled flat around her. Her head was lolling on one shoulder and, from time to time, a painful whimpering bubbled past her puffed lips. Her cap was missing, and her straw-coloured hair was tangled about her face. Her feet and legs were bare. Her dress was torn down to the waist and bunched up to her hips. Her exposed breasts were bruised blue and yellow. Her thighs were spread shamelessly wide, smeared with blood.

Her eyes, too, were wide, but she saw nothing. She didn't see Molly and Annie as they helped her to her feet and covered her as best they could, pulling her skirts down to hide her legs, wrapping her shoulders in a child's cloak that Polly had stolen from a washing line. She saw nothing of Southwark as they half-led, half-carried her away from the Fair, across London Bridge and through the empty north-of-the-river alleys to Wood Street.

'Abigail, get hot water and sour milk. And fetch some brandy from Mother Wickham's room.'

'But Miz Annie, Mother Wickham don't let nobody - '

'Do it! But get the water and the milk first.'

'Yes, Miz Annie.' She scurried away to the kitchen.

'Bring her to my room.' Annie went ahead, while Molly supported Hannah up the stairs, past the Twins' room, past Nan's room, past Polly's room, the hairs prickling on the back of her neck as she relived the journey to the room where the Colonel had ravished her so many times. A flight of stairs short, they led Hannah into Annie's room, a mirror of the Colonel's room.

Annie had a pair of scissors in her hand. 'On the bed,' she directed.

Molly coaxed Hannah onto the bed, put a pillow under her head, arranged the tattered cloak to cover her.

With a fierceness that surprised Molly, Annie flung the cloak aside and thrust the scissors into Molly's hand. 'Cut her dress away,' she commanded.

'But she - '

'Do it!' There was no argument. 'Tell Abigail I've gone for the brandy.'

Molly was a dressmaker. Scissors were a natural extension to her fingers. Without thinking, she snipped along the seams, leaving Hannah nude on the bed without ruining the cloth beyond further use.

Hannah, once naive and bashful. Now face-up and naked, exposed, unaware, dead-eyed. No longer Hannah.

Annie returned with a bottle of brandy at the same time that a sullen-eyed young woman Molly had never seen before arrived with hot water and clean towels.

'Thank you, Bess,' Annie said. The girl left without a word.

Abigail passed her at the door, in one hand a bamboo tube tied with hemp into the opening of a pig's bladder, in the other a jug of sour milk.

There was no need to issue instructions: the older girls had played this scene before. While Annie dribbled the milk down the bamboo tube into the sac, the Twins lifted Hannah off the bed and onto a plain wooden chair; Polly fetched a wide bowl from the table and placed it under the chair. Then, as Nan pinioned Hannah's arms from behind and tipped the chair backwards, the Twins forced her legs apart, and Annie eased the bamboo into her, repeating the rape.

For the first time Hannah reacted. 'No!' she screamed, kicking and writhing in a desperate attempt to get free. 'No! No! No!' The girls clung onto her.

'Hold her still!' Annie compressed the bladder, forcing the liquid into her, squirting it again and again, ignoring the girl's writhings, ignoring the mess that washed over her hands, that splashed out of the waiting bowl and onto the floor, drenching and swilling and sluicing until the last of the milk was spent. She stood, dropped the bladder and bamboo into the bowl. 'Clean her up,' she said.

Between them, Molly and Abigail comforted her, bathed her, swabbed away the caked blood on the inside of her thighs. As they worked, Annie wet her finger with the brandy several times and touched it to Hannah's lips until the girl's face coloured from corpse-grey to high-fever flush.

The Twins soothed an ointment of arnica over her discoloured breasts, then caressed it into her bruised and split labia. Annie let them do enough to assuage her pain, then stopped them and helped Hannah up into the bed, swaddling her in a linen sheet and covering her with blankets.

'Moll will stay here with Hannah tonight,' she announced. 'I'll sleep next door in Polly's room. Polly will sleep upstairs next to Kitty.' She smiled without humour. 'When our visitors arrive, let us be sure to remember which bed we are in. Otherwise it could become crowded in the wrong sort of way.' She corked the brandy bottle and left.

The Twins stood up and wiped their hands on their skirts. Nan and Polly followed Annie. Abigail remained on her knees swabbing up the milk from the douche. The Waif stayed where she was, and slipped a comforting hand into Molly's.

As she opened the door, Annie turned to the rest of the girls. 'Don't tell Mother Wickham,' she said.

＊

Abraham was furious. With Isaac, not Molly.

'This is what your foolishness has achieved!' he shouted, limping up and down the centre of the high-ceilinged salon, his agitation shivering spasms throughout his bent body. 'A poor innocent girl ravished by six of Colonel Charnell's men in plain daylight! And only God can tell what they would have done to Molly if they had caught her instead. Ravished and murdered, probably. Or worse - ravished and disfigured and then murdered. Would you have wanted that?'

'No, father.' Contrite.

As he reached the huge fireplace, he jabbed his finger in Isaac's direction. 'They were in your charge, Isaac - their safety depended on you! And where were you while they were risking their lives in Southwark?

218

Idling in Garraway's, and Change Alley, and the Royal Exchange.' He swung an arm to indicate Molly where she sat cowed on a high-backed chair, her hands folded in her lap. 'Is money so important to you that you'd risk Molly's life for it?'

'No, father.' Less contrite, more indignant.

Abraham dug deep into the pocket of his topcoat, drew out a leather purse and tossed it at Isaac's feet. 'There's gold, Isaac. A lot of gold. It's worth less to me than Molly. Take it. Invest it. I trust you with it.' He paused. 'But I shall never again trust you with Molly.' He turned his back on his son.

Isaac let the purse lie where it had fallen. 'I was escorting Molly and Hannah, father, not looking for investments.' He bit the words out.

'In Change Alley?' The scorn and disbelief in his voice simmered near the surface.

'That's why we were in the City - because Molly wanted to see the Royal Exchange. Because you said I was to take her there!' His own resentment and anger was also bubbling up to boiling point.

'But you don't have sufficient regard for me or her to take proper care of her!'

Danger point. Isaac was youthful enough and angry enough to tell the truth. To claim Molly for his own, and ruin all of them.

As he opened his mouth to reply, Molly came to her feet and interrupted them. 'That's not true, Abraham.' Still they glared at each other, the old ram and the young pretender. 'It were I that asked to see the Royal Exchange,' she continued. 'It were I that asked Isaac if I could see where you conducted your business.'

Isaac was the first to unlock horns; his eyes dropped. Having faced down his adversary, Abraham waited for Molly as she crossed the polished floor, her heels echoing in the hushed room. She stopped in front of him. He was a short man, she was a tall woman, and their faces were at a level. 'And it were I that took Hannah off to Southwark Fair.' She softened her voice, penitently. 'Abraham, it were I that were in the wrong, not Isaac. I know he'd never willingly do anything that would harm me or lead me into danger.' She faced him confidently, knowing that he'd trust her. 'It were I that were foolish, not Isaac.'

Abraham considered. 'Forgive me, my son,' he said. 'You have a skilful advocate. If Shylock had had Molly to speak for him, even

Portia would have been confounded.' Back to Molly. 'Forgive me, my dear. I was so frightened at what might have happened to you, I put blame where there should have been none.' He touched a finger to her lips as she started to speak. 'There is no blame for any of us to bear. I made a misjudgement. Isaac was unfortunate. You didn't see beyond the attractions of the Fair. And poor Hannah was doing only what she was paid to do.' His face darkened. 'If there is blame to be levelled, then let us blame the creature who brought this thing about. Let us blame Colonel Charnell.'

Amen. Please God, strike the Colonel dead.

Molly sat beside Hannah's bed in the servants' quarters, high up under the eaves, watching the flickering eyelids, listening to the almost-sobs of her breathing, seeing the compulsive clenching and unclenching of her fingers, waiting for sleep to claim her.

A week since Southwark, and Molly had swapped roles with her maid. Each morning, she helped her dress, walked with her in the garden, read to her, tried to carry her thoughts away from the church-yard nightmare. Each night, she lit the candles, helped her to bed, sat with her till she slept.

It had been three days before Hannah could speak of what had happened, and then only a murmured phrase. 'Cut her throat.'

Later, 'Cut the throat of the Christian bitch.'

Two days later, more words. 'Cut the throat of the Christian bitch who lives with the Jew.'

Then, chillingly, 'That's what the Colonel wants.' She buried her face in the pillow and wept.

Involuntarily, Molly looked over her shoulder. With trembling hands, anxious not to disturb the already disturbed Hannah, she shifted her chair so that she could see both the door and the window.

The following day, Hannah added more, mumbling, weeping, almost inaudible. 'That's not her. I've never seen her.' That must have been Quince. 'But she can carry a message to the Jew.'

Each day another phrase, a further clue. Always words remembered, never words of her own.

Inch by inch, the curtain drew back to reveal the rest of the picture. And Molly realised, with a pity that made her feel sick, that every-thing she'd endured in all the months she'd been at the Colonel's mercy,

Hannah had been made to suffer in less than an hour.

Hannah's cunny, Hannah's arse, Hannah's mouth, one after the other, all of them twice or more.

Hannah's innocence. Hannah's sanity.

Molly watched helpless as Hannah grew stronger in body, and weaker in resolve. Word by reluctant word, her speech returned to normal. But only to ask would Molly like the fire lit, would she like an extra blanket, would she like to wear the blue gown or the amber or the cream.

As the orchard leaves turned yellow and began to fall, fluttering like broken-winged birds across the meadows, Hannah's lips came slowly alive; but her eyes remained dead.

The Colonel had had nothing to do with it. He was in the country, with friends. The magistrates had his word for it, as a gentleman.

And, of course, Quince had been there with him. The Colonel never went anywhere without Quince.

In October, Hannah missed her monthly blood-flow. Then she began to be sick in the mornings.

Four weeks later, while Molly was busy in the kitchens with Mistress Silver, Hannah walked down the steps at the back of the house, across the meadow where Isaac had once plucked her to safety, and into the racing November river. Nobody saw her and, if anybody ever found her body, they didn't know who to tell.

The house was graveyard-quiet for days. Abraham took Molly to the theatre. But there were so many man-mountain footmen there to guard them, the plays became a sideshow.

There was a ball at a neighbour's house; but a mention of the poor girl who was set upon by thieves at the Fair sent Molly home in tears.

Berry, the biggest of the two mastiffs, died, and everyone suspected poison, though none of them voiced the suspicion.

If Berry could die without warning, if Babu could be snatched silently away and hanged, if Hannah could disappear without anyone seeing her, how safe could any of them feel?

Molly lay content, her arms wrapped around Isaac, listening to the soft fluttering of his breath as he slept naked against her.   She loved him. Loved him.

Not with any hopes that she could marry him, for she couldn't. Not with any hopes that she could share her life with him, for she couldn't. Not with any hopes that they could be together forever, for they couldn't.

She was already betraying her protector. He was already betraying his own father. The only way forward for either of them was to betray each other. Which she could never do. Because she loved him. Loved him. If only she didn't...

She had tossed the matter to and fro in her mind over the last few months. She had spoken of it to poor dead Hannah. She had sought the advice of a fortune-teller, claiming to be the wife of a coal-merchant. She wanted to believe that she didn't love him. That he was just her protector's son. That he had become a dangerous game for her to play. That he was the spice that seasoned her everyday life with his father, a man her own father's age. That he was a fantasy made possible by his father's money.

But... She loved him. Taking care not to wake him, she teased his hair away from his forehead. Outside her door, a floorboard creaked. She froze. Quince? The Colonel himself? Without speaking, she shook Isaac. He didn't wake.

The latch clicked. The door creaked open. Beyond it a candle. She shook Isaac again, harder. His deep breathing continued undisturbed. A shadowy shape shuffled into the room. The candle approached the bed. Molly strained her eyes wide open and filled her lungs in case she had to shout for help.

The footsteps halted. The candle reached forward and hovered. Her heart pounding, Molly squinted to one side of the puckering light, trying to see beyond it, preparing to challenge the intruder. Behind the candle, a face bent towards her. Abraham peered down at her and Isaac.

For the briefest of moments, their eyes met. Then the candle moved away, out through the door, down the stairs.

Still Isaac slept.

Chapter 22

My dear Abraham

I know you can not forgive me, and it is right that you fhould not. You have been always kind to me and generous, and I have more Refpect for you than for any Man I have ever known met, yet all I have brought you in return is Trouble and Pain. I fhall leave London as foon as I am able, and fhall never fee you more. I have taken with me of Value only a few Guineas which I brought with me, and a Gown and my beft Cloak which you bought for me in Covent Garden, and a Ring which is dear to me. Before your Sabbath Day I fhall fend a Carriage for my Trunk, and I pray you by your Goodnefs not to withhold it from me.

Your erftwhile Whore Mistrefs Companion,

Molly

I pray you, be kind to Okoro. He is but a Child.

My deareft Ifaac

While you flept, your Father came into my Room and look'd upon us. He will be angry, but you may fay I was to blame. I pray you, make your Peace with him. He is a good Man. I truly wifh it had been otherwife.

Now I fhall leave London and never return. I beg you, do not try to find me.

Molly

By the time the scowling winter dawn had lightened the rooftops ahead of her, she had already walked the length of Hammersmith and was safe in the side-streets of Kensington. If Abraham sent his footmen to punish her, they'd never find her now.

Even if Isaac... Her head drooped miserably as she trudged past the implacable brick houses, their tall windows flickering into life with the first stirrings of early morning servants. Even if Isaac cared enough to chase after her, by the time he'd made up the miles between them, she'd be lost in the crush that was daytime London.

There was only one place she knew to go.

The smell of people, dogs, horses, filth. The cries of hawkers and harlots, the curses of chair-carriers and coach-drivers, the wailing of babies and beggars. St Alban's cranking out three o'clock.

As she came opposite The Bell's kitchen door in Love Lane, she slowed. She wasn't the rich mistress now. She wasn't even the Colonel's whore. Now she was a beggar.

Without warning, a plump black hand appeared from behind her and clamped a cloth over her mouth. Roughly, she was swept sideways, away from the kitchen, then rushed stumbling up a rickety flight of wooden stairs into a sparse room, suddenly dark as the door slammed behind her.

'Hush, Miz Moll! Hush!' She ceased her struggles. 'Ah'm goin' take dis cloth off you face now. But you must hush!'

The cloth came away from her face, and she sucked in a huge breath. She leant against a chairback, panting, getting used to the dim light creeping past the ill-fitting slats, breathing in the heady smells of cloves and coriander, ginger and chilli. 'Abig... Abigail. Why?'

The negress held up her hand. 'Listen.'

Love Lane was silent, licking its lips. Wood Street was as still as it ever got. The only identifiable sound was the steady clomping of horses, and the grumbling of thick iron wheels over cobbles. And, of course, the excited babble of women.

The York Wagon.

Molly crept to the window, eased the wooden shutter a finger-width and peeped out. The wagoner was lowering the tailgate. The beggars were holding out their bowls to the passengers.

Mother Wickham was eyeing up the newcomers. Two paces behind her was Quince. And, Molly knew, lurking in the doorway, just out of sight, was the Colonel.

There was no immediate danger: the Colonel's mind was riveted on future triumphs, not past disappointments; and Quince was about the business he was paid for. But her chest constricted, and she crept the shutter back into its frame.

Pressing her face against the wooden slats, she could see a sliver of the scene outside the front of The Bell. Mother Wickham, a pious and welcoming smile lighting her face. The wagoner dragging past with an iron-bound trunk, then striding back again, into sight, out of sight, into sight, out again. Quince, gliding through her line of vision without seeming to move his feet. Mother Wickham's gloved hand reaching out to someone unseen, offering help. A young pink hand putting its trust in her. A few moments of hesitation, then a flounce of cream and blue as another lamb was lured into the slaughterhouse.

'You mustn't stay here, Miz Moll. You mustn't stay nowhere near The Bell. Quince come poking in here every day.'

'Just tonight, Abigail.'

She relented. 'Just tonight. But you don't leave this room. And you be gone afore dawn. There's fresh bread by the stove, and yesterday's ham under the cloth, and good ale over yonder.' She leaned over the crude wooden crib beside the bed, tenderly adjusted the baby's shawl. 'If Lily cry, let her cry. We don't want no one asking who comforting her while I'm pouring wine for the visitors.'

She creaked the door open, wiped her hands on her apron, and stomped down into Love Lane.

The hired carriage collected Molly's trunk from Chiswick and delivered it to the cheap, anonymous lodgings she'd taken in Holborn. The driver had instructions to say nothing and, if he were followed, to take the trunk back to Chiswick.

She'd also taken a room opposite her lodgings, and she waited and watched there for two days before venturing out to claim the trunk, and to hire a different driver to take her to Islington.

At Islington, she boarded the York Wagon, travelling north. She gave her name as Mistress Mary Abbott, widow.

Tha name is who th'art, lass. Perhaps a new name would magically transform her into a new person.

My dear Anny

I am gone Home to York, and will never fee you more. I pray you, think of me fometimes, and remember me in your Prayers. Tell Kitty I fhall look for her Name on ye Playbills.

Your loving Friend

Moll

The meagre warmth of Hornsey Toll was behind them, and they were less than a mile onto Finchley Common when the skies closed in and the first flurry of snow swirled into their faces. The wagoner shouted his horses to a stop, tied down the canvas flaps to keep the passengers dry, and whipped his horses into motion again, their feet slipping in the half-frozen mud under them.

Huddled together in the wagon's dim interior to help keep the bone-numbing cold at bay, the passengers had no warning.

The first shot rang out with a flat crack. A blast from the wagoner's carbine was answered by another pistol-shot, and the wagon veered sharply to the left before coming to a halt. All the women squealed, all the men cursed, nobody made any attempt to see what was happening. Molly half-stood, lost her balance as the restless horses trundled forward a few feet, tumbled back onto her bench.

For what seemed an eternity, there was silence; then a third pistol-shot.

A fumbling in the wind-keening silence; a knife sliced through the canvas flaps at the front of the wagon, and the loose ends flapped open. A dim figure peered in at them, a scarf hiding the lower part of the face, a three-cornered hat tilted low over the eyes.

'Out!' The muffled voice was accompanied by the menacing flourish of a pistol. The twelve passengers scrambled out into the snowstorm, wrapping their cloaks around them, huddling for shelter against the side of the wagon.

Molly was one of the last to clamber out, jumping down from the wagoner's seat to the ground. She could see the wagoner sprawled face down beyond the horses, blood seeping out from his shattered cheekbone and eye-socket, leaching into the thin covering of snow. There was a blood-stained wound on his right shoulder, and a scorched bullet-hole in the middle of his back.

She shuddered, took a deep breath, quelled the panic she could feel rising within her. The last time she panicked, Hannah had died. If she tried to run away now, she herself could be the one to die.

Keep calm. Keep your wits about you. There's no saving the wagoner, and they'll rob us whatever we do. Crossing them will only make it worse.

Trembling, she turned away from the spreadeagled corpse and joined the line of passengers beside the wagon.

They'd been captured by three men. One threatened them with a pistol in one hand and the wagoner's carbine in the other, while the other two heaved the travellers' trunks and baskets out of the back of the wagon.

The armed highwayman picked out the four male passengers and waved them to the end of the line. His maimed left arm was tucked into his side; but the pistol in his hand remained steady. 'First, gentlemen, your purses,' he called.

Reluctant, but persuaded by the carbine and the pistol, they reached inside their coats, drew out their purses and put them in the sack he kicked towards them.

'Good,' he said, after the last man in the line had given up his money. 'Now, gentlemen, the keys to your travelling boxes.'

One of his companions scurried across and collected the keys. Within a couple of minutes, the boxes and trunks had been opened and their contents strewn about the common, anything of value dumped into sacks.

While his fellows were busy with the trunks, the leader addressed himself again to his prisoners. 'Gentlemen, I should be much obliged if you'd remove your gloves and unfasten your coats.'

There was no argument. They knew why. Despite the freezing wind whipping round the wagon, they all took off their gloves and opened their coats. Plain rings were plucked from fingers, cheap buckles were sliced from the knees of breeches, anything that glinted in the gloom was torn away or twisted free or cut off and dumped into the sack. Not a rich haul. If the victims had been rich, they wouldn't have been on the York Wagon.

Once he'd filled his sack with everything of value, he treated the men to an exaggerated bow. 'Thank you, gentlemen.' He strutted away to the other end of the line. 'Now, ladies,' he said, 'you'd please me greatly if you'd take off your gloves and open your cloaks. You've seen how easy it was for your menfolk, so I don't suppose it'll be any more difficult for you.'

Molly pulled off her gloves and dropped them behind the wagon-wheel so they wouldn't blow away. Together with the other seven women, she let her cloak fall open.

The highwayman walked along the line. 'I have heard tales, ladies,' he said, raising his voice above the wind as it buffeted across the heath and flapped the wagon's canvas like a ship in a squall, 'that not all of you are to be trusted. I have heard tales that some of you have been known to hide your valuables by stuffing them up your cunnies. So...' He spoke directly to the woman at the far end, a middle-aged matron, her face deep-lined from years of work, wisps of grey hair straggling out from beneath her tight-tied bonnet. 'So you will all greatly oblige me by holding your hands up to your chin for me to see what rings you are wearing - and by holding your skirts up to your chin so I can see what else you are hiding.'

His companions broke away from their work on the trunks to enjoy the sport.

He returned his attention to the matron. 'You first, ma'am, if you please.'

She reared, indignation pursing her features. 'No, you villain, I will not - ' She broke off as he shoved the barrel of the pistol up under her nose.

'There's nothing you've got, mother, that I've not seen before,' he growled. 'And nothing you've got that holds any interest for me. Unless there's a bag of gold up there.' Stooping, he laid the carbine down by his feet. Then, as he stood upright again, he snatched up her skirts and slammed his hand up between her legs. Squealing in outrage, she flailed her fists at him. Dancing out of reach, he lashed the pistol at her, catching her on the side of the head and splitting her face open to the bone. Stunned, she crumpled moaning to the ground, blood splashing across her shoulders.

'Damn you!' Her husband started towards him, a stocky, red-faced carpenter, his gnarled fists clenched.

Thrusting the pistol out at arm's length, the highwayman turned, aimed, fired. At point blank range, the ball took the onrushing man in the throat. He lurched sideways, his scream of pain thickening to a gurgle as the blood filled his windpipe. Crashing against the wheel of the wagon beside Molly, he fell at her feet, clutching both hands to his throat, the blood spurting between his fingers and onto her boots.

The shock was too sudden for her to feel fear. She fell to her knees to help him, cradled her arm round his shoulders, grabbed his fallen white wig and pressed it to his neck, trying to stem the life ebbing out of him, feeling the warmth of the blood pumping over the back of her hand.

Ice-cold, the muzzle of the carbine prodded under her chin and forced her to her feet.

'There's nothing you can do to help him. He'll be dead within the minute.'

'But he's - ' She shrugged away from the threatening weapon and bent towards the dying man.

Again he brought her to her feet, this time with more menace. 'I said there's nothing you can do!' The traveller, choking on his own blood, coughing red gobbets onto the snow, heaved himself up onto his knees and elbows. The highwayman placed his boot against the dying man's ribs and toppled him over again onto his side. 'One minute. Or two. Or maybe three.'

He tucked the discharged pistol into his belt. 'Ladies,' he said, waving the carbine idly, without menace, as if it were nothing more dangerous than a silver-headed cane, 'I'm sure it will be much easier for you now to do as I ask. Pray, take off your gloves and hold up your skirts.'

Now he's killed, he's got nothing to lose. And, since my first day in Wood Street, I've had nothing to lose anyway. If I do as he says, I may live. Better alive and shamed than proud and dead.

She could hear her father's voice: where there's life, lass, there's hope.

Together with the others, she lifted her skirts, feeling the wind icing her naked legs and belly, the feather-touch of snowflakes against her skin, the freezing trickle down her legs as the flakes melted. She could see the shoulders of the two watching men shaking with laughter; she could hear the whimpering of each woman in turn as their captor poked his fingers into their most private parts; she could smell the fear and humiliation of the people around her, women and men alike.

Molly was the last in the line of women. Reaching forward with his pistol, he gently lifted her skirt-holding hands upwards, exposing her fully from waist to boots. Taking a step backwards, he eyed her up and down. And, while he was studying her, she studied what she could see of him. Above his scarf, his brown eyes were flecked with grey. Heavy lids folded down over them, slitting them even more than the weather demanded. Bushed, spiky eyebrows, and virtually no eyelashes. A ridge at the top of his nose where it had been broken some time in the past.

Stepping close to her again, he put the muzzle of the pistol under her chin, and caressed his cold, ungloved fingers into her, exploring deep into her warmth with more pleasure than his search warranted, daring her to protest.

Damn you! Her thighs clamped shut. His hand stilled, and his eyes narrowed almost to nothing. As his lips parted behind the scarf to command her, she eased her thighs apart again and left his way clear. His practised gaze scanned her clothing for anything worth stealing, and alighted on her hands. 'A pretty ring,' he said, continuing to finger her.

Gold, with striped agate. All she had left of Isaac. 'I pray you, leave me the ring,' she said, trying not to plead. ''Tis worth little to you, but 'tis very precious to me.'

He nodded. 'Aye, girl, I believe you. But the shillings it will fetch are even more precious to me. Take it off.'

Nothing left to lose. Except the ring. Time to bargain. 'Leave me the ring, and I'll go into the wagon with you.' Mother Wickham had distilled her wisdom into a few favourite phrases. One of them was: Who will miss a slice from a cut loaf?

His finger paused in its exploration. 'Paddington!' he called. One of the other two left the box he was looting and came to him. 'Reload my pistols for me,' he instructed, handing them to him. 'Matt!' The third man joined them. 'Take this carbine and shoot anyone who tries to escape, or who even tries to speak.' He removed his hand from Molly's crotch, and jerked his head at the wagon.

She dropped her skirts back over her legs, grateful for the comparative warmth as they cut off the flesh-freezing wind, edged past the shot husband, the near-dead breath bubbling out of his mouth, past the red-haloed body of the wagoner, up into the interior of the wagon. The highwayman climbed up after her, unbuckling the belt that clinched his coat tight to his waist, unbuttoning the flap at the front of his breeches, unloosing the swollen flesh within.

Molly lay on the cold wooden floor of the wagon and waited. She didn't look at him, she didn't lift her skirts, she didn't help him, she didn't pretend to enjoy it.

It was over in less than a crude, grunting minute. His fingers digging painfully into her shoulders, he gasped explosively several times, then softened his grip and rolled away from her. 'Wait there,' he said. Without bothering to cover himself, he pushed through the canvas flaps into the gusting snow outside; the wagon rocked as he jumped down. She sat up and covered herself against the icy chill. Outside, she could hear voices and sniggers, but no words.

The floor tilted and creaked as someone climbed up onto the driver's seat. The man called Paddington came into the wagon, his fly hanging loose, his short, squat prick already jutting out towards her.

After him it was the man named Matt.

She climbed down from the wagon, avoiding the eyes of the rest of the passengers, feeling their accusation. The women's skirts were in place, their cloaks wrapped close, one of the younger women comforting the weeping widow. The men were cowed, huddled inside their coats. Paddington was pointing the carbine at them. Matt and the highwayman were tying the necks of the sacks containing their booty. Molly took her place in the line, stooped, retrieved her gloves from behind the wheel, began to put them back on.

The highwayman swung a linked pair of sacks over his horse so that they hung down like panniers, then sauntered over to Molly. He plucked her glove from her hand, seized her right wrist in his left hand, took hold of the ring and tried to wrench it off her finger. She clenched her fist. He let go of her, pulled one of the pistols from his belt and held it close to her face. 'Take off the ring,' he said.

'But you promised me that - '

As she spoke, he rammed the pistol between her lips and into her mouth, banging it painfully against her teeth as she tried to shy away. 'Take off the ring,' he repeated.

She stared helplessly into his eyes. His grey-flecked brown, fold-lidded, bush-browed, eyelashless, broken-nosed eyes. Accepting the inevitable, she opened her hand, removed the ring, held it out for him.

He took it from her, slid the pistol out of her mouth, retreated. With taunting deliberation, he tried the ring on each of his left-hand fingers. Index, no. Middle, no. Ring-finger, no. Finally, yes. With a determined push, the ring slipped over the knuckle and onto the little finger.

Uncocking the pistol and tucking it into his belt, he turned away from her. 'Paddington, the horses!'

Laughing, they galloped away into the falling snow.

Nobody else had ever driven a team, not even a team of plough-horses on a farm. So, after they'd heaved the two stiffening corpses on board, and gathered up what they could salvage and stuffed it back into their trunks, Molly wheeled the York Wagon round and drove it south again, through the gusting snow to the Hornsey Toll.

When she arrived again in London she had less to make her way with than she'd had the first time.

Chapter 23

Annie gave her five guineas.

The Waif promised her another five guineas when she'd spent Annie's five - 'because if you have ten guineas you'll think you're Queen Caroline and you'll spend it all at once.'

Abigail found lodgings for her in Tottenham Court Road, two sparse rooms above a shoemaker's shop, where she was woken every dawn by the tap, tap, tap of hammer on last.

Without Cousin Tom, without the Colonel, without Abraham, without Isaac (oh, God, without Isaac!) she was just another woman in London. But not just another whore in London. Perhaps God's mysterious ways had given her a second chance.

Her father's voice echoed in her memory: In this world, lass, all tha's got is what tha' art.

All I've got is what I am. I've got skills. I'm a willing worker. I can make my own way. I will make my own way.

For five cold weeks, she called on shops in Bond Street, in Covent Garden, in Drury Lane, High Holborn, Chancery Lane, Fleet Street, even in Cheapside, straying perilously close to Wood Street and the ever-lurking Quince. On Christmas Day, she called on the Jewish shops in St Giles.

But nobody had any work for a dressmaker. Mother Wickham was right. London was full of dressmakers. Every silly child who could thread a needle called herself a dressmaker.

As her borrowed money dwindled, and the rent became due, another dewdrop of Mother Wickham's wisdom dripped insidiously into her mind. The prick of a needle is worth pennies. The prick of a man is worth guineas.

❄

He was past his youth, but not yet middle-aged. He was strong-shouldered, curly-haired, clear-eyed. He drank little, worked hard, kept his money close. A butcher, he ran the shop for his father, who was too old and weak to wield a cleaver, but retained wits enough to keep hold of the business. He was awkward, unsure, never yet married. It was tempting. Very tempting. And yet...

'I'm sorry, Francis,' she decided, 'but no. I have no wish to marry again.' Mary Abbott, widow. But there was encouragement in her voice: she didn't want to marry him - but neither did she want to frighten him away.

'Do you not like me?'

'I like you, Francis, more than anyone I know.' She dipped her head. 'But I don't love you.'

It came as no surprise to him. Everybody liked him. Nobody loved him. And the business was his father's, not his. What did he have to offer? 'I'd provide for you, Mary. If you married me, you'd never want for meat again.'

She turned away from him, choosing to bury the unintended double meaning beneath the demureness of her widowhood. What did she need from life? Food, clothes, warmth, a roof over her. A kind word. Francis could provide all these. And, once his father died, even more. What could she offer him in return? An ironic, humourless smile flitted across her lips. Dressmaking. And a commodity that was so common-place, there was not a man in London who couldn't find it in the dark, and not a man who'd recognise it as hers once he'd found it.

The bargain was all on her side. Francis was offering her a comfortable life, the respect of her neighbours, the security of beef and mutton: butchers, like bakers and brewers and burial men, never went out of business for lack of trade. And, though dull, he was a good man. If she were still in York, she'd have been flattered, and betrothed, and married, and... yes, happy - or, at least, content.

But this was London. She'd already tasted the crude openness of The Bell, the casual excitement of the Colonel's money, the educated elegance of Abraham's household. The overwhelming love of her illicit nights with Isaac, the love that tore at her a dozen or more times a day when his memory forced itself into her thoughts. No: she'd already tasted the legend of London, and she didn't want to spend the rest of her life bearing children for a worthy husband in a smothering marriage. Most of all, she didn't want to be beholden.

But. Her lips tightened. Neither did she want Annie's life, giving

234

herself to any man who could afford the price - a price that became smaller with every year, with every blemish, with every moment of uncertainty. Was there a way between? Could she find a path that gave her both the independence of a harlot and the privileges of a wife, without the shame of the one or the obligations of the other?

Aye, she could. The Widow Abbott. A slice from a cut loaf.

'I loved my husband very dearly,' she said, still with her face averted. 'When he died, I thought that I would die, too.' From the corner of her eye, she saw Francis's mouth start to frame the question. She held up her hand to hush him. 'I cannot speak of it.' Mainly because I'm bad at remembering lies. 'I vowed that I would never marry again.' After a few seconds to let him settle, she continued. 'But, Francis, I need meat and bread,' she said. 'You need the warmth of a woman. And, truth to tell, there have been many lonely nights since my husband died.' She lowered her eyes demurely. 'But I cannot marry you.'

She wasn't looking at him; but she knew he was colouring. 'You... you mean...?'

'We would both be the better for it, Francis. And it would cost neither of us more than we could afford.'

He still couldn't believe what he was hearing. 'If I give you cuts of beef and pork and mutton, you'll...?' Too dull to attract a wife, too tight-fisted to spend money on a mistress.

As a child in York, she had often been fishing with her brothers. Teasing the fish with bright-dyed feathers, luring it onto the hook - that was the exciting part. After that, you simply hauled it in, slipped the net under it, took it home and ate it.

She broke away from him with a pretty simper. 'Why, Francis, if I lie with you and you bring me mutton and beef, then it will be as if we are married indeed!'

'Then what must I do?' There was pain in his voice. And longing and lust and uncertainty.

She moved back to him, drew his head down to hers and kissed him gently on the lips. 'If ever you come to my bed, Francis,' she told him, 'you must give me a guinea.' She felt his frame stiffen. 'Then I can spend it in your shop and buy my own mutton and beef.'

She felt him relax again. That was the kind of transaction he understood. Trader and customer, each depending on the other.

And she was doing nothing more than making her own way in a difficult world. Independence, however bought, was better than whoring.

For months, she bought her own mutton and beef with Francis's guineas. Then, too, she began to buy her own oranges and fresh vegetables with Philip's guineas. And her own ale and wine with Will's guineas. A slice from a carved roast. An apple from a broken crate. A sip from an opened bottle.

*

'Tell me, Mary,' said Francis, 'why does your trunk bear the initials MH, when your name is Abbott?' He lay in her bed, his hands behind his head, smugness oiling his well-fed face, watching her as she padded barefoot about the chilly room, draped in a blanket, pouring him a glass of Will's wine, clearing up the sour milk she'd sluiced into herself. For once, he hadn't turned over and gone to sleep after his journeyman humpings.

'What is it to you, Francis?' she asked, carefully keeping her voice light. She handed him the wine, sat on the edge of the bed and combed her fingers through his crinkly hair. He was beginning to bore her. She wished he'd either go to sleep or go home to his own bed.

He balanced the glass on his chest. 'Mary Abbott. MH. I cannot help but ask myself why.'

She teased at one of the sparse hairs on his chest. 'I had a name of my own before I was married,' she said. Why wouldn't he leave?

'I shall guess,' he said. 'Mary Hogg. Mary Hambone. Mary Hare.' Pork and game. What else would a butcher guess at? 'Mary... Horseradish.' Aye, she should have known what else a butcher might guess at.

She stood, walked round to the other side of the bed, climbed in beside him, snuggled up close to him. She was cold, and he was the nearest source of warmth.

He lifted the glass and tilted the wine against his lips. 'Mary Haggis,' he said. 'Mary...'

She didn't hear his next witty suggestion. She'd already gone to sleep.

'Why do you have such an ugly maid?' His voice was low enough not to carry beyond the door into the bedroom, where Cassie was remaking the bed and clearing away the cups they'd been drinking their tea from.

'She's a good woman, Francis.' She wasn't. Abigail had found her. She was a harlot who'd become too old and too raddled to find customers, even in the darkness of late-night Ludgate Hill. 'She's honest.' She wasn't. She'd offered to show Molly how to steal a watch. Molly had refused to listen. 'She's all I can afford. She's cheap.' She wasn't. But a maidservant who could keep five secrets in her head at once was worth a guinea a week.

He set out his stall. 'If we were married, Mary, you could have a pretty young maid. And we could live in much better rooms than these, in... in Chelsea, or... or in Kensington. Or even Richmond.'

Or Chiswick. Isaac. A sudden pricking behind the eyes. She blinked to clear the memory from her mind. Did Francis understand how much it took to live in places like that? 'But you have no money, Francis.'

'My father is old. He won't live forever. When he dies, his money will be shared between me and my brother.'

Brother? He'd never mentioned a brother. To be married to a butcher was small enough ambition. To be married to half a butcher was not what she'd come to London for.

'Marry me, Mary, and I shall keep you in luxury. Just as soon as father dies and leaves his butcher's shop to me and Charlie.'

For a fleeting moment she wondered about Charlie. Was he a bold adventurer? Or was he as dull as Francis? Whatever he was, he was also worth only half a butcher's shop in Tottenham Court Road. She stopped wondering about Charlie.

She ran her hand over the thick, powerful, butcher's fingers where they rested on her arm. 'Promises, Francis?' She remembered a plain gold ring set with rust-coloured agate, the most important thing she'd ever had, more precious to her even than her maidenhead. Yet both had been stolen from her. 'A woman can't live on promises.'

'Then what am I to do, Mary?'

Half a butcher or not, could she bear to be married to a man who asked her always what he should do? Did he want a wife - or a mother? 'Do, Francis?' She broke away from him. 'Give me my guinea, as we agreed. And tomorrow I shall buy the finest, the most expensive cut of beef in your shop.'

She sat astride the cask and swigged from the stout leather tankard. Her voice was tipsy, edging into wantonness. 'This is good ale, Will. Nearly as good as the ale we used to drink in York.'

'York?!' Mock scorn. 'What do York brewers know of good ale? Their water's too soft to brew a good ale.' He tasted from his own tankard and smacked his lips. 'Now, this is a good ale!'

'Have you tasted York ale, Will?'

'Tasted it? No - wouldn't want to, neither. I've heard tell it tastes like dog's piss.' His broad red face sagged into apology. 'Oh, forgive me, Mary. That was... well, it was...'

She put her finger up to her lips to hush him, and made her face as grave as she could. 'In Yorkshire, Will, dog's piss is considered a right treat.'

He gaped at her in astonishment; then his head tipped back and he howled into laughter. His arms flew up in sheer exhilaration, and his tankard slopped beer onto the cellar floor. Molly tried to keep a straight face, but then almost fell off the cask when she joined in. She enjoyed being with Will. Even without the ale. Even without the guineas.

But she didn't want to marry him.

Having dressed herself again, she sat in the obsessively tidy room above the greengrocer's shop, drinking the tea Philip had poured for her, making a pretence of thinking. Even through the thick rugs on the floor, the smell of oranges and cabbage crept up from the shop below and mingled with the odour of his sober pipe. 'No, Philip,' she said at last. 'I am content to be a widow. Your trade is honourable, and you are a good citizen, a good man. But I do not wish to marry again. Even as respectable a man as you are.'

The cleaver crashed into the side of mutton, slicing flesh, splitting bone, burying its point in the wooden block beneath. He left it where it was, and wiped his hands angrily down his blood-stained blue apron. Scrabbling in his purse, he picked out a golden coin and slammed it down on the scarred table in front of him. 'Did you have that many lonely nights?' he shouted. The rest of his customers stared in surprise. 'Here, take the guinea I owe you! To go with the other two guineas you earn every week!'

The other four. But she let it pass. He'd found out about the fruit and the ale. He didn't yet know about the bread and pastries, the butter and cream. She looked to the other women there for sympathy, shook her head in innocent confusion. 'It's most kind of you to pay me back the money I lent you, Master Francis,' she said, allowing bewilderment to spread over her face, 'but I cannot think what I can have done to anger you.' Her head drooped, and her breath caught in a sob. 'I do not deserve to be treated so,' she sniffed through her manufactured tears, and fled from the shop, her handkerchief to her face, the guinea clutched in her hand.

His voice echoed down Tottenham Court Road after her. 'I also peddle meat - but my goods are more wholesome! And they cost less!'

No help for it but to find new lodgings. Heads were turning openly to gawp at her in the street. The widow that wasn't. The Tottenham Court Road Whore.

Even though he'd been, as he saw it, cuckolded, Francis could talk of nothing else to his friends, his customers, his neighbours. Philip, a Puritan in everything except his appetites, would no longer recognise her; the baker and the dairyman had given instructions that she wasn't to be served.

Will's response was quite different. He simply poured a tankard of ale and handed it to her. 'A widow has to make a living as best she can, Mary.' He cocked his head on one side and looked shrewdly at her. 'If you are a widow, that is.' He chuckled. 'And if your name is Mary.'

She took the tankard from him, drank from it, dabbed the froth away from her mouth. 'Will,' she said, 'the truth is - '

'Drink your ale, Mary,' he said. 'I've enjoyed these few months with you, whatever the truth is, and whatever your name is.' He tipped his tankard, took a great gulp from it, then belched a resounding roar that echoed round the cellar. He winked at her and grinned. 'And your company has been worth every single penny.'

From Tottenham Court Road to St Martin's Lane. Together with Cassie, a trunk marked with the initials MH, and a pin of good ale. And enough frugally-saved guineas to pay back Annie, to rent her new room for a month, and to give herself a few weeks in which to decide what to do next.

If five men in Tottenham Court Road could wish to support the Widow Abbott, why not five others in St Martin's Lane?

London was a big city.

Chapter 24

'He even...' Clunk. '...offered...' Clunk. '...to marry her!' Clunk.

The cleaver swung down precisely between the ribs, one after the other, crashing through flesh and bone onto the unyielding beech block. The butcher gathered up the chops, wrapped them in the torn half of a broadsheet, passed them to the pimple-pocked adolescent beside him, who began to tie the parcel with string.

He shook his head in mocking disbelief. 'That's right, he offered to marry her - after she'd been had by every streetseller in Tottenham Court Road, including the chimney-sweep and the dung-farmer!' He positioned the meat, raised his cleaver again. 'And all to save himself a shilling a week!' Clunk, clunk, clunk. 'Maybe that blockhead Francis will learn his lesson one day - but I doubt if it will be before his inheritance has been gobbled up by some woman.'

The youth handed him the other half of the broadsheet. 'Nothing wrong with women, Master John,' he said with a smirk that owed more to imagination than experience.

'I'm not talking about women, boy. I'm talking about wives.' Another parcel was handed over to be tied. 'Mark my words, boy - and be sure you remember 'em. The most expensive harlot in Covent Garden will cost you less than the most frugal wife anywhere in the world.'

Without any reaction at all, Molly moved away from the flayed pigs hanging outside the open-fronted shop, pretended to inspect the eels writhing in their snakepit pots on the stall next door, then continued on her way.

The tale had become more elaborate in the telling. But the Widow Abbott and her friendships clearly had no more future in St Martin's Lane than they did in Tottenham Court Road.

'No, Cassie!' She paced up and down the cramped room, trying to think. 'No! I am not a harlot!'

Cassie poured the tea into two cups, put the unchipped one on a saucer, and held it out to Molly. She didn't bother with a saucer for herself. 'Yer still gotcha looks, Moll. You ain't got the pox - least, not so as I can tell. And yer still got Covent Garden dresses to put on.' She sucked at the tea, slurping it through the gaps in her teeth. 'If yer wanna make a guinea or two, y'could have half the Town outside yer door.'

'I don't want half the Town outside my door!' She took the tea, but didn't drink it.

Cassie stood at her shoulder, a silken thread of temptation creeping into her voice. 'Yer run outta money, Moll. If yer don't get some afore tomorrer, we're out. We're out on the streets, Moll. An' even if yer change yer mind after that, we won't have a bed for 'em to come to.'

'No!'

'S'not as if yer a maid.' A sly, sidelong glance. 'Or even a widder.'

'No.'

'Come on, Moll, yer got nuffin to lose.' She put her cup on the squat-legged table next to the bed. 'Yer got more to offer than nearly all the uvver 'arlots round 'ere, gel. Yer muff's as good as any, and better'n most.'

Defiance clouded Molly's face. 'No, Cassie. I am not a harlot. I'll do any honest work to help us keep alive. But I won't whore for it.'

'S'not as if you ain't done it afore.'

Molly whirled to face her. 'I have not whored before! I were ravished by the Colonel, and I were the companion of Master Abraham Asher. I were not a whore!'

Cassie took the cup and saucer from her, found a place for the crockery among the rest of the debris on the square table by the window: the basin, the pitcher, the unfinished bottle of wine, the fine-tooth comb, the broken mirror. 'And Master Isaac?'

That was different. 'I loved him, Cassie.'

'Maybe so. But yer still let 'im fuck yer, even though his farver was payin' yer to fuck 'im.'

'Have you ever been in love, Cassie?' Angry, challenging.

She shrugged. 'What's to fall in love wiv? One prick's the same as any uvver.'

Molly tossed her head. Thank God my hopes are better than those of a pox-ridden Ludgate Hill up-against-the-wall threepence-a-time buttock-and-file drab. 'If you've never been in love yourself, Cassie, then pray cease lecturing me on the subject.'

Cassie's weary eyes regarded her. 'Francis the butcher,' she said, ticking them off on her fingers. 'Will the brewer. John the baker. Robert the dairyman. Philip the fruiterer.'

Molly turned away from her, and picked at a loose thread hanging from the curtain knotted clumsily round the bedpost. Her mind continued the count. Quince. Three highwaymen. 'Don't be impertinent,' she said. But her voice carried no command.

'I'm not sayin' yer shoulda married 'em, Moll. But the simple truf is, there's men out there wiv money, and there's you in 'ere wiv a muff.' She touched her fingers to her mistress's sleeve. 'And them out there is willin' to pay what they got for what you got.'

Molly froze the cajoling hand. 'I shall do honest work, or I shall starve.'

Cassie nodded. 'That's your choice, Moll. But the first question yer gotta ask is: are yer gonna starve in 'ere, or are yer gonna starve out on the street?' She set about tidying the room. 'The rent's due tomorrer, Moll. And unless yer fancy fuckin' that squint-eyed lardball of a landlord when he knocks on the door, yer'd better have some money to give 'im.'

The Waif lent her the five guineas she'd promised.

And Will not only paid her his usual guinea, but gave her a letter to present to the landlord of The Six Windmills in Cole Yard.

The work was hard, the hours were long, the atmosphere was hot and noisy and smokey and sweat-laden. Every night, Cassie had to rub witch-hazel into the bruises on Molly's thighs and buttocks and breasts where she'd been groped by drunken customers.

Hard, long, painful - and poorly paid.

'Well, o' course 'e don't give yer much money,' Cassie told her. 'E expects yer to make yer money from the customers. That's what tavern wenches do.'

'I am not going to become a common harlot,' she muttered through clenched teeth. She lay face down on the bed, her skirts pushed up to her waist, as Cassie's stubby fingers soothed over her blue and yellow mottled buttocks. 'There must be some business I can set up in that will earn me an honest living.'

'Your man Abraham,' Cassie said, lightly tapping Molly's thigh as a signal to turn over onto her back. 'Now, 'e knows about business matters, don't 'e?'

'Aye, he does. But,' she added sarcastically, 'I hope you're not suggesting I go to him for advice?' She let Cassie loosen the bodice and pull the dress down over her shoulders, exposing the top half of her body.

'Course not. But if yer did, and yer said to 'im Abraham, I got me a business where I can sell what I got, and still 'ave it afterwards to sell it all over again, what d'yer fink he'd say?' She dripped witch-hazel onto Molly's breast and began to smooth it in. ''E'd say You just found the pot o' gold at the end o' the rainbow, gel. And 'e'd be right.' She tipped the bottle again, dripping it onto the other breast. 'Only, yer too proud to see it.'

Molly's fingers bunched themselves into fists. 'Either shut up, Cassie, or get out and leave me alone!'

'All right, Moll. Won't say anuvver word.' She rubbed the aromatic liquid into the bruises, easing the pain.

Abraham. Why did you have to come to me on the wrong night? Why did you have to find out?

✳

The Six Windmills was Drury Lane, not Covent Garden; and its customers reflected its location. Cutpurses, harlots, highwaymen; murderers and thieves; pimps and beggars.

Worst of all, actors from the Theatre Royal, a scant fifty yards away. Not the famous actors who took the leading roles, but the spear-carriers, the ladies-in-waiting, the attendant lords. Not Macbeth, but the Bloody Sergeant. Not Hamlet, but Rosencrantz and Guildenstern. Not Cleopatra, but Charmian and Iras. They came to the tavern late, just embarking on their night's drinking when everyone else was already drunk, armed with a stock of borrowed insults which they fancied set them intellectually apart.

After a performance of Macbeth, a tapster spills some ale. 'The devil damn thee black, thou cream-faced loon!'

After Henry Fourth, Part Two, one of their own number becomes a 'bolting-hutch of beastliness!', and the landlord a 'huge bombard of sack!'

After Julius Caesar, their fellow drinkers become 'You blocks, you stones, you worse than senseless things!' Hoots of appreciation from the actors. Unimpressed silence from the taverners.

No harm in them until... Until The Provok'd Wife.

The actor playing the Tailor - a stammering, frightened, walk-on role - chose to impress the tavern girls with another actor's lines, Constant's protestations of love to Lady Brute. 'Forgive me,' he declaimed, selecting Molly, and taking her by the hand, 'since my hunger rages, if I at last grow wild, and in my frenzy force at least this from you.' With an actor's studied elegance, he bent and kissed her hand.

There was a whoop of encouragement from his fellows; good-humouredly, Molly bobbed a curtsy. He was ridiculous, but harmless.

He continued to hold her hand. 'Or, if you'd have my flame soar higher still, then grant me this.' He kissed her shoulder. 'And this.' Her uncovered neck. 'And this.' She jerked her head aside, and he kissed her jawline instead of her lips. 'And thousands more.' His hand slid into her bodice and scooped her breast free. He bent to kiss it.

She wrenched herself clear, twisted away, uncoiled back, smacked the back of her hand into his mouth. Ale slopped out of the jug in her other hand, splashing onto his breeches and boots. A cry of anger and pain from the Tailor. Goading encouragement from the rest of the actors. An alert silence from the drinkers about them. The Tailor dabbed at his lip, inspected the blood on his fingers and, without warning, lashed out at Molly's face.

But she'd seen his body position change, and her hand was already lifting to her own defence. The blow caught her on the forearm and sent her reeling, cannoning into one of the rough-hewn tables, sprawling across a leather-aproned apprentice, knocking an ink-fingered clerk off his stool, clattering tankards to the floor, smashing glasses, cascading ale from her jug. She rolled off the table and fell to her knees. Out of the corner of her eye she saw the Tailor's feet dance into position next to her. His hand gripped her upper arm, hauled her to her feet, his brandy breath snarling into her face.

But then a rough-edged voice interrupted him. 'Leave her!' The hand that gripped her arm was, in turn, gripped by another. A ham-sized hand, with fingers as gnarled and knotted as an old crab-tree.

The Tailor allowed his hand to be plucked from Molly's arm, and wriggled round to face her rescuer. A dull-eyed ox with an animal instinct for what was proper and what was not.

Rather than confront this unpredictable Hercules, the actor sought

244

refuge in another quotation, affecting a sneer. 'Sir, when you are cool, you'll understand reason better.' He dropped his hand to the hilt of his sword, a poor weapon, more effective on stage than in a fight. 'If not, I wear a sword, sir. And so goodbye to you.' He turned away.

The huge fist swung him back again. 'And I wear this!' The point of a broad-bladed knife pricked into the actor's throat. The ox had found an insult to defend. The beast of burden had become a ground-pawing bull.

The actor found himself staring into a nothing-left face, a face that was already resigned to its own death on the gallows, and would relish a moment of glory before mounting the scaffold. Warily, he took his hand away from his sword, slowly raised it to his throat, carefully eased the knife to one side. He stepped back, removed his hat and swept an elaborate bow. 'Why, prithee, knight, don't quarrel here,' he quoted. Keeping a watchful eye on the blade, he backed away a few paces. 'Leave private animosities to be decided by daylight.' A safe distance between himself and the threat, he beckoned to his nervous companions. 'Let us find elsewhere to spend our poor groats.' They followed him with as much bravado as they could muster.

At the door, he drew himself up to his most actorly height. 'I do not fight with strangers,' he declaimed. He stabbed a dramatic finger in Molly's direction. 'But I have seen you before, girl. And I know who you are.' His body leaned forward, his voice lowered, his eyes narrowed. 'Yes, I know who you are!' Then, head high, drawing his cloak about him, he was gone, the tobacco smoke swirling out into the street after him.

Amid the renewed chatter and laughter, she was down on her hands and knees, picking up the splintered glass, mopping up the spilled ale.

'Who are you?' Down-at-heel boots, frayed white breeches, stained leather apron. Mine Host.

She wrung out the cloth into the bucket, bent, continued swabbing. 'I don't know what you mean, sir.'

'Yon prancing pimp said he knew who you are.' He waited for an answer. When none came, he spelled it out. 'So who are you?'

She snatched a glance at the door of the tavern. The actors had gone. No one else was in earshot. 'You know who I am, sir.' Innocence. 'The

245

Widow Abbott.' Again she bent to her task.

His feet shuffled, and his boot pinned the cloth she was holding to the floor. 'Yes, I know that. The Widow Abbott. And who were you before that?'

'I don't understand you, sir. My husband died.' A contrived hint of tears.

A complete lack of pity. 'Every widow I've ever known had a husband that died. Even though many of them had never been married.' When she didn't reply, his voice hardened into an ultimatum. 'I don't want you bringing trouble here. Tell me who you are.'

'Does it matter who she is, Master Collis?' The voice was lilting, unhurried, persuasive. Irish. A young woman. Polished high-heeled shoes now stood beside the landlord's boots; a gold-brocaded skirt swayed next to the leather apron. 'Should a girl have no secrets?'

The boots held their ground for a few seconds, then brushed past her and stomped away.

A friendly hand helped Molly to her feet. 'Come, Widow Abbott. You should go home.'

'But I have to - ' She half-stooped towards the cloth at her feet.

'Master Collis will understand.' A charming, melting smile. 'Come.' She led Molly to the door. 'Forgive me, ma'am. I should have introduced myself. My name is Colleen. Colleen Murphy.' She held the door open for her. 'Widow,' she added.

The Widow Murphy walked home with the Widow Abbott. The Widow Abbott invited the Widow Murphy into her humble lodgings for a glass of wine.

The Widow Abbott's maid looked up from the stocking she was darning, and spoke. 'What yer doing 'ere, Jenny?'

The Widow Murphy whirled. 'Cassie!' Most of the Irish lilt had vanished.

'She ain't got nuffin left to steal, Jen. An' if yer don' wan' me to make a fuss, yer'll let 'er 'ave back what yer've already tooken.'

Shocked, Molly gaped in confusion at her new friend. 'Jenny?'

The Widow Murphy inclined her head. 'Also known as Jenny Diver, ma'am.' She delved into her placket, plucked out a fistful of items and placed them on the crude table. 'It was never my intention to keep them, ma'am. I would never steal from a fellow... widow.' A brief, ironic hesitation before 'widow'.

Molly stared at the returned booty, then felt anxiously in her pockets. Empty. 'But how...?'

'A trick of my trade, ma'am.'

Molly's shoulders drooped. This was more than a stolen handkerchief, stolen trinkets, a stolen shilling. Under the pretext of help, this had been stolen trust. Jenny Diver's kindness was no more genuine than the Colonel's had been. And, in three and a half years, Molly had learned nothing. For all her experiences, she was still as innocent as she had been in York.

'And the rest, Jen.' Cassie's squat shape was between them and the door.

Her hands spread wide in a gesture of innocence. 'Nothing else, Cassie. I swear it.'

The servant shook her head. She didn't believe it. 'Yer took it, yer brought 'er home, yer give it 'er back agin. Why? Where's the profit for you, Jen?'

The Widow Murphy, Jenny Diver, offered Molly an explanation. 'After a while, Mistress Abbott, when a person has been successful, it becomes difficult for a person to pass unnoticed in the sort of... milieux where a person would best wish to pass. In those sort of circumstances, a person tries to find - '

'What she's sayin', Moll, is that the Town's on to 'er, and she's tryin' to find a good apprentice. An' wiv your looks, an' wiv yer not bein' known around the Town, you could get away wiv it.'

Jenny took both Molly's hands in her own. 'What do you say, Moll? You wouldn't have to scrub floors any more. You'd be the equal of that jackass who hit you tonight. You'd get a lot more money than you earn in the tavern. What do you say?'

'Stealing?'

'Ten times as much money as you're getting now.'

'And a free lengf o' rope when they catch yer.' Cassie's harsh voice behind her.

'I don't...' I don't know what to think, which to choose. Become a thief? No! But spend the rest of my life in that tavern?

Cassie offered the options. 'Steal, and yer'll 'ang. Stay a tavern maid, and yer'll starve. On the uvver 'and...' She bent down to push the simmering kettle from its trivet onto the low fire. 'On the uvver and, yer could make a lot more'n a shillin' or two wivout stealin', and wivout danglin' at the end of a rope.' She stood and faced Molly. 'And wivout givin' up nuffin you ain't already given up anyway.'

Molly pulled herself away from Jenny's coaxing hands, turned her back on Cassie's encouraging leer. 'I will not become a common harlot!'

'No need to become a harlot at all,' Jenny said. 'I have profited well from men, yet I've only ever lain with those I wished to lie with.' Her voice was suddenly close behind her, murmuring into her ear. 'Are you a maid, Moll?'

A simple question with a thousand justifying answers. 'Well, no, I'm not.'

'Then you know the difference, Moll.' Insistent, persuasive. 'Lying with a man for love, for pleasure, for daring - that's what God made our commodities for! But to lie with a man for money?' Her voice betrayed her contempt. 'No, Moll - that is to make ourselves a chattel. That is to become no more than a flower basket or a cooking pot or a donkey-saddle or a - '

Cassie. 'They don't cart cookin' pots off to Tyburn.'

Jenny rounded on her. 'And stealing doesn't give you the pox!' she spat. 'Stealing doesn't make your teeth fall out! Stealing doesn't eat away your face until no man will even look at you, let alone pay you to infect him with your diseases!'

Molly was shocked. 'I pray you, madam, do not speak to my woman like that!' She strode across the room and flung the door open. 'Indeed, madam, I pray you speak to neither of us at all! Good day to you.'

Jenny glanced at Cassie, bobbed her head to Molly, and left. On the landing outside the door, she made her apologies. 'I have offended you,' she said, 'and for that I am sorry. But be sure, ma'am, you haven't offended me.' She smiled. 'You may one day be grateful that you haven't offended me.' At the head of the stairs, she held out her hand; dangling from her finger and thumb was the handkerchief she had already stolen, already given back, and which Molly had already pocketed. 'Just a trick of my trade, ma'am.'

It was three weeks before the actors returned.

They stood in the doorway, peering into the tobacco smoke, the November fog grey and ghostly behind them, before deciding to enter the tavern. They found a place near the roaring stone fireplace, and called for brandy.

'I'll serve them, Moll.' Coarse-featured, heavy-muscled, taller than most men by three or four inches, the grotesquely-named Dainty hefted a full jug of ale and weaved away between the tables. Within moments she was back. 'They'll have no one but you, Moll.' She stacked a tray with glasses and a bottle, handed it to Molly. 'You take them their brandy, and I'll talk to one or two of my friends. Just in case.' She continued her rounds with her ale-jug, occasionally stooping over a table, whispering into an ear, briefly joining a conversation. Wherever she passed, a glance would stray towards the fireplace, or a head would nod without looking, or a customer would find himself cold and rise to move nearer the fire.

The actor who had played the Tailor picked up the bottle from the table where Molly had set down the tray. 'I've not come to bring you trouble, ma'am,' he said. He slopped brandy into his glass, passed the bottle to one of his companions. He drew Molly to one side, his light fingers on her arm as courteous as any gentleman's. 'I want you to be friendly with me.'

She stepped away from him, and he let his hand fall to his side. 'I am paid to serve you,' she said. 'I am not paid to let you shame me in front of all these men.' She swivelled her head to include the whole tavern.

'Nor are you paid to shame me in front of my companions.' There was no sign of anger about him. Nothing but good humour. 'For that, I want you to be friendly with me.'

'Well, sir. I shall be friendly. But now I have other customers to serve.' She turned away from him. Again, the gentlest touch on her arm. Enough to stop her.

'I wish you to be friendly with me, you slut.' His voice remained genteelly modulated, studiously amicable. 'I wish you to come to my bed. I wish you to whore with me the way you have whored with others. And if you don't, I shall...'

She span away and opened her mouth. Dainty made a prepared gesture with her hand. A dozen men rose to their feet.

'...tell my good friend who you are. More important, I shall tell my good friend where you are.'

A twitch of her fingers. Dainty put out a hand. The men held their positions, waiting, watching.

In a low voice, for his ears only. 'Who is your friend?'

His good-humoured performance continued. He'd won.'I'm sure you must have heard of him, ma'am. His name is Quince.'

Chapter 25

As he came out of Molly's room, the actor tugged his cravat fastidiously into position, checked the alignment of his wig, then swaggered past Cassie, pressing a shilling into her hand as he left.

'G'night, yer 'onour.' She shut the door behind him, picked up the waiting jug of sour milk, carried it into the bedroom. Molly was slumped on the edge of the bed, retching into a handkerchief. 'Let's do it,' Cassie said.

Molly reached for the bottle of wine beside the bed, swigged from it, swilled out her mouth, spat into the bowl Cassie was carrying. She flopped backwards, raised her knees, hauled up her skirts, opened her thighs wide, arched her back as Cassie positioned the bowl and towel underneath her and eased the funnel into her before pouring the milk.

Molly stared at the ceiling. 'Revenge,' she muttered.

'Yer want revenge?'

'No. He wanted revenge. He took no pleasure in me. All he wanted was to make me pay, to make me suffer.'

Cassie removed the bowl, mopped her dry with the towel. 'Shouldn'ta let him, Moll.'

'I had no choice.'

'Why, 'acos he freatened to tell Quince if yer didn't?'

Molly continued to stare at the ceiling. 'I'm frightened of Quince, Cassie,' she said. 'I'm more frightened of Quince than I've ever been of anyone or anything else. Quince is worse than the Colonel. The Colonel wants to harm me out of vengeance. I can understand that. Quince simply wants to harm me.' Her thought drifted into the past. Poor Hannah. Poor, poor, dead Hannah. And I'm next. 'Have you ever seen a rabbit cornered by a ferret, Cassie?'

Pause. 'What's a ferrit?'

She didn't hear the question. She'd retreated into her childhood Yorkshire. 'The rabbit knows it's going to be killed, but it doesn't do anything. It doesn't fight. It doesn't try to escape. It just waits.' She rolled onto her side, hugged herself close and drew her knees up. 'That's how I feel, Cassie. That's why I had to do what that actor made me do. Just to keep Quince away for a few more days.'

Cassie snorted. 'D'yer fink that's gonna keep Quince away? D'yer fink you can trust that actor to keep 'is word? They're all mouf, actors. Wivvin a couple o' days, 'alf o' London'll know about it.'

A tear squeezed out, trickled over her nose and down her cheek, dropped onto the pillow. 'What am I going to do, Cassie?'

Cassie collected up the bowl, the towel, the jug. 'Yer gonna stay 'ere till I gets back,' she told her. 'Don't go out. Don't go to The Six Windmills. Don't do nuffin. Just wait till I gets back.'

The door closed behind her. More tears ran down onto Molly's pillow.

'But I haven't got ten guineas!'

'Ten guineas is nuffin for a gel wiv your looks. Yer could get 'em in no time.'

She rolled over on the bed, turned her face to the wall. 'I will not sell myself, even to buy the silence of a bloodsucker like him.'

Cassie belched an abrupt hiccup of a laugh. 'Oh, 'e won't tell Quince nuffin now. No fear o' that. 'E won't tell nobody nuffin, never agin.'

'What?' Molly sat up and swung her legs to the floor. 'What are you saying, Cassie?' Wide-eyed, horror distorting her features. 'You haven't - ? He hasn't been - ?'

'E's still alive.'

'Then...?'

'There's more'n one way to buy someone's silence, Moll. Now all yer gotta do is pay the people what silenced 'im. Ten guineas.'

*

The part of the Doctor in Macbeth was played at short notice by a newcomer to Drury Lane. The actor who should have played the part was indisposed. His tongue had been cut out.

Since Cassie could neither read nor write, it never occurred to her that an actor might be able to do both. Or that a mutilated actor with revenge on his mind might write down names, might draw pictures, might lead his good friend Quince to the lodgings where their prey had gone to earth.

It was the first thing that came to Molly's mind.

When Quince and the bandage-faced actor came to St Martin's Lane, they sought out the puffy, grease-oozing landlord, pinned him sweating to his own wall, punched him and kicked him, slit his nose, razored fat-deep into his throat, let the hot blood run down under his collar with the threat of a slow death from bleeding. But all he could show them was the empty room that Molly and Cassie had left.

'The Captin wants 'is ten guineas, Moll.'

'I haven't got ten guineas!' I've hardly got enough to keep us in these new lodgings for the next week.

The landlord of The Six Windmills owed her a shilling, but she dared not go there to claim it. And she dared not seek work elsewhere. London was full of eyes.

'Better find a way o' gettin' 'em, Moll. The Captin can do some nasty fings to people when they cross 'im.'

I know. Cutting out a man's tongue; destroying a man's life and livelihood while leaving him alive; and all, she suspected, as much for sport as for money. 'If I had ten guineas, Cassie, I'd give them to him. But I haven't.'

The Captain. She'd never met him, never seen him. But she was in thrall to him. And she knew what he was capable of.

A faceless monster. The shadow on the stairs. The darkness lurking under the bed. The Captain.

Even if she escaped the Captain, the Colonel was waiting for her. And always, always Quince. She could feel her chest constricting, her heart breaking its rhythm, the light slipping away from her...

Cassie's voice bumped her back into the cold daylight of her room. 'Yer could get ten guineas easy, Moll.' Simple, direct, insistent.

Molly looked down into Marylebone Road through the grimy panes of their new lodgings. 'I'll get them my way, Cassie, not yours.'

Will filled the leather tankard with ale, passed it to Molly, bent to pour another for himself. 'Francis has taken a sour-faced widow for his wife,' he said. 'She's ten years older than he is, with three daughters, all above fifteen, all unwed - and all ugly! And why?' He answered his own question. 'Because she has fifty pounds a year from her father.'

'Her father?'

He straightened, drained his tankard, wiped the froth from his lips, poured himself another. 'Some sort of speculator. A successful one.' He took his ale, joined Molly in the corner of the cellar beneath the small, semi-circular, barred window. 'He must be very shrewd,' he said.

She leaned her back against the brickwork, feeling its clammy chill through her cloak and gown. 'Why, is he very rich?'

He turned to face her, and she could see the mischief in his eyes. 'No - but he's shrewd enough to pay Francis fifty pounds a year to take her and her ugly daughters off his hands!' His head tipped back, and his laughter echoed back from the brickwork of the cellar.

'Poor Francis,' she said. But, despite herself, she joined in the laughter.

They took their ale up into the warmth of the kitchen, and sat next to each other on the high-backed settle, facing the log-banked fire, basking in its warmth. For several comfortable minutes, neither spoke.

Then, 'Will?'

He sat upright, attentive. 'Some more ale?'

'No, I haven't finished what I have. But I wondered if you'd like to...?' She laid her hand on his thigh. 'Now that I'm here.'

He leaned back into the settle again. He sought her hand and twined his fingers into hers. 'No, Mary, not tonight. I'm tired.' He raised his tankard in an apologetic salute. 'And this isn't the first jug of ale I've had this day.' Again he squeezed her hand. 'But you shall have your guinea.'

She stiffened. 'I didn't come here for - '

'No, of course you didn't, Mary.' He put his tankard on top of an up-turned barrel, leaned back into his seat again. 'My day is filled with barley and yeast, and cleaning out vats, and delivering ale to my customers.' His voice softened. 'I don't have time to go to Covent Garden and buy you the trinkets I'd like to buy you. So I give you a guinea when you come so that you can buy the trinkets instead of me.' He hesitated. 'I know what you're thinking, Mary. But you're wrong. Yes, I give you a guinea now and then - but that doesn't mean I think of you as a harlot.'

'I - '

He was quick to cut her off. 'Mary, we've known each other for nearly a year. Many a time we've shared a bed. Often I've given you some shillings to spend.' He played with her fingers, stroking them gently with his own. 'But if I lost all my money, I believe you'd lie with me to comfort me. And if you lost all your money, you know I'd put some in your purse without asking you to lie with me.' He stared into the fire, ordering his thoughts. 'I once asked you to marry me, but you wouldn't. You were right. You like me, but you don't love me.' The flames flickered their shadows across his face, disguising any feelings that might have showed. 'Many women wouldn't have thought twice. I'd give them a comfortable living, a house of their own, as much ale or wine as they could drink, and as many trinkets as they could buy. And, in return, they'd give me their bodies. For the first few years, anyway. But they wouldn't love me.' He flicked a glance in her direction. 'They are the harlots, Mary, not you.'

She, too, looked into the flames, watching the patterns form themselves into pictures. 'You're a good man, Will.'

He acknowledged the compliment, but disagreed with it. 'No, Mary, I won't confess to being good. But I will claim to be honest.'

Aye, that's what's so different about him. He's honest. He's never lied to me, nor cheated me, nor flattered me. Nor, as far as I know, cheated anybody else.

And more than honest. Generous. She turned to him, kissed him on the side of his face. 'You're wrong, Will,' she murmured. 'You're a good man.' She snuggled against his shoulder.

They sat easily together, enjoying the warmth of the fire. Then he patted her hand and stood up. 'More ale?'

Without speaking, she put her hand over the top of her tankard.

He thought for a moment. 'No, nor me.' He moved to the fireplace, reached out his foot, and stamped the top log further into the grate, turning it to let the uncharred side take fire from the red embers underneath it. For a while he stood with his back to her, watching the new flames spreading along the log. 'Someone's been here,' he said. 'He asked me if I knew where to find you,' he said.

Her breath caught in the back of her throat, and a chill rippled down her back. 'Quince?' Her voice was strangled with fear.

'Quince?' He hastened back to her, put his hands on her shoulders. 'Are you all right, Mary?'

'Was it Quince?'

Her intensity made him draw back. 'No, not Quince. That wasn't his name.' He sat beside her again, took her hand in his, stroked it to calm her. 'He said his name was Isaac.'

Chapter 26

She struggled to swim up through the sea of green and yellow nausea that was swamping her, struggled to catch her breath, struggled to focus on the anxious face above her. Will was chafing her wrists. As her eyes opened, he plucked a rug from the floor and draped it over her. 'Stay where you are!' he told her.

Within less than a minute he had returned from the cellar with a bottle in one hand and a glass in the other. Plucking the cork out with his teeth, he poured a splash of golden liquid. 'Brandy,' he said, placing it in her hand and guiding it up towards her lips. 'Sip it. It will make you feel better.'

The sharp, heady, fruity smell conjured The Bell into her memory. The Colonel, the rising gorge, the shame. She forced her head aside, her eyelids shut tight and her lips pinched together. 'No! Not brandy. It makes me sick. Just a little water, please, Will. Or some ale.'

Without letting go of her hand, he put the brandy on the floor, retrieved his own tankard and put it into her hand. She took a mouthful from the inch or so of flat ale in the bottom, swallowed it, let it give her time to steady herself.

'What did he want? What did you tell him?' Why is he trying to find me? Why now, after a year, after more than a year?

He knelt beside her. 'I told him the truth, Mary. I know nothing of you.'

And, good man that he is, he'd never ask. 'Why was he here? How did he find me?'

'I don't know. He said he'd ridden from York.'

'York?'

'Yes. I remembered that especially, because it's where you told me you grew up.' He released her fingers, rose to his feet, moved to the fire, stood with his back to her. His stocky frame was silhouetted against the flames. 'Who is he?'

How could I begin to tell him about Isaac? The man who unlocked the woman inside me. The man who often frightened me, and just as often made me frightened of myself. The man who still rampages through my dreams, whose name is on my lips when I wake. 'He's...

256

he's someone I used to know.'

He turned. 'Before you were a widow? Or after?' With the fire behind him, she couldn't see his face.

'It were - '

Again, he interrupted her. 'Forgive me, Mary. You have no need to tell me. I have no claim on you. It touches on you, not on me.' A note of concern crept into his voice. 'Is he a threat to you?'

'No.' Perhaps.

'If he should come here again, shall I tell him where to find you?'

'No!'

He nodded his promise, changed the subject. 'One thing puzzled me, Mary.'

'Will, please. I don't want to...' I don't want to hurt you. Please don't ask me any more questions. Please don't ask me about Isaac.

He stared down into the flames. When he spoke, his voice was so low it was almost drowned by the crackling of the logs. 'He called you Molly. I've only ever known you as Mary.' He looked up at her, pasted a jaunty smile onto his lips. 'It doesn't matter what other people call you, whether you like to be known as Molly, or Mary, or Lucy, or Betty. But I'd like to call you by your real name.' Before she could answer, he lost his nerve. 'Forgive me. You probably don't want anyone to know.'

She pushed the rug aside, beckoned him to sit beside her. 'In London, most people know me as Moll,' she said. 'In York, everyone knew me as Molly. Except my mother and my father, God rest their souls. They always called me by my given name. Mary. To you, Will, I shall always be Mary.' She kissed him. 'Molly is for other people.'

Molly is for Isaac.

He'd drunk a lot of his own ale, but not too much. And he was in excellent spirits, a contented man, a happy man.

When she left, she had a guinea in her purse, twice as much as she'd hoped for.

Restless, alone in the midnight of her Marylebone bed, she shifted from her left side onto her belly, from her belly onto her right side, eased her aching neck, pulled the blankets tight round her shoulders.

Isaac. For nearly fifteen months, she'd tried to forget him. She'd tried to blot out his face while Francis was sweating into her, tried not to remember his smell while Philip snored beside her, buried his memory while the actor took his revenge on her.

But why now? What was he looking for? What did he want?

Her broken dreams saw him now as a delivering knight, now as an avenging angel; sometimes with his hand stretched out in love, sometimes with his fist clenched in anger; always with his Jew-black eyes boring into and beyond her own. Her muscles rigid and aching, she rolled herself onto her back, shivering as her feet strayed out of her body-warmed cocoon into the ice-cold of the night air. Had he really sought her all the way to York and back? Where else had he sought her? How had he tracked her to Will? Will knew her by a different name. And...

Bursting into full waking, she sat up in the darkness, ignoring the chill on her shoulders and breasts. If Isaac could hunt her down to Will's house, so could Quince.

✻

My dear Friend Will

I have chang'd my Lodgings but I can not fay where to.

If Ifaac should feek you out again, I pray you do not tell him where I am, even if you have difcover'd. He is a pafsionate Man, and I know not why he purfues me. He has Caufe to hate me, and I freely confefs my Fault, but his Religion claims an Eye for an Eye and a Tooth for a Tooth and I fear his Revenge.

There are Others who would feek me. I pray you, Will, tell No-One that you have ever known me.

Your loving Friend

Mary

Different rooms. A different part of London. The same relentless striving for enough money to live on.

Cassie tipped last night's slops into a bucket, dumped the bucket by the door, returned to straighten the blankets on the bed. 'I tooken meself a job, Moll.'

Molly looked up, accepted the inevitable, went back to the hem she was sewing. She'd expected it. She hadn't paid Cassie for a month. 'When are you leaving?'

'What?' Her face crumpled, and her eyebrows bunched together in a question. 'What d'yer mean?' Her brain put the pieces together, and her face smoothed out. She grinned. 'Nah, I ain't leavin' yer, Moll. I just gotta job, that's all. Wiv Miss Charity downstairs.'

Miss Charity's name suggested she came from a Puritan family; her behaviour belied the possibility. Dark-haired and pale-skinned, wide-eyed and thin-lipped, she claimed she was nineteen, the daughter of a preacher in Portsmouth. She affected dainty airs, played prettily with her Chinese fan, and serviced anything from three to five cullies a night.

Miss Charity rented the whole of the floor at street level, drank French wine, bought her gowns in Covent Garden.

Molly cramped herself into two rooms, hid from men who wanted to murder her, and strayed closer and closer to starvation.

'She's good at what she does, Moll. She gets more offers'n she can 'andle.' Cassie summoned up the most reasonable face she could invent, and squeezed her voice into a wheedle. 'Why don't I bring the extras up the stairs, eh? It'd be good for all of us.'

'No.'

'It's not as if yer was gonna make yer livin' at it, Moll. Yer'd just be 'elpin' out a neighbour, that's all.'

'No!' She put her sewing to one side, rose, stood by the rain-spattered window. To the left, the stark twin towers of Bishopsgate; to the right, the rough road that cut north past the meat-and-potato market of Spitalfields, past the ironmongers' almshouses, then on and on and on to York itself. 'Come here, Cassie. What do you see down there?'

'What?' She leaned over Molly's shoulder, peered down into the street. Two slouching beggars, a loping sedan chair, a couple arguing as they walked, a carriage trotting south, a wagon trundling north.

259

'Nuffin' down there what I can see.'

'Bishopsgate, Cassie.' She turned to face the maid. 'Somebody is looking for me. Somebody who is looking to cut my throat. Somebody who knows the folk who live in Bishopsgate.'

Cassie frowned. 'Why we still livin' 'ere, then? Why don' we get some diff'rent lodgin's?'

Different lodgings. Already Wood Street, Tottenham Court Road, St Martin's Lane, Marylebone, Bishopsgate. East, west, north. All that was left were Southwark's south-of-the-river alleys, and Ludgate Hill, the harlot's mound at the centre of the warren.

But, sooner or later, everyone in London passed through every one of its burrows. It didn't matter where she and Cassie lived, Quince would find them. Even in the stews of Southwark, as poor dead Hannah had found out.

Rabbits and ferrets. 'If the person who's looking for me should find out I'm living here, how long do you think this throat of mine would stay uncut?'

'Ow would he know, Moll? I'd never tell 'im.' Loyal, kind, honest according to her own creed, more aware of the street's demands than most. But unintelligent.

She took Cassie by the hand, led her to the bed, sat her down, sat beside her. 'No, Cassie, of course you'd never tell him. You're a good woman, and I know you love me.' You're a stupid woman, and I can't trust you - not because you don't love me, but because you've got no imagination. 'But if one of Miss Charity's extras happened to be someone who recognised me, they might boast about it. And the person who's looking for me might hear.'

Cassie's brows furrowed as she thought. 'Yeah, yer right Moll.' She stood, collected the bucket of slops by the door, clomped downstairs to empty it.

❋

Cassie was glowing with her own cleverness. 'I 'ad a word wiv the Captin, Moll. Yer can pay him back 'is ten guineas - and yer don't 'ave to fuck nobody.'

Molly stared at the items Cassie had spread out on the bed. A folded black sheet, on which lay a broad-brimmed, point-crowned hat; beside it, a tied bundle of silver birch twigs, three slender glass phials with strange symbols painted on them, and two black candles.

She opened the small lacquered box nestling in her hand, tried to guess at the grey powder inside it, then hastily closed the lid. She waved her other hand at the rest of the theatrical props. 'What am I to do with these?'

'The Captin says it's worf a crown a time against yer debt.'

'Aye, Cassie, but how?'

'Easy. The cully pays 'alf a guinea. You gets a crown, and the Captin gets the rest.' She decided to let Molly into the secret. 'Truf is, Moll, the cully pays a guinea. You gets a crown, an' the Captin gets the uvver sixteen shillins.' She gave an admiring grimace in appreciation of a true professional. 'You does the work, an' the Captin gets the profit.' Serious again. 'But at least yer workin' off yer debt.'

Molly sighed, tried not to let the exasperation make her snap at her maid. 'Aye, Cassie, but what am I to do?' *Whatever it is, I'll have to do it forty times to work off a ten-guinea debt.*

Cassie frowned, puzzled. Birch, pointed hat, potions and powders. There was only one thing it could be. 'Witchcraft,' she said.

'What?'

'Witchcraft. That's what these are for.' She grinned, sly and mischievous. 'Course, what 'e really wants is a witches' sabbaf, only 'e's too mean to pay for a full coven. Fifteen 'arlots all at once ain't cheap.' She narrowed her eyes, and sucked her decaying teeth. 'Mind you, 'e could prob'ly afford it. Maybe 'e's too important to take a chance on bein' seen by a full coven.' Her slow brain chewed over the idea. 'A guinea for just one hour wiv just one 'arlot. Yeah, 'e's scared o' bein' found out.'

'Who? Who's scared of being found out?' *Scared of being found out doing what?*

'Abelard.'

'Abelard?' *Nobody is called Abelard.*

'Least, that's what the Captin says 'is name is. Probably somefin' else, though.'

Molly realised she was still holding the tiny wooden box, and hastily put it down on the bed with the rest of the items. 'But what do I do?' *Witchcraft? Covens? Broomsticks and pointed hats? Bottles of God* knows what? The nearest they'd ever come to anything like this in York was All-Hallowe'en, and that was just children's games, an excuse to be pretend-scared. This was altogether different. 'What will he expect me to do?'

Cassie shrugged. 'Dunno, gel. I on'y ever cleaned up afterwards. I never actually done it meself. But, well, yer got all the bits and pieces there.' She prodded at the assembled oddments. 'The birch is for givin' 'im a good whippin'. The bottles've got some sort 'a potion in 'em. An' the sheet an' the 'at and the candles are there to make him shit 'imself wiv fright.'

None of it made any sense. 'Aye, but what do I do?'

'Don'cha know nuffin about this sort o' fing?'

The more I live in London, the more I realise I know nothing about anything. 'All I know is what you've just told me, Cassie.' And that is so little, there's not even enough to build a guess on.

Cassie's face split into a cheerful grin. 'Don't worry about it, Moll. If 'e's payin' a guinea for it, 'e's bound to tell yer if yer doin' it wrong.'

'I don't know what to do, Annie!' She refused to whore for the money - but at least she knew what whoring entailed. This was straying into the unknown.

The redhead pulled Molly inside, looked nervously up and down Love Lane, then slammed the door behind them. 'You shouldn't have come here without telling me beforehand, Moll. It's dangerous.' She bustled her down into the kitchen, poured cordial into a beaker, tipped gin on top of it, clasped it in Molly's hand, guided it to her lips. 'Drink this.' She waited until Molly had sipped at the rich purple liquid, waited till her mouth had recovered from its tight-lipped spasm. 'Tell me.'

She told her everything. The birch twigs; the black hat, black sheet, black candles; the mysterious phials. 'I don't know what to do, Annie. Cassie brought me all these instruments of devilry, and a man I've never met is coming tonight, and if I don't do what he says - '

'It's a game, Moll.'

'But if I don't - '

'Quiet yourself, Moll. It's only a game.'

Molly wiped her mouth with the back of her hand. 'A game? Dabbling in witchcraft? Endangering my soul? A game?' She couldn't believe

262

that Annie could be so unaware of the dangers.

Annie enclosed her in a reassuring hug. 'Just a game, Moll. It has nothing to do with your soul.' She moved her away to arm's length. 'Nothing to do with your soul, Moll - and not much to do with your body.' She frowned, concentrating hard. 'You said his name was Abelard. I've heard that name, but I can't... Abelard.' Her face cleared. 'Wait here, Moll. I think Kitty will know.'

Kitty knew about Abelard. The Twins knew about witchcraft. Polly knew more than most about birches. Nan and her pock-marks sat sullenly in a corner of the kitchen, and two new girls whispered to each other, sneaking glances at the rest and sniggering to themselves.

The Waif gave them a potted biography of the historical Abelard. 'He had his balls cut off for fucking a nun,' she told them.

It didn't make any sense. 'I don't understand,' Molly admitted. 'Surely he can't want me to...?'

'Maybe he's already had them cut off...' said one of the Twins.

'...and he wants you to cast a spell to bring them back,' said the other. Everyone took a few moments to weigh up the problem.

'Put two pebbles in a purse, and tie it round his prick,' Polly suggested.

'But as soon as he goes off the boil, it'll slide off again,' the Waif objected.

'I don't know what he expects,' Molly said when the lewd laughter had died down.

Nan, sullen and solitary in the corner, brought the subject back from castration to whipping. 'He expects you to use the birch,' she said. The rest of the girls twisted in their chairs to hear what she had to say. 'He wants you to flog him.'

'Flog him?' Molly tried to frame the thoughts in her head. It didn't make sense. 'But why?'

'He likes it. He likes pain.'

'How can anyone like pain?'

Nan shrugged. 'Some do.'

'No, Nan, that can't be true. Nobody likes - '

A flicker of spirit stirred in her tired eyes. 'You watch him. He'll be as limp as a piece of wet string until you flog him. Then he'll get big. Then he'll...'

'Then he'll ram into you like a stallion...' One of the Twins, thin spite pursing her lips.

'...and leave you bruised and bleeding and hurting all over.' The other.

Nan's weary voice contradicted them. 'No he won't. He'll do it himself. He might want to splash it over you, but he won't waste it inside you.' She stood and traipsed towards the above-stairs part of the house. 'He doesn't want a harlot. He wants someone to flog him. But the only way he's going to get what he wants is by paying a harlot to do it, or by breaking the law and being flogged in earnest.'

'That'd be cheaper,' said Polly.

Nan paused at the top of the steps. 'But then he'd be tied to the whipping post. He wouldn't have a hand free to do what he wants most.' The door swung shut behind her.

Molly couldn't believe what she'd just been told. 'I have to put on a silly hat and flog somebody?'

Annie sketched in more detail. 'But you have to take off the rest of your clothes first.'

Molly gaped at her in disbelief, and conjured up a vision of herself. Nude but for a witch's hat, lashing a birch switch at the white buttocks of an overgrown schoolboy, while he jerked furiously at himself.

'No!' Whoring is bad enough. But this is worse. This is turning myself into a burlesque.

The Twins offered their advice. 'Set the candles behind you, and as low to the floor as you can...'

'...then he can't see your face, and all the shadows will be wrong. Upside down shadows are very frightening.'

'When he first arrives, be wrapped in the black sheet up to your armpits...'

'...but leave your arms outside.'

'Offer him some wine...'

'...but spoon powder into it first.'

'Make sure he sees you do it. Then stir it...'

'...and make him drink it.'

Molly began to be apprehensive. Cassie had brought powder. 'What's in it?' Poison? A love potion? A witches' brew?

The Twins had the answer. 'We always used to use dried baby-shit,' one of them said. They fell silent. Everybody fell silent. The Twins didn't have babies any more. Both babies were dead.

But the world went on, whether babies died or lived. The other Twin picked up the story. 'Any powder will do,' she said. 'They never know what it is.'

'When he's drunk it, take the birch...'

'...and let the sheet fall to the floor.'

'Whip his arse as hard as you can...'

'...but never let any marks show on his back.'

Molly was being carried along inside the nightmare. 'How many... When shall I know when to stop?'

The Twins grinned at each other, then turned their grins on Molly. 'You'll know when.'

'When he spills his seed.'

'When he pops, wrap yourself in the black sheet again...'

'...and tell him he's in thrall to your master...'

'...the Great God Pan.'

'Who?'

The Waif leapt in. 'The Great God Pan, one of the Greek - '

Annie cut her off. 'Tell him anything, Moll, but never mention Satan. If you tell him he's in thrall to Satan, you could end up being burned at the stake.'

For several seconds, nobody spoke. For a suspended moment, the School for Harlots linked fingers with the College of Bigots.

It was Polly who broke the silence. 'And before he leaves, make sure you get his money.'

✻

Molly snatched up her gown and covered herself as Cassie barged backwards through the door, both hands intent on not spilling the basin of hot water she was carrying.

'Someone to see yer.' She set the chipped basin down on the table, wiped her hands down her apron.

Molly could feel her resolve fast escaping from her. 'He's early! He's not supposed to be here till six! The clock hasn't struck five yet!' Her shoulders hunched forward, trying to hide behind the brocaded cloth.

'It's not an 'im. It's an 'er.' She stood back to let the visitor pass her.

'Hello, Moll,' the Waif said.

'Kitty! What are you doing here?'

The door closed; as far as Cassie was concerned, it was now Molly's business.

'There's nothing for me at The Bell tonight,' the Waif explained, 'so I thought I'd come and help you.'

'But why? How? What are you going to do? I don't need any help.'

The Waif dumped a shapeless cloth bag on Molly's bed. 'You're scared, Moll. I could see that all the while we were talking at The Bell.' She up-ended the bag and tumbled its contents onto the blankets. Corked pots, twists of paper, coloured sticks. 'You're too much a Christian, Moll. You couldn't birch anyone, not unless you really hated him. And probably not even then. So I've come to help.'

Molly shook her head. 'No, Kitty. I'll try to birch him, if that's what he wants. But I...'

With a light skip, the Waif was beside her. 'Pretend he's the Colonel,' she said, her voice low and intense. 'Just pretend you're birching the Colonel!'

Molly looked into her own soul. Aye, she could birch the Colonel. She could thrash the Colonel. She could whip the cart away from under him as he stood on the gallows. She could cut out the blackened tongue as it protruded through his... through his...

She found herself on her knees beside the bed, the Waif's arms holding her tightly.

'Don't be frightened, Moll. It's only a game.'

Two or three deep breaths, and she was clear again. 'Only a game. Aye, only a game.'

The Waif released her, stood up. Her eyes flashed with mischief. 'If this Abelard wants some magic,' she said, 'let's give him some magic.' She looked around her. 'Where can I hide?'

Molly climbed to her feet, indicated the entire room with a single open-handed gesture. 'There isn't anywhere. This is all I've got.'

'Hmmm.' The Waif knelt beside the bed and lifted the dangling edge of the blanket. 'Yes,' she decided. 'Plenty of room under here.'

'What for? Plenty of room for what?'

The Waif grinned. 'I wonder if your Abelard has ever been to the theatre?'

He was tall, thin, long-nosed, narrow-eyed. Imperious, brusque, used to command. A judge, a bishop, a general. Aristocratic in feature, puritanical in demeanour, a button short of foppish in the silvered lace and gold brocade that hung about his clothes.

Behind him, in the open door, Cassie held out her open palm to show the large silver coin, then backed out and shut the door. The candles, set low, flickered deformed shadows across the walls.

He plucked an engraved watch from the pocket of his embroidered crimson waistcoat, held it up, angled it to catch the light. 'One hour,' he said. He dropped the watch back into his pocket. 'You know what you are being paid for?'

As the Waif had instructed her, Molly gazed past him into the distance. 'Thou commandest a succubus for thy pleasure,' she intoned. 'But thy pleasure must be paid for with pain.'

The idea was foolish, the words were meaningless. Dressed in nothing but a black sheet and a pointed hat, she felt ridiculous.

He nodded his approval that she'd understood, however rudimentally, the rules of the game. Without bothering to look at her, he stripped off his topcoat, draped it neatly over the back of the chair beside the bed, loosened his lace cravat. He unbuckled his sword-belt and laid it precisely, almost mathematically, on the seat of the chair.

She remembered her script. 'Dost thou thirst?'

'A glass of wine relaxeth the body, and prepareth the soul,' he replied, his back to her as he continued with his preparations. Recited as an incantation, but not with any belief. Just a game.

She poured the wine, fighting the urge to giggle. But, when he turned towards her again, her face was composed, her eyes mysteriously hooded.

She handed the wine to him. 'But a magic potion can transport you into a magic world.' It was nonsense, empty, childish chatter.

He gestured a response, urging her to get the ritual out of the way. She opened Cassie's box of powder on the table, scooped out a spoonful, tipped it into the wine. As she stirred, she wondered what Cassie had been given. Baby-shit? Beggar's shit? Or something worse? Abelard took the wine, considered it for a moment, then swigged it back in one

267

draught. He handed the glass back to her, bowed his head. 'Yes,' he murmured. 'Now.'

He fumbled at the front of his breeches, then pushed them down to his knees. His flaccid weapon slopped from side to side as he moved. Hobbling to the bed, he rolled clumsily onto it, contriving to end up in a crouched position. His scarred white buttocks pointed at her in an upside-down heart-shaped target.

'Dost thou command a succubus for thy pleasure?' she asked him. According to the Twins, by asking him this question she was protecting herself against the law. As long as the victim agreed in court that he'd said it.

'Yes, of course I do, girl. Just get on with it, will you.'

When was she supposed to let the sheet fall? Before or after she'd whipped him? She'd forgotten. But, with his face buried in her pillow, he couldn't see her anyway. Go on with the script. 'Thy pleasure must be paid for with pain.'

His voice was muffled by the pillow. 'Get on with it!' he growled.

She reached down the birch switch from the wall, held it at arm's length, then whipped it lightly against the sepulchre-white flesh cocked up at her. A fan of pale pink weals began to glow against the white.

He waited.

She took another tentative stroke.

Again he waited. Then he rolled onto his side and glared up at her. 'My pleasure must be paid for with pain, girl,' he said. 'Pain. Not tickling. Pain.' He rolled onto his face again, tucked up his knees, re-offered the target, and waited.

Molly remembered what the Waif had said. She called up a picture in her mind of the Colonel, remembered her first night at The Bell, piled on top of it all the other nights at The Bell, blamed the Colonel for her lost innocence, her lost ambition, her lost opportunities, blamed the Colonel for everything that was degrading and sordid and unpleasant.

She gathered up nearly four years of guilt and humiliation and self-hatred, and channeled them into a clutch of birch twigs. In front of her, Abelard became the Colonel, kneeling on the bed, his arse in the air. Planting her feet firmly, she balanced the birch in her right hand.

Slowly, she raised it high above her head then, leaning her full weight into it, she slashed it down at him.

'Yes,' he grunted. 'Again.'

Yes. Again. And again, and again, and again. Her anger rose, and the blows grew stronger.

Her virginity. 'Yes.' Cousin Tom. 'Yes!' Quince. 'Yes, yes!' Hannah. 'Yes, yes, yes!!!'

He rolled onto his back. His purple-headed manhood was swollen, blood-gorged, pulsating stiff. He enfolded it in his fist and began to jerk urgently at it. 'Oh, yes!' he cried.

Molly released the black sheet, allowed it to fall away from her, stood naked in front of him. She flung her arms wide and recited the line the Waif had taught her. 'Come, succubus!'

'Eeeeeaaagghhpphhhssssshhh!!!' Hissing and screeching, spitting and howling, the Waif rose up above the bed.

Her head and face were covered with a black hood, sewn about with crows' feathers. In the dim, upward thrust of the candles, she seemed to have no head at all.

Apart from the hood, she was naked.

Painted across each of her half-formed breasts was a gigantic eye, the nipple bright red in the centre. Snarling the width of her waist, a black mouth with pointed, blood-dripping teeth. Her pubic triangle, unshaven for some weeks, sprouted black and curly in the shape of a fuzzy beard. Strapped to her right wrist, a rag doll, its overlong skirt covering her hand.

Molly saw the Waif, made-up and play-acting.

But Abelard was confronted by a grotesque bulging-eyed white head, as big as a cow, its arms sprouting where its ears should be, its legs forking from its bearded chin.

'Aaaaaaaaaaaaaarrrgghhh!!!!' He scrambled howling away from the apparition, backing desperately up against the carved wooden bedhead, his eyes popping in fright.

With pig-squealing venom, the doll shot out towards him. Its skirt dropped over his fear-rigid prick, gripped him tight, carried on where he had stopped, up, down, up, down, squeezing, urging.

Gibbering, he stared into the wide-eyed, unwavering smile of the mewling moppet as it sat on him and ravished him.

Behind the horror, inside the terror, he could feel the seed swelling, rising, spurting, splashing. His consciousness reeling, losing its hold, falling into blackness...

The gentle slapping at his face brought him gibbering back up into consciousness. Molly was leaning over him, covered to the armpits in the black sheet, still wearing the pointed black hat, still holding the birch. 'Would you like some wine?' she asked him.

He shied away from her. 'No!' He scrabbled his feet to the floor on the opposite side of the bed to her. 'No! No wine!' He tried to stand up. But his breeches were round his ankles. He tripped and fell forwards. Grabbing for support, he brought the chair down on top of him, clattering his sword to the floor and tumbling his coat on top of him. He struggled free. 'Witchcraft!' he gasped. He clawed his way to the door, trailing his coat and sword behind him.

The last thing she saw was the purple-red weals slashed across his bare buttocks as he dragged open the door and whimpered over the threshold.

When the Watch thundered on the door a quarter of an hour later to investigate Abelard's complaint, Cassie let them in at once. After all, what was to be hidden?

Molly sat on the chair by her bed, sewing. In a corner, her hair in childish bunches, the Waif sucked the thumb of one hand and nursed her rag doll with the other, humming a cradle song to it. Cassie carried on brushing the floor with the bundle of birch twigs. A simple domestic scene.

The Leader of the Watch, a slow, heavy-framed, red-faced man, searched ponderously through the room, then referred to the scrap of paper in his hand. 'Have you had suckle-busses in here?' he asked.

Molly affected ignorance. 'What?'

'Suckle-busses. Or something what sounds like that. Have you?'

She frowned. 'I don't know what they are. I've never heard of them.'

'They're...' He hesitated. Confused, embarrassed, out of his depth. 'I've been told that they're monsters. With their heads where their bodies ought to be. And they... Well, the gentleman that brought us here said these suckle-busses gave him more of a pleasuring than he's ever had from the most costly harlot.'

Cassie spoke up from the door. 'What's he complainin' about, then?'

The Leader of the Watch took Molly into his confidence. 'I can see there's nothing amiss here. But he's an important man, and I have to ask the questions. Please don't be angry.'

She inclined her head, gracious, forgiving.

He read from his paper again. 'Have you ever had dealings with the Devil?'

She sprang to her feet, horror on her lips. 'Oh, my Lord Jesus Christ, no!'

'Your servant?'

Cassie cast a perfunctory look over her shoulder. 'Not me, yer 'onour.'

'The child?'

Molly lowered her voice. 'Not really a child any more, sir. But...' She circled a finger near her temple. 'But not really a woman, either.'

He studied the Waif briefly, dismissed her from his dim calculations, returned his attention to Molly. 'He said I was to seek a birch and candles and a black sheet. He said that's how I'd know there'd been witchcraft done.'

Molly opened her arms, inviting him to see the room for what it was. She had nothing to hide. 'A birch broom, candles, a sheet.' She feigned embarrassment. 'Dirty, sir, perhaps. But not black.' She admitted the charge. 'It's true, sir, we have all those. What house doesn't?'

'And boxes of powders. And potions.' The pots and boxes on the table in front of her mirror were in plain view.

She led him to one side. 'Sir,' she said, 'sometimes I serve ale at The Six Windmills. I have to work late into the night. And sometimes I have to tempt some of the customers to...' Woman of the world to man of the world. 'A tavern wench doesn't earn much money serving ale.' She touched a fingertip to one of the boxes on the table, the box that contained the powder she'd stirred into Abelard's wine. 'These are a woman's powders and paints, good sir. Just a little help for when we need to look the way we did when we were younger.'

He accepted the explanation, signalled to the three men with him. 'There's no witchcraft here, lads. Our man probably got the wrong street.'

When the Watch had clomped noisily down the stairs and out into the street again, Molly, the Waif and Cassie fell on each other, laughing at their escape.

It was Cassie who brought the bad news. Abelard had complained to the Captain, and the Captain was not pleased. However, he'd decided to be generous - this time. This time, he wouldn't increase the ten guineas she owed him.

But the next ten visitors he sent her were to be serviced the way he wanted them to be serviced, the way they expected to be serviced.

And Molly was to receive not one penny.

Cassie wiped the birch with a filthy cloth, cleaning the worst of the blood off the twigs. 'The rent's due tomorrer,' she said.

'I know, Cassie, I know. But it will be at least a week before I start earning anything from the Captain's callers.' Wearily, she fitted the cap onto a pot of unidentifiable powder and put it back onto the table. 'What am I to do, Cassie? What am I to do?'

Cassie looped a length of string round the birch and hooked it in its place on the wall. She turned to Molly, let her eyes flick to the bed, then back to Molly.

She said nothing.

Chapter 27

It was a day for visitors.

Molly put her sewing to one side as Cassie stood back to let in the first, her neighbour from downstairs. It was early, not yet noon, and the spring sunshine was already angling away from the east-facing windows. Miss Charity took in Molly's lodgings with a single practised glance, noted the birch hanging above the bed, the pointed hat hanging beside it. What she'd heard seemed to be true. 'Miss Moll,' she said, 'I hope you will forgive me calling on you unannounced in this manner. The truth is, I have been neglectful as a neighbour, and I should have made my acquaintance with you long before now.'

Molly said nothing, waited politely for her to go on. *The truth is, you've heard about the succubus, and you want to know how you can profit from it.*

'It's not a subject I'd care to dwell on, Miss Moll, but... Well, you and I are sisters in our chosen livelihood.'

Molly reacted warmly, delighted to help where help was needed. 'You're a seamstress?' she asked, wide-eyed, avoiding any hint of mockery.

Miss Charity's smile scattered, then quickly re-grouped. 'I can sew,' she admitted, 'if I have to. But, like you, I prefer to live by the guineas willingly given by gentlemen rather than the pennies grudgingly doled out by tailors.'

Molly continued to play the innocent, gave no sign that she'd understood Miss Charity's words.

'I seems to me, Miss Moll, that we could come to an arrangement which would be to the advantage of both of us.' Molly said nothing. 'I was wondering whether you might feel able to assist me in a certain matter.'

Molly relented. The poor woman had climbed all the way up a flight of stairs to beg this favour; and, with her night after night exertions, the effort must have tired her. She stood, swept the white and black cat from the room's only chair, offered the seat to her visitor.

Miss Charity sat. 'Cassie tells me there's not a young lady in Town who is more knowledgeable than you in a particular subject that interests me.'

'And that is?'

'The whipping of naughty little boys. And the practice of a certain kind of witchcraft.'

Molly shrank away in terrified revulsion. 'God defend us,' she gasped.

Her visitor acknowledged the performance with the briefest of nods. 'But...' She lowered her voice in case there were listeners; they both knew there were none. 'I have heard tell that you raised a succubus. A real one, not just a raree-show.' Her voice was friendly, her manner was demure, her eyes were ice-cold.

Molly remained standing, her hands clasped modestly in front of her. But she didn't reply. Confess nothing, in case there's trouble in it; deny nothing in case there's a profit in it. One of Cassie's lessons. Cassie's lessons were brutally specific, uncompromisingly pragmatic.

With nothing volunteered, Miss Charity was forced to break her own code of etiquette and ask the question. 'How did you do it?'

As if unwittingly, Molly let her head turn briefly towards the boxes of powders on the table, the phials of potions.

Miss Charity followed her gaze. 'Ah, I see.'

No you don't. You can't begin to imagine. And you're not even interested. All you want is for me to take a certain kind of customer off your hands.

And I'm not surprised. Look at you: you haven't got the shoulders for it. Giving them their money's worth of birching takes the strength of a farmgirl like me, not the pudgy white flesh of a bedbug like you. Your cunny may be as tough as leather, Miss Charity, but your arms are as flabby as bread and milk.

Time to get to the point. Her father's words hovered in her mind: money matters are best painted in black and white. There's no room for grey when your livelihood's at stake. 'How much?'

Miss Charity's demureness held rigid on the surface, but the tone of her voice changed. This was her territory. 'A silver crown for each visitor. Plus a shilling extra for every one who returns a second time.'

Molly made her counter-offer. 'Half a guinea for each visitor, every time, whether they've been here before or not. And, of course, no extra shillings.'

274

The other woman's voice tightened as the bargaining began. 'That is rather de trop, Miss Moll, don't you think?'

She didn't understand the foreign phrase, but she had a close idea of the objection behind it. 'Not at all, Miss Charity.' Cassie had let slip what the visitors expected to pay; and half a guinea a time was a good profit for Miss Charity. 'You make the introductions, I do the work. You get half, I get half.' She leaned forward earnestly. 'Of course, if you prefer, I'll teach you how to wield the birch - and how to mop up the blood and salve the wounds afterwards.' She was painting her own picture now, in vivid colours. Abelard was the only man she'd ever whipped, and she'd not even broken his skin. But Miss Charity didn't know that. 'If you're willing to study, I'll...' She looked nervously over her shoulder, ran her tongue over her lips, made her voice small. '...I'll teach you how to conjure up a succubus. Then,' she added brightly, 'you won't have to pay me anything at all.'

Miss Charity had played her share of tricks on the men who visited her. But she'd heard the tale of the succubus, she'd heard of the gibbering terror it had inspired, she'd heard described its obscene shape, its animal howling, its slavering mouth, the blood dripping from its hooked fangs. And its companion, the rat-sized, baby-faced devil that ravaged the victim. It was beyond anything she could construct. Perhaps, just perhaps, Miss Moll hadn't created it herself. There were, she knew, ancient books handed down from magician to magician, from sorceress to sorceress.

She fought hard not to kick away the white and black sleekness that was rubbing itself against her legs, its purr insistent, obtrusive, unnaturally loud. Every witch had her familiar.

'Half a guinea,' she agreed. She stood, anxious to leave. 'Cassie will be our bond.'

'Aye, Miss Charity.' Meek. Submissive. The transaction had been settled, and she was content with its terms.

Molly opened the door just enough to recognise Jenny Diver, then tried to slam it in her face. But Jenny's foot was already in the gap, holding it open. Molly yelled for her maid. 'Cassie!'

Jenny's smile shone with friendliness. 'Cassie's out buying vegetables. She'll not be back for an hour - more, if she calls into The Hollybush on her way home.'

Molly pushed her weight against the door, peered through the gap. 'What do you want?'

'I want nothing.' She spread her hands innocently, keen to be understood. 'I don't want you to steal. I don't want you to - '

'The last time you were here, you - '

Jenny reinforced her point. 'I don't want you to become a thief, ma'am.' Charming. Scheming. Almost convincing. 'With your scruples, you'd never be a success - and that could give the rest of us a bad name.'

'Then why are you here?'

'May I come in, ma'am?' She looked pointedly at the other two doors leading off the mean landing at the top of the dark stairs. 'I wouldn't care for our conversation to be overheard by people who might not understand what it could be about.'

Try the cold approach. 'Our only conversation has been about stealing, ma'am. And if that is again your subject, then I think there are few who would not understand whatever you might have to say to me.'

Jenny's voice dropped, and her tone became much more familiar. 'But if it were about witchcraft, Moll, there might be many who would misunderstand.' Subtle, an underlying threat of betrayal, a gentle reminder of flames licking their way up a stake.

Accept the inevitable. She stepped back, allowed her in, closed the door behind her. Once Jenny was inside, Molly leaned her back against the door, folded her arms across her chest and waited.

'I will pay you money to help me,' Jenny said.

'I will not steal.'

'You won't have to steal.'

'What, then?'

'Nothing.'

'What must I do?'

'Nothing.'

'Then why will you pay me money?' Owt for nowt? That was not the way of the world - in London less than anywhere.

Jenny glanced at the chair. 'May I sit?' Molly said nothing, did nothing. Jenny took the silence for an invitation and sat. She gathered her thoughts, then decided to come straight to the point. 'You raised a succubus.'

'Who told you that?' Admit nothing, deny nothing.

Jenny smiled; she knew the game even better than Molly. 'It's all round the Town, Moll. A Bishopsgate harlot has raised a succubus. Not a trick, not a raree-show, not an accomplice in gaudy rags, but a real, brimstone-eating, fire-breathing succubus straight from Hell.'

'And why should that be me? I know nothing of witchcraft.'

She grinned. 'I believe you.' Despite her distrust, Molly found it difficult to dislike her. So did everyone else: that was one of Jenny's strengths. 'I don't know how you did it, Moll, but whatever you did has got the Town buzzing.' She lifted a hand to forestall Molly's protests. 'I don't believe you are a harlot, Moll, but you live in Bishopsgate. I don't believe you did raise a succubus, but the Town does. I don't believe in ghosts or succubuses or the Devil. I probably don't even believe in God. But I do believe in using men's gullibility against them to help me make my way in the world. And that, Moll, is where you can be useful to me. And that again, Moll, is why I'm willing to pay you money.'

'For doing nothing?'

'For doing nothing. All I ask is that you come to the theatre with me. And I'll pay for your ticket myself.'

It didn't make sense: nobody gives owt for nowt. 'I don't understand.'

'Let's be open with each other, Moll. I pick pockets. When a gull's attention is drawn to a pretty face, or a drunken brawl, or a notorious highwayman, he's not thinking of his watch or his purse. And that's when my job becomes a lot easier.'

'What has that to do with me?'

'You're the Girl Who Raised A Succubus. Who's not going to crane their necks to get a glimpse of you? All you have to do is walk into the theatre, take your seat, and watch a play. Then, in just a few days, I'll give you a share of everything I take.'

'But they'd have to know who I were.'

'They can't prove anything against you. The Watch have already searched your rooms and found nothing but a cat, a child, and a rag doll.' It was clear that Jenny had asked the right questions of the right people. 'All they have is a tall tale that they want to believe.'

Molly unfolded her arms and let them fall to her sides. 'But they'd have to know who I were,' she repeated.

A flash of impatience. 'Yes, of course they would. It wouldn't work otherwise.'

'And they'd see me.' So obvious, Jenny didn't bother to reply. 'They'd see me.' The audience. Abelard. The mute actor. The Colonel. Quince. The succubus may have terrified Abelard, but the thought of Quince terrified her. 'No!'

'Maidenly modesty, Moll?'

'No!' She shook her head, once, twice, her neck muscles stiff. 'There are people who... I don't wish to be seen.'

'We'll dress you so that your own mother wouldn't recognise you if you spoke to her.' Her voice was low, persuasive. 'Whoever these people are, you'll need have no fear of them.'

Molly reached behind her, unlatched the door, let it swing open. 'I must have time to think about it,' she said.

Jenny stood, stepped out onto the landing, turned back to Molly. 'Don't take too much time,' she said. 'A nine days wonder sometimes doesn't even last as long as that.'

Cassie's advice was predictable. 'They 'angs yer for stealin'. They burns yer at the stake for witchery. Yer a lot safer peddlin' yer muff.'

✣

Abigail screwed her plump lips downwards. 'Like Daniel going into that lion's den, Miz Moll. He come on out again.' She frowned, anxious. 'But you might not.'

Silhouetted against the early evening sun as it slanted into the room, Annie didn't speak. She wasn't sure.

'Annie?' Molly prompted her.

Reluctantly, she ventured her opinion, 'No,' she said. 'Even with new clothes, someone might recognise you. It's dangerous enough staying so close to The Six Windmills, so close to Lincoln's Inn Fields, Drury Lane, the Haymarket. Going to the theatre, where you're almost bound to be under the same roof as the Colonel and Quince is... Moll, it's akin to offering yourself up to them.'

'Like a pagan sacrifice,' the Waif said.

Annie's voice was sharp. 'Enough, Kitty!'

'But it would be. It would be like - '

278

'Enough!' She came forward, out of the sunlight's overspill, into the depth of the room. 'Consider, Moll. What if the Colonel was there? What then? What if your Abelard should be a friend of the Colonel? What if Abelard himself is there?'

Molly let her gaze drift past Annie to the window, beyond it to the sun-hazy reflection of another window opposite, beyond that to a different window in a different time.

When she was no more than twelve or thirteen, one of her brothers had become friendly with a curate at the Minster. One afternoon, when the priest's vanity had overcome his vow of obedience, he'd led her up the steep, echoing stairs to the roof of one of the twin towers high above the west door. She'd leaned out and squinted down at the mannikin people and the toy horses in High Petergate, a hundred and fifty feet below, the gritty grey stone rough under her fingers, her knuckles glinting white through the country-brown skin.

And the daring-devil in her head had whispered its encouragement to climb out onto the crenellated parapet, to stand there above the distant pavement, to cling to the carved stone pinnacle, halfway between earth and heaven, with nothing but her fingertips between her and the flight of a fallen angel.

The fear of tumbling onto the distant flagstones had knotted her stomach. The urge to tempt her destiny tugged at her.

The sight of a deacon striding towards the Minster reminded her guide of his duties; in belated contrition, he'd dragged her away from the parapet and down the stairs, away from his own lapse, away from her fascination with what she most feared.

'And once I picked up a spider,' she murmured.

Annie frowned at her, puzzled. 'What?'

Molly stood. 'I shall go to the theatre,' she said. 'Now you must help me decide what to wear.'

It was Abigail who provided the answer.

❖

Astride Prospero, her knees pressing his lower ribs, her hands gripping his shoulders, her buttocks smarting where his fingernails were digging into them, Miranda bore down on him. And again. And

279

again.

'Yes!' he panted. 'Yes! Yes! Oh, yes!'

She stopped in mid-stroke.

'Now!' he demanded. 'Now! Now!'

'Can you hear that?' she asked him, cocking her head towards the dressing-room door.

'I can't hear anything! I don't want to hear anything!'

'I can't hear anything either,' she admitted. 'You could imagine the theatre empty.'

A spasm racked him; his teeth bared in a skeletal grimace, his breath snorted through his nose, his hips pounded up against her, bouncing her from the couch, his fingers digging into her waist to pull her down against him again, his back arching again and again. 'Aaah! Aaah! Aaah! Aaaa... aaah...'

The great gulping breaths calmed into the heavy sighs of satisfaction. All his muscles relaxed. His right arm slid off the couch, and his fingers trailed on the floor.

She lifted herself off him, put her left foot to the ground, swung her right leg clear and dismounted. Smoothing her skirts perfunctorily into place, she cracked the dressing room door open and listened intently. 'What can have stilled an entire audience?' she asked.

From behind her there was the light riffling of a new-born snore.

*

As she entered, the entire theatre hushed.

Young mens' eyes swung away from their mistresses' bosoms. Wives were left unheeded in mid-sentence. Seasoned whoremasters broke off their banter, ceased their flattery, abandoned their prey. The orange-sellers themselves left off calling their wares.

Ahead of her a waddling dwarf, plucked off the streets by Annie, dressed by Jenny Diver in a crimson velvet mockery of the fashion. Adult-sized buttons on a child-sized coat, fingertip-length lace cuffs, an extravagantly-curled wig flowing over his shoulders and halfway down his chest and back.

Flanking her, a hobbling hunchback in silver-trimmed black; and a cream-clad, puffy-white, hairless eunuch with rouged lips.

Already tall, she'd gained two inches with the heels on the shoes Annie had lent her. Abigail's cunningly wound turban concealed her tucked-up hair and added several inches more, putting her half a foot above most of the men she passed.

And the Waif's burnt cork and pig-fat had darkened her face, neck and hands to a glistening African blackness.

Looking neither to right nor left, she sailed majestically into the theatre. The staff at the door had been warned to expect her; and, since her ticket was already paid for, they hurried to clear a path for her.

The house was full. Everyone had known all day that the Harlot Who Raised a Succubus was coming, and they wanted to see her at first hand. The lure of danger without involvement.

She didn't disappoint them. Unsmiling, erect, her haughty stare not straying an inch to right or left, she followed the scampering dwarf to her place in a private box.

'Impostor!' Craning to see from his seat on the stage, Abelard bridled with indignation. 'That is not the witch who raises succubuses!'

His companion arched a languid eyebrow. 'Really, Sir James? How can you be so certain?'

Abelard affected a cough, covered his mouth with his handkerchief, gave himself time to cover the indiscretion. 'I had heard she was much shorter than that,' he said. 'I was told by... by someone who knows.' He fumbled in his pocket for his watch, mumbled words about the play being late starting, tried to divert the conversation onto horse-racing.

She watched the First Act attentively, but without expression, then left, her three grotesques clearing a way for her. No need to stay any longer: Jenny Diver had already picked her fill of pockets.

Outside the theatre, she climbed into the waiting carriage. By the time she dismissed it at St Paul's, her familiars had melted back into the streets, the cork was scrubbed from her face and hands, the gown and turban were stowed in a canvas bag.

The African Sorceress had become just another night-girl trudging the streets of Bishopsgate.

Abraham smiled past his son to the beautiful, dark-eyed young woman beyond him. 'And what of that, Rachel? Did we not avow you excitement?'

She inclined her head, her flirting eyes acknowledging a promise fulfilled, her full lips puckering with amusement. 'So.'

Abraham drew back and winked knowingly at his son. 'A new sensation for the Town to gossip about, eh, Isaac?'

'No, father.' Isaac's voice was low, intense. 'That was nobody new. That was Molly. Our Molly.'

Chapter 28

'I saw him, Annie!' Distracted, agitated, Molly paced the twelve yards of The Bell's kitchen and back again, clenching and unclenching her fingers, plucking at her skirts, brushing at the tears that welled from the corners of her eyes.

'You must have expected him to be there?'

I hoped he'd be there. 'I didn't think.' I didn't think I'd see him with his new mistress. A handsome woman three or four years older than him, her hair glossy and black, her arms firm and white, her gown richer than anything I used to wear in Chiswick. I watched him laughing with her, teasing her, kissing her hand. 'I saw how he looked at her, Annie.'

Annie took her by the arms, waited for her to quieten. 'It's been well over a year, Moll. More than a year since you walked out in the middle of the night with only a note to say that you'd gone. Is he to blame if he thinks you didn't want him any more? If he thinks you wanted somebody else? If he's grown tired of waiting, and has found somebody to take your place?'

'But...' But he rode all the way to York and back. He tracked me as far as Will's. Why? To tell me he'd found someone better?

A hard thought dripped into her mind. Or did he want the agate ring back to give to his new mistress?

She turned away from Annie. She wasn't tearful any more. 'Aye, of course you're right. I'm to blame, not him. But nevertheless, I thought... perhaps...'

Annie's voice was close behind her, low, comforting. 'Women can wait, Moll. Men can't. Men don't have the faith that women have.' The clock of St Alban's began to whirr as it prepared to clunk out six o'clock. She broke away. 'I have a visitor soon, Moll. I have to go.'

Molly picked up her cloak and swung it over her shoulders. 'I shouldn't have come here. I should never come here. It's dangerous for both of us.'

Annie disagreed. 'It's not dangerous for me, Moll. I live here. And unless you encounter Mother Wickham or the Colonel, it's not dangerous for you.' She touched her on the arm. 'Nobody here will betray you. Even the Twins hate Mother Wickham. And everybody hates the Colonel - including, I have no doubt, his own mother.'

Molly nodded her acceptance of Annie's judgement. Then, without farewells, they went their separate ways, Annie up to her working-bed, Molly out into the slanting shadows of Love Lane.

The Colonel paused, the wine halfway to his lips. He gazed into the distance for a few moments. 'Yes...' he breathed. 'Yes...' He replaced his glass carefully on the table, dabbed at his lips with a napkin, rose to his feet. 'Tell the girl I shall not be needing her tonight,' he told Mother Wickham. He waved away any possible protest. 'Quince will pay you - and her - anyway.'

Mother Wickham also rose anxiously. What had gone wrong? 'Has the girl offended you, Colonel?'

'The girl?' He'd forgotten her already. 'Oh, the girl. No, she's done nothing wrong, Mother Wickham.' He moved to the door. 'I've been puzzling, Quince, over the harlot we saw at the playhouse. The one they called the Harlot Who Raised a Succubus.' He'd already forgotten Mother Wickham. 'Upon my life, I could not recall where I'd seen her before. But now...'

Quince counted out the coins into Mother Wickham's open palm. 'But now, Colonel?

'But now, Quince, I have remembered.' He strode down the passage-way and out into the pale spring sunshine of Wood Street.

It was less than a dozen paces from the kitchen to the banquet-room, the orgy-room, the room where seductions began with brandy and honey.

As the Colonel and Quince went in search of Molly, and Molly went in search of the rest of her life, they passed within twelve paces of each other.

She walked.

For over six hours, she walked the streets of a London she thought she knew. But the London she saw was not the London she had ever taken in before.

From the stinking gutters of Love Lane to the bustling reek of Wood Street, the sweetness of horseshit mixed with the sourness of sweat, the comfortable smell of her York farmyard clashing with the threatening odour of a predatory city.

From Wood Street into Cheapside, seeing for the first time the bundled rags of flesh begging on the corners, seeing beyond the imploring bowls to the sores that wept down the skull-tight grey faces, seeing the twisted limbs, the makeshift crutches, the crabbed and crippled hands stretching out for pity as the embroidered gowns and velvet cloaks swept past them. But what pity was there in London? What pity had Mother Wickham or the Colonel shown her? What pity had Quince shown Hannah?

From Cheapside down to the river, swirling, filthy, lapping grey and greasy against the muddy embankments and slime-green steps. Watching the rats scuttling from hawser to hulk, the sailors scuttling from capstan to cargo. The river that Hannah had chosen to wash away the corruption smeared on her by Quince and his men.

Across London Bridge, its raddled face patched and painted like the harlots who lurked in the doorways of its shops and houses. Downstream, the onion-capped turrets of the Tower; upstream, the loop of river that hid Chiswick from her now, and hid Isaac from her for ever.

For an hour, she stared upstream, remembering picnics and sunshine, parties and snowballs. Remembering Isaac, conjuring up a might-have-been life of happy-ever-afters, feeling his touch against her nakedness, the gasping oneness of their passion, the dangerous thrill of their love.

The despair inside her was too deep for tears. And all the time she stood there, not one buck approached her with an offer, not one harlot begrudged her the space around her. Her wretchedness had made her invisible.

At last she stumbled onwards, into the warren of Southwark, empty now of fairgoers, peopled with its all-year-round swarm of harlots and beggars, cutthroats and pickpockets. Past the churchyard where Hannah was ravished into a slow death. More memories, but still no tears.

Back over the twilight Bridge, and up the frost-slippery cobbles to Ludgate Hill, past the coarse cackle of harlots warming their hands at a watchman's brazier as they waited for a shillingsworth of custom to pass by, or lifting their skirts waist-high to display their temptations to a drunken reveller, or passing mugs of gin from mouth to swigging mouth. Ahead of her, a dead-eyed, matt-haired harlot of Molly's own age rucked up her skirts, straddled her legs apart, half crouched and pissed onto the cobbles, vacantly watching the thin rivulet steam downhill towards the Fleet.

The hell-shrieks fell away behind her as she crossed Fetter Lane, deserted but for a scurrying lawyer on his way to the Temple, and the last of the afternoon drinkers lurching home. Even the beggars were elsewhere, waiting for the playhouses to disgorge their patrons onto the streets.

Chancery Lane, empty of people, but filled with eyes. Eyes that saw a lone, trudging woman, but which saw no prey. There was no sport to be had here: a slump-shouldered wraith with nothing to steal, and nothing to lose.

Into the emptiness of Lincoln's Inn Fields. Past the theatre, where warmth, light and laughter spilled out into the night, and where the Colonel, Quince and depravity held court inside. Past the waiting carriages, the horses stamping and fluttering their breath into the night air, the coachmen huddled in groups, smoking their stubby clay pipes, arguing their individual policies to end the world's ills.

Was Isaac inside, forgetting to watch the play as he smiled into the eyes of the dark-haired woman? Was he in Chiswick, holding her in his arms, stroking her hair, kissing the soft down at the nape of her neck? Or was he in her bed, powerful and gentle at once, smelling of garlic and rose-water, sighing with passion and whispering sweet words?

She didn't see the playbills outside the theatre. She didn't glance at the light-spilling doors. None of the coachmen noticed her as she passed.

On and on, out of the wide, moonlit streets, through the night-black dangers of Clare Market, into the echoing walls and narrow alleys that led to Drury Lane. And out again, unhindered, unmolested, unharmed into the Strand and back east again along Fleet Street.

Over the Fleet Bridge, flanked and confronted by prisons: debtors in The Fleet, harlots and cheats in Bridewell, gallows-bound thieves and murderers in Newgate. Close as it was to Ludgate Hill, still nobody approached her.

Keeping outside the line of the old wall, she trudged on past the grandiose carvings of Aldersgate, the stinking dunghills outside

Smithfield, the crenellated towers of Cripplegate, the ten-windowed block of Moorgate, thinking, remembering, weighing, rejecting. By the time she arrived home in Bishopsgate, she'd considered her world and made up her mind.

*

Isaac leaned against the fireplace and stamped on one of the dying logs. It collapsed with a crashing sound louder than its movement promised; sparks cascaded upwards, caught in the updraft and flickered like fireflies up the chimney.

He turned to his father and Rachel, both sitting at the low table, sipping tea, and looked from one to the other, wonderment lighting up his face. 'I don't think I shall ever forgive you, father,' he said, his grin, pure joy, giving the lie to his words.

'Has he been so wicked to you, Isaac?' She put down her cup, rose, moved to him, linked her arm with his and kissed him lightly on the cheek.'I am a man - ' Isaac began.

'Huh!' Abraham mocked him, the loving mockery of a proud father.

Isaac pretended to ignore him. 'I am a man,' he repeated, 'and my wicked father has let me come to manhood without ever telling me I had a sister.'

Abraham corrected him. 'A half-sister.'

'A sister,' Isaac insisted. He smiled at Rachel. 'And such a beautiful sister.'

She accepted the compliment gracefully. 'You must not blame your father, Isaac.' She corrected herself. 'Our father. So. My mother was not kind to him.' She disengaged herself from Isaac and came back to the table. She bent and kissed Abraham on the forehead, pulled a chair forward and sat next to him. 'My mother was not kind to anyone.'

Isaac followed her, sat opposite her. 'Tell me again about Virginia,' he said. 'Is it really so big? Can a man really ride all day and still never reach the end of his land?'

She nodded. 'Land is cheap. So. Most of the men - and the women - have been transported from Newgate. And many of them will steal from you. So.' The faintest of blushes coloured her cheeks. 'But there are gentlemen there, with land and servants, who have a branded

287

palm. And no one thinks any the worse of them.'

'And some think the more of them for their courage,' Abraham added.

Isaac took her hand in his. 'When you are married to your Brendan, I shall travel to Virginia to visit you.' He kissed her fingers. 'I'm sure I like him already. To insist you have the permission of your father is the mark of a gentleman.'

Abraham raised his eyebrows in pretended surprise at this unexpected tolerance in his son's views. 'A gentleman, and a Christian?'

Isaac's eyes lost their sparkle, and his jaw tightened. 'The most gentle person I have ever met was a Christian,' he said.

Behind him, another log collapsed, and another shower of sparks leapt into the air.

❋

Past midnight, but Cassie was waiting. 'Yer late,' she said.

Molly lowered herself onto the bed, unlaced her boots, dropped them on the floor. She flopped backwards, drained.

'The Captin was 'ere. 'E wanted to know where yer was.' No response. 'Musta bin an 'our he waited afore 'e went away again. Don't fink 'e was pleased, Moll.' Still no response. 'Moll?'

She shrugged. What difference did it make? She'd made up her mind. 'What did he want?'

'Dunno. 'e didn't say.' She sat on the bed and took Molly's hand in her own. Having taken hold of it, she didn't quite know what to do with it. Awkward, but kind. 'Where yer bin, Moll?'

Molly patted Cassie's hand, then let it go. Repay warmth with warmth, but don't let the warmth worm its way into you. 'Walking,' she said. 'Walking and deciding.' Nothing to lose. Nowhere to go but up. Or perhaps down. It didn't matter which any more.

'Decidin' what?'

She rolled away from the maidservant, lay on her side. 'I've changed my mind, Cassie,' she said. Her voice was dull. 'If Miss Charity has any extras, I'd be pleased to help take the burden off her.'

Chapter 29

Men climbed the stairs, unbuttoned themselves, thrust into her, trumpeted their own manliness, swaggered down the stairs again.

Cassie collected the money, plucked out and replaced the half lemon, sluiced her with sour milk, inspected her for signs of the pox.

Molly spread her legs for the visitors, spread her legs for Cassie's remedies, spread her legs alone at night to ease the soreness.

Miss Charity took half the money. The landlord took most of the rest.

After three weeks the Captain, having lost at cards, grew impatient for the money she owed him. The grunting gorilla he sent to collect was delighted when Molly was unable to pay. It gave him an excuse to carry out the Captain's orders.

Molly flinched away, but Abigail twined her fingers into her hair to keep her head still. Her forefinger carried on tracing the high line of Molly's nose, her thumb and middle finger squeezing gently down from the puffy purple and yellow that almost closed her eyes to the split nostril that was weeping mucous onto the swollen lip beneath it.

She released Molly, took her hand away, wiped it on her apron. 'It ain't broken, Miz Moll.' She turned to Cassie. 'Who done this? One of Miz Moll's visitors?'

'Nah. One of the Captin's men done it.'

Annie jerked upright, suddenly alert. 'The Captain?'

'She was late wiv 'er payments.' To Cassie, that was a full and reasonable explanation.

'What has Moll to do with the Captain?' Annie's voice had tensed. She jerked her head from servant to mistress. 'Moll?'

Molly's bruised lips tried to work, but failed. 'Ah oh m tn gniz.'

Cassie translated. 'She owes 'im ten guineas.'

Annie walked away to the other end of the kitchen, pushed the blackened kettle further onto its trivet in the great fireplace. 'Big man, this Captain?' she asked casually. 'Big, with black hair?'

Molly grimaced non-committally and winced. She'd never seen him.

Cassie sifted through the dim pictures in her memory, then shook her head. 'Nah. Ordinary size, wiv red hair. An' a twisted arm.' A detail scummed to the surface. 'Got no bollocks. 'Ad 'em kicked in by some-body's 'usband.'

'Captain Jack,' Annie breathed, almost inaudibly.

But Abigail heard her. She glanced at Annie and repeated the name. 'Captain Jack.'

Annie poked the fire into a blaze. 'Where is he now?'

Molly couldn't help. 'Nev met m.'

Cassie's face screwed up in an effort to dredge up an answer, then crumpled as it failed to come. ''E comes, 'e goes. 'E never tells me nuffin. 'Cept when he's got a cully for Moll to whip.' Her face brightened as she remembered something that might be useful. 'The Golden Fleece is where 'e drinks.' Her confidence faded away again. 'But not always.'

Annie led Cassie into a corner of the kitchen, sat her at the table, cut her a thick slice of good ham, put a freshly-baked loaf in front of her, filled a glass to the brim with gin and fruit cordial. 'Tell me about this Captain, Cassie. What more do you know of him?'

She no longer cared. The Captain had sent messages via Cassie, for-bidding her to lie with anyone but the men he sent to her, the men who had already paid him. Until she'd paid the ten guinea debt, he said, he owned her.

She ignored him. If Isaac had forsaken her, what more could the Captain do to her?

Lying passive on her back, she looked into the distance, beyond the veins and knotted sinews standing out on the neck of the fat, bearded burgher sweating up and down on her. Her elbows dug into the sparse mattress, and her hands gripped his shoulders, not with desire, but fending his pork-fed weight off her. Her legs were parted to make way for him, but she didn't join in. Not since Will had she raised her knees for a man; and only ever for Isaac had she wrapped her legs around him and locked her ankles together, gasping with pleasure and passion and love, clutching him to her as if to pour him, molten, into the crucible of her body.

On the bed-canopy above her, she watched two mating flies mir-roring the action below; lurking behind a fold in the stained crimson cloth, a spider stalked them.

Somewhere in London, lurking behind a fold in the stained grey cloth of the city, Quince stalked her. But she no longer cared.

Three or four times a week, she donned the black hat and the black sheet, and wielded the birch, cutting red swathes of vengeance into the buttocks of willing victims.

She concealed her contempt as they floundered onto their backs like landed fish and spurted onto her sheets or into their own hands or over their own bellies; then, when their breathing had slackened and their shuddering bodies had stilled, she held the towel out for them to swab themselves clean.

She never mentioned the succubus. The African Sorceress's robe remained hidden.

Some of them were sent to her by the Captain. Most were sent to her by Miss Charity. Within weeks, she had enough to pay off the Captain's debt. But she dared not, for fear he would ask how she'd come by the money.

But, whipping by whipping, the debt shrank. From three guineas to two to one to a half...

Abelard was the last one. It had taken him two months of resolve to climb her stairs, and he was panting with apprehension as Cassie ushered him in.

Molly played the game. Black hat, black sheet up to her armpits, floor-level candles. But Abelard's game was now different from all the others. 'Thou commandest a succubus for thy pleasure,' she intoned. 'But thy pleasure must be paid for with pain.'

'No succubus,' he muttered.

She continued with the ritual. 'Dost thou thirst?'

'No wine.'

She reached for the box of powder. 'A magic potion can transport you into a magic world.'

With an effort, he straightened his shoulders. The tendons stood out on his neck, and his whole body was trembling. 'No potion.' He fumbled with his fly-buttons, pushed his breeches down over his thighs. He stood there, pink and shrivelled and limp.

Molly picked up the birch, hefted it in her hand. 'No succubus?' she said.

His eyes darted from the birch to the room beyond her, back to the birch, to left, to right, back to the birch. Beads of sweat joined together on his forehead, coalesced into droplets on the bridge of his nose, then

291

joined forces and ran down, over his upper lip and mouth, onto his chin. 'No - no succubus.'

Between his shirt and his half-mast breeches, he stirred, then began to swell. The head poked free of the foreskin; it pointed straight out, then up and up.

Molly leaned closer, her face within two inches of his. 'No succubus?' she whispered.

'No... no... no...' The sweat dripped off his chin.

Closer, closer. 'Dost thou remember the succubus, Abelard?' No more than a breath.

'I... I...'

She put a finger to his chest, nudged him backwards. A few inches. Then a few inches more. A final menacing caress, and he tripped, as she knew he would, over the squat table with the potions on it. Stumbling backwards, his legs pinioned at the knee by his breeches, he flailed his arms to get his balance, glimpsed the chair behind him, allowed himself to collapse onto it.

And onto the black and white cat that was sleeping on it.

Screeching, spitting, howling, the slash of hooked claws across naked buttocks, the memory of a huge, grotesque face-cum-torso, the vision of a ravaging moppet.

No need for the birch. No need for the doll. No need even to touch him. He boiled to his feet, his rictus mouth choking on a scream, his entire body juddering into a convulsion, his head shaking and bouncing, his arms flapping, his pelvis jerking, his knees sagging, his breath pumping. Staggering wide-legged with both hands to his head, he spurted onto the bare floorboards, and again, and again, then fell to his knees, onto all fours, crawling towards the door, his ankles tangled in his breeches, moaning with fear and drained lust and panic and not enough blood and...

When he recovered consciousness, he was lying on his back on Molly's bed. A practised hand was mopping him clean with a warm wet cloth. But it wasn't Molly's face that swam into view. Instead, he was gazing up at the wrinkled, raddled warts and pustules of Cassie.

'Yer didn't want the suckyerbus this time, then?' she said. Expertly, she lifted his spent prick, put her thumb and finger to its base, milked the last of the semen from it, wiped it dry. She treated him to a lewd

292

grin. 'Didn't make much difference, though, did it?'

Forty whippings at half a guinea a time, plus ten she'd not been paid for. After just two months, she was clear of the Captain's debt.

The man at her door stood tall, his pale cheeks sunken from abstinence rather than hunger, his eyes bright with a zeal that had fought and lost the battle against his desires. 'The Widow Abbott?'

'That's right.'

He stepped past her into the room and began to peel off his gloves. 'The Captain said you would know why I have come.'

She remained by the door, holding it open. 'Pray give my compliments to the Captain, sir, and remind him that my debt is discharged.'

A moment's hesitation. 'Indeed, madam, I shall,' he said. No anger, no disappointment, nothing but the thin, cold smile of courtesy. But the slightest flaring of his nostrils hinted at a malice lurking underneath, the frustrated hunger that could so quickly turn to righteous condemnation. He pulled his glove back on, and went down the stairs.

The following day at eight in the morning, acting on information laid before them, the Watch, led by a magistrate, burst into Molly's lodgings and arrested her and Cassie for harlotry.

And for possession of a gentleman's watch, a far more serious offence. However, when they saw Abelard's real name engraved inside the case, they remembered the witchcraft episode and accepted that it had fallen from the pocket of a customer, and was being kept safe until his next visit.

Within the hour, the magistrate had convened a court in the main hall of his own Thames Street house, and sentenced both of them to three days in a house of correction, 'which, with God's help, will encourage you to mend your ways'.

As Molly was led from the dock, he looked straight through her. Just another harlot sent to ponder the arguments of Bridewell.

Perhaps he knew who the Widow Abbott really was. Perhaps not. The last time he'd seen her, she'd been fifteen years old.

But she recognised him.

She'd just been committed to prison by the man she'd travelled two hundred miles from York to be with. The man she'd dreamed of marrying. The glow of happiness the Colonel had snuffed out for ever.

Her cousin Tom.

Chapter 30

She stood in the balustraded cart, swaying to keep her balance as it bounced over the cobbles, averting her face as the ragged street-children ran alongside jeering, trying not to hear the honest citizens as they spat their hatred. She was squashed between a fat, gin-reeking harlot and a thin, tobacco-reeking card-sharper. Cassie's belly butted against her own, her rancid breath just a few inches away as she kept a protective eye on her mistress.

Cassie had told her what to expect. 'Better'n Newgit. Not as good as the Fleet.'

The distinction was lost on Molly. Prison was prison. The shame of being paraded through the streets. The danger of being seen by people she didn't want to be seen by. Quince. The Colonel. Isaac.

But this was Cassie's world. In these matters, the servant knew more than the mistress. 'The Fleet's easy. Long as yer got money, o' course. That's where debtors go. If yer got enough money, yer can live nearly as well in the Fleet as you can at 'ome.'

Molly sighed, superior. 'And where, Cassie, do you think debtors get enough money to live well in prison? They're debtors. That's why they're there.'

Cassie gave her a patronising, lopsided grin. 'Yer too honest, Moll. Yer don't know nuffin about the way the world really works. Most debtors've got more money than the people they owe it to. They just don't wanna let go of it, that's all.' Her grin decayed into a frown. 'But if yer 'aven't got any money, the Fleet ain't where yer'd choose to be.' Her face cleared, and she wheezed a foul-breathed laugh. 'Not as bad as Newgit, though!'

'Well, Newgate is... we all know what Newgate is... it's...'

'It's a lodgin'ouse between this world an' Tyburn.' Her face cracked into an appreciation of her own wit to come. 'You ever heard folk say that Tyburn don't take no prisoners?' she asked Molly. But she wasn't waiting for an answer. 'Well, it does. It takes all the prisoners Newgit can give it!' Her laugh cackled out again; the harlot next to Molly joined in; the card-sharper on the other side twitched his lips wanly, more because he wanted the thin companionship of joining in than because he'd heard Cassie's joke.

The laughter died. The jolting journey continued.

'And Bridewell?'

Cassie screwed up her mouth, tipped her head, spread her hands. 'Better'n Newgit, not as good as the Fleet. They'll flog us - but they won't 'ang us.'

Molly stared at her. 'Flog us? They're going to flog us?'

'Better'n Tyburn's tree.'

Her body drooped in dejection. 'I refused to flog one of the Captain's friends,' she said, 'so now I'm to be flogged instead.' The world must have its whippings, and any back will do.

The irony was lost on Cassie, but she understood the story. 'An' I'll tell you somefin' else, Moll. It was the Captin 'imself what brought the Watch down on us.'

Molly looked away, past her fellow prisoners, past the cat-calling spectators, past the streets of London.

Since the moment I arrived here, I've been afraid. I've been afraid of the Colonel, afraid of Quince, afraid of Mother Wickham, afraid of the Captain. But what difference has my fear made to the way they've treated me? Whether I've done what they wanted or not, they've still betrayed me.

She stood upright, staring out over the heads of the jeering crowd. Head high, shoulders back, jaw set. If Quince and the Colonel and the Captain are watching me now, so be it. I will not try to hide. If I'm to die, I shall die my own woman, not theirs.

The cart rumbled over Fleet Bridge, laboured up Ludgate Hill, manoeuvred awkwardly into Blackfriars, doubled back again over the stinking, sluggish trickle of the Fleet, paused outside the gaunt stone walls of Bridewell, then trundled through the great oak gates. Their hinges squealing, the gates crashed shut behind them with an abandon-hope finality.

Molly stepped down. Down from the cart, down from York, down from Chiswick, down even from Bishopsgate.

Down into a House of Correction.

'Welcome to the University of Bridewell, my dears.' With mocking courtesy, the bulbous-nosed, leather-aproned gaoler flourished a hand at the door which led from the courtyard into the noisy, noisome dimness that was to be their prison for the next few days. 'Here you will learn how to become better citizens than you are now.' He laughed, his blackened teeth silhouetted against the gaping black hole of his mouth.

Bare stone walls. A filthy stone floor. A leaking slate roof nailed crudely to the pitched wooden rafters. High, barred, open windows that admitted little light and less air.

The stench of confined bodies, the constant scuttling touch of lice, the snarls and curses of prisoners and gaolers alike, the squeaks of rats, the shrieks of men and women in despair.

And, as soon as their names had been checked off the gaoler's list, the muscle-draining, palm-blistering, lung-burning, deafening pounding of mallets on hemp-laden blocks. More than a hundred sweating miscreants learning that the virtues of honest toil were better than the sins of cheating, whoring and stealing.

I'm out of place here. I don't belong with these drabs and vagabonds, these frayed-at-the-edges sharpers at cards, these cheats and petty thieves. I'm out of place, and my gown is out of place. One of the fashionable gowns Abraham bought for me.

I can't hide. I can't disappear into the background like the pine moths above the farm, the same colour as the bark they sit on. In this gown, I'm more like a Painted Lady among the nettles.

She leant on the long handle of her mallet, remembering the wild summers of her childhood, chasing the gaudy butterflies, plucking armfuls of wild flowers, blowing dandelion clocks.

'Faster! More effort!' The cane swished, stung her across the back of the legs. 'You're beating hemp in Bridewell, not cracking hazelnuts in Covent Garden!'

Her gown drew attention to her; but it also attracted small privileges. The cane didn't land as often on her as it did on the older, uglier harlots. It fell less often than it did on the children, the crippled, the men with faraway eyes, the women who plucked at their own skirts and talked to themselves. An embroidered gown might mean that the harlot was known to wealthy men. Even Bridewell had its pecking order.

Molly put her farmgirl's strength to work, more from prudence than fear. Beating hemp was no more arduous than chopping logs, less demeaning than beating the Captain's customers, and a lot less painful than standing in the stocks behind her, dangling by the wrists under the sign proclaiming that it was Better to Work than Stand thus.

'No need to work so hard, Moll,' Cassie hissed to her out of the corner of her mouth. Thump with the mallet; half on, half off the hemp; lots of noise against the wooden block, not much effort. 'All yer gotta do is enough to stop 'im usin' the cane on yer, and enough to make sure 'e puts the leg-irons on someone else.' Thump with the mallet. 'And 'e's only got two lots o' leg-irons, anyway. 'E can't put all of us in 'em.' She jerked her head at the broken-nosed harlot behind them. 'She'll be next. She ain't got nuffin left.' Thump with the mallet.

A few swings later, there was a clatter as the harlot Cassie had picked out dropped her mallet to the floor and sank to her knees.

The cane lashed down onto her shoulders. The gaoler grabbed her by the collar and hauled her upright again. 'Work, strumpet!' he shouted at her.

'No!' She wrenched herself free, and stumbled towards the door. The cane caught her again, and again, on the back, the neck, the exposed forearm. As she scrambled up the steps to the door, he caught her, threw her bruisingly back onto the floor of the workshop. In three quick strides he was beside her; stooping, he plucked off her mobcap, twined his fingers in her greasy hair and dragged her to the block where Molly was working, one of the two blocks with the leg-irons attached. Shoving Molly roughly out of the way, he shackled the iron sleeve round the exhausted harlot's leg, and forced a mallet into her hands.

'An extra hour for you tonight!' He turned to the room at large, tapping the cane menacingly against his own palm. 'Work!' he roared. The interlude over, the stolen moments of unplanned respite at an end, the rest of the prisoners hefted their mallets and attacked the hemp again.

'See?' Cassie said when he was out of earshot. 'The rest of us is safe now till tomorrer.'

They all slept together, men and women, uncovered on the slimy stone floor. Stiff, aching, unable to sleep in the fetid darkness, Molly listened to the night-sounds of Bridewell. Snores, groans, farts, sighs; the wordless cries of nightmares; the moans and grunts of a snatched coupling.

As the first glimmer of dawn picked out the bars of the window high on the workshop's east wall, she fell asleep. Within minutes, it seemed, she was awake again, forcing down the lumpy, tasteless porridge, summoning up the strength and the will to stand at her block for another day's labour.

The second day stretched out for an eternity, punctuated with enough edible slops to keep them alive, and a few brief periods of rest to let them catch their breath.

That night Molly slept without dreaming, and awoke cramped and aching, every bruise a punishment in itself.

Day three was one of the week's two flogging days.

'It ain't so bad,' Cassie told her in the morning. Thump with the mallet. 'It'll 'urt for a few days, and yer'll have a few scars on yer back. But they won't show in the dark.' Thump with the mallet. She grinned. 'And who gets to see an 'arlot's back anyway? None of 'er cullies, that's for sure!' She squawked loudly at her own joke then, before the gaoler sought her out to see what she found amusing in his workshop, she thumped the mallet down on her block.

Molly gripped her own mallet and set it to work.

I am not a harlot! Not a harlot! Thump on the block. And again... and again... crushing the hemp... against the wood... bruising its fibres... ready for its journey... to the rope-makers... and Tyburn... and the noose... about the neck... of the Colonel... or Quince... or the Captain -

'Moll!' Cassie's hand on her arm. 'Don't work yerself out!'

She paused, trembling, the blanket of red in front of her eyes clearing to pink, then to the grey of Bridewell.

'Jesus damn them all to hell!' she cursed. Grasping the mallet by the end of its shaft to give it her full weight, she took a pace backwards, hefted it behind her and upwards in a huge circle over her head and brought it arcing down again. The mallet crashed against the block, vibrating painfully up her arms and into her shoulders. The handle shattered. The head bounced away, hit the wall, span to rest.

Molly leaned both hands on the block, panting with exertion, her knees threatening to betray her.

The gaoler took her skein of hemp, tossed it onto the pile for collection, signalled for another to be put in front of her. 'That is how I want to see you working,' he told the rest of the prisoners. 'That is how you'll become better citizens.'

This day, there were thirteen of them to be flogged.

'...until your back be bloody, as the court has pronounced.' The President of the Court sat at his table in the courtyard outside Bridewell, and signalled to the Junior Beadle, a thickset, no-neck brute in shirt-sleeves and a leather apron.

The first of the prisoners, stick-boned and pale, was already standing shirtless in the stocks, his fingers cunningly and inescapably pinched between two of the grooved boards.

The nine lead-tipped tails hummed through the air and cracked a fraction of an inch away from the prisoner. Gobbets of flesh leapt into the air. Blood streamed down his back.

The watching crowd, separated from the stage by a semi-circle of iron railings, roared their approval.

But it wasn't enough for the President. Another signal. Another swing. Another bouquet of blood. And another, and another.

After the fourth swing the prisoner cried out for the first time. And, for the first time, the waiting crowd laughed.

Six swings with nine tails. Over fifty stripes, until there was nothing left of his back to be bloodied.

The President knocked on his table, and the Junior Beadle laid aside his whip. The stocks were released. The prisoner slumped to his knees. Two other beadles dragged him away to rub salt into his wounds against infection. Bridewell prided itself on its humanity.

Six more men, beaten to a sodden red mess.

Then the women.

Like the men, they were stripped to the waist. But now the crowd had an added sport: comparing the sizes and shapes of the prisoners' breasts, and making lewd jokes.

The President played to the crowd, savoured the theatricality of the moment, saved the best till last.

First, Cassie. The oldest, the ugliest, the least interesting of the women. The drooping sacks of her dugs wobbled against her belly as she walked unconcerned past the faces peering up through the railings. She hunched her shoulders, clutched herself tight against the centre post of the stocks, accepted her three strokes without a single cry.

Three more women, three more bosoms to ogle at, three lashes each.

The fifth taunted the President with a curse, cupped her bare breasts in both hands and jiggled them at the crowd. 'Yours for a shilling!' she offered. The crowd laughed. She lifted her skirt up to her waist and thrust her naked pelvis at them. They cheered and called obscenities back at her.

The beadles bundled her to the stocks and locked her fingers into place. The President of the Court let her take five blood-spraying lashes before he rapped for the punishment to end. Not once did she cry out.

As the beadles dragged her away, she summoned up the strength to caress the crotch of one of her captors.

Molly was pushed forward into view, stripped to the waist. In York, she would have cowered and wept for shame. Outside Bridewell, she was just another spectacle for London's fools to gawp at.

In her head, she could hear Cassie's voice: Yer can't use whatcher ain't got. All yer can use is whatcher 'ave got.

Her breasts were younger and firmer than any that had been on show that afternoon. So why not use them as more than a handful of flesh for drunks to grope, or for lechers to kiss, or for silly old men to crawl into and relive their infancy?

Ignoring the crowd, she moved with as much dignity as she could to the stocks. As she reached the blood-spattered boards, she turned to face the President, holding herself erect, letting him see the full shape of her body. 'I pray you, sir,' she said, without fear, without pleading, without brazenly catching his eye, 'be merciful.'

She allowed her fingers to be hooked into the stocks, followed Cassie's instructions to huddle as close to the whipping post as she could, tucked her elbows in as far as the splayed position would allow, bit on the wooden dowel the beadle put between her teeth, waited for the pain to strike.

When it came, it exceeded anything she'd expected.

She heard the hiss of leather slicing the air a moment before the thongs laid themselves across her naked skin. And then the lead tips curled round her ribs and bit into the soft flesh at the side of her breast. She was prepared for pain on her back. She wasn't prepared for the carpet of agony that enveloped her entire being, as if twenty executioners had plunged knives into her heart, into her liver, into every muscle in her body.

The shock had locked her breathing. Her lungs were going to burst. She was about to die.

The second swing found fresh ground. The weighted tips tore into the thin flesh over her stretched ribs.

The pain shot into every nerve, from her fingertips to her toes, from the inside of her brain to the depths of her belly.

Nothing existed outside this white-hot crucible.

The blow broke the spell and sucked a great breath into her lungs. But only so that she could howl it out again in agony and outrage and despair.

The crowd cheered with delight.

Gasping, she clenched her eyes shut, her jaw, her whole body, tensing herself for the next lash.

Instead, a sharp rap on the President's table.

Just two strokes.

As the beadles hustled her away, a disappointed voice from the crowd shouted out 'Somebody paid money for you, girl!'

'They was right,' Cassie said. Back again in Bishopsgate, she swabbed the dried blood away from Molly's white back, rubbed salt into the open wounds, then soothed witch-hazel into the purple-striped bruises. 'Someone bribed the President to let yer off.'

'I showed him my body.' she gritted as Cassie's treatment seared into her. 'I begged him to be merciful.'

'Nah. He sees tits all the time. Yours ain't no better'n some o' the uvvers he sees. Not even as young as some o' the uvvers. Bastards like that don't stop a good whippin' for the sake of a pair o' tits.' She smoothed the last of the oil into Molly's skin, tapped her on the buttocks to indicate that she'd finished. 'Nah, someone slipped 'im a few guineas to tap 'is table early.'

Painfully, Molly rolled over, sat up and eased the gown back over the top half of her body.

'Lie down, Cassie,' she said.

Cassie wriggled out of her bodice, grunting as the cloth peeled the dried scabs from her flesh and set the blood running again, and settled herself stoically face down on the bed.

Molly sponged her clean, rubbed fresh salt into the criss-cross red wounds that overlaid the lattice of white scars from other whippings, picked up the bottle of witch-hazel.

Cassie was right. Somebody had bought leniency for her.

But who?

Chapter 31

She brooded and sulked in her room for six days, spurning visitors, refusing customers, her back stiff and sore. Twice Cassie had to break the scabs as they became infected, scraping the wounds clean and rubbing salt into them.

How had she, Molly Huckerby, honest daughter of an honest farmer, church-going Molly, Molly the York virgin... How had she become a scar-backed Bishopsgate harlot with nowhere to go but Ludgate Hill - or, God forbid, Newgate?

The road from York to Bridewell had been signposted with men.

The Colonel, who had debauched her. Quince, who was looking to kill her. The highwayman, who had cheated her. The actor, whose threats had driven her into the Captain's slave-world. The faceless Captain himself, who had used her and betrayed her. Most of all, her cousin Tom, who had first spurned her, then condemned her, and scarred her both inside and out.

She stirred on her bed, wincing as the wounds caught and cracked. 'Forgive me, God,' she muttered, 'but I hate them all, and I wish them ill.'

Not Abraham. Despite the danger she'd brought down on him, he'd never once blamed her, never once been less than kind.

And Isaac?

She couldn't wish Isaac ill. But she couldn't forgive him, either. Not much more than a year, and already... Had his love for her really been that shallow?

Or had it all been just another game? Had he simply been challenging his father, like a young bull?

But if he'd only wanted to tup her, why swear that he loved her? And if it were just a game, why be angry with himself for breaking the commandments of his faith, for dishonouring his father, for committing fornication? Why bother to pretend?

The Colonel had never pretended. None of the others had pretended. Abraham had been open and honest. But Isaac...

She'd seen his excitement at the theatre as he kissed the dark-haired woman's hand, the pleasure in his face, the wonder that she was sitting beside him. Nobody else that night had existed for him. Not even the Harlot Who Raised a Succubus.

A year and a quarter, and he'd forgotten her already.

She shifted uneasily. 'I don't wish him ill,' she mumbled to herself. 'But when he asks her to marry him, I hope she says no.'

Farmgirl, dressmaker, kept whore, mistress, tavern-wench, harlot. Learn the trade, earn the wage. In this world, lass, tha must toil for what tha eats.

Neatly, tidily, she established her own routine. On Mondays, Wednesdays and Fridays, she flogged fops and Puritans, magistrates and freemasons. Sometimes the Captain sent them, sometimes they returned of their own will and ignored the Captain, sometimes they came unannounced upon a recommendation.On Tuesdays, Thursdays and Saturdays, she hung up her birch and received Miss Charity's extras. Each Sunday, she found a different church to pray in.

The weeks warmed into May, sweated into June. And still the days revolved. Lemon halves, grunting flesh, sour milk. The birch, the ridiculous hat and sheet, the jerking hands, the sharp-smelling splashes. The routine became a way of life. She didn't think about it. Lie down, spread the legs, feed it in, wait. Ease it out, wipe it clean, fake a smile, wait. Say the words, swing the birch, drop the sheet, wait. Watch it spurt, wipe it clean, fake a smile, wait.

Cassie ushered in the visitors. Cassie collected the money. Cassie cleaned up afterwards.

Sunday. A quarter past five in the morning. Molly eased the latch out of its metal holder and inched the door open.

She was on her way to meet Annie, to worship at the tiny, hidden-away church of St Ethelburga-the-Virgin less than a hundred yards away in Bishopsgate. Annie was free to roam the City at will; the less Molly ventured out into the open, the safer she felt.

Annie hadn't wanted to go to church at all, and Molly had had to plead with her. Two harlots meeting at a virgin's shrine. But better this irony than not to meet at all.

She nursed the door shut behind her, careful not to wake the snoring Cassie. As she started down the stairs, she heard voices. The door to the street opened, and the indefatigable Miss Charity entered, brushing the light June rain from her cloak.

'In here, dear sir.' She guided her visitor out of the morning-grey light of Bishopsgate, and into the dimness that led to her rooms.

Unassuming, Molly waited on the bottom stair for them to pass.

Miss Charity offered a genteel acknowledgement. 'Thank you,' she murmured.

The man with her flicked a casual glance at Molly; with the attentive, paid-for meat cooing him forward to a few minutes of pleasure, he had no time to waste on her sulky neighbour, half-hidden in the shadows.

But in that one glance, Molly recognised him. Eyebrows like spiked bushes. Heavy-lidded brown eyes, flecked with grey. A broken-nosed ridge between them.

And, on the little finger of his left hand, a ring. A delicate ring of gold, set with rust-coloured striped agate. Isaac's ring.

Miss Charity led him into her rooms.

Molly felt the deadness drain from her, felt the warmth of anger flush through her as she remembered Finchley Common, a man's blood spurting over her feet, the highwayman's cold fingers probing between her thighs, the animal coupling with one, then two, then three of her travelling companions' murderers, all in a bid to save a simple band of gold set with agate.

And the shame of it all being for nothing, of losing the ring anyway, of being cheated.

Unhurried, she turned, went back up the stairs. 'Cassie,' she said, 'Miss Charity has a visitor.'

The sleepy-eyed servant nodded at the quivering walnut-sized bell near the door, the bell that had woken her and summoned her downstairs. 'I know. I'm just goin' down there.'

'Not yet. First, you must dress me.'

'But Miss Charity's got - '

'Aye, Miss Charity has got a visitor. But she can undress herself. Or she can ask her visitor to undress her.'

'Yes, but - '

No arguing. 'She will only need you when she's finished. I need you now, Cassie, before she's started.'

She dragged the chair next to the bed, stood on it, reached down the hatbox resting above the bed's canopy, opened it, took out the loaded pistol one of her since-hanged regular visitors had given her for safe keeping.

Leaving the hatbox on the bed, she took a candle, lit it with a taper from the fire, lodged it in a candlestick on the table. She lifted the chair back into the middle of the room, pulled her gown down over her shoulders. 'First, Cassie,' she said, 'let us burn some cork.'

Miss Charity knelt on the bed, her back to the door, naked from head to hips, her skirts up around her waist, sitting astride her customer, her hands on his shoulders.

She eased down onto him, then eased away. Down... away... Her thighs tightened, and she thrust forcefully down as far as she could go, withdrew almost completely, teased at the tip of him, then thrust again, hovered, tantalised, waited a fraction of a second more than he wanted, pretended to thrust, hesitated, pushed down on him, drew him up into her as far as he would go, used her inner muscles to squeeze him, squeeze him again.

And all the time she watched his eyes in the curtained half-light, mapping his reactions, judging the right moment, the perfect moment, the moment when he lost all awareness of self and became a blistering bubble of white heat, the moment when the world slipped away from him.

Her moment.

His eyes drifted out of focus, their grey-flecked brown began to swim up under his eyelids, his mouth opened wide, his breath shortened to explosive gasps, his hips heaved up against her.

Abruptly, he refocused. His body tensed, writhed, spasmed as the climax shook him. But his concentration was locked onto the partly obscured shiny black face looming over Miss Charity's shoulder, the burning hatred of the eyes between the tall headdress and the figured half-veil concealing the bottom half of the face.

And the cocked pistol that rested between his teeth.

'Get off him.' The eyes never wavered from the highwayman's. But Miss Charity obeyed, just the same. In the breath-held silence, the faint sucking squelch as she lifted herself clear was the only sound.

Molly tossed a coil of thin rope towards Miss Charity. 'Tie him wrist.' Her voice was the best imitation she could manage of Abigail's thick accent. It wasn't African, but it was alien.

Miss Charity stooped, picked up the rope, tied it tightly to the high-wayman's left wrist.

Slowly, very slowly, Molly withdrew the pistol from his mouth. But she kept it close to his face. 'Turn over.'

He glared ferociously at her, tried to intimidate her. 'Do you know who I am?'

She slid the pistol up from his mouth to the centrepoint between his eyes. 'You are nobody,' she said. 'Turn over.'

His lips curling into a silent curse, he rolled over onto his front. The pistol traced the shape of his head as he moved, never leaving his skin from forehead to temple, from temple to above the ear, following the hairline to the hollow at the base of his skull.

'Tie him wrist to de post at de head of de bed,' she said.

Miss Charity obeyed. She didn't want blood and brains splattered all over her room. She didn't want the Watch investigating her. She didn't want to lose a valuable customer. 'Forgive me, Captain,' she said.

Captain! A tremor ran through Molly's body, a tremor of fear and loathing and triumph. Was it the same Captain? Every footpad who could ride a stolen horse called himself Captain. But this Captain had already used her, cheated her, robbed her. Perhaps he was also the Captain who had terrified her, exploited her, had her beaten. So many scores to be settled. So many wrongs to be righted. So many injuries to be revenged.

But her resolve didn't waver. 'Take de rest of de rope and tie him other wrist to de other post.' Miss Charity did as she was told. 'Now tie him legs to de posts at de foot of de bed.'

Within a minute, the Captain was spreadeagled on his face, exposed from waist to knees.

'Take off him jacket and him shirt.'

Miss Charity had future trade to think of. 'I can't. He's lying on the buttons and I - '

With a simple movement of the wrist, Molly took the pistol away from the Captain's neck and pressed it into Miss Charity's belly. 'Get yo' knife. Cut him clothes away.'

The Captain squirmed, tried to look over his shoulder. 'You bitch! I'll hunt you down and make you wish you had never been born!'

She bent her mouth over his ear and breathed into it. 'I never was born. I was summoned up from de depths of hell to punish you for all you have done in yo' miserable life.'

Miss Charity opened a drawer in the table beside the bed and took out a pair of scissors; raggedly, ignoring the seams, she slit the back of the Captain's jacket and shirt, left them lying open, his white back and legs exposed from neck to calf.

'Loop de rest of de rope round him neck.' Now the pistol was free to wave in her direction, Miss Charity was quick to obey. The rope looped once, twice. And still there was length left over.

'Hold onto de bedpost.' She did. Molly tied Miss Charity's wrist to the bedpost, looped the rope round the post at the foot of the bed and twice round Miss Charity's slender white neck, then knotted it to her other wrist before tying it off to the Captain's ankle.

Harlot and highwayman, woven together like an ill-made rigging. Any attempt to struggle would at least garrotte the other, and possibly both of them.

'Before de Day of Judgement,' Molly intoned, 'come de Day of Atonement.' The words flowed unrehearsed into her head. Her own Christianity and Abraham's Judaism mixed up in a non-orthodox threat.

Now the pistol had served its purpose, she eased its hammer into the safe position, placed it next to the bowl and jug on the washstand, and plucked one of the pair of crossed birch switches from the wall above the bed, where they were angled artistically beneath a pointed witch hat. The slippery layer of dust under her fingers confirmed what she already knew: they were there for effect, not for use.

She hefted it in her hand to gauge its weight, then began.

For a full quarter of an hour she swung and swung, lashing at the Captain's back and buttocks until every inch of his skin ran with blood. She stopped only when her arms were too leaden to lift the birch, her lungs burning with effort, her shoulders heaving as she sucked in great rasping breaths.

The Captain had gone through threats of violence, through blustering defiance, through howls of pain, through promises of money, through to an exhausted whimpering.

Miss Charity had begun by observing, unafraid. She'd seen men and women beaten before. This was the sport Bridewell offered twice a week. This was what the woman Molly upstairs was paid to do: whip them, satisfy them, take their money.

But, as the birch continued to slash down and down, with no sign of wearying, with no President's gavel to halt it, with its singing arc breathing within inches of her noose-captured face, as she watched the blood run and drip and spray from the Captain's flayed back, as the towering hell-black figure whipped on, and on, and on.

Miss Charity began to doubt the strength that could keep up this assault without tiring. She began to fear what this avenging angel would do when it had finished punishing the Captain. She began to believe that there had been a Harlot Who Had Raised a Succubus. Crouched beside the bed, she began to shake uncontrollably.

Molly dropped the birch to the floor, leant against one of the bed's four posts, caught her breath. Then she pushed herself upright, wobbled three paces on trembling legs, retrieved the pistol from the washstand, cocked it, came back to the bed.

The Captain, exhausted, barely conscious, dripping with blood, forced his head round to peer at her over his own shoulder. He saw the pistol. He saw the pistol from the same angle as his own victims had seen it. He prepared himself to die in the only way he knew how. 'Damn you!' he gasped. 'Kill me and be damned!'

She put the muzzle against his temple. 'I want to kill you,' she said. 'But my master don' want you dead. Not yet. My master saving you fo' de Day of Judgement.'

The Captain bit his lip against the pain, but said nothing.

Keeping the pistol against his head, she stretched out her free hand, wrenched the agate and gold ring from his little finger, held it between finger and thumb in front of his face. 'Look upon this,' she said. 'This ring is your key to de gates of hell.' She brought it close to his eye, next to the muzzle of the pistol. 'By this token will my master know you,' she said.

The Captain managed to form his lips and tongue sufficiently to spit defiance.

Miss Charity's small voice croaked into the silence. 'Who... who is your master?' She'd shrunk. Crouched beside the bed, she was pale, quaking, wide-eyed with fright. Sweat ran down her face, between her naked breasts and into the bunched-up clothes at her waist. Unnoticed, a pool of her own urine was puddling outwards from her knees.

Molly took the pistol away from the Captain's head, eased the hammer safely back into place, backed away to the door. 'My master's name is written in letters of fire,' she said. She'd heard the phrase somewhere before, but she had no idea where. Kitty, probably. It was the sort of thing the Waif might have said in these circumstances.

Outside, she opened the front door, slammed it noisily shut, took off her shoes, and crept up the edge of the stairs so that they wouldn't creak. Inside her own room she hastily, but thoroughly, washed off the burnt cork and pig-fat, buried the African gown and veil in their secret tomb under the loose floorboard beside the bed, together with the pistol and the ring, and sent Cassie down to attend to Miss Charity and her visitor.

Creeping downstairs after her, she let herself silently out of the front door, put on her shoes in the street outside, and hurried away to keep her appointment with Annie and with God.

As she untied her pay-mistress, Cassie swore she'd seen no one in the house except Molly, who had gone to church an hour ago. Miss Charity knew that to be true. She'd seen her.

Cassie unraveled the Captain, helped him to his feet. And then she took pleasure in treating his wounds with salt. After all, he hadn't only betrayed Molly for a whipping in Bridewell. Cassie's own back had been striped, too.

But even Cassie knew the Captain wouldn't be content to leave it at that.

Chapter 32

The door splintered open and crashed against the wall.

Molly leapt to her feet, backed away from the austere figure that stumbled in towards her, and from the raging creature behind him that blocked the light from the door.

'Is that her?!!' A spitting fury that only blood could assuage.

Sprawling at Molly's feet, Abelard cowered away from her and gibbered a reply. 'I don't... I... she... I don't know... it didn't...'

'Is that the Harlot Who Raised a Succubus?!!'

'She's... she's not black.'

The Captain took two paces into the room, bent, hauled Abelard up by the front of his shirt. 'You said she raised a succubus! Is this her?'

'She... it... it was the cat. I sat on the cat. I was... I thought...'

The Captain flung him back onto the floor. 'A cat!' He rounded on Molly. 'Where's your birch? Your birch for flogging creatures like him?' He jerked his head contemptuously at Abelard.

She pointed to where it hung beside the bed. Heavier, more workmanlike than Miss Charity's.

He ran his fingers along one of the whip-thin branches, then spread a hand to indicate the sparsely-furnished room. 'Where's the ring?'

'Ring?'

A single stride took him to her. His hand struck upwards and seized her by the throat, slamming her against the wall. 'What do you know of letters burned in fire?'

'I... I...' She couldn't speak. She couldn't breathe.

'Tell me!'

She coughed and heaved as he relaxed his hold. 'What letters? I've not burned any letters!'

He shoved her away from him. She fell awkwardly, cannoning into the table and spilling pots of cosmetic powders onto the floor. 'The ring,' he snarled. 'The pistol. An Afric dress.'

'I know nothing of pistols! I'm a harlot, not a highwayman!' She never in her life thought she'd have uttered such words.

He knew about loose floorboards. After half a dozen stamps of his foot he'd found the hiding place by the bed, found the battered leather purse with the two golden guineas in it, shoved the coins into his own pocket, thrown the empty purse onto the floor. The purse that had been left there to be found.

But he didn't know how to sew. He didn't know how to stuff a pillow with an African dress and sew it tight again. He didn't know how to sew an agate ring into the hem of a bed-curtain. Not even Cassie knew that.

And the pistol had been at the bottom of the Thames these two days past.

Smouldering with anger, the Captain made for the door. As he passed the cowering Abelard, he aimed a brutal kick into his ribs.

'Agh!' Abelard groaned, curled himself round the pain, pushed himself to his knees, clutching his side. 'You'll regret this,' he wheezed. 'I'm a Justice of the Law.'

'I shall regret nothing,' the Captain told him. 'And you are simple enough to be in Bedlam.' Another kick thudded into Abelard's belly. The Captain spat on him, turned away, stormed down the stairs and out into the street. The door creaked loosely on its broken hinges.

After a few minutes to regain his breath and his composure, Abelard staggered after him.

❋

Molly huddled beside the hearth in the kitchen at The Bell.

'I don't know why I said it,' she said. 'It just came into my head. I don't know what it means. I must have heard it somewhere.'

'Yes, maybe.' Annie wasn't listening. She was staring into the flames, conjuring up pictures, toying with an idea.

'It sounds good enough to be Shakespeare,' the Waif said. She put on a deep, lugubrious voice. 'My master's name is written in letters of fire!'

Annie stooped, picked up the metal poker that leaned against the hearth, worked it into the heart of the fire which flickered fitfully despite the warm June day outside. 'Wait here,' she said. She climbed purposefully up the steps and out into the main body of the house. In the afternoon stillness, they could hear her feet pattering up the stairs.

312

By the time she returned, three or four sheets of paper in her hand, the poker's shaft was glowing bright red. Scooping up a handful of her skirts in her right hand, she gripped the metal handle, brought the poker-tip to within a quarter-inch of the paper, and traced a ragged circle. The paper charred. More shapes, more charring. A word began to form.

The paper flared into flame. Annie snatched her fingers away from it, and stamped it out on the stone floor.

A re-heated poker, another sheet of paper, another scattering of ashes.

Annie thought for a moment, went back to her room, came back with a twelve-inch square of torn-edged calico. This time, she paused between each pass with the fiery sword of the poker, blowing the thin spirals of smoke away, giving the cloth time to cool. Twice she had to snuff out the flicker of a flame but, when she'd finished, the material was intact. She held it up for Molly and the Waif to see.

Charred into the off-white surface was a name, written in letters of fire.

It said QUINCE.

This was a job that Molly had to do herself. She couldn't trust Cassie even to know about it.

She waited till Cassie was at the market, and Miss Charity out looking for her first customer of the day, then stole into the rooms below her own.

When she left, the scorched calico was flying like a battle-banner from the tips of the bloodied birch.

Miss Charity wouldn't touch it, wouldn't go near it, wouldn't stay in the same room with it.

She ran to the Golden Fleece, found the Captain, trotted alongside him as he strode along Poultry through the beating rain of a late spring thunderstorm, stood at the door in Bishopsgate while he went in.

He considered the calico square with its unequivocal message, plucked it down, tucked it into his belt.

Without a word, he returned to the Golden Fleece.

Chapter 33

'Kitty's not here. She's run away.' Annie's voice was tense, shrill, louder than usual. For the first time in two years or more, she had a glass in her hand. Molly could smell the gin on her breath.

'Where's she gone?'

'Don't know.' Behind her, a clutch of faces at the kitchen table watched and listened. Nan, the Twins, a couple of faces Molly had seen before, a couple of others she hadn't. 'She's run away.' Annie drained the glass, refilled it from the squat green bottle on the table. 'Jed's gone after her.'

Jed! Unspeaking, unshakable, implacable, uncaring, cruel. 'When did she go?'

A past-caring shrug. 'Three, four days ago. She said she was going to help Polly find somewhere to live.'

'Polly?'

'Mother Wickham cast her out.'

'Why?' What could she have done? Polly always did exactly what Mother Wickham told her to do. She never complained. She never argued. She never rebelled. 'What did she do?'

Annie's mouth twisted. 'She caught the pox.' Her eyes were years away. Again, she drained the glass and reached for the bottle. 'Now she's dying, and the visitors don't want her, and she's no use to Mother Wickham, and Mother Wickham needs her bed, and Mother Wickham has got a new girl to lie in it.' She jerked her hand in an ungainly gesture that took in the whole of the table; one of the new faces looked away and pretended to be hungry enough to finish her porridge. 'And Mother Wickham has cast Polly out into the streets.' She filled the empty glass with gin. Plain gin. No fruit cordial. 'And Kitty has gone with her.'

Molly reached out and gently stayed Annie's hand as she lifted the glass to her mouth. She dropped her voice so that only Annie could hear. 'I know where Kitty will be,' she said. 'Sooner or later, Kitty will be where I can find her.' She turned to go, then turned back. 'Don't tell Mother Wickham,' she said.

Cassie huddled inside her cloak. After a blazing June day, the cloudless evening had brought a contrasting chill with it. 'She ain't comin', Moll,' she said.

Molly watched the latecomers straggling into the theatre, glanced briefly up at the impassive pinpricks of light in the moonless sky, then back down to the waiting carriages. In the guttering light of the linkboys' torches, the horses blew their hot breath into the cold air of Lincoln's Inn Fields. Leaf-laden branches loomed black against the near-black sky. The liquid burst of a nightingale's song mingled with the laughter of the coachmen.

'You're right, Cassie.' Perhaps she's chosen Drury Lane or Goodman's Fields or the Haymarket tonight. But, some other night, she'll come here. All I have to do is wait. 'Let's go back to Bishopsgate.'

She'd hoped to see Kitty. But Kitty hadn't come.

She'd hoped to catch a glimpse of Isaac. But it was Friday. Isaac never went to the theatre on a Friday.

Cassie coughed damply, wiped her mouth on her sleeve. 'Four times, Moll.' They leaned against the tree, sheltering against the steady drizzle. Water filtered down through the leaves, dripped off the branches, splashed off their cloaks, caught their foreheads and ran down their faces. 'Four times, and she still ain't come.'

Molly peered into the blurred night, watched the yellow smudge of light by the door to the theatre, struggling to make out each face, trying to read each walk, straining to catch each voice. 'She'll come.' She must come.

'Why don't we go and stand outside one of the uvvers? There's a bit o' shelter to be 'ad by some o' the uvvers.'

Molly shook her head. Water flicked from the front of her close-fitting hat, showered over her shoulders, joined the rivulets that ran down her cloak and onto her shoes. 'Then we'll miss her. She'll come, Cassie. If we wait long enough, she'll come.'

Again, Cassie rumbled the loose cough of a summer cold, hawked up the phlegm, then turned away and gobbed it against the foot of the tree. 'If we waits long enough, she can come to our funerals.'

Molly pointed. 'There she is! Come, Cassie. We mustn't lose her.'

'Wait!' Cassie spat on her hands, rubbed Molly's face, blending away the lines where the dripping rain had cut channels into the swarthy complexion they'd worked so hard to effect earlier in the evening.

Inside the theatre, the air was thick with tobacco and the cloying smell of wet clothes drying in the body heat of their wearers. The babel of voices bulged with the hearty relief of cold people who had come into the warm. Orange girls cried their wares, harlots whispered their promises, husbands forswore their marriage oaths. Fluttering fans hid the details of assignations, fawning lips hid the menace of threats, the bustling distraction of an audience hid the pocket-picking fingers.

Jenny Diver took in Molly's gipsy skin, the large hooped earrings, the flamboyant shawl that hid her hair and most of her face, then passed on, choosing not to recognise her. Live and let live.

Above the pit in his private box, the Colonel noted the gipsy girl, saw nothing to interest him, turned his attention to more exciting challenges such as the fifteen-year-old daughter of a fellow officer on her first visit to the theatre. Then a frown creased his forehead, and he bent to share a few words with Quince. They both craned their necks towards Molly, then nodded their agreement.

Molly fixed her eyes on the stage. On Abraham, on Isaac, on the pretty young woman between them. Then she broke away. No time. Must find Kitty. She stood on tiptoe, scanned the packed pit, recoiled as she caught sight of the Colonel and Quince, pulled the cloak further across her face, kept them in the corner of her eye.

They were staring down into the maggot mass of people below them. She followed their gaze. She nudged Cassie. 'There she is,' she muttered. She began to shove a path through the crowded pit. The Waif, of course, was trying to get as near to the stage as she could.

As she came up behind Kitty, she sneaked a sidelong glance up at the Colonel. He'd been joined by the scowling Jed, and Quince was pointing down into the pit. 'Kitty! You must come away!'

'Moll!' She jumped up and down with excitement. 'Moll, I've been to every theatre in London, and I'm going to become a famous actress, and - '

'Shut up!' She grabbed her by the arm. 'Mother Wickham has sent Jed after you, and he's here in the theatre, and he's seen you, and your life is in danger! Come away - now!'

Kitty's baby-face lost its excitement. 'Where?'

Another glance up at the Colonel. He seemed to be staring straight at her. The icy fingers of the grave tightened round her heart. He's seen me. 'Anywhere! Just go! Just go!'

The Waif saw the panic on her face, believed her and, without looking back, ducked away and began wriggling between the milling bodies. Molly followed, elbowing, barging. Cassie let them go, chose a different direction, became a faceless drab in the crowd, moving slowly so as not to create any eddies in the surface of the semi-stagnant pond of the theatre's auditorium.

From each side of the Colonel a figure slipped away, the dogged Jed to seek out Kitty, the pitiless Quince to destroy Molly.

❁

'Father - the gipsy!' Isaac stood and pointed.

Rachel pretended to admonish him. 'Are you so burning with lust that you must have a gipsy girl, brother?' She drew Abraham into her joke. 'Father, what sort of a whoremaster have you bred here in London?'

Abraham's lips smiled indulgence. But his eyes were sharp as they followed Isaac's arm and the stiffly pointing finger. 'Yes, Isaac, I see her.' Without fuss, he laid his fingers on his son's arm, persuaded him back into his seat where he no longer called attention to himself.

'It's Molly, father!'

Birdlike, Abraham's head twitched as he scanned the rest of the audience. 'Colonel Charnell is here,' he said. 'I think he, too, has seen her.'

No more thought. Isaac leapt to his feet, thrust Rachel to one side, pushed past his father, vaulted over the waist-high screen, ran to the front of the stage, leapt into the pit. Swinging, kicking, punching, he fought his way after Molly, shouting her name above the chatter and the catcalls, the vendors' cries and the screeches of drunken laughter.

❁

Like a hawk, Quince fixed his prey, judged the obstacles between them, prepared to swoop on her.

His lips parted in anticipation, and his tongue licked over his yellow teeth. Almost dancing with the thrill of the kill to come, he slipped through the curtain at the back of the Colonel's box, hovered at the end of the gallery, then prowled towards the head of the stairs that led down into the pit.

Suddenly, in mid-stride, he stopped.

A hoarse grunt squeezed from his throat, his shoulders hunched up and back, his neck arched upwards towards the ceiling, his eyes slitted, his teeth bared in a grimace of pain. He craned his neck back over his shoulder, then stumbled two half-paces towards the stairs.

Behind him, the Captain viciously twisted the long-bladed dagger in its wound, jerked it free, swung his arm back and scythed the steel upwards again into Quince's side.

This time, Quince fell to his knees, reaching limp-armed behind him as the blade ripped clear. He coughed. Blood trickled out of his mouth, ran down his chin and dripped onto the floor. He coughed again. His arm flopped from behind his back, his hand leant for a moment on the floor, then collapsed. Slowly, he folded forwards onto his elbows. His wig, already skewed, slid to one side and fell off. His head dropped, his forehead touched the floor, and the blood from his mouth began to run upwards, into his nose, into his eyes, into his close-cropped hair. He toppled sideways, curled into a ball, put his tightly clenched fists up to his cheeks. His breath squeaked and wheezed and bubbled through the blood that was filling his lungs.

As the people around him screamed and backed away, the Colonel brushed through the curtains, unhurriedly drew his sword, reversed it, swung it by the blade like a club, and crashed the jewel-encrusted hilt into the back of the Captain's skull.

The dagger arced from the Captain's fingers to the floor, skidded into the wall, bounced back, stayed spinning for a couple of revolutions before coming to rest, pointing at the bunched up Quince like an accusing, blood-stained finger.

As the Captain crumpled to the floor, the Colonel changed his grip, took the hilt in both hands, and drove the sword downwards like a ceremonial dagger in a blood sacrifice. The blade skewered the Captain's upper arm and pinned him to the wooden boards of the gallery. The Colonel stepped away from the blood that spurted onto the floor, to avoid soiling his polished boots. The sword's natural flex kept it swaying backwards and forwards.

Raising his voice a fraction above a conversation level, the Colonel turned away and said 'Call for the Watch.'

For the first time in twenty years, Quince didn't rush to do his bidding.

✻

By the time Isaac had fought clear of the surging, scandal-lapping crowds and out into the lowering drizzle of Lincoln's Inn Fields, Molly had disappeared.

By the time he'd returned to his father and his half-sister, the Captain was already chained to a wall in Newgate.

Safe home in Bishopsgate, Molly leapt to her feet as Cassie closed the door behind her and shook the water off her cape. 'Did you find her? Did Jed see her? Did he follow her?'

Cassie frowned with concentration as she tried to understand the questions. 'Who's Jed?'

'You don't know him,' she said. Half-crazed Jed, dogged Jed, Jed the faithful and brutal hound of Mother Wickham. 'Did you find Kitty?'

'Didn't look.'

'What? Why not?'

The squat woman defended herself. 'When I come out, she'd gone. You'd gone.' She gurgled with coarse mirth. 'Alf the featre'd gone by the time the Watch come.'

'The Watch?'

Time to relish the excitement all over again. 'The Captin's bin took,' she said. 'Turned somebody off wiv 'is knife, right there in front of everyone.'

Molly sat down on the room's only chair. Her head was spinning. Too much had happened too quickly. 'Who?' Did it matter? If the Captain had been taken, there was one less person to pursue her.

'That man yer said was a colonel - '

Her heart jumped. 'He killed the Colonel?'

'Nah. He killed the Colonel's man.'

'Quince?' She couldn't believe it. Had the scorched calico really done its job so well?

319

Cassie lifted her shoulders up around her ears. 'Dunno. If that's 'is name, yeah.'

No more Captain. No more Quince. But still the Colonel. And still Jed. 'We've got to find Kitty.'

The servant wasn't enthusiastic. 'More 'anging about outside play'ouse doors?'

'No. After tonight, she'd have to be a madwoman to go near a theatre - at least for a while.' She remembered her two years of theatre-going. 'Anyway, they close at the end of this week. They'll be shut now for the whole of the summer.'

'So what we gonna do?'

I don't know. But somehow, anyhow, I've got to find her before Jed finds her.

Outside Molly's rooms, lurking in the doorways of Bishopsgate, Jed waited, his scarred face patient and impassive.

Mother Wickham had charged him with finding Kitty. He didn't know where to find her. But before she'd run away he'd seen Moll Huckerby talking with her, sharing secrets with her, sneaking into The Bell's kitchen with her.

Sooner or later, Moll Huckerby would lead him to her.

Chapter 34

For the first time in a year and a half, Molly felt safe on the streets of London. But, lurking in the shadows of her mind, there was another anxiety. The Waif.

Sitting on a low stone wall with Annie, she could feel the hot sun beating down on the top of head. Stooping, she picked up a crumbled piece of stone from the slippery green steps beneath her and tossed it towards the river. With a barely-audible plop, it buried itself in the ebb-tide mud. The silt oozed back over it, and all trace of it was gone.

'Where do you think she is, Annie?'

The redhead tilted the ever-present bottle to her lips. 'I don't want to think where she is. If I think where she is, I might say where she is. If I say where she is, somebody will tell Mother Wickham where she is. If Mother Wickham knows where she is, she'll have her dragged back to The Bell. And she'll break her. I've seen her do it a dozen times with girls that ran away.'

'But I wouldn't tell Mother Wickham. I wouldn't tell anyone. I'd find Kitty and help her.'

More gin from the bottle. 'If you find her, Jed will find her.'

'I'd be careful.'

A short laugh. No hint of humour. 'Wherever you go, Jed goes. Haven't you seen him?'

Molly whirled to look behind her, seeking right, left, along the waterside cobbles, past the lumbering carts on their way to the wharves, along the wood and plaster fronts of the sun-bright houses, up to the glinting windows, over the steep-pitched roofs outlined against the cloudless June sky. 'Where?'

Annie continued to watch the greasy brown water eddying past them. 'You won't see him. But he's there. Once Mother Wickham's told him what to do, he's not got the wit to do anything else.'

Molly, too, gazed out across the river. The stench of the low-tide Thames mud drying in the hot sun was unpleasant but familiar. Jed, too, was unpleasant but familiar. She knew how to cope with both.

During the summer months, Miss Charity's trade slackened. Her wealthier visitors forsook the Town for the country; the tradesmen worked extra summer hours; and the young apprentices had sun-lazy serving-girls who'd spread their legs for nothing.

Molly had time on her hands. Miss Charity could satisfy all her cullies without help. And there were few who sought Molly's birch. Being whipped was a cold sport, ill-suited to the sweating days of high summer.

Jed followed her everywhere. To the fields of Islington, to the shops in Covent Garden, to the inns of Southwark.

And, while he wasted his days trailing after Molly, Cassie set herself to find the whereabouts of the Waif.

'Little,' Cassie said. 'Ardly old enough to have tits. Calls 'erself Kitty. Or Cleo-sumfin. Or Feelya. Or Desmonia.' She sucked her teeth in concentration. 'Yeah, an' Eleanor Troy.'

The Ludgate drabs lounging in the sun listened without comment. They, too, had a different name for every day of the week.

'What she done?' A tall, gap-toothed harlot picked her nose, inspected the dried bogey on her fingernail, wiped it on her skirt. Like the rest of the waiting trade, she'd never heard of Eleanor Troy, and she didn't care. But, on a slow day, even a meaningless conversation was better than none.

Cassie leaned back against the stone wall behind her, magicked a bottle of gin from her copious skirts, and offered it. 'Nuffin. Jus' tryin' to find 'er, that's all.'

The harlot uncorked it, swigged at it, passed it to her neighbour. 'Why?'

'There's no money in it, if that's what yer finkin.'

'Then why?' Suspicion. Who does anything if not for money?

Cassie's mouth stretched grotesquely into a leer. 'She's me own long-lost daughter. I'm tryin' to save 'er from a life o' sin.'

The general laughter broke the tension. 'What was 'er name again?'

Cassie levered herself away from the wall. 'Sometimes she's called Kitty. But if yer finds a gel wiv a name what don't sound right, that'll be 'er.' She waved away the bottle as it was held out to her. 'Keep it. I never touches a drop.' More laughter. She knew her audience, and they'd warmed to her. 'I'll be 'ere again tomorrer. If yer sees 'er, foller 'er till yer finds out where she lives.' She started down the hill, then turned back. 'Now, that's worf money,' she said.

322

Mother Wickham sat in her room, self-congratulation playing at the corner of her lips. Yes, she had the answer. 'Enquire at all the church-yards inside the City wall,' she said. 'Talk to the magistrates' clerks. Find out all the burials.'

Jed's brows knitted uncertainly. 'Can't do that and follow Moll Huckerby.'

She lifted her head. 'Forget Moll Huckerby. We've wasted too many weeks on her already. If she's looking for Kitty in Islington and Covent Garden, then she's a fool.' Her eyes narrowed. 'Or she's very clever.'

Jed repeated his instructions, just to make sure he'd got them right. 'All the burials in the City,' he said.

She stopped him. 'Not all the burials, Jed. Only the women. The young women.'

'You think Kitty's dead?' He didn't care if she were dead or alive. But if she were dead, he could carry on with chopping the firewood and fetching the coal and carrying the rubbish, the comfortable jobs he knew and understood.

Her voice was cold, pitiless. 'Kitty's not dead. But Polly soon will be. And when she dies, Kitty will bury her. That's when we find Kitty and bring her home.' A smile tightened her thin lips, a smile that an-ticipated the satisfaction to come. 'It's not a difficult task, Jed. When there's no plague, it's only the old folk who die in summer. Old folk - and Polly.'

Molly was outraged. 'Ludgate Hill? You've been seeking Kitty on Ludgate Hill?!!'

Cassie was surprised at Molly's reaction. 'Why not? She's gotta make a livin' somewhere. An' what else can she do?'

Molly turned her back on her, stood looking down into the dingy street below. Cassie was right, of course. 'I know, I know. But Kitty? On Ludgate Hill?'

'Nuffin wrong wiv Ludgit 'ill, Moll, if yer needs to earn yerself a shillin' or two for yer lodgin'. I bin there meself, many a time.' The voice of reality.

'I'm sorry, Cassie, I didn't mean...'

Cassie tipped her head to one side. 'Course, if they finds 'er, it's gonna cost yer.'

'Aye, of course.'

'Could be 'alf a guinea.' To Cassie, this was a fortune to pay one harlot for tracking down another.

To Molly, it was as cheap as a friend's ransom could get.

Will leaned his back against the cool brickwork of his own cellar. 'I haven't seen her since I last saw you,' he said.

Isaac slammed his fist down on the table. 'Dammit!' he swore fiercely. 'Do you know where she's living?'

A non-committal shrug. 'I never asked her. When she wants to see me, she comes here.'

'If she comes here again, ask her!'

'No.' Will shook his head slowly, deliberately, resolutely. 'I won't do that. If she wished me to know where she lives, she would have told me.'

'I can pay you well.' He saw the change on Will's face, the chilling of the eyes, the tightening of the lips. He took a deep breath. 'I'm sorry. Please accept my apologies. That was insulting.'

'Yes, it was.'

The two men faced each other, motionless. Isaac was the first to break away. His shoulders dropped, and he sank onto one of the rough-hewn three-legged stools that were provided for the brewers when they were working. 'Forgive me, Will. I've searched for her for a year and more. I was told in London that she'd gone home to York, and I followed her there. I was told in York that she'd gone to London, and had never been heard of since. I sought her in every town between York and London.' He clenched and unclenched his fist several times. 'One of the girls at The Bell told me that she'd... A butcher in Tottenham Court Road told me that you and she...'

Will pulled a stool to the table and sat down opposite him. 'What is she to you, Isaac?'

Isaac stared at him, confused emotions flickering across his face. 'She's... I...' He boiled to his feet, clattering the stool across the stone flags. 'Damn her! Damn her! I love her!'

Will waited for Isaac to calm himself. He indicated the stool. Isaac retrieved it and sat down again. 'I, too, have an apology to make,' Will told him. 'I lied to you. I have seen Mary. Molly. I have seen her since you and I last met. Twice.'

Isaac leaned forward. 'Tell me.'

Will took a deep breath. 'You won't like what I tell you.'

'Tell me.'

'She's frightened of you, Isaac.'

'Of me? Of me? How could she be frightened of me?'

'She didn't know why you'd been hunting her all the way to York and back.' He watched Isaac wrench his head aside, his teeth bared in frustration. 'And I can see why she might have been frightened. You're a passionate man, Isaac. And passion can often be mistaken for violence. Did you ever tell her you loved her?'

'I was forbidden to love her.' A tight-lipped mutter.

'Forbidden?'

A flash of anger. 'Forbidden by the laws of my religion! She belonged to my father!'

Will frowned his disagreement. 'Mary has never belonged to anyone. She's not to be bought.' He held up a hand. 'Yes, men have given her money. We all have to pay our way in the world. But she is not to be bought.' He pushed a bottle of wine and a glass towards Isaac. A shake of the head. 'But you didn't answer my question. Did you ever tell her you loved her?'

He spat out his reply. 'I couldn't!'

'Then do you wonder she was frightened? If you never told her you loved her, why should you pursue her up and down the country? Hatred? Revenge? Malice?' He waited for Isaac to answer. When none came, he pressed his point. 'How was she to know?'

Isaac sat staring at his clasped hands in front of him. 'You said you'd seen her twice.'

It was Will's turn to look uncomfortable. 'Yes.'

'Where?'

Pause. Avoid the question if possible. 'It will profit neither of us to talk of where I last saw - '

'Where?'

Another pause, longer, more tense. Eventually, 'Bridewell.'

'Bridewell? Bridewell!' He knew what happened in Bridewell. 'They flogged her? They flogged my Molly?' He rose to his feet and stormed away from the table, slamming his right fist into the open palm of his left, again and again.

Will waited until the worst of Isaac's passion had subsided. Remaining

325

at the table, he said 'She took two strokes, that's all.'

'Two? Only two?' The disbelieving curl to his lips was almost an accusation of lying.

'I softened the President of the Court with a few guineas.'

A prolonged moment of stillness in which nothing was said, but much was understood. Then Isaac returned to the table and lowered himself onto a stool. His rage had muted into concern. 'Do you love her, Will?'

More time for thinking, for choosing exactly the right words. 'Yes, I love her, Isaac. But not in the way you do. Whatever will make Mary... Molly... Whatever will make her happy, I'll do everything I can to bring about. If that means letting you know where she is, then so be it. But only if she says she wants you to know where she is.'

Isaac offered his hand to Will to seal the bargain. 'Agreed,' he said. 'You're a good man, Will. And more generous in your love than I could ever have been.'

Annie hovered some ten yards away, sheltering in the shadow of St Paul's from the late August sun.

Stumpy Jack balanced himself on his crutches and faced Molly. 'Annie says she don't want to know where Kitty is. But she says you do.' Molly waited. 'How much is it worth?'

'A guinea.' Annie had already set the price for her.

'Two.'

'One.'

Stumpy Jack stood his ground. 'Two, or you'll never know.'

Molly walked past him, towards Annie. 'Then I'll never know.' Her father's voice in her head. Keep your eye on what it's worth to the seller, lass. No matter how much you may want it, it's only worth what he'll settle for.

The beggar's voice behind her. 'A guinea and a half.' She ignored him. She heard the hasty clopping of his crutches behind her, as he called out to Annie. 'Tell her, Miss Annie. It's worth a guinea and a half, ain't it?'

Annie waited for Molly to join her, then they made a show of returning towards Cheapside.

'Miss Annie? Miss Annie!'

Annie put her arm on Molly's sleeve to stay her, and walked back to Stumpy Jack. After a few words, she put enough distance between herself and him not to hear anything that was said.

The beggar hobbled the few yards to Molly, defeat slumping his face. 'Now, then, Jack,' she asked him, 'where is she?'

'Kill-Cat Lane,' he muttered. 'Off Eastcheap. Behind the Boar's Head. House of Betty Bulliver.'

'How do you know this?'

His eyes were resentful. 'The harlots were looking for her on Ludgate Hill. But I knew her better'n that. So I kept close to the actors, to see if they'd been fucking anyone worth talking about. Sure enough, she came to them. And I had one of the brothers follow her home.' He held out his hand for the money. 'Kill-Cat Lane. Eastcheap. Betty Bulliver.'

She gave him his guinea. Anchoring his crutch on the cobbles, he swivelled away from her. 'Wait.'

He stopped, but didn't turn. She came to him, took his hand, pressed a second guinea into it. 'Thank you, Jack,' she said. 'That were important to me. And it's just as important to me that nobody else should know. Do you understand me?'

He slipped the extra guinea into his pocket. 'I've forgotten all about it already, Miss Moll.'

❉

Mother Wickham dropped the guineas into her placket without counting them; he'd never cheated her yet. 'Is the new girl to your taste, Colonel?'

He took the crone's hand and caressed it courteously with a kiss, acknowledging her skill in choosing girls. 'This goose will lay you golden eggs, Mother Wickham. Last Friday, she was a reluctant virgin. On Sunday, she had accepted her new life. On Tuesday, she was ready for me. Tonight, I hardly had time to get through the door before her clothes were off, and she was spread out before me like a feast.' He settled himself into one of the deep, comfortable chairs in Mother Wickham's room. 'She'll bring you a chest of gold. But no, she's not to my taste. I prefer a pinch more spice in my victuals.'

She frowned as she poured a glass of her best brandy and put it on the delicate, lacquered table beside him. 'I pray you forgive me, Colonel. If

I'd known - '

He dismissed the matter with a brief gesture. ''Tis of no consequence. There will be others.' He put his fingertips together and gazed at her over the top of them. 'Others like Moll Huckerby.'

She made a small moue, and dipped her head in impatience. 'Fallen from grace, Colonel. A common harlot now, selling herself in Bishopsgate. You'd get no excitement from her.' She poured brandy for herself. 'But maybe it's time to find something different for you.'

He picked up his glass and sipped at it. 'Bishopsgate, you say. Do you know whereabouts in Bishopsgate?'

'No. But Jed knows. He's been following her.' The Colonel tilted his head in an unspoken question. Mother Wickham's ingratiating smile tightened into malice. 'Since Kitty ran away, I've been doing everything possible to bring her back again. So I set Jed to following Moll Huckerby. If anyone can find Kitty, Moll can. Sooner or later, she'll lead us to her.'

'It is clearly important that Kitty be brought back to the nest,' he agreed. 'However, I would be interested to know where I can find Moll Huckerby for myself. Call Jed.'

She spread her hands in an extravagant apology. 'Jed isn't here. Jed is out seeking Kitty.'

He placed his glass on the table, rose to his feet, moved to the door. 'When he returns, send him to me.'

'Yes, Colonel. Of course.'

But he'd already gone.

Chapter 35

Kitty led the way up the narrow stairs, pushed open the door and stood back to let Molly and Cassie pass her.

'Polly?' Molly squinted into the gloom, turned her face away, wrinkled her nose against the stench. What would Kitty know about finding rooms? She'd only ever lived at The Bell, with Abigail and the day-women to clean and cook and make the beds. Hidden in a corner of Eastcheap, this was a squalid, flea-ridden, damp, overpriced hovel, reeking of the dung-heap that piled against the outside walls.

And several miles too near Mother Wickham. At least Jed hadn't found her yet.

The Waif stood just inside the door, not knowing what to do. 'I didn't know where else to look.' Her voice was the baby-girl voice her visitors used to pay for. But now she wasn't acting.

Cassie took in the broken furniture, the cracked windows, the trodden-in grime. She distorted her mouth in scornful disapproval. 'Why dintcha come an' ask?'

Polly was dying. There was no doubt of that. Despite the late August heat, she was huddled in a chair by a smouldering coal fire. Her whole body fluttered in tiny twitches as she gasped for breath. Her skin, where it showed, was the waxy yellow-white of tallow. Her lips trembled as she forced out words, words addressed to nobody, words that flitted round the fringes of sense, but made no sense at all.

As Molly got close to her, she could smell the pungent odour of this dying woman's last indignity. Polly's bowels had emptied themselves where she sat.

The hook-nosed landlady, paid by Kitty to keep watch over Polly, was slouched on a four-legged stool opposite her charge, her arms folded, her back against the wall, snoring. A bottle of gin rested uncorked on the floor beside her, and her glass had emptied itself over her skirts.

Above her, a line of carelessly swilled washing dripped onto the hearth, provoking an occasional faint hiss as the water struck the grate.

Between her and Polly, a boy-child, three or four years old, sat on the hearth, gripping a piece of charred meat in a pair of coal-tongs and holding it over the fire, blowing out the flames when the fat caught fire, and gnawing what flesh he could whenever it cooled down enough for him to risk his lips and tongue on it.

Cassie kicked the stool from under the sleeping landlady, plucked the child away from the fire and shoved him howling into a corner. Wrapping her skirts round her hand, she gripped the handle of the crude poker buried in the coals and stirred the fire into flame. Once it was burning to her satisfaction, she dragged Polly and her chair in front of it, loosened the grubby cloth wound round her head, pulled the threadbare blanket away from her throat and chest, let the fire's warmth play over her naked, sepulchre-white body.

As the landlady picked herself up from the floor, shrieking threats, Cassie snatched the poker from the fire and thrust its red-hot tip within a few inches of her face. 'Get out!' she said.

The landlady backed away, muted her threats to a sullen mumble, grabbed the child by the arm and stumbled past Molly onto the landing. The door slammed shut behind her, then creaked open again on its ill-fitting hinges. One of the pieces of paper that had been stuffing the cracks between the crude planks fell out and dropped to the bare floorboards.

'I've already paid for two physicians to give her a cure,' Kitty said, 'but all they did was argue with each other. Neither of their cures made any difference to Polly.'

'Save yer money,' Cassie growled. She rubbed Polly's wrist in both hands, trying to warm her. 'There ain't no cure for brain fever.'

Molly had never been in a room so neglected, so filthy. 'Is she well enough to be moved?' she asked 'Can we get her somewhere better than this?'

'What for? She ain't gonna live more'n a few days. She can die 'ere as well as she can die anywhere else.'

'Sh!' Molly was shocked at Cassie's lack of sensitivity. 'Don't say that in front of her,' she whispered.

Cassie made no effort to speak quietly. 'She can't 'ear me. She can't 'ear nuffin. She's as good as dead already.' She reached above her to the washing line, felt along the garments, found one that was more or less dry, plucked it down. She handed it to Kitty. 'Old that for a minit.' She pointed to the bed. 'Get me anuvver blanket,' she told Molly.

Molly reached through the bed's moth-holed curtains, bundled up a stained blanket, stood waiting for Cassie's instructions.

'Lay it down on the floor. In front o' the fire.'

Molly kicked the fallen stool out of the way, toed a few stray lumps of coal back into the meagre heap beside the hearth, spread the blanket out as neatly as she could.

Cassie bent over Polly, put her hands under her armpits, flexed her knees. 'When I got 'er standin', you take the blanket off 'er.' With a bunched effort, she heaved Polly upright.

Molly stripped the soiled blanket away, let it lie where it fell on top of the pile of coal, hastened to help Cassie with the dead weight of Polly's limp body.

But Cassie had done this before. Taking small steps backwards, she half-crouched, let the white, wasted frame down onto her knees, then lowered her face-down onto the blanket by the fire. Standing upright, she lifted down the wettest of the garments hanging on the line, knelt, began swabbing the worst of the mess from Polly's brown-smeared buttocks and thighs.

When she'd finished, she dropped the filthy rag into an even filthier bucket of water, snapped her fingers at Kitty for the smock she was holding.

'Every time she eats something, she shits it out again soon after,' Kitty warned her.

'Yeah, I know.' But instead of dressing Polly in the smock, she rolled her over onto her back. 'Old 'er legs up in the air.'

Molly and Kitty looked at each other, but did as they were told. Cassie slid the smock under Polly, drew the bottom of it up between her legs, wrapped the arms round her waist, tied the three ends together. Then she draped the unsoiled blanket round her. 'Put 'er back in the chair.' They lifted her, slumped her into the chair, heaved her and the chair round to face the fire. Her head drooped on her chest. The muttering had tailed off into silence. A trickle of saliva dribbled out of her mouth and ran down her chin.

Is this how I shall pass my life? From baby to child to harlot to baby again, without ever being a woman? Without ever being loved, without ever being wanted, without ever having any choice?

'The Captin done yer a favour,' Cassie told Molly. 'That Quince ain't after yer any more.' She turned to the Waif. 'But you still got that Jed chasin' yer.' She wiped her hands down her skirt. 'D'yer want 'im stopped?'

'No!' Molly answered for her. Cassie's solution to the problem of the actor had been worse than the problem itself.

Cassie shrugged. 'It ain't gonna be 'ard to find yer.' She jerked a thumb in the direction of the blanketed sack that was Polly. 'In a few days time, yer gonna 'ave to get rid of a dead body.'

As if on cue, Polly's head shot upright. Her eyes sprang wide open. 'Don't tell Mother Wickham!' Her voice was clear, lucid, urgent, frightened. Her awareness flittered about the room, saw only ghosts, clouded over, closed. Her head sank down onto her chest again.

'Kitty, you must earn enough for all of us.' Molly spooned bread and milk into Polly's mouth, then wiped away the surplus where it squeezed out of her slack lips and ran down her chin.

'Better if yer bof earn some money,' Cassie said, 'an' let me take care of 'er.'

Molly shook her head. 'No. Miss Charity needs you, Cassie. And she also needs either me or Kitty to take her extras.' She smiled ruefully at the Waif. 'We can either of us satisfy Miss Charity's extras, Kitty. But you don't know how to look after Polly.' She spooned some more pap into the dying girl's slack mouth. 'I had baby brothers to bring up. I know what needs to be done.' She put the spoon into the bowl, balanced the bowl on the stool beside her, wiped Polly's mouth with a cloth. 'I've made out a list of things I need. Some for Polly, some for me.' She drew out a scrap of paper from her placket, handed it to the Waif.

She read it, then read it again. 'Where do I get cinnamon? What's agri... ag-ri-mo-ny?' Confusion coloured her voice; if such things had been needed at The Bell, Abigail was the one to make them appear.

'I'm giving it to you, Kitty,' she said, 'because Cassie can't read. But Cassie knows where to get things. And she knows where I keep everything. Cassie, let Kitty have the guineas the Captain didn't find.' Cassie didn't protest; they were Molly's guineas to do with what she wanted. 'And leave her alone in our rooms for a while. There's a secret matter I wish her to think about.' Isaac's ring, sewn into the hem of the bed-curtain.

The Waif continued down the list. 'Blankets, petticoats, blue gown, birch, witch's hat...' She looked up. 'Witch's hat? Birch?' She stared at Molly in disbelief. 'Here?'

Molly nodded tentatively. 'Perhaps.' I don't want the Waif playing games, pretending she can raise a succubus, bringing Jed down on herself - and bringing Quince's successors down on me. Just because Quince is dead, the Colonel won't blot me out of his mind. 'Put everything in my trunk, and bring it here.'

They left. Molly wedged the door shut behind them.

From Polly, a soft, liquid, bubbling fart, and a sudden, different foul smell among the other foul smells.

Molly pulled the bucket of already soiled water towards her.

Feeding, sleeping, shitting. The life of a baby with everything to come. The life of a dying harlot with nothing left. A near-corpse that had once been a baby.

The wheel of fortune.

'Go to the 'anging,' Cassie told her. 'I'll tend to Polly.'

'But Miss Charity will expect you to - '

'Miss Charity won't expect nuffin. From now till Sunday, she'll have her usual number, and she'll need you for the extras. On Monday, she won't 'ave no cullies at all till after the 'angings.' She grinned with a ribald satisfaction. 'Then she'll 'ave so many, she'll be glad to pay for any 'elp she can get. She'll need you and Miss Kitty a lot more'n she'll need me.' She picked up a lump of coal, stacked it at the back of the fire, trod it into place, pushed the battered kettle over the red and black glow, wiped her hands down her thighs. 'Dunno what it is about an 'anging,' she said, 'but it makes a man's prick spring into life like nuffin else I've ever known.' She turned to Molly with the ardent expectation of a storyteller confronting an audience who'd never heard the joke before. 'Specially the man what's being 'anged!'

Molly heard the words, but they didn't register. There'd been far fewer hangings in York, and she'd never seen any of them. She'd never wanted to see any of them. But her brothers had told her about them. The life being choked out of a man, the kicking feet, the baying crowds.

The Captain had been tried, and judged, and sentenced. The Captain was to hang. Cassie bobbed encouragement at Molly and repeated the punchline. 'Specially the man what's being 'anged!'

Molly pretended to enjoy the joke. 'Thank you, Cassie. I'll come back as soon as I've seen... as soon as justice has been done.'

But Cassie had a better idea. 'Nah, don't come back 'ere, Moll. Go back to Bishopsgit. Miss Charity'll be payin' double, just so as to keep 'er regulars 'appy.' She prodded the fire again with her foot.

'Yes, you're right.' Molly left, leaving the door open to let some air into the room.

Cassie slipped off her overdress to relieve the oppressive heat, and tossed it onto the bed. It landed half on, half off, then slithered to the floor.

'Dunno what it is about an 'anging...' she chortled to herself.

Mother Wickham was still in her nightcap and gown when the Watch burst into her room.

It took the Captain of the Watch less than a minute to read out the charge to her. Ten minutes later, she was dressed and on her way to the magistrate's court. Within the hour she'd been convicted and sentenced, and was entering the dark confines of Bridewell.

When it wished to, the law could move with bewildering speed.

Annie stood at the head of the oval table in The Bell's eating room; despite the early evening sunshine outside, the curtains were fully drawn. Like the five girls in front of her, she was gowned, wigged, powdered, ready for the evening's work.

But it was Mother Wickham who should have been standing there, not Annie, and the girls were clearly apprehensive. Annie answered their unspoken question. 'Mother Wickham has been arrested on a charge of keeping a bawdy house. She is to be pilloried tomorrow morning.' She leaned her hands on the table. 'She has friends who will protect her. But she also has enemies who may seek retaliation.' She stood upright again. 'Mother Wickham is to be paraded, and maybe pelted, on Ludgate Hill. Pray for Mother Wickham. Without Mother Wickham, Ludgate Hill could become your destiny, too.' She put her hands together. 'Let us all pray for Mother Wickham.'

The rest of the girls closed their eyes and mumbled under their breath. None of their mumblings were prayers.

Annie's voice became brisk. 'Tomorrow's a Tyburn day. You know what that means. Men with iron in their pricks, and gold in their purses. Nobody is to leave The Bell until Mother Wickham says they can.'

'What if Mother Wickham doesn't come back from Ludgate Hill?' One of the Twins.

'What if they stone her to death?' The other Twin.

Annie's face was impassive. 'Whatever happens, nobody is to leave The Bell until Mother Wickham says they can.'

Chapter 36

Colonel Charnell admired himself in the mirror, straightened his wig so that the two tight curls on either side fell symmetrically about his ears, plucked a wisp of fluff from the collar of his military-red jacket.

The day ahead was a busy one. He had vengeance to attend to - not only at Tyburn, but on Ludgate Hill, too.

The hard, red, pea-sized pimple that had formed where his foreskin met the glans hadn't come to a head. Instead, it had flattened out into a sore, the size of a fingernail. The pimple hadn't been painful; neither had the ulcer. And now nothing remained of either.

But the Colonel didn't need a physician to tell him what these symptoms foreshadowed. He had the pox.

And where could he have caught it? Mother Wickham had only these few weeks past turned one of her girls out of doors for becoming poxed. But she must have had the disease long before Mother Wickham found out - unless Mother Wickham didn't turn her out until she was so pox-ridden that even the visitors were beginning to notice.

And what of Quince? Who betrayed Quince to that murderous highwayman? Mother Wickham knew they would be at the theatre that night: he had visited one of her girls - he forgot which - that same afternoon.

Wasn't there some tale of the Captain - Captain? That slovenly foot-soldier, that rabble! - some tattle of Quince's killer fathering a bastard on Mother Wickham's black servant?

It was plain: Mother Wickham was his enemy. And Mother Wickham must be punished. A formal complaint about a woman in Wood Street keeping a bawdy house; a swift hearing in front of a magistrate; a sentence handed down with no more than a cursory glance at the offender.

He'd chosen the magistrate well. A man with no vices, no weaknesses, and no mercy. A man who could be neither bullied nor tempted. A man with the reputation of being the only magistrate east of St Paul's who couldn't be bought.

Mother Wickham's conviction had been inevitable.

And even if she'd had some hold over the magistrate, as she had over so many of her other customers, who could she have complained to? The other magistrates? The justices? The Lord Chancellor? The Colonel notched his belt about his waist, buckled on his sword with a professional's ease, smiled with self-satisfaction at his own reflection. When did lawyers ever turn against their own?

He manoeuvred the knot of his lace cravat to the exact centre of his throat. The smile died, and he gazed with unflinching resolve into his own eyes. He had a busy day ahead of him.

Tyburn.

But first, Ludgate Hill.

No cordial. Just gin. 'Go before me, Abigail.' Annie drained the glass, refilled it. 'I shall be there.' Again, she tipped the clear spirit down her throat, poured more. The neck of the bottle rattled against the rim of the glass.

Abigail took a hesitant step forward. 'Let me stay with you, Miz Annie. You ain't well.'

She let her eyes wander to the window, where the early morning mist was hugging the grimy panes. 'Go on to Tyburn!' She swigged at the gin. 'There is something I must do.'

＊

Abraham considered the proposition. 'Is it evil to destroy evil?' he asked.

Rachel wiped her lips and fingers, folded her napkin, laid it neatly on the breakfast table. 'How can it be?'

He continued his argument. 'Is it evil to murder a murderer?'

'An eye for an eye, a tooth for a tooth,' Isaac growled. 'A life for a life.'

Abraham reached his conclusion. 'Then, by murdering Quince, this Captain Jack has committed no evil. By ridding the world of an assassin, he should deserve our thanks.' He took a crust of bread, wiped his plate with it, chewed it with obvious satisfaction, swallowed. 'He has observed the law of Moses, and yet we applaud those who prepare to hang him.'

Rachel saw it differently. 'Vengeance is mine, saith the Lord.' She cocked her head to one side as she formed her reply. 'The man Quince murdered people, you say. So. Perhaps he deserved to die. So. But your Captain Jack is not Jahweh. When he murders - no matter who it might be - he, too, is a murderer, and must be treated so.'

'So who will hang the hangman?' Abraham challenged her. Rachel and Isaac stared at him in astonishment. 'As you say, Captain Jack is not Jahweh. But neither is the hangman,' he explained. 'Yet he presumes to take the life of Captain Jack. Is he not a murderer for murdering Captain Jack?'

Isaac glowered, threw his napkin onto the table, scraped his chair back as he stood. 'This talk is foolish, father!' He strode to the door, turned. 'Are you coming to Tyburn with me?'

Abraham looked at Rachel, offering a silent invitation.

'Not I,' she said.

'Nor I,' Abraham agreed. 'I have seen men hanged, my son. I have no desire to see more.'

Silver had the carriage waiting, the horses fresh, a groom holding their heads. With the ground sun-baked, and the promise of a clear sky, the Chiswick road should be easy.

Isaac's footsteps rang out on the courtyard cobbles as he hurried past the stables. 'Fetch me all the men you can spare.' Silver raised an enquiring eyebrow. 'Miss Molly has reason to be at Tyburn today. I want her found.'

'And brought here, sir?' His tone was polite, restrained, the perfect servant. And disapproving.

'No, not here. I want her followed. I want to know where she's living.'

Silver took the reins from the groom. 'All the men except Fisher,' he told him. The groom ran towards the house. 'Fisher is new,' Silver reminded Isaac. 'He wouldn't recognise her.' He leaned on the reins as one of the horses skittered sideways. 'Are you sure she'll be there, sir?'

'She'll be there.' Molly had told Will about the Captain and his hold over her. Isaac had visited Will often, hoping for news, hoping for an address. It had taken weeks for Will to trust Isaac; but when that trust came, he told him about the Captain.

'Yes, she'll be there,' he repeated.

Jed, too, had his orders. Unquestioning, he closed the Love Lane door behind him and set off for Tyburn.

The gaoler's key grated in the lock of the Captain's fetters. The loud rattle of the chain as it dragged through the ring in the wall echoed back from the slimy stone walls. The heavy metal links clanked as they dropped onto the flagstones. The gaoler retrieved the manacle, refastened it around the Captain's wrist, pushing the bloodstained sling further up the highwayman's forearm to make room for it. The key rasped again as he locked it into place. Stooping, he lifted up the slack noose and slipped it over the Captain's head. This was the Captain's own private rope; it would accompany him on his journey to Tyburn. And beyond.

Apart from the coughs and grunts of the shackled, and the painful groans and mutterings of the sick, Newgate was still. Tyburn day was a time for reflection, not conversation.

The Captain stumbled out into the first glimmers of grey daylight, allowed himself to be prodded into the spike-sided cart that was already loaded with his own coffin, hauling himself up with one hand. A parson climbed in behind him. The rest of the Tyburn travellers were crowded into a second cart. The Captain was good enough entertainment to warrant a parade of his own.

The gates of Newgate creaked open. The cart moved out into the just-after-dawn mist, lumbered north and west down Snow Hill, over the tiny bridge spanning the Fleet, then up again to the top of Holborn Hill. Ahead lay two miles of Holborn, High Holborn and the Tyburn Way.

Already, jeering crowds were lining the route.

The quickest path from Bishopsgate to Tyburn was through the early morning mists of St Paul's Churchyard, a familiar route that took them dangerously close to Cheapside and Wood Street, then up and over Ludgate Hill.

As they passed, Molly peered into the grey pall at the twenty or thirty wraiths already gathered there. 'Someone's to be pilloried,' she said.

'Let's not wait,' the Waif said. 'I've already been to one of those, and I didn't much like it.' She giggled at her own joke.

As they crossed the Fleet Bridge, Molly could see the dim square outline of Bridewell. Aye, let's not wait. I've also been here. And I didn't much like it either.

They carried on into Fleet Street.

On Ludgate Hill, a much smaller gathering than would normally be expected. A notorious bawd in the pillory was good sport. But it was no match for a seven-rope hanging at Tyburn.

The magistrate climbed up beside the T-shaped structure to read out the charges. 'That Elizabeth Wickham, known as Mother Wickham, now of this parish, did entertain divers loose persons, men and women suspected to have committed bawdry, the said Mother Wickham being the proprietress of the ale-house known as The Bell in Wood Street, whereunto many persons well-habited have resorted by day as by night...'

When the charges had been read out, the Watch led the impassive Mother Wickham to the pillory, placed her head and hands into its three holes, swung down the securing board and locked it into place. Above her head, the accusing paper named her and promised that So fhall fuffer all Bawds.

Her sharp features showed nothing. Not hatred. Not bravado. Not even her customary avarice.

Until she saw the freckle-faced young woman appear out of the mist, make her way to the front of the thin crowd, stoop, pick up a stone, brush her long red hair away from her eyes, draw back her arm.

'No! Annie, no!' Mother Wickham's impassive face broke into disbelief and fear; her desperate plea prompted a pitiless cackle of laughter.

The stone missed by a yard, rattled onto the cobbles beyond, skipped and bounded down Ludgate Hill. The red-headed girl vanished back into the crowd.

Colonel Charnell looked away from Mother Wickham's terrified face, turned to his left, lifted a finger in a pre-arranged signal.

A burly man in a torn calico shirt stepped forward. He was already hefting a large stone in his hand. 'Let us rid the world of bawds and harlotry!' he shouted. But he shouted it with such little conviction, it was easy to guess it had been rehearsed. His arm arced back, lining him up side-on to the pillory. His coiled body unwound, and his arm snaked out. The stone flew hard, flat, accurate.

Mother Wickham wrenched her head to one side, dislodging her cap; but the pillory held her firmly in place. The stone caught her above the ear, cannoned off the pillory board and bounced back towards the watchers. Blood welled out of the wound, into her grey hair and down the side of her neck.

A second man, shorter but wirier, joined the first. 'Kill the bawd!' His stone was hurled just as hard, just as straight. It took the dazed Mother Wickham on the top of the head. Her face jerked upwards, her eyes screwed shut with pain. Blood splashed across the scrawled accusation above her.

The third stone caught her full in the face, splitting open her lips and nose, splintering her teeth.

As the first stone had been cast, some of the respectable townspeople had scuttled away to watch from a safe and pious distance. But many of them had stayed, searching for stones to fling, cheering each direct hit, congratulating each other on their aim.

Within less than five minutes, Mother Wickham's rag-doll body dangled lifeless from her wrists and from the bloody, splintered pulp that had once been her head.

The Colonel unfolded his arms, tugged his cuffs neatly into place, turned his back on her, and signalled for his coach to collect him.

Ludgate Hill was over. Tyburn beckoned.

Chapter 37

The early mist was thickened with the warm breath of the gathering spectators. The atmosphere lay choking on Molly and the Waif as they weaseled further and further into the thickest of the throng.

Suddenly, there it was ahead of them, looming out of the thin grey curtain that hung between sky and hill. Three massive oak pillars, joined by an equally massive open triangle laid flat across the top of them.

'The Tyburn tree,' the Waif said. They both stared up at it.

The Tyburn tree...

The festival mood had started before dawn, with vendors staking their claim to the most favourable pitches.

Late risers could breakfast on oranges and flat round biscuits flavoured with cinnamon, and slake their thirst with ale.

A ragged woman with a baby in her arms was doing brisk business selling The laſt dying Speech & Confeſsion of John Fletcher, alſo known as Captain Jack, alſo known as ye Captain. Last Tyburn day, the same speech had sold just as briskly with a different name on the title-page.

Jenny Diver moved quietly among the excited crowd, selecting her victims. For now, she touched nothing. But, during the few minutes between the first and last dying kicks of the condemned prisoners, her fingers would be ant-swarm busy.

The day began to clear. The air became brighter, the mist melted, the hills beyond shimmered as the hot breath of eight thousand spectators rose up to meet the September sun in its cornflower-blue sky.

From the top of the high wooden stands above Molly, a pigeon was released into the air to signal the prisoners' arrival. Twice, three times it circled over the three-cornered gallows, then beat away eastward, silhouetted against the still-rising sun.

The babble of voices swelled from gossip to anticipation. The entertainment was about to begin.

Isaac jumped down from the carriage, pushed towards the guarded entrance to the stands. 'Come with me, Silver.'

'Yes, Master Isaac.' Courteous compliance. No enthusiasm.

'We'll be able to see better from there. We'll be higher up. The moment you spy her, you must point her out to me.'

'Yes, Master Isaac.'

Isaac sighed in annoyance. Silver's disapproval was irrelevant. But it was irritating, just the same. 'And tell your men to keep an eye on me. If we see her first, we'll point them to her.'

'Yes, Master Isaac.'

At the head of the procession, a solitary drummer beat out a warning rhythm, a crisp death-rattle that foreshadowed the retribution to come.

Behind him, the Newgate Ordinary's carriage trundled its slow way through the crowd, its driver astride the lead horse, two footmen beating back the revellers who tried to leap aboard for a free ride.

Inside, the Ordinary himself, the Newgate chaplain, the man charged with preparing the prisoners for their death, yawned, removed his wig, scratched his shaven pate, put the wig back on. Without a mirror to check for lopsidedness, it was now a good inch askew.

'Rabble,' he sneered at the flushed faces outside, keeping his mouth half-closed so that they couldn't hear him. He leaned out and regarded the carts behind. No sympathy, no compassion, no excuses. There was nothing he could do for these condemned men and women. They'd been prepared for their own deaths every day since they were born. Whore, cheat, steal, murder, be hanged. That was the beginning-to-end story of their lives. Some managed to be hanged for stealing before they took their first step into murder. Sometimes they murdered each other, and nobody complained to the Watch. Others, like the Captain, stalked the whole world as their prey, rich men and paupers alike, stealing, raping, maiming, murdering, with no fear of the powerful and no pity for the weak. But, whether stealing a watch or murdering a Watchman, the end was the same. This rabble was born to be hanged.

A rotten orange spattered against the frame of the carriage window, showering him with musty-sweet juice. Hastily, he pulled his head inside.

'Murderers and thieves!' he spat, brushing at his shoulder. 'Wastrels and harlots! Rats and lice!'

Sometimes he wondered why the Ordinary was required to be at a hanging at all. The most he could do was ask them if they repented of their sins. No, of course they didn't repent of their sins. They simply regretted being careless enough to be caught committing them.

'Repent,' he told them, 'and you may yet go to Heaven instead of Hell.'

Some of them shrugged cynically, played the odds and repented. Not with any conviction, of course. But who knew how lenient God could be? It was worth a few mumbled words.

Some of them ventured a brave joke about preferring to be in Hell, about meeting old friends there, inviting the Ordinary to join them there to meet his own old friends.

Most of them snarled curses at him, blasphemed the name of the Lord, prepared for their own death with boiling hatred in their hearts.

And the ones who could afford brandy were so drunk, they couldn't remember their own names, let alone the sins they had committed.

But it was the Ordinary's job to give them spiritual comfort during their last moments on earth. And that's why he was required to be present at every hanging.

'Scum.' He leaned back in his seat, wriggled himself into a comfortable slouch, yawned again.

Seven hangings. Seven attempts to gain a dying confession, seven vain exhortations to repentance, seven readings from the Holy Bible, seven prayers for the Lord to have mercy on their souls, seven dying speeches, most of them incoherent. And anything up to a quarter of an hour before the last of them finished kicking.

Seven! He'd be lucky if he managed to get them all despatched before lunch.

At least, he thanked the good Lord, seven unmarked graves in unhallowed ground didn't require even one burial service.

Behind the Ordinary's coach, the main attraction, the Captain.

Since he had a fearless reputation to protect, he ignored the parson's pious readings and carried on a surly communion with the crowds lining the way. Defiant insults to the pious who condemned him; gallows jokes with his friends and former confederates; bawdy exchanges with the harlots; viciously obscene suggestions to the burghers' wives and daughters.

As the cart began the shallow ascent up the mound they called Tyburn Hill, he scanned the wooden stands, caught the eye of the Colonel, rose unsteadily to his feet, holding onto one of the side-spikes with his good hand, the noose draped about his neck like a loose collar.

'Colonel Charnell!' he yelled above the clamour of the crowd. Hundreds of heads craned towards him, hundreds of voices hushed so as not to miss the sport.

High above him, the Colonel cast a pitiless eye on him.

'Colonel Charnell, I salute you!' He played to his audience for maximum effect. 'You showed the true mark of a gentleman. Only an officer would be coward enough to hit a man from behind!'

The Colonel turned away; the crowd broke into a turmoil of mocking laughter.

Molly sidled behind a fat man and his fatter wife, hiding from the Colonel. 'Who is he to speak of cowardice?' she asked the Waif, contempt and loathing in her eyes and on her lips. 'I've seen him shoot a defenceless man for trying to protect his wife. And he stabbed Quince in the back.'

The Waif nodded. 'He stabbed Bull in the back.'

Bull? The Captain had killed Bull? She hadn't realised until now how tightly this one man had been woven into the fabric of her life in London. She looked towards what she could see of him, some thirty yards away from her, swaying above the heads of the crowd. He stabbed Bull in the back. He stabbed Quince in the back.

And when I birched him, she remembered with satisfaction, I left him without enough of his own back even to be stabbed in.

Behind the Captain's cart, the supporting cast: three hanged-men to be, two hanged-women to be, one hanged-child to be.

Behind them, a company of eight or nine guards, three on horses, the rest straggling in double file, their pikes waving raggedly in the air above them.

Ahead, the Tyburn gallows welcomed them, glistening in the sun, their impassive pillars framing the misty outlines of Finchley's hills to the north. Room for nine hangings at a time, with a comfortable space between each dangler.

But today there were only to be seven.

'Come, Lily, climb up onto Mama.' Abigail scooped the four-year-old up to her bosom, forced a path through the crowds.

The half-white child wrapped her arms round her mother's neck and clung on. 'Where we goin', Mama?'

Abigail stroked her hand down the child's back. 'We goin' see God punish an evil man,' she murmured. 'But pray God he repent afore he die, so he don't get burned in the everlasting fire.' She hugged the child close to her. 'Pray God...'

The hangman lounged comfortably astride one of Tyburn's three hanging-beams, leisurely puffing at his pipe. No need for him to fight for a place at the front. No need for him to pay out a pocketful of guineas to sit in the precarious wooden stands. No need for him to bribe a gardener to let him sit on top of one of the walls nearby. If he weren't an actor in the show himself, he'd have the best seat in the house.

The distant shouting, the sudden stir of excitement, made him raise his eyes. The edge of the crowd was parting, like the Red Sea at the command of Moses. He squinted through the shimmering breath of eight thousand people, and made out the shape of a horse-drawn cart. Above him, a solitary pigeon flapped for height, circled for its bearings, then headed east to Newgate, carrying news of the prisoners' safe arrival.

He spat a gobbet of tobacco-brown spittle, watched it sail down to the cobbles below, where it splashed away a patch of grime and replaced it with a wet stain that glinted in the bright sunlight.

'Here they come, Wat,' he called down to his assistant. 'Stand ready to throw me up the ropes.'

'Annie!' Molly hugged the redhead to her.

Anxiety creased the Waif's young face. She looked nervously in all directions. 'Where's Mother Wickham?' she hissed. 'Where's Jed?'

Annie ignored her, pushed herself away from Molly, stood on tiptoe, craned her neck above the crowd. 'Where's Abigail and Lily?'

Molly was shocked. 'Are they here?' A baby at a hanging?

'Of course they're here!' The words were bitten short, poisoned with hatred. 'She's brought Lily here to see her father die!'

'Her father? But Bull was her – '

'Captain Jack is Lily's father. And he's also the murdering pig who left her fatherless!'

Of course. Annie's own words came back to her: 'He was bedding Abigail, while Bull was bedding me.' Three strands braided together like a pigtail. The Captain and Abigail; Bull and Annie; Molly and the

Captain. The Captain as seducer, murderer, thief.

Annie snatched her arm away as Molly tried to comfort her. 'Don't let Abigail ease his passage to Hell. I want Captain Jack to die slowly!' Her eyes had the gin-glaze Molly had seen so often, but with a blazing hatred shining through the fog. Again, she craned her neck, searching for Abigail.

As if piecing together a broken pot, the pattern suddenly became clear. Annie wanted revenge for the death of her lover. Abigail wanted revenge for the death of her husband - but she also wanted mercy for the father of her child.

Annie crouched, gripped Molly's arm with one hand, the Waif's with the other, her fingers digging white into their flesh. 'Don't let him die easy,' she growled. 'Stop Abigail from letting him die easy!'

As close to the gallows as he could get, Jed climbed up onto the wheel of a wagon hired by a dozen cheerful, gin-swigging harlots.

One of the girls waved her glass merrily in his direction. 'You'll have to wait. No fucking till after the hanging.'

He scanned the crowd. 'Mother Wickham has charged me to find a girl,' he said without looking at her.

She'd never heard of Mother Wickham. She cupped her hand under her breast and jiggled it suggestively at him. 'Do you think she'd pay for a willing girl like me?'

He ignored her. 'Not you. Another girl. I shall stay here awhile.'

Her mood changed, and she thrust at him with both hands. 'Find your own wagon!' she shouted. 'This one's ours!'

He turned his dead eyes on her. 'I shall stay here awhile,' he repeated. There was no possibility of argument.

She'd met enough dangerous men in her life to recognise when to back down. She huddled close to her fellow harlots, sought the bottle, poured herself more gin.

The Captain had a beam to himself.

Three men on one beam. Two women and a fourteen-year-old boy on the second. The Captain on the beam facing the stands.

One by one, the hangman's assistant tossed the loose ends of the nooses up to his master, who looped them over the beam, tied them expertly, leaving enough slack to allow the prisoners to stand in comfort, not enough to let their feet reach the ground when the cart was driven

347

away.

The Newgate Ordinary climbed onto the cart and did his rounds. 'Do you repent you of your sins? Do you hope to come into the grace of God? Do you hope for resurrection and the promise of eternal life?'

The Captain hoped for nothing. 'If the life eternal is anything like this life here,' he answered defiantly, 'then give me damnation!'

The hangman, having climbed down from his perch, followed the Ordinary along the cart, pinioning the arms of sinner and repentant sinner alike behind their backs, checking each noose for snugness, casting a practised eye aloft to make sure the ropes weren't near enough to each other to tangle when the kicking began.

The Captain winced as his bandaged arm was wrenched out of its sling, twisted behind him and bound at the elbow to his other arm. He could feel the blood trickling down from the re-opened wound, and dripping off the ends of his fingers.

Annie was on tiptoe, trying to spot Abigail.

Molly pulled the Waif aside. 'I don't understand. How is it in Abigail's power to let the Captain die easy?' Witchcraft? A potion? She'd never been to a hanging before.

'She'll hang on his legs to tighten the noose.' Neither had the Waif ever been to a hanging. But she'd heard the Twins describing it, moment by grisly moment.

Molly shook her head. She didn't understand. 'How does that make him die easier?'

The Waif shrugged. 'Maybe not easier. Just quicker.'

The hangman jumped down from the cart, greeted the Ordinary, then presented the tableau above him for the priest's approval.

The seven prisoners stood pinioned, prepared, resigned. Some scared, some defiant, some drunk, at least one of them innocent.

Molly evaded the guards, stood below the Captain, caught his eye, lifted her hand towards him, turned it so that the sun caught the agate ring on her finger.

He frowned. Then, as he recognised the ring that had previously graced his own little finger, his puzzlement changed to understanding. He didn't remember her face, but he remembered the incident. A passenger on the York Wagon; she'd bargained her body for the ring; he'd fucked her, then taken it anyway. She, or someone in her pay, had flayed him alive, and taken it back. Honours even. 'You must treasure it highly,' he called down to her.

'You'll never know how highly,' she called back.

He jerked his head upwards at the rope that led from his neck to the gallows-tree. 'This high?'

'Higher!'

The guards shoved her back into the crowd with the shafts of their pikes. The Captain's eyes stayed locked on hers

'There!' Isaac nudged Silver and pointed. 'There, right by the gallows! Organise your men!'

Elbowing, pushing, treading on feet, he fought clear of the stands and into the crowd.

From his vantage point, Jed saw Molly. Scanning the immediate neighbourhood, he caught a glimpse of the Waif.

Simultaneously, the Waif caught sight of Jed, standing head and shoulders above the crowd.

Jed jumped down from the harlots' cart, and was instantly invisible; but Kitty knew he'd seen her.

She grabbed Molly, kissed her warmly on the cheek, hugged her briefly to her. 'Look for my name on the playbills,' she said. 'God bless you, Moll.' Before disappearing into the crowd, she flung a last instruction over her shoulder. 'Save my books for me.'

She grinned, wrinkled her nose, and was gone.

The drummer beat a roll on his drum.

The crowd held its breath.

The hangman gave the signal.

The driver whipped his horses forward.

The prisoners danced as nimbly as they could along the moving cart until there was no cart beneath their feet to dance on.

Nothing at all beneath their feet.

But still they danced.

Chapter 38

As he stumbled to the tail-end of the cart, the Captain snarled a curse in Molly's direction.

In a flurry of kicking limbs, he and his six fellow-travellers stepped out of this life and into the next.

Four thousand respectable, upright citizens bayed their approval. Another four thousand less upright spectators screamed abuse at the hangman, or contemplated their own futures in silence.

The ropes stretched to their full length and jerked to a halt. The Captain's curse choked into a strangled rasp.

The danse macabre began, and the uproar continued as the seven dancers went through their unrehearsed steps.

Mouths gaping, tongues protruding, eyes bulging, legs thrashing, bodies twisting, a bloody froth spraying from the lips, a hoarse gargling that grew thinner within seconds and died, a sharp smell of urine and shit and fear.

Seven sacrifices to the law.

The Captain's face, thin as a weasel, started to swell. His flecked eyes popped, the whites blossomed with a map of red. His face turned crimson, then purple. His tongue squeezed out a protest, then croaked into silence, poking out to taste the bitter air that would never reach his lungs.

At an ungiven signal, a stampede of wives, mothers, sisters, lovers, friends converged on the writhing bodies, hoping to shorten the agony, doubling the weight on the noose, dragging their loved ones to a quicker death.

'God forgive you, Captain Jack!' Abigail rushed towards the scaffold with the rest.

'God damn you, Captain Jack!' Annie also dashed forward. But it was Abigail that she clasped round the waist, Abigail she gave her weight to, Abigail who came crashing to the floor among the milling feet of the victims' would-be saviours.

'Miz Annie!' Shock, disbelief, confusion.

Annie pinned her to the ground. 'He killed Bull!'

'He give me Lily!' She struggled frantically, trying to fight clear, scrambling for purchase. Above them, the Captain's legs kicked and kicked, trying to climb up the air to relieve the weight on his throat.

Annie wrestled her full weight onto Abigail. 'Let the murdering pig die hard!'

On the inner fringes of the crowd, the spectators began to divide their attention between the choking thieves above them and the fighting whores at their feet.

Molly looked away from Abigail and Annie, up at the Captain. There was still a light in his eyes, though he saw nothing. Still strength in his wracked limbs, but no control. Still a life in him, but a life that was seeping away from him agony by agony.

Should any man die like this?

She decided. Die, yes. Like this, no.

She stepped forward, staggered as a boot slammed into her shoulder, clutched her arms round the Captain's waist, let her legs slump down, added her weight to his, tensing herself as his feet drummed into her thighs. She could feel the wetness of his breeches, smell the stench of his shit. But she steeled herself and clung on.

Juddering down through his jerking body, she felt the bones cracking in his neck. The legs lost their power, twitched feebly a few times, went limp. The Captain hung quiet from the gibbet.

Annie tore herself away from Abigail, clambered to her feet. 'Why?' Hatred distorted her features as she confronted Molly. 'Why?!!'

Molly clawed herself upright, then left the Captain to dangle in peace. 'He's dead, Annie. We are both avenged. He won't trouble us any more.' She held out a hand each to Annie and Abigail, helped them to their feet. 'And Abigail still has Lily.'

Abigail turned her back on Annie, Molly and the Captain, took the hand of the uncomprehending black-white child, pushed herself into the crowd and out of sight.

Annie sagged, looked as if she might fall. Molly caught her, supported her. Silent sobs began to shake her. 'I loved Bull,' she half-mumbled, half-sniffed. 'I loved him, Moll. And... and Captain Jack killed him.'

And you're drunk, and you're not going to get home on your own.

And the Colonel must have seen me, and I've not got a much better chance of getting home than you have.

A carriage. We need a carriage. But how to pay for it? When the Waif

351

needed money at Southwark Fair, she earned it. So...

She weighed up the spectators close by, chose one with a prosperous air, one on his own. A butcher, perhaps, or a greengrocer. She knew butchers and greengrocers. Francis and Philip. And she knew what they wanted. Something for nothing. Or, if not nothing, then cheap.

'Sir.' She plucked at his sleeve, hesitant, not over-bold. Reluctantly, he turned away from the jerking figure of one of the women on the gallows. 'Sir, I pray you help me.' A brief gesture led his gaze to the drooping figure of Annie. 'My friend is overcome with grief.' She flashed a glance at the gallows. 'Her sister...' she explained.

He shied away from her, put one hand to his watch and the other to his purse, just to make sure they were still where they should be. 'What is that to me?'

'Please, sir, I must get her to her bed.' Plaintive. Desolate. Damsel in distress. 'If you could ask your driver to take you home by way of Wood Street, you'd have the gratitude, sir, of a poor widow. And her friend.'

His driver? Flattery. He had no carriage. But he could hire a carriage. He weighed the offer. 'And her friend?' His leer in Annie's direction faded as a suspicious scowl settled on his face. 'You're not expecting me to pay for this, are you?'

Molly let a flicker of naivety pass over her face. 'I beg your pardon, sir? Pay, sir? No, sir, I just wish to get my friend home to safety, where she can grieve in private.'

'And you'd be... grateful?'

Again her fingers found his arm, and her eyes sought his, this time with a hint of promise. 'Oh, yes, sir. Very grateful.'

He swallowed the bait. 'Come with me.' He set off into the crowd. If he were to find a carriage for hire, it had to be now, before the bodies kicked their last, before the sport had ended, before the rest of London's law-abiding citizens wished to go home.

Molly put her arm round Annie's shoulders as she followed him. 'Come with me, Annie.'

'Whe... where we going?'

'Say nothing. Do as I tell you to do. We're going home.'

The Colonel watched from the stands.

Abigail and Annie squabbling over who should speed the Captain's exit, and Moll Huckerby cheating them both.

Abigail sulking off with her half-breed bastard, Moll cozening a by-stander, Annie lurching drunkenly behind her.

And where would they go? Abigail would return to The Bell. Annie was no longer capable of knowing in which direction The Bell lay. But Moll was soft. Before going back to wherever it was in Bishopsgate that Jed had discovered her, Moll would take Annie home. To The Bell.

How fitting. After betraying him nearly four years ago, she'd finally crept back to her own rathole. But revenge would be all the sweeter for that. A pleasure delayed is a pleasure doubly savoured.

He snapped his fingers. A servant came running. 'Fetch the carriage.'

'Yes, Colonel. Where shall we be going, sir?'

Quince wouldn't have needed to ask.

Silver was enjoying himself.

Different from hunting the fox, of course, with the hounds baying about your feet. But exciting, nevertheless.

Following the hired cab through the semi-deserted streets of west London, across the City, into the east, hanging back so as not to be spotted, keeping near enough not to lose them. Drury Lane, Fleet Street, St Paul's, Cheapside.

Yes, he knew where they were heading. The Bell.

The butcher (who, he claimed, was a silversmith) couldn't even cope with Molly, let alone Annie as well.

Under her teasing fingers, he stood just long enough to go into her when she sat on him, then faded into a flaccid jelly. He gave up trying. Since it was costing him nothing but the fare for the carriage, there was nothing lost.

Lifting herself off his lap, Molly sat beside him on the leather seat, continued to play with him.

The carriage turned north into Wood Street. Molly knocked on the ceiling of the carriage. 'On the right,' she called out to the driver. She peered out of the window as they neared their destination.

Outside The Bell, a carriage. A carriage she recognised. Hunching her face away from it, she threw her free hand up to rap on the ceiling again. 'Keep driving!'

The silversmith/butcher slapped her teasing hand away. 'You said you wanted to go to Wood Street, and we're already in Wood Street!' How much extra was this going to cost him? 'Driver, stop!'

Roused by the sound of his voice, Annie stirred. As they passed The Bell, she blurrily recognised the monogram on the door of the Colonel's carriage.

'Drive on!' shouted Molly. 'We dare not stop!'

'Stop!'

'Drive! Drive on!'

From beneath the fogging layers of gin, Annie understood Molly's fear, and took action to make everything right.

Dropping to her knees on the carriage floor, she took the passenger in her mouth, worked him with her lips and tongue, her head bobbing rhythmically, waited for his body to cease its jerking and his breath to slow, then lifted herself back onto her seat, spat out of the carriage's open window, smiled at the man opposite, and lapsed back into her drunken dozing. By then, the carriage was beyond Cripplegate and almost into Moorfields, well out of reach of The Bell.

The stench was choking, nauseating, a hundred times worse than any dunghill. And the swarming flies kept up a constant drone.

'She's dead,' Cassie said. Polly's green-tinged body, puffed up with rotting gases to nearly twice its size, was laid out under a stained sheet on the fouled bed. 'She died after yer left on Thursday.' She sucked her teeth. 'We got trouble, Moll.'

'Trouble?' Polly's dead. The Waif's fleeing from Jed. The Colonel's chasing me. And now there's even more trouble? 'What's happened?'

'Well, I didn't fink yer'd be back until tomorrer, but I waited till the time o' the 'anging just in case. Then I told that poxy landlady to go and fetch the searchers.'

'Searchers?' To search for what?

'The old women what tells the parish clerk what she died of.'

Molly didn't understand. 'But we already know what she died of. We could have told the parish clerk ourselves.'

Cassie shook her head. 'Nah, that's not the way it's done, Moll. We 'as to 'ave the searchers.' Sometimes she wondered whether Moll knew anything about the way things were done in London.

'But why does that mean we've got trouble?'

'Well, as soon as she clapped eyes on the dead body, she ran out o' the 'ouse squealin' about witchcraft an' murder an' all sorts of uvver fings.'

Molly tried to pull all the pieces together in her mind. 'But the... the searchers?' Cassie nodded. 'The searchers will be able to tell that she wasn't murdered.'

'Yeah - if that's where she goes. More likely she'll go to a magistrate. Then, if there's anyfing they can take us up for, she'll get forty pounds reward.' Her face cleared. 'On the uvver 'and,' she said, 'if the magistrate says she died natural, that poxy landlady could be doin' us a favour.'

Molly was puzzled. 'Why?'

'Cos all we 'as to do then, is say we don' know who she is, an' we only took 'er in out o' charity 'cos we could see she was dyin'.'

'But why should we say that?' *Should we be ashamed of trying to make Polly's last hours a tiny bit more comfortable?*

Carefully, as if to a child, Cassie explained. 'Cos then the parish 'as to put 'er in the ground.'

'But - '

'They pays for the coffin. They pays for the gravedigger. An' they pays for the parson to say a few words over 'er.'

Four years in London, and it was still a different world.

'Poor Polly.' Annie touched the dead girl's face with her fingertips, staggered away to the room's only table, sat, buried her face in her hands. 'Mother Wickham could have...' She sank into herself.

An officious rap on the door broke into Molly's thoughts. 'The searchers?' she guessed.

'The Law,' said Cassie, heavy irony creasing her features. 'Only the Law knocks like that.' She didn't bother to stand or cross to the door. As she knew it would, it opened anyway, uninvited.

Molly stared at the two figures on the threshold, the two last figures she ever thought to see again, and felt the world starting to slip away from her. 'No,' she said. 'No...'

Chapter 39

All the girls stood dutifully as the Colonel pushed open the door to the high-panelled room.

'Come,' he said, beckoning to the new girl Mother Wickham had provided for him. A sad-eyed, cringing virgin; a pious country girl who thought all Town gentlemen must be honest because they were rich; a delicious piece of innocence to be melted down into corruption. He'd forgotten her name.

One of the Twins spoke up. 'Mother Wickham isn't back yet.'

The other Twin explained. 'She was sent to the pillory this morning.'

The Colonel gave them the news. 'Mother Wickham won't be returning. Mother Wickham is dead.' He waited for the new girl, tears dribbling down her cheeks, to edge past him into the corridor, then followed her.

And four of his men waited, out of sight: two inside The Bell's front entrance, two inside the door to the kitchen. They had their instructions.

Annie on one side of her, splashing stinking water into her face. Cassie on the other. 'Yer all right, Moll. 'Ere, drink some o' this.'

Molly gagged at the raw gin that was tipped against her lips, and twisted her head away. 'No.'

Cousin Tom, stiffer and colder than Polly's exposed corpse, stood by the open window, a handkerchief to his nose and mouth, still choosing not to recognise her. A hint of lavender mingled with the pervading putrefaction.

Beyond him, by the door, the angry features of Isaac.

Behind Isaac, the squeamish faces of the Watch, keeping outside the room as long as they could.

Thomas Heppenstall could see no knife or bullet wounds, no bruising on the throat, none of the tell-tale facial contortions that spoke of poison. 'This woman has clearly not been murdered,' he pronounced. Dismissed, the landlady slouched sullenly from the room. The Watch followed her down the stairs and out into relatively untainted air.

'I told yer,' said Cassie. 'She died o' the French pox.'

The magistrate accepted the diagnosis. 'Just so. Cover her up again.'

Cassie tugged the sheet back into place. 'Who was she?'

Molly looked around her, saw the room as he saw it. The filthy squalor. The stench of decay. A huddle of four harlots, one of whom was already dead. The shame dropped her head, quivered her lip, forced tears up into her eyes.

'Who was the dead woman?' Cousin Tom the magistrate, unbending, insistent.

Annie slurred into the conversation. 'Her name is Polly.'

'Polly what?'

She shrugged. 'Don't know her other name.' Nobody at The Bell had a second name. She pulled the gin bottle towards her.

Molly began to tremble, a light tremor running through her belly, her chest. Enough to feel, not enough to show. There was a chance, the slightest chance, that Cousin Tom might be merciful, might bend just a little. The slightest chance that he might help distract the Colonel long enough for her to get away from London.

Pray God, let Cousin Tom have pity on me. She raised her head and looked him fully in the eyes. 'It's not Polly.'

Everybody stared at her in amazement, then at Polly's bloated corpse. Everyone but Cousin Tom.

'Then who is it? I need to know the name of the dead woman.'

Despite the overwhelming stench, she took a deep breath. 'Her name is Molly, not Polly.' The trembling became more violent, spilled into her voice. 'M-Molly... Molly Huckerby.' Tha name is who th'art, lass. And now she'd given it away to a dead person. The urge to fall to her knees in prayer as she announced her own death was almost irresistible.

Isaac, Cassie, Annie gaped at her, thoroughly confused.

Even Cousin Tom was taken aback. 'Molly Huckerby?'

She swallowed, struggled to force out the words, fought to control the stammer. 'Molly Huckerby is dead.' Her father's voice cautioned her: Always be careful what tha wishes for, lass - just in case it's granted thee. Too late: she'd already taken the gamble. 'With God's help, she has mended her ways,' she said. Would Cousin Tom remember his own words, the words he had spoken when he sentenced her to be whipped in Bridewell?

He collected himself, considered, decided. 'So be it.' He moved to the table, opened his satchel, took out a sheet of paper, a quill, a sealed pot of ink. Meticulously, he inspected the tip of the quill, uncorked the ink, smoothed the paper, wrote a name at the head of it. Although she could only see it upside down, she could read what it said. Molly Huckerby.

'When did she die?' he asked.

'Dunno,' said Cassie. 'I wasn't 'ere.' Cassie was following her own advice: never tell the Law more than you have to. 'By the look of 'er - and by the smell of 'er - prob'ly last Thursday or Friday.'

The magistrate's pen scratched into the silence. 'How old was the dead woman?'

Me? Or Polly? In less than a sevenight I shall be twenty one years old.

Annie took the initiative. 'Twenty three,' she slurred. 'On the last day of April.'

Unhurriedly, Cousin Tom wiped the point of his quill, sharpened it with a penknife, dipped it in the ink, penned a note in a small, fastidious hand, inspected it for errors, then fashioned a baroque signature at the bottom. 'Did you know the dead woman?' he asked Molly.

She nodded. Her throat was too constricted to speak.

'The law requires this certification of death to be witnessed.' He dipped the pen in his inkwell, poised it over the paper. 'And what is your name?'

Panic fluttered round her lips. Name? Molly Huckerby is dead. Polly Something? The Widow Abbott?

From the doorway, Isaac's voice broke in. 'Her name is Molly Asher.' He corrected himself. 'Mary Asher.' He drew himself up to his full height. 'She's my wife.'

Everybody recognised the lie. But nobody spoke.

Eventually, Cousin Tom bent to his paper. The only sound was the scratching of his pen. He glanced up at Molly. 'Of where?'

Isaac answered for her. 'Of Chiswick.'

Cousin Tom finished his deposition, sprinkled sand on it, shook it free, placed it carefully in front of Molly, dipped his pen in the inkwell. 'Your signature, please.'

Isaac stepped forward, took the pen, scribbled a name. 'I have signed for her. She cannot write.' He held out the pen. 'Come, my dear, make your mark.'

Molly looked down at the paper. Molly Huckerby. Died of ye pox

358

2nd September 1731 in Cheapfide, aged 23. Attefted by Miftrefs Mary Afher, Wife of Mafter Ifaac Afher, Citizen of Chifwick. Below, the signature, Mary Afher, in Isaac's large, impulsive hand.

She understood. Pray God she understood aright. Taking the pen from Isaac, she made a cross against the lower signature.

But still Cousin Tom was cautious. 'Forgive me, Master Asher,' he said. 'You are a gentleman, and I have had the pleasure of meeting your father. But if there should be questions asked...' He allowed his eyes to stray towards Molly for a moment. 'I understand there are people who might be seeking Mistress Huckerby.' He lifted his hand in acknowledgement. 'Even though she is now dead.'

'Of course, sir,' Isaac agreed. Man of the world to man of the world. 'As a magistrate these are the questions you must ask. But, as you can see...' He indicated the dead Polly. '...Mistress Huckerby has departed this life. The people who seek her need seek no more. And, in due time, they should be made aware of this circumstance.' He took Molly's hand in his. 'My wife and I depart from London very shortly. I doubt we shall ever return.'

Cousin Tom met Molly's eyes. 'Then there is nothing more to be said.' He packed up his ink, his quill, his signed and witnessed document, and stowed them in his satchel. 'I trust you will have a safe journey, Master Asher. You and your... wife.' An unsmiling bob of the head and he was gone.

Isaac dug into his pocket, handed a heavy leather purse to Cassie. 'A good coffin, a good burial, a good priest. Molly Huckerby deserves the best.' Cassie weighed it with a practised touch. By the feel of it, there'd be plenty left over.

The carriage jolted and bounced over the hard September ruts. Crooked in Isaac's arm, her face against his breast, Molly hardly dared breathe in case the dream faded away and the Colonel took his place. After all that had happened, could Isaac be in earnest?

'What of your father?' she asked. Will I be turned out of the house? And what will Isaac do then? Abandon me? And then where will I go?

Isaac reached for her hand, caressed it, let his fingers stray over the striped agate ring. He knew nothing of its history between the day he had given it to her and now. 'My father will give me his blessing. He

359

will give us his blessing.'

'But we betrayed him.' Abraham's face in the candlelight, peering down at them as they lay naked in the bed he had provided for her. His own son and his own mistress, between them breaking commandments and promises, transactions and trust.

A violent shake of the head. 'He knows nothing of that. He will give us his blessing.' Even Isaac's words of love ripped past his lips in a growl.

'But he saw us!'

'He saw nothing! He was walking in his sleep. I have known him do that many times.' He looked down at her with a fierce resolve. 'He came to see that you were safe. He saw that you were safe. He went back to bed.' He pulled her to him. 'My father loves you, Molly. Enough to let me marry you if it will make you happy.'

She twined her fingers in his, said nothing, remembered. Since leaving Chiswick, she'd been cheated on Finchley Common, in hope of saving the ring. Bought by Francis and Philip and Will and the others. Humiliated in The Six Windmills. Blackmailed by the Actor. Terrorised by the Captain. Risked burning for Abelard. Flogged in Bridewell. And she'd whored for Miss Charity. Nearly two years of living in a nightmare because she hadn't realised that Abraham was in a dream.

She squeezed his hand and smiled. 'It will make me very happy, Isaac,' she said. 'I love your father as a father.' She snuggled into him. 'I love you as a lover. And I will ever be faithful to you as a wife.'

Dozens, scores, perhaps a hundred men or more. None of them of any worth, none of them to be remembered. Except Will for his humour and Abraham for his kindness.

'Yes, my dearest Isaac,' she murmured, 'that will make me very happy.'

If the Colonel doesn't discover where we're living.

Annie was eager to help. After all, the Colonel was a good customer.

She led him and his men through the streets of east London to the evil-smelling lodgings in Cheapside.

But, when they arrived, the rooms were empty. Even poor dead Polly was gone.

The landlady, of course, knew nothing.

360

Chapter 40

To my deareft Anny, whom I fhall ever think of as Red Anny.

Since leaving you at ye Hanging I have left London and have taken up with a Company of Actors and I will not return until my Name is at ye Top of ye Playbills at Drury Lane or Lincoln's Inn Fields or ye Haymarket.

Being an Actrefs is very pleafurable and almoft as eafy as being a Harlot but ye Words I have to learn are more and are written by famous Authors fuch as William Shakefpeare and I cannot invent them as I am ufed to at Ye Bell!

We have play'd in grand Houfes and Inn-yards and once in a Barn and in Newbury we play'd in a real Theatre. I have already play'd a Lady and a Serving Woman and a Young Boy - becaufe my Bubs are ftill not as big as ye other Actrefses - and a Countrywoman and a Princefs - but only a Princefs of Morocco, and I had no Words to fay - and ye Manager fays I will be a fine Actrefs one Day with his Help but his Help moftly means fucking me before I go on ye Stage but I give no Mind to that becaufe he fays every Actrefs who becomes fuccefsful is fo becaufe they work hard at what they are beft at!

At Oxford I fancy'd I faw Jed but Nobody tried to abduct me fo maybe it was fome other Man with a fcowling Face.

I pray you do not let Mother Wickham sell my Books or throw them away. Give them to Moll and tell her to keep them fafe for me and to read as many of them as fhe can.

Your loving Pupil who taught me to read and made me to love Books and made me to love Shakefpeare and made me to love the Theatre,

Her Royal Highnefs ye Princefs of Morocco.

My dear Anny.

*Iſaac was true to his Word, and Abraham has given us his Bleſſing.
I am now no longer Molly Huckerby, but Miſtreſs Mary Aſher! We
were marry'd in ye Houſe at Chiſwick by a Rabbi, which is a Jewiſh
Prieſt, and Iſaac ſays that when we get to Virginia in ye Spring we
ſhall be marry'd again by a Chriſtian Pastor, as his Siſter Rachel was to
her Huſband Brendan, who is a Papiſt, tho' we have to wait until then
becauſe no Prieſt in England would do the Same, for they would curſe
Iſaac as an Infidel.*

*Abraham has given Iſaac his Inheritance now instead of waiting until
he dies, and Rachel and her Huſband are ſeeking to buy a Farm for us
near them, which is a great Joy to me, for I lived on a Farm all my Life
before I came to London, and it will remind me of my happieſt Days in
York.*

*Beſt of all, my deareſt Anny, I think I am with Child. Nay, I am certain
I am with Child!*

*If he is a Boy-child, we ſhall name him Walter Abraham for my Father
and for ye kindeſt Man I ever have known. And if a Girl-child, ſhe ſhall
be call'd Ann Catherin for ye only Friends I had during my darkeſt
Days.*

I pray you, write to me and aſſure me that you are well.

God bleſ you, Anny, and all of us.

Your eternal Friend,

Miſtreſs Mary Aſher.

✻

St Alban's announced midday. As the final chime rang out, Annie opened the door and made her way down the steps into the kitchen.

The giggling babble ceased.

'Good afternoon, girls,' she greeted them. She brandished the two sheets of paper. 'I have news of Kitty and Moll.' She addressed herself to the new girls. 'They used to work here at The Bell,' she explained. She scanned the faces at the breakfast table. 'Shall I read their letters to you?'

The Twins looked at each other and sniggered. Nan sulked in a corner as she always did.

It was one of the new girls, Kate, who voiced what was expected. 'Yes, if you please, Mother Wickham,' she said

New Releases for 2010

"Annie's Quest"

The next episode in The Harlot's Progress trilogy

The Peter Mottley Collection

Plays